THE
GOOSE
FRITZ

Sergei Lebedev

TRANSLATED BY ANTONINA W. BOUIS

NEW VESSEL PRESS
NEW YORK

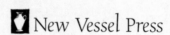

New Vessel Press

www.newvesselpress.com

First published in Russian in 2018 as *Gus' Frits*
Copyright © 2018 Sergei Lebedev
Translation Copyright © 2019 Antonina W. Bouis

Library of Congress Cataloging-in-Publication Data
Lebedev, Sergei
[Gus' Frits, English]
The Goose Fritz/ Sergei Lebedev; translation by Antonina W. Bouis.
p. cm.
ISBN 978-1-939931-64-1
Library of Congress Control Number 2018963467
I. Russia—Fiction

He drove bulls, dogs, and white-fleeced sheep, tied together. Here the massacre began; some he struck in the head, others in the throat, others he chopped in half with his sword; some he tortured in fetters—he must have seen men in them and not mute beasts.

Ajax, Sophocles

A sound.

The sound of water gushing into the rain barrel outside the house.

The overturned geyser pounds water to the very bottom. The small carp caught yesterday, half the size of your palm, swim back and forth, crazed. Swirling in the barrel, the pollen-yellow foam, the pink apple blossoms, last year's brown leaves and dried apples with yellow spots of rot that had all washed through the rain spout; the spider web with bugs caught in its spiral is swirling, too—there, the flash of mica in the broken wing of a dragonfly!

The storm tears down and carries off everything that has faded and died, as well as everything that was just born and has not yet grown strong or well fastened: the remains of the past and the fruits of the future.

In the morning, when the storm has passed, the beaten grass around the barrel reveals the overflow of the night: the shriveling flakes of foam, the blossoms washed to fatal translucency. The carp will float white belly up, death depriving them of the only dignity of creatures—being properly positioned in space.

And you will stand there, a small child, your cheek still remembering the pillow's warmth. And you will pity no one and no thing: not the fish, not the blossoms, not the fruits, as if you've seen it all dozens of times, in different places and at different times; as if of earth's many sounds you love only one.

The sound of water gushing into the rain barrel.

* * *

*K*irill took another sip of wine, lit a cigarette, closed the file with the text he'd started writing, and set aside his laptop.

Now that there was no one in the house, he could smoke inside. There's the corner where he slept as a child. But they'd moved the couch. And the rain was absent now. But the season was the same—early June.

Why had he started the text that way, with his memory of the storm?

In the distance, the commuter train started out of the station—probably the last one to Moscow … Until morning … The train left, which meant the crossing would be closed.

Kirill thought about how he had been lined up at that crossing six hours ago.

The wind had cooled the dew on the grass and caused the dewdrops on hot hoods of cars to swell. To the left—houses behind impenetrable fences, silent, unlit. To the right—a small river in a hollow, looping through stands of reeds, surrounded by meadows. It was from those meadows, where the cattle were not yet pastured—the marshy soil had not dried out from spring—that the heavy fog rolled in, creating deceptive rainbows in the headlight reflections.

The wind stopped. The fog dampened the sounds. Suddenly from within the fog, illuminating its floating veils, came a blurred glow, turning into a bright yellow moving ball of light. All the drivers turned. Out of the gloom there came something as mystically ominous as a halo around the sun, a sign of coming events so horrible that they could extract an inarticulate symbol from mute matter.

An instant later, the terrible sensation vanished. Braking in the heavy fog, the Moscow train quietly rolled up to the crossing; its headlight shone brightly.

A ball of light. It set off a chain of associations that led Kirill to the night of rain.

A ball of light. The image was tied to Grandmother Lina.

8

Kirill closed his eyes, trying to recall that stormy night long ago.

He was a child again, he heard the announcement through the hiss of interference and the singsong moans of radio waves: "Forecasting a strong storm in the Moscow region, with winds gusting to eighty kilometers per hour."

That storm had been gathering for over a week, its heat oppressive and enervating. Grandmother Lina's joints ached, but she went out and set supports under the fruit-laden apple trees. It was a good harvest year, she said, she didn't remember that many apples ever, except right before the war, in June, forty-one.

And on the seventh day, when it seemed that the storm would dissipate, exhausting itself in a protracted warm-up, or bypass them, thundering beyond the horizon, the radio said in the morning: "Forecasting a strong storm in the Moscow region, with winds gusting to eighty kilometers per hour."

Kirill did not believe the forecast: the sky was pale, the grass and branches lifeless; even the water seemed to hunker down, weakened by the heat, and the forest brook moved listlessly.

After noon a blue-gray wall of clouds appeared in the distance. Seeing it, Grandmother Lina stopped eating—an unheard-of event, for she believed in finishing every task, movement, gesture, and phrase—and hurried into the garden to hide tools and things, telling Kirill to shut the windows tight, every single latch.

Something happened with her that Kirill had never seen. It was as if ghosts of terrible, unimaginable catastrophes, wars, fires, floods, were nipping at her heels. His grandmother didn't rush around pointlessly, she picked things up with tight, precise movements, and the trajectories of her steps followed the shortest, most economical path, as if they had been calculated and rehearsed.

She was taking her own possessions out of harm's way—the

old pup tent she used to carry hay, the bench they used when picking gooseberries. A stray cat was rubbing itself against the porch, but she paid no attention to it—the invisible dome of her concern covered only people and people's things.

Kirill ran through the rooms, checking the window latches; he came out on the porch, annoyed by Grandmother's anxious precautions—it was just rain, what was there to be afraid of?

Then they secured the greenhouse beds. Kirill brought smooth stones to hold down the plastic, and their weight gradually made him internalize the power of the coming storm; when the cucumbers and tomatoes were covered tight, he straightened up and turned to look—and froze.

The separate mass of clouds coming from the north was gone. The sky itself was changing color and materiality, as if a fatal and fast-moving gangrene were devouring the heavens.

A violet tongue lashed out, as if from a snake's mouth, and licked something beyond the forest.

There was a deafening thunderclap.

The slowly rotating weathervane made from aluminum at the military aviation factory—a gift from grandfather's army friends—suddenly whined, its propeller humming and turning into a bright shimmering disk.

The wind gently pushed against the walls. The windowpanes reinforced by nails moved and jangled. The tree crowns moved as one.

The weathervane slowed down and froze, like the reel on a fishing rod when a pike touches the bait and leaves.

The rain started—tap, tap, tap, tap-tap, tap-tap-tap ... The pure, large drops made noise on the leaves and on the roof. Nothing terrible. A summer shower, maybe a little harder than usual.

If not for the purple boil of the sky!

Grandmother Lina, a raincoat over her shoulders, walked around the yard, picking up everything metal—a hoe forgotten in the beds, a dustpan, the compost bucket, a frying pan filled with soapy water.

She always worried about lightning during storms.

She had long been asking her son, Kirill's father, to chop down the big birch trees on the property. Tall trees attract lightning, she would say. She seemed to think that the storm's electricity was looking for her, trying to get her.

They considered it an eccentricity: lots of people have odd fears. And Grandmother laughed about it when the weather was good. But the storm was approaching and Kirill sensed that there was a reason for her fear. She seemed to know what could happen and she put away everything that could attract evil and conduct it—literally and figuratively.

The rain, having wet the grass and leaves, was almost over. The weathervane spun lazily.

The sky had turned to glass, its belly low to the ground, thickening with inky toxic murk.

Then the weathervane sang again; they say the reel sings when the pike has swallowed the hook and disappears into the depths.

Kirill instinctively looked at the homemade lightning rod, sticking up above the television antenna: a stripped branch with a metal rod on top and a wire running into the ground. He had picked up his grandmother's tense anticipation and he felt that the clumsy construction was their only defense.

The lights flickered. From way up high, with a great swoop, a wall of water pounded the house. The dampness fogged up the windows. Turbulent rivers flowed from the drainpipes into the barrels, the rain lashed at the windows with such ferocity that water seeped through the cracks in the putty.

Grandmother Lina was taking off her raincoat in the entry. Kirill went up to the attic, one floor closer to the thunder.

The lights blinked convulsively. Blue lightning ripped through the dark. The storm's whirlwind spun the apple tree foliage.

A branch broke off the Arcad apple tree that Grandmother was treating for lichen on the bark. An Antonovka tree was split down the middle, fell, bounced, and scattered apples in every direction. The crowns of the enormous birches were tossed at a height beyond his vision, but he could see the thick trunks straining in the wind. Any of the birches could fall on the house, destroy the thin apex of the roof resting upon the rafters.

The lights went out.

Hail. Icy clumps, a strange summer sugar. It banged and drummed on the panes.

Water fell from the ceiling, dripped from the window frames—the old house wasn't made for a storm like this.

The mice scurried, climbed up the stairs; the cellar must be flooded; there were so many of them!

Primal fire cast long shadows. Grandmother lit a candle on the first floor.

There were lots of people around, in the neighboring houses. But he and grandmother were alone with the wind, dark, and rain.

Usually Kirill sensed that Grandmother Lina knew where he was in the house, kept him in her field of diffuse but still sensitive attention; that field was gone. Grandmother Lina was walking around with the candle, rechecking the latches. Her figure was reflected in the sweaty windows. She moved like a sleepwalker.

A thud—and the window smashed, broken by an apple tree. The candle fell from her hands and rolled along the floor, without going out. Grandmother picked up a kitchen tray and covered the hole, as if expecting someone to try to climb in. He picked up the candle, not feeling the hot wax burning his fingers, and stood behind her. The neighbor's window reflected the flame—not as a narrow sharp tongue but as a glowing rainbow sphere. Grandmother shuddered and backed up, holding the tray before her like a shield; she was terrified of the flickering sphere.

The wind blew into the broken window and put out the candle; the ball of light reflected in the window vanished.

Grandmother Lina sank to the floor. Kirill hurried over. Her breathing was weak and quiet but light and clean, as if the person breathing were the little girl Grandmother used to be, and not an old woman sick with asthma.

A minute. Two. Three. The breathing did not change.

He saw the white cabinet on the wall with the medicine kit; the pale word "faint" floated in his mind and then the sharp, stinky, and bracing "ammonia."

Kirill brought a wad of ammonia-soaked cotton to his grandmother's nose. He remembered how she used ammonia to remove old stains and had cleaned a silver ring's patina. He believed in that liquid as an alchemist would, believed that it would chase out whatever had settled inside her, preventing her from breathing fully. The ammonia did not let him down, Grandmother opened her eyes, pushed away his hand holding the cotton, and muttered weakly, "That's enough, enough, don't, Father …"

Kirill did not notice the word "Father," it had sounded to him, in his happiness, like "don't bother."

"Please bring me some water," she asked; if she was as polite as ever that meant that she was herself again and the strange fear was gone.

Kirill helped her up. He wanted to ask why she'd been frightened by the glowing reflection in the window, but he sensed that she did not want questions.

"I'll go to bed," he said and kissed her cheek.

"Go, my dearest," she said tenderly. "The storm is passing."

He shut the door behind him.

The rain was no longer pelting, it was drumming steadily; the frenzy was gone. Kirill was tired, as if the tempest had lifted him into the air and then thrown him to the ground, breaking him, twisting him, whipping him with sudden bursts. His muscles ached. Kirill realized that he had lived through the storm *with* the apple trees; mentally and emotionally he had struggled, held up trunks, supported the branches; his strength was gone, physical and spiritual. Without making the bed, he fell onto his couch in the corner and fell asleep. The water fell noisily into the rain barrels. He felt the strain of their metal hoops.

Kirill slept without dreaming—dreams require effort; he fell into the depth of nonexistence.

He woke close to noon; opening his eyes, he listened to his body, empty and new, not lived in yet.

When he came out on the porch he thought he was still asleep and had stepped into a chaotic world where things had not yet returned to reality, found their place and assumed the usual order.

The branches of a fallen apple tree blocked the porch. Emptiness gaped where the crowns and trunks used to be, as if some evil force had abducted them and removed them to another dimension, removing the usual supports of vision, consciousness, and memory.

Juice still foamed out of the snapped trunks, but the leaves were faded; yesterday the foliage had been full of life, and now life was gone, all at once. The apples in the grass were shiny, washed by the rain.

A poplar had been toppled by the fence. Its leaves were still glossy and firm. He thought, if you could raise the poplar it would easily grow back into its previous place. The apple trees, exhausted by the ripening apples, died instantly, but a fruitless tree was tougher; a repulsive law of nature was revealed to Kirill.

The yard was thoroughly destroyed. The plastic vegetable bed covers, which they'd patched and mended, were torn to shreds. The currants and plums were ruined, only the smaller and prickly gooseberries survived, clinging to the sharp branches. The beds were washed away, and the pathetic, childlike bodies of immature carrots, turnips, and beets stuck out of the ground. The cucumber netting was pounded into the mud; the infantlike tiny cucumbers floated in dirty puddles—only yesterday they were in the silvery sweat of birth, in a tender fluff.

The neighbors hadn't had time to take down the wash. Now an old cotton dress with big roses hung on the fence, children's shirts lay on the grass like evidence of desperate flight, running through the dark with demons of the night at their heels; the disheveled traces of the chase were still in the air, you could feel them in your nostrils.

Only now did Kirill notice that the storm-washed air carried a burning smell. Smoke of a dying fire rose over the village.

He understood where the smoke was coming from, whose house had burned down.

The Sergeant's house, recently left ownerless.

* * *

*E*ven decades later Kirill remembered the old man as if it were yesterday.

The Sergeant had a special aura.

He was of medium height, nothing remarkable about him, with an ordinary face, pockmarked in an ordinary way; his clothing was slightly shabby—a missing button, worn cuffs, a spot on a trouser leg, but a lot of village men dressed like that.

But everyone in the village and in the dachas knew that he had been recommended twice for a Hero of the Soviet Union award and both times he was not given the Gold Star. He did not brag about the many other orders and medals he had, he kept them in a box under his workbench. He didn't show them to just anybody—they were personal—but he didn't pay much attention to them, either. He was not invited to speak to the Pioneer volunteer group or to lay a wreath at the obelisk marking the war graves.

Only the most perceptive guessed that the Sergeant was eaten by his envy of commanders who had received the Red Stars and Red Banners on *his* blood, as well as the Khmelnitsky and Suvorov medals, for which he was not eligible as a noncommissioned officer; envy for everyone who stole glory and a piece of the big victory pie, who brought home German trophy goods by the truck- and train-load and then wrote memoirs about the division's glorious war, something like *Beneath the Guards' Banner* or *Frontline Roads*. And what was he? A sergeant. There were millions of sergeants like him, dead and buried.

The Sergeant was born in this village, served as a scout in the war, and came back afterward. They whispered—secretly—that he had gotten into mischief after the war, for Moscow was nearby and there were lots of hotheads like him there. But then he gave it up, got a job as a watchman at the vegetable warehouse; he made money from "unofficial" truckers—but these were just rumors; sometimes the police car was parked by his house, the chief of the regional crime division would come to share a bottle. He, too, was a former scout, they had fought on the same front.

Of course, the village respected the Sergeant for not sticking his medals in everyone's face, but that's not enough. There was something else. Say, when a man is chopping wood, it's a peaceful picture. Whatever the Sergeant picked up—ax, saw, chisel, curved pruning knife—the metal took on a different meaning in his hands; it became menacing, and not peaceful. The teeth of the saw, the blade of the ax, the point of the chisel, sated by birches and aspens, dulled on bast and bark, suddenly seemed to show their predatory fangs, with a thirst for salty blood, hot, and not the innocent juice of trees; that is what the villagers sensed, and that's why the Sergeant was the Sergeant, with a capital *S*.

Only his close neighbor, Fedoseyevna, a city woman sent to work in the village, had her own opinion of the Sergeant. She had once been a Komsomol member, was full of ideals, and had married his neighbor, a shock-worker tractor driver, before the war; he burned to death in a tank beyond the Oder River, when the German Tigers and Panthers were counted in tens, not hundreds. However, two tanks ambushed and burned the entire unit while they were bumbling around like orphans at the canal, looking for a way to get across.

Fedoseyevna wore mourning for her husband longer than customary in the village. And then she became the head teacher—she taught history—and decided to create a local history museum at the school and interview natives about how they fought and what they saw in the war.

This is how their feud started. Before, they'd lived without conflict, greeted each other in a neighborly way, the Sergeant even helping repair her greenhouses. She was a widow, after all, and he had certain ideas about that. He respected her in his own way for her long mourning, that she remained faithful to the twenty-five-year-old dead man, his childhood friend, whose remains, mere ashes and soot, were scraped out of the tank by the funeral squad. Why the hell did she have to start questioning him, and bring two Pioneers with her, a boy and girl, to write down the conversation?

"Ask your dead husband," the Sergeant told Fedoseyevna. She'd asked about the war, wanted him to talk so that the village children would be brought up on the example of veterans. And he shut the door.

Had she been a man, the Sergeant would have punched him. He could not admit that Fedoseyevna had wounded him deeply: in fact, his inner desire was to talk things out with her. And it had seemed to him that she'd discerned his inner desire, and that infuriated him. Hanging over this disagreement was the shadow of misfortune that no one had ever seen.

The villagers knew that in July, on the anniversary of the day the Sergeant was wounded in the Battle of Kursk, he closed his shutters and drank. Some said he took down the picture of Stalin from the wall, filled his glass, put it right up to the mustache, and drank with the Leader. Others maintained that he was perturbed about the only wound he'd received that wasn't, strictly speaking, military, and took this day to drink in anger over the mine shard that had clipped a chunk of meat from his buttock. He drank in the shuttered house, pouring himself a full measure of his old hatred for the enemy, but the booze didn't work on him, with his calloused heart. In the evening he went out onto the street with a steady gait, not swaying, looking for *Germans*.

The villagers understood, and didn't tell him that the war had ended almost forty years ago. They said that the Germans who had been there were chased away by heroes, just a week ago, and then headed West. Our soldiers hadn't left a garrison behind, after all, it was a small village, just one well. They presented the Sergeant, a hero liberator, with a glass of samogon moonshine with a hard-boiled egg and a crust of bread and coarse salt. That's the strong kind, the Sergeant always said, rejecting fine-grained salt from the store.

The kids reacted by hiding in ravines and bushes, it was all a game to them, but the adults took it seriously. No one scolded the Sergeant later for going around the village and upsetting people. Once the Sergeant beat up the new postman, some-body's nephew on a summer job who bicycled around in a stylish jacket; the jacket looked like a German uniform from a distance, and so the Sergeant decided that he was a German messenger. The Germans often traveled on two wheels, and the bike was shiny, from somewhere else, the Baltics perhaps. The Sergeant grabbed the postman and gave him a beating, but the village took his side and the aunt made it clear to her nephew that he could not write a complaint to the police.

One spring Fedoseyevna was given a new gander; it was either Polish or Hungarian—a distant relative worked in the socialist countries and gave the old woman a present. The gander truly was fine-looking—exceptionally white, like fresh snow; the orange beak was brighter than a tangerine; the body was pow-erful but not heavy, as it preferred flying to walking; mean and angry, it had killed the old gander, even though it was younger and weaker-looking. In short, an exceptional gander.

Fedoseyevna called it Martyn—she liked the brazen sound of the name, it suited the gander. But the Sergeant gave it a different name. One day—it was a moonshine day, he was in his cups—the Sergeant came out onto the street and the gan-der blocked his way, hissing. The Sergeant didn't count domestic animals and fowl or forest creatures among the living; he was called in to slaughter pigs, kill fowl, he shot rabbits in the woods for the sheer pleasure of killing, he visited old wartime friends in Siberia and hunted bears in their den, and here was some goose. But the Sergeant, drunken to a state of terrible sobriety,

looked at the gander and said with a nasty smile and a murder-
ous amazement:

"Why, he's a real Fritz! Freeeeeetz!"

And as he patted its long neck, he added, as if sizing it up,
"You grow up, Fritz! Grow up! And then …"

The gander let him pass—probably for the first time in its
life, for it did not fear dogs or cats; it shook its head in confusion, then hissed at the Sergeant's back and coiled its neck.

That's how the gander got its new name—Fritz. The kids
told their parents, the grannies gossiped, and the whole village
began calling the gander Fritz to spite the feisty Fedoseyevna,
who after all wasn't from the village. Fedoseyevna resisted, but
the gander forgot its former name, the boys teased it—Fritz,
Fritz, watch the blitz—and it got angry, not flapping its wings,
but stretching its neck and trying to bite. Fedoseyevna cried a
bit—the neighbor after all had stolen her gander, in a sense, by
renaming it—but then she got used to it, eventually even taking
pride, and considered the gander to be German, even though it
had never seen the German Democratic Republic or the Federal
Republic.

It happened about three years later, when Fritz reached his
prime. He had intimidated every small creature, his goslings
were growing up—with their father's temper, troublemakers, but
without his coloring, they were all grayish; apparently a flawed
breed, the villagers gloated.

Kirill saw it all that day; he and his pals were playing soldiers on the sand hill. They had roads in the sand, and one of
the boys—acting like a German driver—pulled a toy truck on
a string. The partisans had laid "mines" by tying strings to some
sticks; if they pulled the string in time, the stick would hit the
truck from underneath and knock it over; if they were too slow,
the sand would fly in all directions, and the German convoy

would keep going. The sand hill was by the pond, near the Sergeant's and Fedoseyevna's houses.

The Sergeant was drinking on that July day, the anniversary of when the German shard had torn his ass off as he was crawling along. He went out the gate, stared at the kids, and the boy "driving" the truck no longer wanted to drive; the Sergeant came over, examined the disposition, snorted—*shitty partisans*—and looked at each of them. He didn't like children, considered them the plague and let them know it, but he never touched them. For the first time, Kirill noticed the Sergeant's enormous hands, as if they belonged to a seven-foot giant but had been sewn onto him at the hospital; he saw the gray lupine hairs on his fingers and the thick yellow nails.

"Scram!" the Sergeant ordered. Kirill's friends scooted along the fence and ravines back to the village, but Kirill himself was going back to the dachas. He stalled, but the Sergeant had already turned around. He knew that no one would stick around when he told them to go.

Kirill pressed himself down into the sand pile.

The Sergeant went to the pond; and once again Kirill saw the huge hands that wouldn't fit in a pocket, he thought; they weren't human, they were bull-like, bear-like.

Fedoseyevna's geese were swimming in the pond; Fritz strode along the swampy bank, protecting the goslings testing the water. Seeing the Sergeant, the goose turned and headed toward him; Fritz hissed, and his eyes turned furious, recognizing his enemy. The Sergeant, when sober, teased him frequently. It seemed like the Sergeant would back off, maybe even run away, because a drunk could not handle a devious and agile goose; the Sergeant's anger was stale and rotten, like a two-year-old pickle; the gander was filled with pure fury, as if he had been waiting a long time to get even.

But the Sergeant had been waiting for the goose to attack. With a swift movement of his arm, which suddenly became too long, telescopic, he grabbed the gander by the neck and raised him in the air, squeezing the throat tighter. The bird struggled, beating his wings, he must have weighed fifteen kilograms, how could he hold that weight with an extended arm? But the Sergeant held him, and Kirill felt what strength lived in the old man's body, a slow, crushing strength, like a vise; he felt it as if he were the goose, feeling the steel fingers on his own throat.

The gander sagged, the tips of his wings trembling. The eyes had lost the madness of the attack and were meek and rolled backward; the Sergeant patted the bird's head with his left hand, saying, "That's it, Fritz. Gotcha. That's it, Fritz. Don't struggle. You'll only make it worse. That's it, Fritz. Your time has come. It's come."

The Sergeant looked into the gander's eyes. Kirill realized that he wasn't seeing a bird but some German corporal or camp cook who made the mistake of stepping away from the bunker just then. It was important for that little German to die quietly—he was of no use for the scouts, his rank was too low—no screams, no sobs, and so the Sergeant was seeing him off into death, whispering almost gently, to keep him on the road to death, not wanting to return even for a second, dying obediently, without any unnecessary fuss.

Kirill wanted to run out and latch onto the Sergeant's hand, to release the goose. But he sensed that the Sergeant would take him for someone else: he wasn't seeing the pond or the geese or the village houses; he was there, in the war, in the swamps near the Dnieper River or in some German town. He couldn't be pulled out of there, because it was all mixed up in his head; the Sergeant wouldn't see you, a boy from the nearby dachas, he would see a young soldier in the *Volkssturm*, and not vaguely, as in a deceptive dream, but determinedly. His memory would transform your clothing, your face, place an anti-tank rocket in your hands.

Kirill was afraid of many things, but this kind of fear was new. He sensed he had wet himself. The King of Fears came in the guise of the Sergeant, strangling the gander Fritz. The Sergeant believed he was killing a real German; the horror was in the very existence of such a situation, because it meant that nothing had any foundation, there were no laws among people.

The Sergeant put both hands around Fritz's neck, interlaced his fingers, and the goose's neck began to turn. It was then that Kirill heard the goose screaming, not hissing or honking, but screaming, and his cry was close to human speech, as if Fritz were trying to explain to his killer that he was not a German soldier and was calling on the world as witness. But the head was already moving unnaturally, the way a living thing cannot. Then there was a crunch, the thread of life broke, and the head fell to the side; a green mass oozed from the beak.

The Sergeant laid the goose on the ground carefully, stood staring at the dead bird. Then he looked around, saw the rest of the geese as if anew, clustered by the pond, clucking softly. Fritz's son, the second eldest gander in the flock, had gathered them and stood a bit in front, both to declare his leadership and not to irritate the Sergeant with excessive bravery.

Kirill wanted to shout—fly, run, save yourselves!—but he couldn't speak. The Sergeant muttered with icy zeal: "Fritzes! Oh-ho, how many! Fritzes!" He went to his house, repeating "Oho! Oho!"

Kirill hoped that the Sergeant was off for another drink and he would be able to chase the geese into the bushes or the reeds or summon an adult. The Sergeant went into the house; Kirill wanted to run, but a soldier's sense told him to wait: don't hurry, don't show yourself. And sure enough, the Sergeant came out on the porch with a hunting rifle; he sat down by the fence, stuck the barrel between the boards, and looked through the sight. Kirill thought that the sight would bring the geese closer, make the Sergeant's gaze sharp—optics, clean glass, they don't lie—and he would come to his senses, understand with whom he was warring on a hot July day, who was hiding by the pond stretching their long necks; then he noticed that the Sergeant's trouser pockets were bulging with cartridges.

The first shots were like the crack of a shepherd's whip. The pointed bullet tore right through the goose; *bang, bang, bang*— the geese fell, bloodied feathers flying; the Sergeant did not miss. Then the rifle jammed. His fingers had stumbled, with the samogon pumping through the veins, they had not loaded the cartridge properly. He jerked the magazine and then froze—as if the resistance of the mechanism twisted something in him as well.

Fedoseyevna ran out to the geese; they were sprawled on the grass, one fluttering a wing, the Sergeant's aim was slightly off. You couldn't see the blood from a distance, but you could see they were dead; a dead man can look alive in death, but a bird lies there like a sack. The bullets had taken away everything—grace and personality.

The Sergeant stood, turned, and looked straight at Kirill, hidden behind the sand pile. Kirill wanted to bury himself in the sand, but it was too late—the Sergeant had seen him, seen him with the vision that turns geese into Germans. Kirill felt he was the gander Fritz, felt those hands on his neck. He realized that the Sergeant was going to kill him, boy or goose, it made no difference to him.

"What have you done, you Herod! Herod!" Fedoseyevna attacked the Sergeant, pushed him in the chest. "Herod! Herod! Herod!"

Herod; Kirill did not know the word, but it struck the Sergeant, penetrated his drunken head. Maybe he remembered the priest's words from childhood, back when there was a chapel that stood at the head of the spring, and a brick church, too—now it was a kolkhoz warehouse.

Kirill thought the Sergeant would kill Fedoseyevna. He never allowed anyone to touch him, and here she had him by his shirt lapels. But he sank to the logs, shook his head, and then fell to his side. Fedoseyevna forgot about the geese, ran into the house, her worn heels kicking up the hem of her unwashed slip; she returned with a pail and poured the well water, icy cold, over the Sergeant.

He came to. People were watching over their fences, but did not come out into the street, understanding this was between the two of them. He shook his wet sleeves, looked around, as if he didn't know who he was or where; he saw Fedoseyevna with the pail and asked peacefully, but with surprise, "Have you lost your mind, old woman? It's my day today. I have the right to drink."

The Sergeant was so quiet that Kirill climbed out from the sand hill to get a better look at the old man: Where was the killer who shot the geese three minutes ago? A harmless old man sat drying in the sun, as if Kirill had had a nightmare that would not be repeated.

But Kirill realized that it would. There would be another day, just as sunny, portending no disasters, and the Sergeant would come out, half-mad from the samogon, and whatever came his way—a dog, a suckling calf, the electrician with a folding ladder—would be a fascist. And Kirill won't have time to run away again, because the others were faster, smarter, and braver, and he would be the one who must remain for the Sergeant to punish.

Kirill hated the Sergeant for the knowledge that would never give him any peace; his fate was determined.

In the meantime, the Sergeant noticed the dead geese. After a pause, he asked grimly, "Me?"

"You," Fedoseyevna replied and burst into weeping, not the way she usually cried, with scant tears, but sobbing, bitterly and helplessly; even an infant would see that she loved the Sergeant.

The Sergeant hiccupped, once, twice, three times, as if the large demons had already left him, and now much smaller demons, harmless, like flies, were crawling from his mouth. Still weeping, Fedoseyevna struck his back and sobbed, "Not you, you didn't do it! It's the damned war inside you!"

Kirill thought she had forgiven him, completely, and would forgive him another ten times, even if he shot the whole village and butchered all the innocent animals. And had the Sergeant shot Kirill, Fedoseyevna would have wept for the boy, but she would have also forgiven it.

The hiccupping stopped. The Sergeant put his arm around her and led her to her house, but he did not lower his eyes at the sight of the dead geese—as if to say, it's my fault, I know, but I won't let anyone blame me.

***

*T*he following spring when Kirill was brought to the dacha, the Sergeant was no longer among the living. They said he went hunting in the winter and died. There had been a lot of snow and the hares went over the fence covered by snowbanks to gnaw on the new branches of the apple trees. The Sergeant didn't notice the old communications ditch, left over from the war, covered by the snow, and rammed one ski into it, fell, and broke his leg; an open break. But he did not give up, he took off the skis and crawled back to the village; he shot his rifle, thinking someone would hear his distress call.

He would have made it, but a blizzard came up, covering the ski trail, and he lost his way. The hard cold came after the snow, chilling the forest; the air froze between the firs, there wasn't a sound or a rustle, everything was clenched by the frost, except for the water frozen in the trunks, which broke the trees from within.

The cold stopped the Sergeant's heart. They found him, stiff, and they brought him out of the woods on a sled, like firewood. They whispered in the village that the communications ditch had belonged to the Germans, and so, in a way, the ghost of a German killed in the winter of 1941 crossed over from the other world, grabbed the Sergeant by the leg, and dragged him to his death.

Kirill learned of the death by accident, overhearing a neighbor's conversation. The world felt roomier to him, as if the man had taken up a huge space; a menacing cloud gone from the sky.

But Kirill avoided the goose pond and no longer played in the sand pile. The geese were there, a new gander, Fritz's son, was the leader, and Kirill was amazed that the geese remembered nothing, just lived their goosey lives in which last summer was far beyond the horizon; no memory—no fear. He wanted to learn not to remember, so he forced himself to forget—he started small, for instance, he tried to forget what they had for breakfast Sunday, and in despair saw that his memory was getting better, deeper, and willful, as if Kirill were its servant. He dreamed of having the power to erase bad memories, destroy places and things that reminded him of fear.

That was why Kirill ran as fast as he could to the Sergeant's empty house when he realized it was burning—the path was covered with water, which splashed up into the air, frogs leapt this way and that. He unlatched the gate, the chain clanged, and the dog behind the fence barked at him. Here's the turn, here are the three firs that survived the storm, and here ...

A pile of horrifying black logs; the fire was extinguished but below, in the bricks of the foundation, in the coals and ashes, the heat was still alive; dirty and stinking steam rose over the ashes.

The house had burned to the ground. Kirill guessed that the gas tank had exploded. But to burn to the ground …

"It was lightning," someone muttered. "It hit the antenna."

People didn't seem to know for sure whether it had been lightning or not. But people believed it already; it wasn't a random coal rolling from the grate—it was lightning, which made it more significant and scarier.

"You see how God made his judgment," one of the old men said, without sorrow or sympathy, accepting the higher sentence.

Kirill stood there unable to believe it. Fedoseyevna wept in the arms of her women friends, while he, even though he knew it was shameful and wrong, thanked the storm. He saw the geese indifferently feeding at the pond, and he thought they had overcome the Sergeant together; there would be no fear.

But the next week he was traveling away from the village, from the dacha, with his mother. An old man got on the train at the Belorussian station. He was dressed too warmly for the season; he must have suffered from rheumatism. People blocked his view, and Kirill saw only a hand, against the old military coat and raffish boots, the tops of white felt that belonged to a colonel or general, the patent leather, embroidered in triple stitching. Kirill recognized that hand, immobile, wearily lowered, but full of old strength, a strength that is not in the flesh but in the bone, ossified, ancient.

Kirill thought it was the Sergeant, still alive—or that he'd come back to life—that he'd come to the city, gotten off the train and onto the Metro. Kirill hid behind his mother, peering out: he thought the Sergeant had come for him.

The crowd eased and Kirill saw that this was a different old man who didn't look like the Sergeant at all. The old man got out two stops later, leaning on his cane and shuffling his boots; Kirill could still see the hand. It all came back:

"You grow up, Fritz! Grow up! And then …"

He was cold, afraid, had a sense of doom: the renewed knowledge that there are Sergeants and geese Fritz in the world, and they are brought together by life, because they are meant for one another, and nothing had changed with the death of a single Sergeant from the dacha.

Everything was coupled together and lay in his memory. When there was a rainstorm, with hail—wherever he was, Kirill recalled that night at the dacha, the tempest, falling apple trees, grandmother at the window in fear, the burning smell from the village, the charred giblets of the burned house, Fedoseyevna and the Sergeant, the sand pile where he hid, the dead geese, the Sergeant's voice: You grow up, Fritz, grow up and then, the Sergeant's huge hand. It felt as if everyone in the world was an adult and he was still a child, feeling his immaturity; the Sergeant had *removed* something important for achieving adulthood from him when he killed the geese he took for German soldiers in front of him.

The night at the dacha … the tempest … The sound of water falling heavily into the rain barrels.

He fell asleep, like diving into the dark whirlpool of the barrel, the swirling foam and fallen leaves.

***

Kirill woke early, it was just getting light. He wasn't hungover, but he felt weak, as if the past had sucked out his strength through the narrow straw of memory. He had a powerful sensation of something squeezing his right wrist—as if the Sergeant's stone hand had caught him and wouldn't let go.

Kirill pulled his hand out from the blanket, afraid he would see the bruises made by the dead man's fingers.

No, nothing there. It was memory. The memory of handcuffs.

Kirill realized with indifferent surprise that last night was the first time in six months that he had not thought about what had happened. The arrest. Imprisonment, which was commuted to not being allowed to leave the country. He no longer pictured himself without those thoughts, used to running through all the events and their consequences, testing every point—could he have done something different then, foresee, avoid? But on the way to the dacha Kirill forgot. He had not been here for a long time, the house remembered him as a free man, and the air in the rooms was locked since fall, slightly sour, cold, redolent of mice, dried St. John's wort, old wood, as well as something lingering from earlier times, like the antique furniture in the rooms and the black-and-white family photos; a thick, magical brew of oblivion.

But his thoughts ran in circles. A May afternoon, a rally, thousands of people; flags, posters, a naïve feeling of victory to which Kirill succumbed, even though he had gone there as a historian, to see live what he studied; then—police, shields, helmets, truncheons, dozens of telephones filming the mass of people, the tangle of arms and legs, the smoke from burning flares, someone being dragged, someone fighting off the police—and somewhere in the midst of bodies and faces there was an unnoticed video camera held by an operative dressed in civilian clothes; there, captured by the lens, was a miniature, digitized Kirill running around, trying to cry out to his life-size self, to warn him of the danger.

The airport, the flight from Berlin, the strange holdup at passport control—the border guard spent a long time flipping through his passport; at last Kirill was let through and he was immediately approached by a policeman; "Let's go," and he went, asking "What's the problem?" but he was walking … The questioning, the road to the detention unit, darkness, he remembers nothing, as if his inner light had been put out; all he saw before him was the luggage rolling on the baggage claim belt.

Once again the rally, faces, more faces in the camera's eye, from which the investigators would choose the accused, charge them with resisting the police; and once again the thoughts—why did they pick him, for which secret reasons? Kirill knew it was random, but believing in pure randomness was even scarier than thinking that he had made a misstep somewhere, had behaved incorrectly somewhere, and that was why events turned out as they did.

He had that feeling again that had tormented him in jail: the arrest and imprisonment weren't happening to him, Kirill, but to some component part of him as grandson Kirill, great-grandson Kirill. Not an individual, but a unit of the line, the heir to the family fate. Sometimes Kirill even thought that this feeling was saving him, it explained what happened, it answered the question "why."

When they announced that he was amnestied, incommensurately and inappropriately, Kirill recalled walking through the woods alone as a child, and suddenly being overwhelmed by an inexpressible fear. He thought that someone enormous, bodiless, and blind was moving through the woods, and that the enormity had sensed Kirill's presence inside itself, the way a human feels a prickly fir needle under his shirt; the thing stopped and tried to feel him; the cool forest air blowing on his skin became the touch of that creature. A second, two, three—and it moved on, dissolving into the forest, leaving only the memory of touch and fear.

With the news of the amnesty, Kirill experienced something similar; the same blind something had touched his fate and then was gone, but he remained standing and listening to the sounds of the forest.

Kirill slowly walked through the house and looked into the study where he had been working on the computer the night before.

In the light of day, the study looked different. The oblique sunshine illuminated books, copies of documents made in libraries, files, photographs, maps—his work, his project of the last few years; retyped and revised ten times, familiar in every dog-eared page; everything that he could find about his family history.

But now, thanks to the bright sunlight, Kirill felt that what had happened to him cast an altered light on the past, a sunspot that shifted the shadows; the letters, numbers, and images under the covers seemed to wake up, sussing out among them new connections of connotations that had not existed before; they formed themselves into a book that he had been wanting to write and was unable to begin.

For many years he had been in the position of an author who collected other people's lives and had a retrospective view of the past. But, like his characters—his ancestors—Kirill was blind regarding the future, the new future that did not continue the past but eliminated it. The moment had come when he had learned everything he wanted to learn and was ready to start the book, but at that very moment he moved from author to *character* life picked up his text and willfully added a new chapter.

He had not yet decided whether he would leave the country

or stay. But now he clearly sensed that the path to the future lay in the book.

Here, in this house outside the city, were papers from family archives of various years, letters, diaries, photographs, the materials he had collected: documents, articles, extracts; thousands upon thousands of pages, handwritten and printed, still open, ready to talk to him, connected to him by thousands of threads of memory, retaining a conceptual unity, preserving the misunderstood and the unseen, waiting to be learned and to perform their duty. He needed to follow the path of the book—from the origin, from his childhood when he first felt his special connection to the past—in order for the family fate to let him go.

With a cup of coffee, Kirill came out on the porch.

He took a sip and lit a cigarette. He had to combine all the plotlines, facts, his own recollections and those of others, surrounding him like a galaxy; a galaxy that takes its start and spreads to the four points of the world from a single milestone that connects time: the old limestone monument, covered in green and black moss, at the German Cemetery in Moscow.

***

*I*n his childhood, once a month, not less, Grandmother Lina told Kirill: "Saturday we're going to the German Cemetery."

She packed her bag ahead of time—a trowel for the flowers, a stubby broom for sweeping leaves, a box of tooth powder to polish the marble that darkened quickly from the damp and rot. Grandfather suggested going by car, Grandmother refused; for some private reasons she preferred walking along the road that led from the highway.

Grandfather, Mother, and Father rarely went with her. Once Kirill started school, Grandmother Lina started asking for his help, without pressure, almost shyly, saying his going would make things easier for her. His parents and grandfather did not contradict the plan, and Kirill, while feeling it strange that Grandmother had chosen him as her constant companion, found the mysterious attraction of ritual in these trips.

And so they walked down Aviamotornaya Street past the unusual houses of postwar construction: four stories high with sharply steeped roofs, subtly German, and Kirill thought that this previously German neighborhood was spreading its imperceptible influence and changing the local architecture. Lettuce green, with slate roofs, these houses had formerly had tile roofs and were painted white, according to his grandmother.

Then they turned left, walked past the school and the ponds with non-working fountains. Through the thick poplars encircling the pond, there were glimpses of a high wall, puce, Kirill had never seen that color anywhere else, and it seemed alien to him, brought from abroad. Three rows of shallow brick niches were set in the wall, resembling crosses and also abstract human figures—many buried souls. The same kind of trees grew behind the wall, but a sensitive heart ascribed a different meaning to them—these were the poplars and lindens of the cemetery, looking down from the crowns into the dark abyss of the graves.

One more turn to the right, along the asphalt path, and beyond the stands with artificial flowers, the gates: red brick, with five pointy towers and silver-plated spires that resembled the façade of a Catholic church.

Kirill shuddered going through the gates. The city in which everything was familiar, including the old mansions and the new concrete buildings, remained outside, beyond the cemetery wall. Inside the gates a new space revealed itself, one that was entirely unfamiliar, as if an unknown power had brought a huge piece of land from far away, and Moscow grasses grew upon it, Moscow lindens set roots in it, but still you could tell: this was foreign terrain.

Your own, but alien. Alien, but your own.

Following the example of his elders, Kirill never told anyone that their family plot was in the German Cemetery. That was the custom in the family; Kirill valued being privy to the mystery that resembled a curse.

Grandmother Lina never led him to the grave by the direct and simple path along the main allée. She turned left then right along narrow paths among the decrepit, shuttered vaults and listing memorials with inscriptions in German, English, and French. Sometimes she stopped to catch her breath—the paths clambered the slopes of a hill over the Sinichka River where the water had been channeled into pipes—as if paying the tribute of memory to some unknown person. Kirill quickly realized that she always stopped in the same places—either her strength gave out at exactly the same distances or she truly was silently commemorating someone. Kirill started looking closely at the spots, but he didn't understand a thing: black diabase monuments resembling slabs of darkness, dug out of the grim depths of the night, bore foreign names that said nothing to him, and with all his imagination he could not connect the names with his grandmother.

Then they came to a low border sunken into the ground; among the ferns stood a small tombstone of gray marble: Sofia Uksusova, 1884–1941. This was the mother of Grandmother Lina, Kirill's great-grandmother. To the left and right—also inside the border—were two limestone monuments. The one on the right looked like a chest of drawers, the Gothic script, worn by frosts, rain, and wind, barely visible. The left was like an altar; the stone table was covered by a stone altar cloth with tassels, with an open book of stone on top of it.

Kirill did not understand church symbols, no one in the

family prayed or went to church. He felt the heavy significance of the stone book, and when his grandmother turned away, he stole furtive looks: were there letters on the stone pages? Kirill knew there weren't, but he believed that the letters existed and would appear someday.

He never looked closely at the inscription on the right obelisk; he felt the letters repelled his gaze, did not allow themselves to be read, as if the person beneath the stone was locked in his death and wanted nothing from the world of the living.

The book. He was deeply moved only by the stone book in the edifying simplicity of its empty pages.

Kirill felt a vague challenge coming from it: the one who has the right can read it. He went to the cemetery with his Grandmother for the sake of that book, as if it were calling him, reminding him, in some sense cultivating him for itself.

Kirill could not understand why his great-grandmother was buried in the German Cemetery. In foreign soil. Who had led her soul through the foreign, turreted gates?

Grandmother Lina always said: great-grandfather had worked in the military hospital diagonally opposite the cemetery. The family lived in the hospital wing. When Great-grandmother Sofia died, she was buried near the house, where the authorities had allocated space over the old graves.

The explanation seemed believable: among the old grave markers there were many new, Soviet ones—generals and officers who died in the hospital, engineers, professors, actors; Russian, Ukrainian, Belorussian, and Jewish names mixed with German ones in a multilayered, squabbling palimpsest.

Kirill believed the very convincing explanation—yet he did not believe it fully; the stone book hinted at another truth. Kirill waited for that truth to be revealed, in letters on the limestone pages.

Sometimes, his grandmother would go to the Donskoy Cemetery the next day, on Sunday. She did not take Kirill with her, and his parents rarely accompanied her. It was just "a trip to the cemetery," not to visit anyone in particular, just a pastime. Grandmother said that friends from her youth were buried there, but she did not name them; of course, she did not go often. Only once, in early autumn, she took Kirill along; it must have been in 1982.

They took the tram from Shabolovskaya. Grandmother, usually careful with money, even stingy, bought a big bouquet of red carnations. Kirill carried it. He felt the weight of the fading flowers that had drunk the murky water in the store's vase, poisoned by that water, already invisibly rotting; he felt the weakening stems, losing their firmness, and he thought the carnations would liquefy and pour from his hands in a sticky goo like slippery bark.

They headed straight for the crematorium. Kirill had seen it from afar: an industrial death machine, a modernist pavilion crowned by an evil crenelated tower. Funereal lanterns at the door, a heavy crude archway leading to the twilight of the portico; a construction that seemed completely opposite in form and sense to the light and festive Metro pavilions ornamented with columns and plasterwork, flowers and garlands. Kirill recognized it—the grim entrance to the underworld, to the Metro of the Dead.

Kirill came up with the idea of the Metro of the Dead on his own.

Some buildings in town that did not seem remarkable—an abandoned house, a transformer box, a grass-covered mound of a bomb shelter—gave him inexplicable shivers. He thought they were entrances to the other world, connected by dark underground tunnels.

He must have heard rumors about the secret Metro lines that led from the Kremlin to Stalin's dacha, Blizhnyaya; heard whispers of the military bunkers beneath Moscow.

Those rumors turned into the image of a different, upside-down Moscow that could be reached through the Lenin Mausoleum or other inconspicuous stations—a Moscow in which corpses rode eternally in ghostly trains along ghostly rails, penetrating stone, and the trains were very old, with cushioned seats and yellow paneling, the ones that were living out their days on the old lines.

Who the dead were and why they were doomed to travel underground, unlike his great-grandmother who slept honestly in her grave, Kirill did not know. He rarely thought about the Metro of the Dead: only when he saw an old building that might serve as an entrance, or one of the Stalinist high-rises near Krasnye Vorota, where there was an ordinary Metro exit on the first floor—and he imagined the same pyramid-shaped high-rises, inverted and mirroring the ones above ground, where the people who had once lived upstairs, now existed below; buildings with stores where they sold dead waxen food, with windows open to the bowels of the earth.

Kirill thought the crematorium at Donskoy to be the second main entrance, after the Lenin Mausoleum, to the Metro of the Dead. People milled about, and a large yellow bus, not a special one from the morgue but an ordinary passenger one, which some relative had managed to "borrow," was backing away. The crowd was made up primarily of men, in clumsy suits that sat heavily on their bodies, graying, balding, grim and flustered, not knowing where to stand or how to behave, as if there were no instruction manuals for such occasions and they felt lost.

Swallowing their curses, six men with black armbands pulled a coffin through the passenger doors: a scarlet woven ribbon caught on the door and fell off. A worker in blue overalls unlocked the doors of the auditorium.

The mourners straggled in, and with them Grandmother Lina. She slipped into the line and laid the bouquet of carnations at the foot of the coffin. Kirill did not understand what was happening, but her hand pressed his shoulder: stand and watch. Their bouquet along with the other flowers was covered, and the coffin rode down small, toylike tracks, bouncing on the bumps, into the crematorium, past all the doors, past the steel curtain, into the oven, into death.

Later they strolled along the cemetery paths. Kirill, who was accustomed to his grandmother being always a grandmother, soft and velvety, the velvet cushion for her needles, the glittering knitting needles making a gentle wool scarf, the flannel cloth with sewn edges to clean her tortoiseshell glasses, suddenly realized that her habitual elderliness was in part for show, that there was another person inside her, an old person he did not know, as hard as ivory, with the elderliness of stubborn things that had survived wars, evacuations, and deprivation not because people took care of them, saved them, carried them away in suitcases and bundles, but because they were inherently able to survive whatever their owners did; they had the ability to resist dispersion and not get lost in resistance.

Grandmother walked along the paths as if in conversation with the cemetery, all the graves, trees, falling leaves, the walls of the columbarium, the church, the houses beyond the cemetery fence, the monastery towers, the noisy roads, aloof and leading out of town to the thinning autumn forests where winter's deadly dream is born, the rivers growing quieter and shallower.

Kirill sensed that her words were seeking someone whose ghost might flitter here in the cemetery—and in a hundred other places; he strode silently, setting aside all his questions, trying to guess who had been given the carnations, already burned and adding nothing to the smoke rising above the crematorium.

Great-Grandfather Arseny. The one who wasn't in a grave at the German Cemetery. It would have made sense for him to be there, but he was not; Kirill knew only that he had been a military doctor and had died at the front. His grave was lost in the desperate chaos of retreat, and then, when three years later the Red Army, attacking the West, reached those areas, there was no one to remember who was buried where; all the soldiers and officers of the early drafts were killed outright; they were all in the ground.

Kirill thought that his grandmother was burning an offering to her missing father with the carnations, as if part of his soul was still in the air and could sense the bitter smoke. What amazed him later, as an adult, was that he had not seen anything strange in her action. His life had prepared him to invent unlikely but still viable explanations, connected to reality, for the strange behavior of adults, their inexplicable rituals, their omissions about the past.

Year after year Kirill went to the German Cemetery with his grandmother, year after year—until he was a teenager—he felt the allure of the stone book on the stone altar.

Grandmother Lina was aging and losing energy. Now he watered the flowers, raked up the leaves, while she sat on the small cast-iron bench, made just for one person to sit and grieve for a beloved. Sometimes his grandmother asked him to clean both limestone monuments—when spiders spread their webs on them or when melting snow left dirty smears.

Kirill came, on his grandmother's instructions, to tend the orphaned monuments that had lost their living people. And Grandmother stayed home more and more and he went to the cemetery alone.

Sometimes Kirill didn't even go to the family plots, he simply roamed around, peering into the faces of statues, laughing at vainglorious epitaphs, stern photos in oval frames—they were equally suited for honor roll plaques and for gravestones. The residents here no longer had the habits of Soviet people, they had left the Party, did not participate in parades on May Day and November 7, did not read the reports on harvests in *Pravda*, did not listen to the speeches of the Secretary General—and Kirill relaxed with them, as if with pleasant and easygoing neighbors.

The German Cemetery became part of his inner landscape: he recalled its trees, avenues, monuments when he looked for images of contemplation on destiny, history, generational connections, love, family, alienation, and loneliness.

Kirill studied the cemetery's history—written and unwritten. One of the vaults had a mosaic: Charon rowing a soul to a steep island covered with cypresses. The cemetery seemed to be such an island, which even the Soviet regime could do nothing about. After the putsch, after the collapse of the Soviet Union, he unconsciously waited for something like a return, a resurrection of the dead—for it was the end of the afterlife reign of the pharaoh who lay in the granite pyramid in Red Square.

One day that fall Grandmother Lina told Kirill that they had to go to the cemetery the next day to clear leaves. The trees were not completely bare yet, but Kirill paid no attention to that detail: she had been feeling poorly, and if she suggested going that meant she was getting better.

In the morning they took their usual route, but at the entrance, Grandmother led him to the flower store, which shared a space with the granite workshop. Kirill's family never brought flowers to graves, even on memorial days. They occasionally brought flowers from the dacha, a bouquet of meadow flowers, daisies, buttercups, bellflowers, and salvia wrapped in a wet rag.

This homely bouquet stressed that *our* dead needed *nothing*, that they were modest in their requests to the living, they did not expect roses, hyacinths, or chrysanthemums—just the insignificant flowers of the fields where they had liked to walk, just the meek, scrawny blooms that had not known care or love, who faded just as they had grown, without individual value and beauty.

Kirill and his grandmother went into the store. Carnations, tulips, and roses of several varieties. One kind stood out, deep red, large and fresh, with large hooked thorns on the stems, as if they had not come from a garden in paradise, where plants live in concord, but from a hellish one, where flowers compete with one another, rip other flowers' leaves with their thorns, sink a sharp thorn into the heart of an unborn bud.

To his amazement, she chose those roses, and she bought the entire bouquet, thirty or forty stems. She didn't like roses, and if someone brought them for her, she put the vase far away on the windowsill. She loved violet irises, she embroidered them on pillow cases, transporting them from a long-ago happy summer of memory.

The seller tied the roses with string. They moved through the German gates, their pointed towers covered in silver scales, the simple, foreign cross, lacking the lower crossbeam of the Orthodox cross, the grim gates of red brick.

There had been a storm the night before. The cemetery, a center of tranquility, was transformed. Gaps showed in the crowns of trees, broken trunks lay among the graves—the wind was so fierce it did not topple trees gradually by swaying them but broke them in one blow. The marker railings were bent, metallic contorted grimaces, and gravestones were knocked down by heavy branches. The cemetery workers were sawing an overturned old poplar; its roots had pulled out a rotted coffin and the bones of the dead.

Kirill had never worried that something could happen to the graves. The apartment could be flooded by the upstairs neighbors, the dacha might get struck by lightning. But the darkened marble gravestone, the limestone altar with the book—all events were in the past here, and there was only the eternal aging of stone. He felt that the tempest was only an echo of a posthumous storm; for a day, an hour, the cemetery had come to life.

They passed the chapel, covered in graffiti with superstitious promises of mutual love and requests for success on exams; past the chain-encircled grave of the prison doctor, a German named Haas, past the arrow that read NORMANDY-NEMAN, pointing to the mass grave of French pilots of a fighter squadron that battled the Luftwaffe, buried either by accident or with irony next to a stele surrounded by cannon barrels, the burial place for Napoleon's soldiers who died in Moscow hospitals.

Someone must have been burning fallen branches nearby, but to Kirill it was the smoke of history, the smoke of Moscow burning in 1812, after which a new city was built, the city where people came in the nineteenth century to start a business or to work, the people who were buried in the cemetery: generals with stone medals on their chests; chocolate manufacturing kings buried under black diabase headstones; engineers, doctors, traders, and priests who served in churches of other denominations.

In his Soviet childhood he had seen the posthumous traces of their existence, the futile symbols of a distant past. Now he unexpectedly felt that the cemetery was *alive*. In the cursive fonts of German, French, English, and a dozen other languages, the dead were stating, they were born in a town that may no longer exist, or belongs to another country, and the house is gone, bombed by a Junker or a Boeing B-17, razed by a ship's artillery, destroyed by howitzers or Katyusha rockets, the church archives with birth records burned down, and the last relatives emigrated across the ocean, died in Auschwitz, were deported to Siberia—the dead were hidden here, in a randomly saved cemetery, as in an ark, and now gave witness before God about themselves, their perished descendants, scattered around the world, deprived of tombstones, unable to join their fathers, grandfathers, and great-grandfathers in the family vault.

The orphaned dead. Kirill saw the astounding, outrageous orphanhood of the dead, realizing how many abandoned graves there were here, how many stones bore a date inscribed before the revolution—and then nothing, a break, an abyss … He remembered the moss-covered gravestone on their plot belonging to no one—whose was it, whose name was carved on it?

Grandmother Lina walked slowly, leaning on his arm. He felt the weight of her body, the rustling sounds, the whoosh of her tired blood, the gasps of her lungs. Here it was, the burden of existence, though Kirill realized that his grandmother would be here at the cemetery forever. He was embarrassed by the thought, and he guessed from her look at him that she understood but was not offended; from her end of life the thought looked different than from his.

At the turn from the main allée lay a mound of broken maple branches. The leaves, which had been fresh yesterday, were drying, turning into parchment, their veins bending and hardening, like bird feet; the leaves had such a powerful fragrance that it seemed their green, light being was flying off with the scent.

She let Kirill go first at the turn—the path was too narrow for both of them. He went, remembering that she had always led him; was he in front now by accident?

Here on the path, as if in his courtyard, he recognized their neighbors. On the left, a lieutenant general, an honored artillery man, who in Soviet times had the unwritten right to a luxurious, individualized tombstone, a sharp-cornered slab of labradorite; on the right, the proprietor of the German pharmacy, Karl Gottlieb Shultz, and his children, who had shed the German name in the third generation; then the engineer Colonel Votyakin; an Englishwoman—governess, boardinghouse landlady—who died in the first year of the new, twentieth century. Her grave was opposite a nameless rusted cross, and then there was the Simpelson family, who always stood out in Kirill's memory because their daughter Radochka died at just eleven months, in 1941; the peasant faces of the Semenovs, who names were engraved over the former German ones on the old obelisk; then another Brit, "Why did you leave your homeland Wales," written as if it were a line from a song, and maybe it was; the weed-covered grave of the Pole Ludwikowski—who would have buried him in 1937 in the middle of the Great Terror, when even association with a Pole was dangerous?—and then the welcoming elderberry bush, the familiar wrought-iron border sunken into the ground with a small gate, little towers on the posts, and a heavy latch that needed lubricating with a little sewing-machine oil—they were there.

He opened the gate—Grandmother had always done that. She sat down to rest on the small mourning bench, as she called it; Kirill took out the broom, as usual.

"Wait," she said. "Not now."

She took a new shiny piece of steel wool from her purse.

Grandmother stood up with determination, went over to the stranger's monument, the limestone monolith framed with carvings along the edges that resembled an enlarged clock. Rain, dust, and mud made the stone wild, host to lichen and moss, covered with a greenish patina, and only with difficulty could you make out that something was written on it.

She approached it as if she had the right to do so, as if the monument had been waiting for her. She was no longer the familiar grandmother, mother of his father, but someone with a connection with the unknown, wife of someone lost in action, sister of nocturnal wastelands, daughter of the Civil War, granddaughter of the Tsushima catastrophe, great-granddaughter of emancipated serfs.

She rubbed the scrubber over the stone once, twice, three times; the dried lichen and fine limestone dust fell away. Beneath her hand clearing away the crust of time there appeared clear, firmly carved letters of the German alphabet: Ba; Baltha; Balthasar; Balthasar Sc; Balthasar Schwe; Balthasar Schwerdt; 1805–1; 1805–1883.

BALTHASAR SCHWERDT
1805–1883

Grandmother stepped aside, delicately, so as not to trample the ferns on the graves, looked at the monument, as if checking it against her memory, and then scrubbed beneath the first inscription, closer to the ground, where the moss and lichen were thicker and the dirt blacker; and once again, with the scrape of metal on the soft stone, deep, clear letters began to appear.

CLOTHILDE SCHWERDT
1818–1887

ANDREAS SCHWERDT
1856–1917

With her eyes, she told Kirill to come closer; she let him stand nearer to the grave, put her hands on his shoulders, turned him to face the monument, holding him tight, the way she had when she straightened his posture when he was a child, not noticing that she was hurting him, her fingers pressing with a strength that belied her age.

The enormous inner energy that had kept the knowledge of the names on the stone under lock and key was about to gush out in an instant—and Grandmother Lina did not know what to do with it, how to handle it, and so she kept squeezing Kirill's shoulders, while he, as if reading Latin letters for the first time, tried to pronounce the shuffling SCHW sound.

"Shverdt," she said. "Balthasar Schwerdt. One of the three wise men. Caspar, Balthasar, Melchior. Clothilde Schwerdt. Andreas SH-VER-DT," she repeated, and Kirill imaged that the sounds were intoxicating her, bubbling like champagne in her alveoli. Schwerdt—and the rock blocking the cave entrance rolls away, and out comes the resurrected in his shroud, touched by corruption but unharmed.

Grandmother Lina whispered something in German, as if to fix the letters in place and keep them from disappearing again.

Kirill did not know she spoke German, and the shock was as if the stone had spoken; and the stone had spoken, in fact.

"This is your great-great-great-grandfather," she said, apparently enjoying the repetition of *great-great*. "And your great-great-great-grandmother. And their son. Mr. and Mrs. Schwerdt," she said with a German accent, and Kirill was impressed by her pronunciation.

It was only then he understood *what* she had said, how she had connected herself, him, and the monument.

BALTHASAR SCHWERDT
CLOTHILDE SCHWERDT
ANDREAS SCHWERDT

Forever, for his whole life, until death, which would occur here, beneath these trees, in this earth.

"Hand me the flowers, please," said Grandmother Lina.

Now he understood why she had chosen the roses. Not irises from the summer garden of memory but conquering roses that signify not nostalgia but triumph, victory over oblivion.

Kirill took out a penknife to cut the twine around the stems. The knife slipped and cut his index finger, and a drop of blood was released. Kirill stared at the blood—for the first time it was not simply a physiological substance, the crimson, innocent moisture of the body, but the concentration of dark secrets. Before his blood had been his own blood, but now it was someone else's, flowing in his veins but not fully his own.

He now saw it as a mixture of bloods carrying different inheritances, different possible destinies, boiling from contact with one another, eternally arguing for primacy. This argument suddenly explained why his life was so unstable and drifted in multiple directions, why he did not know how to apply himself, why he was so restless and wasteful of time.

Standing by the border around the grave, he saw the stone book on the altar, the one from which he had expected a miracle, believing that letters would appear on the empty pages. As a child he thought it was the only one in the world; now he knew it was a genre of memorial, there were others in the cemetery exactly like it, with a stone altar cloth and woven tassels in the corners. But either through an amazing accident or through oversight, the pages in the other books had edifying inscriptions, for instance, "Come unto me all ye that labor and are heavy laden and I will give you rest" or "In the sweat of thy face shalt thou eat bread, till thou return unto the ground from which thou hast been taken." But *their* book, his book—the only one!—was blank.

With a grown-up's heavy feeling, he understood that his earlier presentiment was right: the book that revealed the secret of the Schwerdt family, that brought together everyone lying here at the German Cemetery and in the soil of various countries, who died on the ocean floor or who dissipated into smoke, would have to be written by him.

Looking away from the stone book, Kirill suddenly saw the cemetery with new eyes. He used to see it superficially, noting and remembering forms and colors: trees, paths, vaults, obelisks, flowers, crosses. Now, as if his grandmother had wiped away the patina, the gray moss from the space, giving his view sharpness and depth, he began to make out what he had never seen before. The cemetery tried to speak with him, to reveal its hidden symbols. They were everywhere, peeking out of the shadows, from behind branches and on monuments.

The first one he noticed was a Masonic triangle with the All-Seeing Eye, the eye of God, in the center of a stone sun with sharp rays resembling ancient swords; overgrown with reddish and greenish mosses, the Eye—the size of a hand—hid under the monument's relief arch that cast it in shadow.

Kirill shuddered: he thought the stone eye was looking at him. Having met the stony gaze, he began making out other signs scattered about.

Stars inside a circle; stars in bas- and haut-relief; crosses, Gothic, Roman, Celtic, carved in stone; crosses entwined with fabric and ribbons; crosses entwined with vines; wheat sheaves and grape clusters; chains; medallions with angel wings; leaf and flower ornaments; marble wreaths in which every flower was recognizable—here's a daisy, here's a rose, here's a campanula; trident anchors suspended from the wreaths; amphorae, the vessels of grief, tapering toward the bottom and tied by ribbons on their narrow throats; majestic cubes; six-pointed stars inscribed into a wreath; laurel branches, olive branches, palm branches, also tied by ribbons at the cleanly cut stalks; colored mosaics—blue squares, green rhombuses, black triangles, blue triangles; crossed swords and crossed scimitars; lions roaring and lions sleeping; eagles with wings spread; swimming fish; hammers, axes, and picks; interwoven rings, arrows, quivers, bats; other signs whose meaning Kirill could not decipher.

These symbols were as distant as Egyptian hieroglyphs or Sumerian cuneiform; he was *mute* in this language, he could name the signs—ivied cross, cloverleaf, amphora, crossed swords—but he didn't know what they meant. He was seeing the cemetery with his grandmother's eyes for the first time, and for her these images were a natural part of life, but for him, born in the Soviet Union and knowing only red stars, hammers, and sickles, they were dead.

He understood Soviet symbols; reading the tombstone "First Deputy Minister of Medium Machine Building," he could decipher the abracadabra of MINSREDMASH, which in the language of state secrets was the minister responsible for the atomic project, and he could weigh the place in the hierarchy of some lieutenant general by the orders incised into the stone; but even though he had read the Bible, and could tell the meaning of a cross covered in ivy, he could not accept it in his heart.

Grandmother gave him more than unexpected ancestors. The world of another culture appeared before him, a silent but living world to which he belonged by inheritance, by the right of wild, inexhaustible blood in which all eras and the starry sky flowed. Kirill would have to learn that old language, speak it, for it was the road into the past, where the shadows of Balthasar Schwerdt and Clothilde Schwerdt wandered in the pale asphodel meadows.

Grandmother was watching Kirill in expectation: Would he hurry to ask questions? Would he rebuke her silently? Even though the words were on the tip of his tongue, he said nothing, knowing that it was not only his grandmother evaluating him now—there was the Eye of God, and dozens of other invisible eyes. Is he the one? Will he manage? With great conviction he promised himself that he would manage—the last of the line, who now knew why he was born, what life had been preparing him for, sending signs and setting out the nets.

Grandmother signaled it was time to leave; Kirill shut the iron gate, looked back at the rose bouquet, red at the foot of the monument that had been simply a mound of stone half an hour ago and was now the axis of the world.

She went down the paths where she used to take Kirill as a child, stopping seemingly at random in several places. Kirill now guessed that each stop had indeed meant something, marked something. The cemetery was turning into a mysterious labyrinth, into a spectral reunion, as if all of Balthasar and Clothilde Schwerdt's friends and relatives, whom they used to see in Moscow and were now also lying here, had awakened and were reaching out to the living visiting their kingdom.

Leaving the underworld of Erebus,
The souls of people who had left life came to
the pit.
Women, youths, old men who had seen much
grief,
Tender maidens, feeling grief for the first time,
Many men fallen in cruel battle, with wounds
from sharp spears,
In bloody pierced armor.
This horde of the dead thronged to the blood
from everywhere ...

The Odyssey, Homer

Kirill recalled the lines. With his perfect memory for texts, one of his best university skills, when he got a boring question on the oral exam on *The Iliad* and *The Odyssey*, he chose instead to talk about Homer's metaphysical topography, how his heroes as they die move from the upper world to the lower one and how we can imagine a narrative where men who have killed, betrayed, poisoned, dishonored each other meet again—and this meeting is eternal, for they have nothing but eternity before them, an eternity without Christian suffering.

At that time he merely sensed the divine ease of his memory and sharpness of thought. Now, for the first time he thought of how many ancestors had studied Homer in different languages, sharpening the skills he would inherit; how many had hoped for the future, prayed for it, lived for it, giving up the past and the present—and now Kirill was that future. The one where everything came together, where all lines led.

Grandmother stopped. The narrow path, the thick damp shade. A tombstone of gray granite looked like a throne: the tall stele was the back, and the armrests on either side were granite blocks topped with bronze vases. Four steps led to the platform before the stele, scattered with dry leaves and twigs. At the top was a niche with a bronze face, a king of the Dark Ages, descended from barbarian rulers who worshipped fire and mistletoe. Thick bronze curls brushed back; a heavy mustache that could hide a couple of margraves; a well-fed chin; Neanderthal ears, ready to catch the sound of hunting and animal roars; narrow squinting eyes gazing into the unfurnished space with thoughts of bridges, roads, troops, ambassadors from foreign lands; a monumental nose, pitted with metal, smelling battles and gold; a hilly plain of a forehead; lips eager to suck out bone marrow; and a strange and incongruous detail—a bronze dickey with a tie encircling the tree-trunk-thick neck. Teuton, forest ruler in a dickey, conqueror of Rome, a sovereign whose statues were easy to imagine all over the country, equestrian, on foot, with a sword or scepter, taming a lion or pointing the way beyond the ocean, to the country of Eldorado (Kirill even thought he could see him in Lenin's place), a cast-down god, whose shrine was forgotten, whose adepts were scattered, but here, in this holy place, an echo still remained of the ancient faith.

The person was completely alien to Kirill. It was no accident he'd never noticed this monument during his walks with Grandmother Lina—the way you wouldn't notice a luxury car if that wasn't part of your world.

GUSTAV SCHMIDT
1839–1916

Schmidt … Kirill sighed in relief, for he had been on the lookout for Schwerdts. Here was Schmidt, some stranger Schmidt, judging by the headstone a millionaire, a Rabelaisian character with an appetite for quail by the dozens, villain of heartrending popular novels of early last century, owner of factories where poor souls toiled tied to furnaces and lathes. Grandmother must know a story about him, thought Kirill. He couldn't imagine being related to anyone in possession of more than an apartment, a simple country house, a car, ten thousand rubles in the bank.

"I never understood why they made the face in bronze," Grandmother said. "He was Iron Gustav. A steel magnate. I missed his funeral, I was with Papa at the front. But I remember Gustav. He's your great-great-great-grandfather. He's my mother's father—she was married to Andreas. Her maiden name was

Elizaveta Schmidt, and then she became Elizaveta Schwerdt. I would have made the bas-relief in steel."

Kirill regarded the bronze face, seeking at least some similarity or family features. He looked at his grandmother. Back at the monument. Not a thing. Then he realized that no matter how dominant *essential identity* can be and how powerfully it manifests itself, it can be hidden by performing a kind of natural selection on oneself. In the Soviet period his closest ancestors lived by chasing away Schmidt's legacy from themselves, afraid of being his grandchildren, and apparently they succeeded in this self-neutering; they renounced the primal power, the talent to own and control, for there was no outlet for that talent except making a career as a Soviet manager, general director or ruler of a gigantic construction project, plant, canal, or an entire region. But thank God they did not aim for that role, otherwise Kirill would have inherited very different ancestral sins.

"I've shown you everything," Grandmother Lina said. "There are also graves here of people I knew, but we can do that later."

Kirill did not know what to say. He had an urge for time to roll back, for the car to have broken down, for them never to have made it to the cemetery today.

He used to be protected by the innocence of not knowing, and now his fate was controlled by the same forces that had controlled the destiny of his ancestors. Kirill could not know for sure what those forces were, their nature, but he sensed that they were like a storm raging outside, piercing the sky with lightning, chasing travelers on nighttime roads, burning old oaks to their roots; they formerly had no entry into the *house* of his life—and now suddenly, ball lightning might fly in through the window opened by accident and turn *everything* to ashes.

Storm. A storm. The noise of water gushing heavily from the roof into the rain barrel. The moist, cold, dripping windows. The drooping grass. The heavenly sugar of hail, landing in cups and glasses left outside, resounding, melting, vanishing. The wildness of agitated tree crowns, violet slashes of blinding lightning.

That recollection reverberated like the tempest that had traveled across the cemetery, strewing broken branches and fallen railings. The echo was weak in his memory: the smell of burned wood, fallen apple trees, green apples hitting the grass like large shrapnel; Grandmother, her terror, the spherical reflection of the candle in the trembling window …

"Let's go," she said. "It's time. The sun is going down."

Kirill looked at the sky. The sun of course had moved past noon, but it was still high in the sky. He and his grandmother lived at different speeds, her time flowed much faster, her inner sun was setting, had been for a long time, was nearly in twilight, and that was what she saw now, illuminated by the declining sun, touched but not warmed by its weak rays.

The ones who were not in the cemetery, who had no tombstone anywhere, who were tied to these *named* monuments by the spectral thread of her memory—she was with them now, she saw *them*, conversed with them.

"Tomorrow we'll go to the Donskoy," she said.

Kirill was no longer surprised. He nodded. They stepped onto the main allée, walked through the cemetery gates beneath the sorrowful face of Mary, Mother of God—and the noise of the street, the sparrows' chirps, the distant thump of a ball, the trolley bell, children playing jump rope, dogs barking, snatches of conversations, engines running, the *rat-tat-tat* of a jackhammer, the click of high heels rolled all around them, like change from a torn pocket, deafening them, slicing through the veils of silence as if they had truly come from the kingdom of the dead.

Kirill started the car and pictured his grandmother as a little girl in a horse-drawn carriage, the strong horses setting off in rhythm, powering uphill, and the cobblestones sounding beneath their hooves instead of asphalt. The little girl, wrapped in fur—for some reason Kirill pictured a fox coat—beloved by those now dead, still a daughter, still a sister, granddaughter, great-granddaughter, and niece, goddaughter—not yet knowing that a steely wind would soon carry away the adults, and she would be left alone, one-on-one with the century.

At home Grandmother Lina did not let on to his parents in any way what she had told Kirill at the cemetery. He realized she wanted to give him time to process the new information without general conversation and discussion; to his surprise, he recognized that he did not want to share what he had learned, as if while the facts belonged to them all, they had a deeper meaning for him alone.

In the morning, the two of them went to the Donskoy Cemetery. It was drizzling, the trolley bells rang on the boulevards, old men on folding chairs in front of the Fisherman store sold worms. It was all—the rain, the worms—so insignificant, petty, important but to very few people in the city, that Kirill began to feel that this trip, after yesterday's stunning revelation, was a minor and unnecessary tautology: he would encounter the same red brick cemetery wall, the same faded plastic flowers …

Kirill knew that the Donskoy would not have the wealth of symbols that had amazed him at the German Cemetery, no lions or griffins roamed there, stone ivy did not grow there, and the stone Eye of God did not peer out of a Masonic triangle.

They entered the cemetery. Here the names were Russian, the old graves of nobles, officials, actors—but there was no sense of secrets, his eyes slid steadily over the stones, recognizing his native language, the familiar images.

The rain came down harder; there was so much polished stone around that the sound of the rain was strangely dry, as if thousands of cricket drummers were striking mica timpani; the sound came in waves of a funeral march, increasing, diminishing, carried by wind gusts. Kirill sensed an acute internal shiver in time with the music; the sound seemed to be coming from below, from underground.

He remembered the Metro of the Dead he had invented as a child; when his grandmother had brought him to Donskoy, he "identified" the crematorium as the entrance to the Metro. Now he thought he heard the corpses banging rhythmically on the coffin lids, demanding truth and revenge. This was not the noise of the rain falling from the sky, but the dull thud of bones coming from under the earth. It softens the soil for landslides, chases away rats, penetrates foundations, warps cobblestones. It is carried by the water of underground rivers trapped in pipes, it flows over rails and wires, it gushes out of the ground, soaring to the Ural Mountains, to the Siberian swamps, to the edge of the continent, breaking off into the Sea of Okhotsk and the Arctic Ocean near Magadan and Pevek.

Kirill felt sick, as if he were losing his mind—but he sensed that hammering with extraordinary clarity; the world had revealed its other side; he thought that his grandmother could also hear the sound, knew about it.

He wanted to open the umbrella, but she stopped him. She had always been markedly neat and tidy, could not bear damp and dirt, as if in response to the years of poverty when there was no place to find shelter, dry off, get a new dress or shoes to replace the soiled ones. But now Grandmother Lina did not want protection or anything to separate her from the voices of the dead pretending to be rain.

They passed the crematorium and turned left—Kirill vaguely remembered this path—then left again, where the crumbling towers of the old monastery stood beyond the trees, and stopped at the crossroads of the allées, by a granite flowerbed filled with self-seeded blooms. The bed was an unfinished project: they were planning a fountain or a pavilion where one might rest, but the result was a flowerbed to fill the empty space.

"Papa is here somewhere," Grandmother Lina said softly, sadly, looking at the flowerbed.

Kirill did not understand which father she meant. Her own? Great-Grandfather Arseny? He'd been killed in the war and buried in the battlefield. Somewhere in an imaginary landscape with woods and river, wheat and village, where a hawk circles and soars on currents of hot air, and in the winter a vixen catches the mice that feed on the leftover grain from harvest.

"He's here," Grandmother said. "In the grave of unknown remains. I learned many years later. We had a KGB supervisor at work. High up. He had been in the service back in the 1930s. And he survived. So he," she stumbled over her words, "he knew that I was half-German, even though I had taken Kostya's surname. It was all in the records. And he," here she stumbled again, "he found pleasure in playing with me. Once he said that he knew where my father was. It was twenty years since his arrest. I still had faith. I believed that maybe he was someplace where they wouldn't let him send us word. That colonel said that Papa was at the Donskoy. They shot people in prisons. The bodies were brought here. Burned in the crematorium. And buried here. Somewhere here." Grandmother sighed deeply. "Under this flowerbed."

Kirill recalled their trip here years ago, the flowers she put on a stranger's coffin so that they would be incinerated and spread as smoke. Grandmother first lied to her son, telling him the story of the soldier missing in action so he would not ask unnecessary questions and could live without a shadow at his back;

then he inherited the lie. The revealed lie separated them, tore the threads of confidence established in his childhood. But he sensed that she had nothing more to hide and suffered enough from living in silence.

Kirill embraced her and whispered, "Grandmother, Grandmother"—wanting her to understand that he loved her and did not judge her. He felt the old fear in her, like a poisonous piece of shrapnel, of being accused, exposed, losing everything in a moment, a fear stealing a day from the week, taking away taste from drink, and luminescence from light.

Now he understood why they didn't bring flowers to Donskoy—any flowers would be too much here at the empty flowerbed hiding the remains of thousands of people. In that unimaginable mix of atoms there was what was left of Great-Grandfather Arseny, the man in the photo at home in a military cap with a red star on the cockade. He was inseparable now from the others who were burned and concealed.

Still, Kirill felt that destiny could exist separately from the one who had lived it, destiny could continue *after* death.

Being secretly executed, secretly cremated, and tossed into a common pit meant not dying but landing in the Metro of the Dead, the underground world of ghosts, wandering souls deprived of funerals, deprived of the death that takes place in the hearts of the living, in an open farewell ceremony. In that sense Arseny's destiny was not completed: Kirill had to fulfill it.

"Schwerdt," Grandmother said suddenly. "I was Karolina Schwerdt until I married Konstantin."

So she was not Lina Vesnyanskaya, as he knew her, whose surname—Vesnyansky—he bore, but Karolina Schwerdt, who took her husband's name the way people put on other people's clothes that make them unrecognizable, in order to be saved, in order to escape. Karolina became Lina, to make the name sound Russian.

"Schwerdt," she repeated. "Schwerdt. I used to avoid saying the name, even to myself. They all died because of it. Papa. Mama. My sisters and brothers. Gustav and Andreas. Everyone. When I became Vesnyanskaya in 1945 and changed my documents," she rubbed her hands along her face, as if throwing back a veil, "I swore that I would never again say Schwerdt. I would remember them by their given names.

"I didn't come to the cemetery for many years, afraid that someone would see me by the grave and realize that I was Schwerdt and not Vesnyanskaya. Many years. ... The grave was overgrown. After the war no one took care of the cemetery. At night bandits hung out in the vaults. In the daytime there were hoodlums. People were afraid to go there. I wanted it to be like that forever. So that the monument would sink into the earth. So that the word Schwerdt would disappear.

"Then I started coming. Like a thief. Early in the morning. Or in the evening, when everyone was gone. In the worst weather, snow and rain. So no one would see me. I walked down the main allée as if I were taking a shortcut to the Hospital Rampart.

"Other women came, too. Also in bad weather. I met one at the well, we had come to get water. I watched where she went: to the old grave of a colonel in the imperial army, a German. And she watched me secretly."

Grandmother stopped.

"They all died in different ways," she said simply. "Maybe they would have been killed in any case. I don't know. There's no point in trying to figure it out. But the fact is, the fact is ... The fact is that they died because their name was Schwerdt. It was a stone that sank them to the bottom. Proof that did not need to be invented. An excuse not to save them. A justification for betrayal: why feel sorry for Germans?"

She stopped again. Kirill looked at the flowerbed, at the sparse, untended grass. He hid from Grandmother—Karolina, not Lina, all of a sudden—as if still listening to her previous incarnation; he pretended to himself that Grandmother was talking about someone else's terrible past, not her own—upsetting, but not inevitable—about a past that could be opened and shut like a book, coupled and uncoupled like a train wagon.

Probably sensing Kirill's state, Grandmother said, without looking at him, "They all died, and I remained alive. How can I die if they die with me? I promised Papa, in my mind, even though he was already dead, that I would not forget."

Kirill was aware that he was hearing a testament. He wanted to make a joke of it, to say it was too soon for Grandmother to think about death, but he realized how unbearable was the sight of that dusty, dreary, pathetic grass growing on human remains, as if the grass, too, was doomed, as if the grass knew grief and anger; he quietly took her hand in his, brought it to his lips, and kissed it the way you would kiss the cross.

***

*G*randmother Lina died at the dacha. She went out in the fall to spray potassium permanganate on the peony beds and replant the phloxes; the flowers were her connection to her late husband, Konstantin, who died when Kirill was still in grade school. His grandfather was an antiquarian capable of talking for hours about the pattern of a Meissen porcelain plate. Yet he loved the flashy, shaggy flowers, disheveled by wind, sparkling with rain drops—as if his peasant background found relief in them—and Grandmother continued planting them along the path after his death.

She left in the morning, one of those rare October days that actually belong in August; the last unexpended forces of summer ferment in them, like the juice in overripe apples. The clear morning was followed by a hot day, but rain, persistent and cold, came in the evening.

Grandmother had not returned the following evening. The phone in the dacha guard booth went unanswered; in this weather the guard went to his house in the village to warm his rheumatism by the stove. Kirill drove out in his grandfather's old Volga with the unreliable carburetor, the "barge," as he called it; the motor died on him twice, and twice restarted—the Volga liked shamanism, knocking, pauses on the trip—and finally turned onto the familiar country road, and light from the family windows glowed through the rowan trees by the gate. He was happy until he thought what light in the windows meant at 3:00 a.m., probably burning since the night before.

Grandmother left sooner than her time, Kirill later understood. The remains of her days, the precious remainder of life, she had invested in the dacha house, in the trees on their property, in the forest around them; she used up the time to create ties that could not be put into words: not guilt, not duty, but the strange tugging feeling that she was present in the rustles of the house, the busyness of the wasps under the beam, in the appearance of mushrooms in the old spots that she had shown Kirill when he was a child, in the alpine strawberry swoon of forest meadows—reminding him politely, asking for something, appearing in a beam of light cleaving the forest, breaking against its fir limbs, or in the fall of an aged leaf, or the quick fading of phlox, dropping petals onto the apples that had rolled into the drainage ditch.

When they buried her, the weather had changed. At the German Cemetery, snow fell in tiny grains that did not melt on the shoveled clumps of reddish clay. When Grandfather Konstantin had died, Kirill was in summer camp and did not get home in time; this was the first time he saw the cemetery earth open, and Kirill imagined that the gravediggers were knocking on the coffin lids of Balthasar and Clothilde.

Grandmother's coffin was a cheap one—the family was not doing well by then—and she was not buried deep—the grave-diggers didn't want to keep banging at the soil,—but Kirill imagined that the dead were pushing up from below, piled one on top of the other; once again he saw the signs, the Masonic Eye of God, the clover leafs, crossed swords, and knew that no one noticed them, no one cared about the stone book on the limestone altar; this was an inheritance intended for him alone.

The death of Grandmother Lina somehow released the fam-ily, the way an unfinished knitting project held by a needle falls apart. Neither his father or mother nor Kirill had understood how much Grandmother held them together; it seemed she lived unnoticed and quietly, rereading books, taking care of ancient things left by his grandfather, and herself was an ancient thing. But it turned out that it was Grandmother—not by word or advice but by being there—who balanced the differences in vari-ous personalities, multiplied by the vicissitudes of life.

Misfortunes visited the family after her death. There were cuts at Father's institute and he lost his job, then Mother slipped on the ice and spent a long time in the hospital, where it was now necessary to buy medicine and the attention of the staff. Then—and subsequently Kirill would see a direct parallel with the family history during the 1917 revolution—bandits showed up to take away the five-room apartment in the Stalinist building near the Oktyabrskaya Metro station, inherited from Grandfa-ther Konstantin; they came the way the revolutionary sailors entered the houses of parasites to enjoy the spoils. The bandits had been given a tip, they knew an antiquarian, a collector, had lived there and that was why they wanted that apartment and not the one next door. The family was rescued by a KGB general who had been a patron of the late Grandfather Konstantin, but he rescued them according to the "rules" of the new times: they had to move to a three-room apartment in a worse neighborhood, but they got to keep Grandfather's collection and their lives.

Father started selling off some of the antiques, getting into affairs he didn't much understand, tricked more than once. And the money received for trophies of a long-ago war—Grandfather's collection was mostly that—did not stay in their hands, did not bring joy or sufficiency.

Kirill did not notice the poverty, he even felt resigned about the bandits who came to throw them out into the street—a sense of gaining a second, belated, and real youth made up for the criminals.

Fifteen years later, when he thought about his generation, which had come into adulthood in the 1990s, he felt that the ancient alchemy of history was still alive. Fire, water, air, earth—they were the children of fire and air, never knowing water and earth. The children of the great mirages that rose over Russia—the generation of the pause, when the monster of Russian statehood had almost died, was weak and wraithlike. When the atmosphere changed and one could barely breathe, it turned out that they had nothing to lean on, that their existence was founded upon the play of air currents.

The Union fell apart without great bloodshed, as if on its own, and they were corrupted by the ease of the collapse and therefore unprepared for resistance. They thought that all evil had been contained in the USSR and now that there was no Union, things would take the right path; they did not understand that evil was a part of history and that democracy was a system for minimizing evil and not for the triumph of good. Now they were twice orphaned because the country of their birth was gone and the country in which they grew up was also gone.

Kirill liked the nineties; dust had been blown off things and events, a veil had been removed, and they were free. He worked, wrote, taught, received grants, spoke at conferences, and unable to develop a smart strategy and pick one topic, he worked on the history of collaborationism during World War II, then dekulakization in the national republics, then the Comintern.

In Soviet times, his father was close to dissident circles, read *The Gulag Archipelago,* and even once contributed money to some cause. Kirill zealously, to his own surprise, wished that everything they had whispered in kitchens would be said aloud at full voice, that there would be books, films, monuments; but in fact he was simply trying to avoid his personal mission. Defending the abstract truth of history and talking about others was more comfortable than digging—to the bottom—in his own family's past.

The family—because of the determinism of kin, the causality of births that form irrevocable ties—began to personify what he feared most of all: the inability to manage and control—in this case, the past. Kirill feared that dark waters of the elemental past would rush into his life, that which could not be changed and could not be accepted.

As a child suffering from morbid attacks of dreaminess, he imagined that he was no one's son, no one's grandson, no one had borne him into the world, he was *superfluous*, a stranger to all, related to no one, not even his beloved Grandmother Lina.

As a youth he began hating words denoting kinship. Mother-in-law, second cousin twice removed—they seemed antiquated, hoary, from the tribal intimacy of language. Kirill could not imagine he could be the subject of those terms; it would mean being covered in animal fur, forest moss, turning into half-human half-animal, bound by pagan ties not only with others like him but also groves, springs, meadows, trees, and animals.

Kirill was afraid that if he went down the family tree even into the 1930s, to the torture cellars reeking of blood, he would learn something that would take away his right to determine his own life, make him one of the men—he had met a few—who were *killed alive* by the terrible truths of the past, appearing to others as ghosts of conscience, forced to sacrifice themselves to expiate the sins of their fathers.

Sometimes Kirill opened his grandmother's tabletop desk with wooden cubbyholes, where she kept papers that had survived a century. He opened it but did not touch the papers, looked at the soiled, worn corners of envelopes, and thought that poison might seep out of those holes, as if sent by an assassin. He would shut the desk and return to his books, articles, and lectures, promising himself that one day he would definitely read her archives and write a text.

Kirill thought he had to take care of his own destiny first and acquire independence. He worked steadily, defended his doctoral degree on the Russian Liberation Army, made a name for himself. He was invited to America for a project on the deportation of Jews from the Russian Empire during World War I.

It wasn't his topic. Kirill drafted the proposal on the margins of his other studies, so to speak, and sent it in, telling himself that he had no chance but he was fully aware that it would arouse some interest.

The answer came: Harvard, two years, an enormous stipend, the prospect of extended work and residency; a prestigious offer at the highest level. Kirill accepted instantly, telling himself that those years would allow him to fully establish himself as a scholar. But secretly he know that he would not return to Russia, he would separate himself by an ocean from the destiny of Europe, where the destiny of his family lay, he would reject the idea of the book willed to him by Grandmother Lina, would work on a topic that he did not need but that meant something to others, he would write a completely different book, and move to another continent—forever.

Her legacy kept reminding him of her testament and his promise. Without noticing, he thought of her more rarely. Her things suddenly became unwanted witnesses; her lamp, desk, bookshelves, even the sugar bowl in the kitchen, which she filled by using tongs shaped like a bird's beak, started to seem like obsolete relics, unneeded, cluttering up the house, kept only because they had become ridiculous and fetishistic embodiments of memory. Under various excuses, he began ridding himself of witnesses, hiding the sugar bowl in the cupboard and moving other things into the storeroom or her old room, which stood empty. He did not see this as a hidden war, regarding it instead as a concern for the spatial functionality; he thought—and it's so easy to think in the name of the dead—that Grandmother Lina would be happier than anyone else at his success and his coming trip to America.

In the preparations for the trip, Kirill felt he was forgetting something, but wrote it off as inevitable travel jitters. One evening about two weeks before his departure, his father said casually, "Maybe you should visit the cemetery? To bid farewell?"

Kirill was ashamed. The simple thought that he should visit the graves, to say goodbye, had not occurred to him. Previously he would have thought of it himself, it would have been natural; and now, what was happening to him? Kirill looked at his father, who seemed to have fallen behind the times, and realized that his father loved him.

He embraced his father. Now he had to go to the German Cemetery, stand at the gravesites, and the anxiety would vanish, because it arose from his nonobservance of ritual, his stepping away from the duty of memory and respect.

His father peered into the dark of the corridor that led to Grandmother Lina's old room, and said nothing, merely shut his eyes and shook his head.

Kirill went to the cemetery in early spring, when the days are warm but the nights still frosty. He went, as it seemed to him, in a good mood, to bid farewell for a long time or forever to his family on this sunny, cheerful day, and to remember the graves, paths, and gates looking like this. But the closer he came, the less confident he felt. He wanted to turn back, or buy flowers, or not buy flowers—the flowers would be a misguided attempt at asking for forgiveness; the engine light started blinking, he knew there was nothing wrong with the engine, it was the light that was broken, but he grew angry as he did whenever something was wrong. At the entrance a family in black stood next to a coffin cart waiting for the hearse to arrive and a handyman was sprinkling the road with salt; the cart was rusty, the salt fell in large clumps, and an old woman in a black coat gave Kirill a dirty look as if his green jacket offended her.

Kirill walked along the allée and then took the path. The snow banks accumulated over the winter were melting, and the whitened, squashed plastic flowers showed through the snow.

The stone monument of Balthasar and Clothilde was visible in the distance. There was the altar with the book, there was the bench, and there was …

Grandmother's marble stone was split in two. The fissure separated first name from surname and birth date from death date.

At first Kirill thought the crack was due to a cavity in the stone that had filled with water, then froze, then thawed, then froze, throughout the winter.

He felt remorse about the broken object. He considered going to the cemetery office and finding the mason, to see whether the stone could be repaired or if it needed to be replaced.

The harsh scraping sound of a handyman's sleigh against stone somewhere changed Kirill's perception as if in a kaleidoscope: he saw the peeling paint on the railings, the dirt on the snow, feathers of a dead bird, branches broken by the snow, and most importantly, the line of the crack in the stone, random but well-defined, like the zigzag of lightning—the blackness inside the crack, the very essence of blackness that did not seem to belong to this world.

The trolley rang its bell in the distance; the sound was of farewell, as if the trolley was traveling toward death, as if it knew that today it would kill someone with its heavy wheels. With that sound—he used to come back with Grandmother on a trolley, a red trolley with a beige stripe and round yellow headlights—Kirill understood the meaning of the sign given to him. He did not believe in the materiality of spirits, that his late grandmother literally existed somewhere and could interfere in events in this world. His fear was that this simply had been water gathering in the cavity and breaking the marble headstone in half, but the rationality of the explanation underlined the subtle *coincidence*, with the lifespan of a flash, between his departure and the appearance of the crack.

Kirill realized that he wasn't going anywhere, that he would turn in his tickets, give some excuse to the directors of the Harvard program, because otherwise that damned crack would not let him alone to the end of his days, would leave a mark on everything otherwise solid and whole, things would break apart, feelings, relations, attachments, that crack would run though the lines of his life like a black snake of meaninglessness.

He felt relieved. Kirill ran his hand over the stone folds of the cloth on the limestone altar, over the empty stone pages of the open book. Kirill regarded its surface as if it were a country, a continent; he peered closely at the dark stone, its potholes, craters, ribbed edges of moss, the valley of pages broken on the spine, and began to see mountains, forests, roads, cities, vague shadows of the past and future, moving like the shadows of clouds on a plain. He saw the book of destiny and he could conceive all eras at once, saw himself standing at the cemetery, which alone was unchanging and unmoving; the rest flickered, hid in shadows, appeared and vanished; the foggy seas splashed the continent of the book, and ships sailed for it; cities were built and disappeared, troops marched along the roads. Only the stone altar with its stone cover, with the stone book on top, stood immutable in the flickering, smoke, sparks, and changes of night and day—like the axis of the world.

Kirill turned. Grandmother was looking at him from the photograph on the split tombstone. Her gaze was joyous.

Kirill wandered the cemetery for a long time. He felt as if he were at the Great Hall of the Conservatory, the orchestra members in place and the marvelous instruments ready to produce sound. He sensed that the music was nearby, as if the singing of the organ pipes, hidden by a curtain of metal sunbeams, could break through the noise of the day.

His parents received the news that he was not going to Harvard with relief. His mother was simply happy he was not leaving her. His father urged him to consider his decision and not be hasty. But Kirill saw that his father was also happy, but for a different reason, and Kirill could not understand the reason.

***

*L*ater that evening Kirill thought about his father.

He thought about him as a man profoundly alien to him, so much so that this alienation contained a paradoxical closeness: it was his father, through rejection and dislike, who made him who he was. He went over dates, circumstances, historical contexts, unhurriedly trying to distill the alchemy of fate from them.

His father grew up seeing the *nomenklatura* friends of Kirill's grandfather. The army bureaucrats, suppliers, and specialists in reparations impressed the boy with their tailored uniforms, array of medals, ceremonial weapons, and trophy furnishings.

The beneficiaries of the World War II victory, who had received Pobeda cars, they wanted to appear like real soldiers—at least in the eyes of a child—and their talk was full of boasting and exaggerated or false exploits. Grandfather Konstantin knew their worth, but he had to put up with them; Grandmother despised them, but did not dare disagree with her husband. So they came to carouse, brought the boy to Red Square to watch parades, took him to the shooting range, gave him extravagant presents inappropriate for his age.

Having spent eight years after the war under Stalin, afraid of him even dead, they drank vodka and ate fatty steaks to suppress their fear of Him and continued to celebrate the leader's birthday—for they were afraid he would return, reach them from the other world, grind them into labor camp dust.

During the war they took out their fear of Stalin on subordinates, humiliating, beating, shooting them. Afterward, when the leader was dead, they joyfully sang along with stage music, movies, and memoirs of senior officers that portrayed them as fearless heroes.

They tried to exorcise their fear, bury it under corpses, drown it out with Katyusha gunfire in movie soundtracks, conquer it once and for all. But no matter how many bravura marches played on the screen and how many black-and-white tanks rolled past the signpost "To Berlin," the fear was always with them, wearing a military jacket, smoking a pipe, and speaking in the voice of Mikhail Gelovani, the actor who always played Stalin.

The boy didn't know. And so he took the former slaves of the leader for worthy men; he played with their children, studied with them in an elite school and then at university.

But there was something in him—probably from his mother—that made him a loner, so he avoided sitting in the front row, among the activists and heroes—not courage but the ability to become, if necessary, *inconvenient* prey, like a turtle or a sea urchin.

He never got in anyone's way, never competed with anyone, he belonged to the Komsomol, joined the Party. Supported by his father's connections, he was not a careerist; he neither knew nor desired to know how to devour people, he was cool toward big ideas, but persistent in science. He studied his archeology as if he wanted to hide deep in time, in history, take cover in ruined palaces and temples of Central Asian rulers, in the houses of merchants who died during the Mongol invasion, to shrink, to disappear in the coals of ancient fires, in clay, in sand.

His mother never told him about his German ancestors. But he wisely never delved into the family history, as if blind to recent historical eras, and had an innate historical longsighted-ness, discerning only things centuries away. In his archeological expeditions in Asia he encountered the archeology of recent times, fresh ruins of camps, the settlements of exiled nations, quarries and mines built by the slaves of the Gulag, but he did not pay them any mind.

It was there in Asia that he met his wife, Kirill's future

mother. After graduation, she was sent to oversee the planting of windbreaks and fight the dry winds that destroyed the virgin chernozem soil plowed on Khrushchev's orders. Her father had died of wounds soon after the war, and her mother, exhausted by wartime evacuations, died shortly before the wedding.

The windbreaks were inadequate; the trees did not take well, ailed, dried at the root as young transplants; but Kirill's mother had the strips replanted, fought with the regional authorities, demanded tireless work from the laborers, as if the struggle with the desert's lungs were a tribute to her parents' memory. And there, at the edge of the world, Kirill's father met her.

In truth, he stole her, arranging the transfer of the young specialist to Moscow without her knowledge—one of Grandfather Konstantin's military pals was a big shot in the Ministry of Forest Industry; he stole her, loving her simplicity and firmness, sensing that he, a refugee from the present, needed a wife who could take on daily life, leaving him the safe and distant past.

Initially, she was unsettled by their Moscow home, Grandfather's big apartment. The first time she was left there alone, she wept—not from fear but from the foreignness of the ancient objects. Soon Kirill was born, and through him, who had no idea of the age or value of things, crawling, walking, climbing—his grandfather worried about damage to the antiques but forbade nothing—she began mastering the world of the Moscow apartment. When Grandfather Konstantin died, she took his place as guardian of the house.

But Kirill guessed that this house and this life were never truly hers. With the same stubbornness with which she planted windbreaks, she expended a lot of effort to fit into the world of her husband, his parents, and son. But Kirill feared she had exhausted herself, and in her old age, when that time came, she would not find real support in the house and these things.

Kirill hoped that his book would be a lifeboat, an ark, for his father and mother.

***

*K*irill opened the little portable desk that held the papers of Grandmother Karolina—he couldn't call her Lina anymore—the next day. It didn't look as small as he had remembered it. He set it on his desk. The wooden box seemed much heavier than the papers in it, as if the contents of the letters had weight—the events, fates, and deaths imprinted on the papers.

There were worn leather albums filled with postcards, collections of letters in envelopes and without. Neatly written books, old school notebooks, photograph albums with cracked leather bindings. Newspaper clippings, school reports, imperial certificates, money: imperial banknotes, the million ruble notes of the revolutionary period, Soviet rubles. A small stamp album with stamps cut from envelopes; handwritten pages with typed copy on the reverse—someone was using old paper from an office. Some completely illegible bits, crumpled and then ironed, notes with ink blurred by tears, trolley tickets perforated by a five-toothed punch, math division problems, and more notepads, old telephone books with short numbers that were no longer in use in his lifetime, Soviet greeting cards with the flag and state seal, his father's third-grade exercise book, children's scrawls—drawings, kindergarten colored-paper appliques for Women's Day, evaluations from the workplace typed on a machine with a sticky *E*, IDs, passes, bank books, and badges featuring the astronaut Gagarin. Patterns for a wedding dress with a piece of fine lace pinned to them; soup and dumpling recipes written on loose pages; carbon paper worn through in places, reused so that lines covered other lines, forming strange patterns of ghostly words; two tickets to the planetarium, used, with the stubs torn off; two unused tickets to *Eugene Onegin* at the Bolshoi Theater; blueprints for the dacha house on waxed paper; the wrapper of a Polyot chocolate candy (who ate it and why had they saved the wrapper?); prescriptions; and a newspaper cutting of Grandfather Konstantin's obituary. And more of Grandmother's letters, photos of her brothers and sisters, several notebooks with perforated pages; a heavy notebook filled with unfamiliar handwriting with old-style orthography, state bonds, an old map of Moscow trolley lines; another notebook in Grandmother's handwriting, clean, neat lines, she wrote without errors, she must have made the clean copy from a crossed-out draft; more documents, more letters, an envelope with negatives, a library card, a receipt for watch repair ...

Grandmother, who could not tolerate disorder, should have organized the papers by topic and year, placed them in envelopes, and labeled them in a neat hand, almost like a penmanship lesson. For some reason, she did not do that. Was she putting if off for later? Did she mix everything up on purpose?

Kirill thought that she probably did not want to *neaten* the past, that is, in some sense *bury* it, dressing it in a corpse's fancy clothing. In this mixture of everything together, important and unimportant, random and serious, the past was still alive, breathing melodically, and Grandmother Karolina kept it that way.

Kirill spent several months going through the contents, sorting, reading papers, making piles, inventing classifications: by people, by era, by genre. Every classification fell apart: she wrote about the years before the revolution and the Civil War to her love in the 1930s—a tragedy, her letters were returned, without envelopes, in a pile, and all that remained was the name Arkady—had he stopped loving her, had he been arrested, had he died in the war? The nineteenth century was described in

Great-Grandfather Arseny's diary, written in the winter of 1917, while the events of that winter were in Grandmother Karolina's most recent handwritten reminiscences in a separate notebook, with a few photographs. The few surviving letters among the brothers and sisters either reported on the sender's daily cares or referred in a paragraph to the childhood or adolescence of the recipient, events known to the correspondents but not to Kirill.

Postcards, signatures under photographs in albums, everything echoed, complemented, leaped across time, called like lost mushroom hunters in the woods, gaped with omissions and torn lines, peered myopically with faded postmarks, hid cut-out and torn-out pages, bristled with dark crossed-out lines, and ran off in all directions, vanishing, vanishing, vanishing …

Kirill ruined his eyesight sorting out handwriting, old type fonts, following the changes in spelling, the loss of some words and the birth of others. He noticed that some of the letter writers kept their language pure while others littered theirs with words from newspaper headlines; intonations in relationships changed, events were reflected differently in the mirrors of opinion, and the old family legend of Balthasar Schwerdt and his descendants was forgotten, covered in weeds, and gone from letters and recollections.

Kirill assumed he had only a small part of what was once a large whole. He saw this in the gaps in correspondence, in the mentions of other diaries he did not have. Only a small fraction, five or three percent, had survived, and there wasn't a single paper in German. Kirill understood that the archive had survived many purges, those in turn elicited by various purges, large and small, in the country, ideological campaigns, show trials, from the early Taganstev case in 1921 to the Doctors' Plot in 1953. Threats came from various directions, requiring the removal and destruction of a single page or an entire stratum of life. What was safe yesterday became dubious today, what is dubious today will be fatal tomorrow; the archive grew smaller, parts of it were burned, burned like fuel for the undiminishing fear that broke though in febrile flashes.

Some lives survived only by a half, others by a third or fourth. Some, like Grandmother's brothers, left only remnants, particles, bits of biography, the way the dead lie shattered on the battlefield after being hit by a howitzer shell.

Kirill would have found it easier to read if he had known that there really had been a howitzer shell, a single historical cataclysm, but he saw how people spent decades excising things, aborting the past; he felt he was witnessing a crime committed out of deadly fear and cowardice. This was the crime he had to expiate.

He hung posterboard on the wall and drew schemes and graphs. A family tree appeared before him—with a broken trunk, fallen branches, lost leaves; he had seen such trees in photographs of battle scenes. This *ghost tree* came to him in his dreams, grew into him like a restless spirit.

He, who had avoided kinship, began to feel in his nightmares like the final branch of the ghost tree, the last shoot tied by its stem to the other world, growing out of it and existing in two realms. He would waken with a powerful revulsion for the tree metaphor, its vegetative literalness, associating a person with a branch or leaf; but he felt he had to live through this association, accept the identification, for it would give him strength, the way a mask does to an actor, to continue along the path and the keys to hundreds of locked doors waiting for him.

For months and years, Kirill traveled in ever-widening circles of research. He wrote down all the names he found in the archives, looked for those names in memoirs and histories; he leafed through hundreds of books, archive files, manuscripts, finding precious grains of mentions, lost fragments from his puzzle. He journeyed to the places where his ancestors had lived, looked for witnesses, and if he didn't find any, turned the place itself into a witness, using it in his attempts to restore the contours of the past. Letters in response to his questions arrived from Siberia, Europe, Australia, both Americas, where grandchildren and great-grandchildren had also preserved the remains of papers that had come from grandparents and great-grandparents, papers carried out under a coat, in a suitcase, saved from night searches, fires, artillery, and submarine torpedoes in the Atlantic.

Things gradually came together, and torn threads were restored; Kirill wrote drafts and sketches, but he couldn't capture the character or genre of the future book; it remained a stone, unresponsive to his efforts. He taught at the university, wrote articles, defended his PhD, early, incredibly early in terms of the post-Soviet scholarly world, but he knew he was working at a third of his talent; his strength belonged to the book, put into it in advance, into the need to keep the variegated ghosts in his mind, his memory, alive. The book was with him always, maturing, rewriting itself, and he was its tribute payer, but he could not begin it, as if the book said: it is not time.

Time, real time, prompted: run. Move away.

Two newspapers where he wrote columns about history were shut down. When he refused to sign a bootlicking open letter, they cut his teaching hours. The grants ended. Invitations to Russian conferences petered out. His foes said behind his back that he denigrated the Russian people, he was a slanderer; they called his dissertation on the Russian Liberation Army "anti-patriotic."

Kirill felt the noose of his unwritten book tighten; he thought sometimes that there would never be a book, that it was a dream, a Grail, merely an expression of his acute and unmistakable sense that his life was beholden to fate but that the book only masked this feeling, fracturing it, reflecting it in the circumstances of the past, allotting it to the characters of his narrative—in other words, made that feeling tolerable, since in its pure, undiluted form it was as deadly as the Gorgon's gaze.

**

*K*irill has long known *whom* the book would be about.

About faces and masks, fractured fluid personalities, the Januses of history. Those for whom doors are wide open. The shoots of the family tree that bear strange fruit. The bizarre scions in whom the line ends and simultaneously unfolds in full possibility, unrelated by conditions and traditions. About people leaving old ties behind and moving into the unknown. Secret heroes of history, invisibly harnessed to its reins. The ones whose destiny is a letter in a bottle. About the unusual links in the chain of events—a different color, a different material. About those whose actions determine the destiny of subsequent generations.

Kirill sees the blueprint of the family tree. He remembers all the branches, all the names, relatives remote and close, hundreds of people. The tree's roots reach back into the fifteenth century, but Kirill doesn't need to go so deep. For his family history that is a prehistoric era, like the reverse calculation of time before the birth of Christ, before our common era.

In 1774 the new era had not yet begun, but the one who made it possible was born in Anhalt-Zerbst: Thomas Benjamin Schwerdt, son of a pastor and the niece of August Gottlieb Richter, a prominent professor of medicine.

Thomas had studied medicine in Jena, where he lived with his uncle, professor of anatomy and surgery Justus Christian Loder;

his other medical mentor was Christoph Wilhelm Hufeland.

Richter, Loder, Hufeland were the leading medical minds of the era, confidants and physicians of august persons, and friends of Goethe and Schiller. Members of secret societies, masters of Masonic lodges, researchers in nontraditional practices like Tibetan medicine, and authors of learned works; teachers of generations of doctors in Europe; participants in great events related to Russia: Hufeland treated the mortally ill Field Marshall of the Russian Empire Kutuzov, Loder set up the Russian Army hospital in the war with the French and became the personal physician of Emperor Alexander I, and Richter trained them both; and all three greats, like muses or midwives, influenced Thomas Schwerdt's medical career.

Naturally, with that kind of patronage, his future was guaranteed. However, he would have flourished on his own, thanks to his abilities, the greatest of which was obstetrics: many noble and wealthy families were indebted to him for their descendants.

But he did not acquire the outstanding talent of his mentors. He was received in their homes, took part in discussions, but he never equaled them in science or society. Fate set him back a few times: his first wife died young, and he had not been able to save her; in 1812 he was almost executed by the French for sabotage—just before the execution, while he was receiving communion in prison, the city was liberated by the Prussians.

Thomas changed cities, universities, medical specialties, as if hoping to come across a place where his gift would flourish and yield fruit worthy of his teachers. Everywhere he was under their patronage, everywhere he was called in to oversee childbirth in the most noble families—but with every year he sensed more clearly that he would not enter the pantheon of medicine's greats.

In 1805 his first son, Balthasar, was born. That was the start of "our era" in Kirill's family, because Balthasar was the first to step onto Russian soil. Thomas and Balthasar were part of the Big Family, whose boundaries were wide and flexible—part of the changing union of several families united in the interests of the clan as well as by various degrees of kinship. Patronage, politics, and money intertwined; various branches of the Big Family belonged to different hierarchies, social circles, professional corporations, worked for kings, built careers for generations in the army, navy, and in foreign colonies. Anyone born into the Big Family was like one of its organs, belonged to it like an infantry solider to his unit, and was subject to the decision of the elders—to marry, to be assigned a regiment at birth, to be designated a priest, physician, admiral, scientist. The Big Family was always playing the career game, promoting its own, reinforcing its positions, capturing new resources and posts, planning two, three, four generations ahead, competing with other Big Families. Balthasar, like his younger brothers, like his father, Thomas, was a piece in this game.

Kirill had learned to see the family tree from this angle, too: not only as a network of relations but a network of mutual support, a scheme for multiplying influence, capital, social capital, a map of geographic, social, and professional expansion; the tree's crown sometimes appeared to him as a hive, a hive of gold-bearing bees, gathering earthly and heavenly treasures.

Balthasar, naturally, was to have his place in the game, become a pawn, a knight, a rook. But he broke off relations with his father, while maintaining some support from the Big Family, the clan, and headed to Russia. That was the total knowledge that Great-Grandfather Arseny and Grandmother Karolina had; it's possible that Balthasar, when telling his children about the past, downplayed his starting position for certain reasons, and so his descendants took him to be a simple doctor rather than the emissary of mighty forces.

Kirill could see further.

Balthasar graduated from the medical school at Leipzig University. His father was a surgeon, and more importantly, an obstetrician who practiced at the court of Zerbst and had friends in high places. Behind him, in the shadow of eternity, were the figures of three titans—Richter, Loder, Hufeland, great physicians who cared for the health of the men who ran Europe. There were probably other patrons who remained in the wings of the family history. A marvelous beginning, a grand future: follow the plan, trust in the Lord, and perhaps you will be a titan in your old age, having enriched medical science and brought glory to the family name.

Balthasar became his father's assistant, joined his practice— his father was growing old, his hands were not as firm holding a scalpel or forceps—and he needed an heir. There was more: his father, the junior comrade of great men, with a clear understanding of his own abilities and knowing he would never equal them, must have hoped that Balthasar would surpass him, would be not only worthy of patronage but would heal the father's injured pride, proving that a Schwerdt could do more, that the court of Zerbst was not the limit.

Balthasar met his father's expectations. He was still very young, but he was knowledgeable and even daring as a physician. He worked for three years with his father, diligently preparing his dissertation—something on treating goiters was all Kirill could remember—and wrote articles; he defended his dissertation and his father was ready to retire, turn over his practice, and introduce him into the circle of old friends not as a son but as a doctor. Balthasar seemed to be eager to follow his father's plans and counsel; the middle brother, Bertold, was at the same medical school in Leipzig, and the youngest, Andreas, was still little, and Balthasar would soon be Doctor Schwerdt—in the future, the famous Doctor Schwerdt.

Suddenly, when everything was decided, Balthasar broke with his father and with traditional medicine, allopathy, and became a homeopath. Inexplicable. Great-Grandfather Arseny wrote that Balthasar had experienced a personal crisis, but he did not know why: it was a mystery to him.

Arseny did not know what Kirill had learned from his research in the archives: before the crisis Balthasar, probably influenced by his father, had been a critic, even a persecutor of homeopathy: he took part in debates, wrote sarcastic articles about "charlatans," sharpening his scientific arguments on his enemies, creating his medical credo. In that period homeopathy for Balthasar was like a dangerous heresy perverting the Holy Writ, and Balthasar acted with an inquisitor's fire, probably—although there is no direct evidence for this, but Kirill thought so—stooping to intrigues at work or socially; his father, long schooled in court life, must have given him his first lessons.

But why were homeopathic doctors the chosen victim of Balthasar's wrath? The archives were silent on this. Why not alchemists or healers of all sorts? Kirill imagined that it was the father's influence: perhaps a homeopath had taken away a valuable client. But still, Kirill felt that this passion was inexplicable. Balthasar must have believed in medicine as a deity, believed in the physician's prophetic role as intermediary between God and the suffering. He persecuted homeopaths, claiming the truth of medicine, worshipping the scalpel that cut off mortal flesh.

Then, like Saul on the road to Damascus: "Suddenly a light shone around him from heaven. Then he fell to the ground, and heard a voice saying to him, 'Saul, Saul, why are you persecuting Me?'"

The false became the truth, the former truth—false.

Kirill searched for even a hint of what caused the transformation. At first he thought that Balthasar had lost a contest between doctors: he couldn't heal someone who was then healed by a homeopath. But there was something missing in that hypothesis, a final precision that was commensurate with the scale of self-rejection and change.

Balthasar then wrote several articles on homeopathy, about how he had been in the darkness of ignorance, deprived of true light, until God's providence gave him the true measure of things. But he never explained how God gave him the revelation. Was he embarrassed? Couldn't explain a vague sign? Or, did he not want to reveal the depth of his shock and upheaval and considered it between himself and God and no one else?

Balthasar was trying to spare his father's feelings, his professional ego. That guess, based on nothing, allowed Kirill to delve into the ancient plans of fate. Balthasar was mortally ill with a disease that could send him to the grave or at best leave him crippled—blind or deaf, legless or maimed. Thomas could not cure him, his son, his hope. The father could not, his friends could not, but a homeopath, called in secretly by family, perhaps, did. A homeopath. A damned heretic.

His obstinate father would have preferred his son to die—as if with that cure he had sold his soul to the devil. Young Balthasar, who fearlessly challenged death when he was dealing with other people's lives, for the first time felt its heavy imprint on himself; he changed, for before he had believed in his great future and thought himself invulnerable. Saved, he simply admitted the truth of homeopathy—he saw his work, his path in it.

"So he, trembling and astonished, said, 'Lord, what do You want me to do?'

"Then the Lord said to him, 'Arise and go into the city, and you will be told what you must do.'

"And the men who journeyed with him stood speechless, hearing a voice but seeing no one. Then Saul arose from the ground, and when his eyes were opened he saw no one. But they led him by the hand and brought him into Damascus. And he was three days without sight, and neither ate nor drank."

Kirill had reread those lines many times until he realized—belatedly because he had grown up as an atheist in an atheist country, that Balthasar, grandson of a pastor and son of a pious father, had certainly known the Bible well and must have viewed his experience through the prism of the Acts of the Apostles, the incident on the road to Damascus. And he was probably a passionate and ecstatic man who in the fever of his illness and the joy of being healed could have imagined a Voice—or heard the homeopath's speech as such.

But why did the new Balthasar, Balthasar the homeopath, go to Russia? Was it because the northern country was wild, medicine not very developed, and it would be easier to win converts there than among Europeans, who were ossified in old medical superstitions?

What was the role of the three titans, Richter, Loder, and Hufeland, and the Big Family? How could they benefit from the unexpected impulse of the young doctor, how could they direct and control the paladin?

The result of Balthasar's travels Kirill knew, but not the true, inner source. Kirill set out to visit the five cities where Balthasar had lived with his father, before he became a homeopath and headed to the North. Leipzig, Grimma, Zerbst, Wittenburg, Halle—somewhere there his character was formed, the knot of his fate tied, and Kirill hoped to undo that knot, not in the state archives but on the streets where Balthasar walked, in his buildings and churches, amid his rivers and hills, by the things of life that create the forces of destiny, its attraction and repulsion, its secret calls, whispers, night phantoms, and starry blueprints.

***

*K*irill spent several days walking around Leipzig. But the city did not want to tell him anything. Jaws open wide, three-toed paws extended, blind eyes bulging, the patina-green chimeras looked at him from the church cornices on the corner near his hotel; they were the embodiment of the monstrous power of oblivion, for their jaws seemed to emit the meaningless, convulsive roar of a creature that did not know why and for what it was born.

Limestone griffins with ram horns, dog tails, and wings folded on their backs supported balconies and were squashed by the weight of the stone; round-eyed demons with bird claws and lion manes immured in medallions over the arches of doorways strained to escape and were ossified by their fury—the city looked at him with dozens of hellish eyes, as if demonic forces had been mixed by stone masons into the cement and were now creeping out of all the crevices, blending into a mocking devil's mask with a long tongue, sophisticated in the art of lying.

Kirill was ready to leave. There was only one place left that he had not visited—the monument to the Battle of the Nations. Not looking forward to the crowds of tourists, but reminding himself that the Lake of Tears on the Mamayev Mound in Volgograd had been copied by the sculptor Evgeny Vuchetich from the Leipzig monument, he traveled to the memorial site in the morning. It was pouring rain, the wind turned his umbrella inside out; there was no line at the ticket counter.

He went up to the observation deck. The rain stopped while he was ascending and the sky cleared over the tower. Leaning on the parapet, he looked at the low houses with tile roofs, the brick water tower, the television tower in the distance, in the grim fog. Gradually, looking deeper, he understood that he had chosen the right place; whatever the city had to tell him could only be seen from here, from above and at a remove.

The Battle of the Nations ... 1813 ... Balthasar's father, Thomas Benjamin, was almost shot by the French ... Suddenly Kirill's vision changed, and he saw how the plain beneath looked after a decade of Napoleonic wars—burned houses, rivers poisoned by corpses, fertile fields trampled by troops. This plain was defenseless, open to the winds of war, all passing armies; the city was crucified on the crossroads of trade routes, doomed to be ravaged—over and over.

This is what Balthasar grew up in, this is what he left, this was his childhood memory. Kirill had unconsciously placed his ancestor in today's Germany, but in fact, Schwerdt had departed from the small kingdom of Saxony, a place devastated by war: from a smaller, fractured world into a larger one, stable and secure.

"Seemingly stable and secure," Kirill automatically corrected himself.

The vision vanished. He was standing on the square top of a granite tower. The rain had returned, and the view was enveloped by drizzle.

He was back in the center of town by noon. The day seemed replete with what he had found. He sloped aimlessly around town, thought about calling his father but did not want to share his discovery for fear the line of revelations would break. Leipzig still had not told him everything; there was a detail, small but important.

Where to find it? Would it be found? Kirill decided to go where he had had no intention of going: the museum of city history. Just that morning he thought that the museum would tell him nothing because the museum holds only what the city wants to show, but now he thought he was being tested—would he be able to overcome his prejudice?

A teddy bear with a Nazi armband. Mannequins dressed up as East German police in helmets with plastic face shields. A Soviet poster: "We Won." An antique desk of lacquered oak—on the polished lid the drawing of the tree's growth was executed with same unconscious power as the movement of God's hand in Michelangelo's *The Creation of Adam*. An oversize fly swatter made of rough stitched tarpaulin, to put out fires spreading from firebombs.

Kirill wandered the halls of the museum, not focusing on any particular era. He waited for a secret inhabitant of some object, a wooden casket or a cuckoo clock, to peek out and check that the guards were gone, and jump down and head over to visit a neighbor in a nearby exhibit, say, a coal boy wearing an old fire helmet with brass wings. Of course, Kirill was only using the image to sharpen his focus, even though he enjoyed imagining how official portraits of old people exchanged winks or how a porcelain service that survived the bombing cried piteously over its cracks. He expected objects, seemingly condemned to physical roles and to the muteness of the obvious—here is an oil lamp, here is a printing press—to yield a glimmer that overcame the inertia of matter, and allowed them to bear witness beyond themselves.

Red trousers. A man in a picture had red trousers. In the background, a crowd, behind it the Old Town Hall, the very one that now housed the museum in which Kirill was standing and looking at the painting.

Red trousers—there was something so incongruous about them that Kirill stopped.

"Influenced by the July Revolution in Paris, demonstrations

also took place in Leipzig in September 1830. Furious citizens wrecked the apartment of a high-ranking police official."

September 1830.

A bloody echo of the French Revolution. Citizens with swords, soldiers with rifles. A matron hurries her children away. A dog runs underfoot. Burghers have crossed swords holding them aloft—a vow? A child with a toy saber does not want to leave. A woman with blue ribbons gives him a reproachful look.

A month later Balthasar Schwerdt would leave Leipzig for Russia.

The boy with the toy saber does not want to leave.

Schwerdt would leave.

"What was it?" Kirill wondered. "The last straw? The last argument for leaving? No. The decision was made long before. The agitation on the town square was merely a sign that he had made the right decision. A sign that made Balthasar feel better. He set off on his journey unburdened by doubts.

"Red trousers," Kirill laughed, "red trousers."

Leaving the merry and dangerous red trousers to head to colder climes, to Nicholas's Russia, where the emperor prescribed food according to status and rank; had power over the dress of his subjects, where no one could wear freethinking red trousers; to the frigid, eternal authority, to the north with its lifeless lights.

He thought of Tutchev's poem addressed to the Decembrists:

There won't be enough of your blood
To warm the eternal pole!
No sooner did it flash, steaming,
On the age-old hulk of ice,
Than iron winter breathed—
And not a trace was left.

Tutchev wrote the poem in Munich in 1827, two years after the rebellion. It was unlikely that young Balthasar read it, but he could look at the northern kingdom from a similar German perspective: as a frozen regime protected by the aristocracy from the lower element splashing out onto the public squares, from the ferocity of the mob that did not want to know higher truths, a regime that could use homeopathy as an instrument of enlightenment.

The rebel's red trousers, the ghost of the red rooster singing with fiery craving under dry roofs. Red trousers would be awarded to revolutionary commanders of the Red Army in Soviet Russia. In the 1920s red trousers would appear as a red rash on the canvases of Soviet painters of battle scenes, along with scarlet banners and red ribbons on hats. Red Trousers, tucked into soldiers' boots, would come for Balthasar's descendants, throw them out of estates and apartments, grabbing the wealth of the *krauts*, the damned Germans, the foreign bloodsuckers; and Balthasar had fled from red trousers to the Russian imperial throne, which had seemed to him, and to Tutchev, to be immutable.

Kirill recalled the impact of a simple episode in the notes of the French ambassador Maurice Paléologue, who was himself recalling someone else's words: that Nicholas II, who had abdicated, was being held under guard at Tsarskoe Selo and amused himself as the winter was coming to an end by shattering a pool of ice with a pickax. The guards mocked him and shouted at the former autocrat: what will you do when the ice melts?

What will you do when the ice melts? Kirill never forgot that question, as a postscript to Tutchev's certainty that the age-old hulk of ice, the foundation of the northern throne, would never melt. Now he thought those lines were a retrospective epigraph to Balthasar's departure for Russia.

Grimma, Wittenberg, Zerbst.

Grimma, Zerbst, Wittenberg.

Wittenberg, Grimma, Zerbst.

Zerbst, Grimma, Wittenberg.

Kirill shuffled the names of the cities, thinking about the order in which to visit them. He decided on the simplest way— following the biographies of Balthasar and his father, Thomas, and the changes in their lives.

"Grimma, Zerbst, Wittenberg," he said falling asleep, as if repeating a childhood spell, a magic counting game that would bring out the old *domovoi*, the spirit who lives in the cellar and knows everything about the previous residents of a house, its builders, and what used to be on this land, on this field, before the cornerstone was laid.

***

*H*e was the only one to leave the train at Grimma—or was that his imagination? The station was boarded up and covered with graffiti. There was a Soviet monument in the nearby park— pathetic, abandoned, the kind you see and can't recall a minute later if it was a stele or a star.

A monument to a Hussar regiment. A man with a swampy green face—you can sense the proximity of a river, the stone is mossy—has his hand on the withers of a horse, his greatcoat open, revealing his richly embroidered uniform festooned with braids; pigeon droppings on his temple resemble a scar; the characteristic outline of the Iron Cross on his chest.

Why did Kirill care about this sculpture, that the Iron Cross hung on the chest of a hussar from World War I—and yet it hit him with a wave of alienation.

He turned and went in the opposite direction. A school on a

hill. Balthasar had studied in another one, this was newer, more bourgeois, more pompous.

Towers, bay windows, Gothic trefoils, a marble Minerva Owl over the door. And suddenly, like recognizing an old friend in a crowd: a concrete bust of Rosa Luxembourg, familiar in the dreary manner of depiction, the abstraction of the face, which was supposed to express unlimited humanism and love for progressive humanity, but expressed nothing.

Oddly, this made Kirill feel better. He could not imagine being born in this city, studying in this school, living in one of these houses that resembled sandcastles. Grimma not only had a unity of style, it had a solidity of style; he could not enter it, just as he would not have been able to plunge into the salt-heavy water of the Dead Sea. Everything here was too real—the window frames of pink sandstone, the bronze weathervanes and guild signs, ornaments with white dancing griffins and idyllic maidens.

Born under a red star, hammer and sickle, and made—in the way a resident picks up the building's defects—of crumbling concrete, faulty, cracking bricks, damp spackling that has lost its adhesive nature, Kirill sensed that his lack of pedigree bestowed freedom. He felt that he understood one of the sources of Balthasar Schwerdt's destiny: the desire to break into the *easy* world, where your life is not determined by your ancestors, their bulky houses full of wealth, their emblems and coats of arms, the very materiality of their lives—oak, gold, silk—as high quality as heavy.

"Goodbye," Kirill said, kissing Rosa Luxembourg's concrete cheek.

He walked past the city archive. He wanted to look in but changed his mind, saying, Next time, knowing there would be no next time.

He imagined the archive as the quintessence of urban existence; the city lived to produce orderly posthumous documents on shelves, where the papers of good neighbors continued to reside side by side; where a son follows his father, the grandson his grandfather, and the yellowed wills of former lovers touch the way their balconies once touched, too closely.

The archive seemed defenseless in the face of his intrusion, like furniture in a house with new owners. Besides, he had more faith in his own ability to understand someone else's fate, its spirit, than in archival information.

Down the street, toward the expansive town hall with a gold clock and the date of 1515. How many minutes had passed in five centuries, yet the town hall still had a tavern in the cellar, and a golden lion recumbent beneath the blue vault of the arch across the street still looked at the clock.

Down, down, toward the old granite bridge. A factory would be to the right, and beyond it, the secondary school where Thomas, Balthasar's father, had taught, and where the boy had studied.

Kirill crossed the river for a view of the school from afar—so large was the building.

The school looked into the emptiness of the opposite bank. Cut off by the river, it opened up to the eye entirely: three stories with thirty windows on each floor. How long could the corridors be, thought Kirill; the school was bigger than the city, bigger than the narrow river valley, taller than the granite cliffs.

The façade, lined by white cornices, was a lesson in drafting geometry. The bank opposite bristled with steep stones; rough cliffs were festooned with moss. The school looked out like an ancient battleship with a threatening cannon at the chaotic forms of nature, saying every substance would be counted, all matter would be told its place. The gymnasium school, like the enormous Ark, had everything—except the secret of the universe; its universe was limited, comprehensible.

Kirill imagined how young Balthasar had chafed at the school, how he wanted those windows and those corridors to hold no power over him.

Kirill walked several kilometers along the river, upstream, past the weir and the hanging bridge. He thought about the gymnasium, its grim majesty, the severe brick building stretching along the bank like the local paper factories. He thought about how a man truly could flee to the end of the world to get away from this factory of biographies, that then settled as fragile papers in the archives. The archives, with its flaking tower and weathervane, the only moving thing in the city—that and the river.

But why Russia? The school must have had an enormous globe on a bronze stand: pick any continent, any country. Kirill knew the answer. It was waiting for him in the next town, in Zerbst. He walked back across the rose sandstone bridge, past blue, green, and violet Easter eggs in the shop windows, the gray concrete wall behind which the city hid from floods, through the heavy steel gates, past watermarks from different years on the corner of a ruined building, a graph of catastrophes that had become habit—to the red train that would take him back to Leipzig.

* * *

*H*e knew Zerbst better than the other cities on his list—naturally, thanks to Catherine the Great, Sophia Frederika Augusta Anhalt-Zerbst.

Even though she had lived in Stettin, where her father served the Prussian king, and not in Zerbst, her marriage to the heir to the Russian throne in 1744 and her coronation in 1762 connected the courts of the Zerbst principality and the Russian Empire with dozens, hundreds of various threads.

Surely, thought Kirill, some of the grandees of the small principality had visited St. Petersburg, been blinded by the splendor of the empire (as had the empress herself at one time, before she became empress), enjoyed the ruler's favor, and brought back stories about the mighty northern state, the enlightened monarch who listened to the counsel of wise men and corresponded with the most outstanding minds of Europe.

Kirill arrived in Zerbst around noon. The streets were deserted, and the houses seemed to have shutters tightly closed, curtains drawn, shades lowered.

Right, then left, along Pushkin Promenade, to the old castle. Kirill was always uncomfortable in Germany with all those street names—Gagarin Allée, Pushkin Promenade, and Lermontov Strasse—that had replaced the original German names. But here, on the way to Catherine's family home, Pushkin Promenade was appropriate. "Foreign writers showered Catherine with praise," Pushkin had written. "Quite naturally: they knew her only through her correspondence with Voltaire and the stories of those she allowed to travel."

Stories, stories, stories. Kirill passed the tower on the marketplace, turned into the palace park to the small and restored palace and the large one left in ruins, and the new statue of Catherine.

The deceitful bronze vestal in a dress embroidered with innocent flowers, inadvertently extending her hand toward the imperial scepter and crown on the pedestal. "The nice old lady lived pleasantly and slightly sinfully," Kirill muttered, pleased to have Pushkin's ironic line.

Catherine had died two hundred fifty years ago. Apparently, the oath breaker and husband killer still elicited illusions among enlightened Europeans—or, her figure lent significance to the place, turning it from a backwater to the birthplace of a great empress.

Kirill imagined the Germans and Russians fawning and flattering, how the burgomaster and officials delivered insipid speeches—nonsense about "cultural bridges" and "ages of unity"—how infirm nobles, representatives of societies of friendship and memory, drank champagne while watching reflections of fireworks in the palace pond. He googled and found that even the organizers of the memorial society for Peter III in Kiel came for the festivities; a fine story, he thought, when the murdered man's executors come to honor the killer; Catherine would have laughed heartily!

But, despite his sorrowful disdain, Kirill sensed that he was on the right track. All this posthumous bustle, the division of the dividends of glory two and a half centuries later, showed how great the cult of the empress had been in the days of Balthasar and his father.

Kirill looked at the ruined Grand Palace, light gaping through the missing windows of the top floor, at the blackened statues on the gable, and tried to imagine how Balthasar had seen those windows. His father delivered babies in this palace, had entrée to the court where there were conversations about German careers in Russia, governors and generals, scientists accepted into the Academy of Sciences; about Pallas, who had studied nearby in Halle and was now on an expedition in the East, to uninhabited places promising discoveries in all areas of knowledge; about Euler, who was given a house in the capital by the empress; about others, celebrated and unknown, who rushed to Russia to benefit from its wildness, vastness, to encounter wonders that if in fact still existed would be found only in that still unexplored country.

In the fourteenth year of the new, nineteenth, century, Nicholas, grandson of Catherine and brother of Alexander, who vanquished Napoleon, came to Germany. Soon after, Nicholas and Charlotte, Frederick's daughter, were married; she converted to Orthodoxy and became Alexandra Fedorovna. Russia married Prussia; this was examined and re-examined in Zerbst, where a different family ruled, not related by blood to the late empress but remembering the golden, pearl, and emerald mirages from the East.

Kirill reached the gymnasium where Balthasar had studied. The tall and narrow Gothic windows made it look like a church, and the lower rows of stones, rough cobbles, seemed to grow out of the ground, taking on honed, polished forms the higher they went. To the right a tower peeked over the city wall. The façade turned to the city retained traces of how the building had grown, tripling in size. Another façade had windows: narrow, monastic ones below and a very large one with stained glass and a Gothic quatrefoil over it. Kirill recognized the quatrefoil, he had seen it on headstones at the German Cemetery—so this is where those signs were born that ornamented gravestones in the faraway northern country.

Balthasar had been a pupil at this school, which had not changed since the Middle Ages. A pupil who took not only the lessons seriously but also the school's spirit, grim, stubbornly monastic, striving for higher mysteries hidden in matter and the mystical revelations of the heavens—the vanishing spirit of an age when people believed in the existence of the Holy Grail, krakens, and witches, when alchemists sought the philosopher's stone, and magicians tried to catch a salamander or find the mandragora that bestowed immortality.

Of course, when Balthasar was at the gymnasium, the lectures were completely different; the clear light of new science chased away the shadows of the old mystical knowledge. But it lived on in the very ribs of the walls, the candle-sooted vaults, the foundation stones and the shape of the wizard's tower, the shelter for wise men above the earth. Arriving here after Grimma, a school of the new times, Balthasar took the first step toward his future transformation into a homeopath, a step toward the ability to combine knowledge and ecstatic faith.

But what was the source of Balthasar's strength for transformation? What inculcated the apostolic power and turned homeopathy into messianic passion? Zerbst did not have the answers. Tomorrow Kirill would follow them to Wittenberg, where the Schwerdts had moved from Zerbst.

* * *

"Lutherstadt Wittenberg," announced the sign at the station.

Kirill had the impression that in every German city he had visited, Luther had lived, preached, or studied, a fact that was mentioned in guidebooks and on memorial plaques; in the USSR every building where Lenin had stopped was similarly marked, and the familiar pathos repulsed him.

He had read Luther's theses, by coincidence right after reading three volumes of Lenin's collected works, the articles written in 1916–1917. He was taken by the similarity of two powerful but narrow minds and the style of their rhetorical constructions; Luther's rebellion against spiritual capitalism, the use of indulgences, and Lenin's rebellion against material capitalism. He had thought about writing an article on Lutheranism in Russian socialism, but as often happened, he was too lazy to go beyond the hypothesis.

As if driven by a persistent pop melody, he wandered around the city. Luther peered out from beer bottles and café windows.

Luther was a refrigerator magnet. A florist sold "Luther" gladiolus bulbs. Farmers offered *Luther-tomaten* in the main square, and the fiery reformer looked down sadly from his picture on the price list at the tiny tomatoes selling for eight euros a kilo. Luther is more alive than all the living, Kirill said to himself. He was jammed into the narrow little streets, where everyone knew you were another tourist visiting the city because it was Lutherstadt Wittenberg.

Hemmed in by the immense cathedral—no longer a place of God but the place of Luther—Kirill left the old city, walking along the river into the emptiness of the fields. It was noon, the sun shone almost straight down, and the trees seemed to grow out of the edge of their own shadows. After a kilometer or two, watching only the river flowing between huge slopes, the swaying of red and green buoys, he forgot about Luther and Wittenberg.

The image he had noted excited him: the tree growing out of the edge of its shadow, as if the shadow were its root. He saw that the tree was Balthasar and the shadow, Luther; one was not possible without the other.

Kirill saw the young man so clearly, living in Luther's city, a city where Giordano Bruno had studied. In the small town by a river, where the transformation into a prophet occurred and a new epoch began; where word and faith turned the world upside down.

What had turned into the dross of culture in Kirill's day, into refrigerator magnets and tacky souvenirs, had still been alive as a triumph of the spirit in Balthasar's. Then the memory, transmitted from generation to generation, still lingered of wars over faith, the victory over Tilly and Wallenstein; missionaries were still traveling to primitive places, and the New World was arising across the ocean, the continent of Protestant faith, crowned by an evangelical city on a mountaintop.

Balthasar—it's not clear how deep his faith in God was or the nature of his faith—could read that very fact that he was in Wittenberg as a providential sign. He was seduced by spiritual temptation. He was chosen, like Luther, chosen to become a homeopath, an apostle of the new medical truth.

Standing on the bank of the silent river, listening to the wind in the fields, the rustle of dry, obedient grass, Kirill sensed for the first time—tangentially, an echo—the scale and strength of the temptation that made Balthasar go to Russia. He sensed it as something unimaginable, impossible for a modern man, who would call it foolhardiness, self-deception, naiveté, while for Balthasar it was passion.

Kirill thought about the varieties of human passions that propel history. That there was a special sort among them: not the dark passions of tyrants, traitors, executioners—and not the radiant passions of saints, fighters for truth, defenders of the oppressed.

The special sort of passions were the ones born of illusion. Balthasar, heading off to convert Russia to a new medical faith, expected to find the unenlightened and savage, that is, non-existence, no identity. He would be received at court, he would pronounce the true word (with the help of or through the mouth of the monarch)—and everything would be transformed in an instant.

But the supposed non-existence gave a counterresponse to Balthasar. He thought the Russians would change, become his flock—but the soil reflected his intentions in a crooked mirror, and it was he who changed, who became its hostage.

Kirill saw, as if himself witnessing scenes from Greek myths, how false dreams and deceitful illusions fell on fertile ground and created new creatures—vicious chimeras that gave rise to fate as dragon teeth planted in the furrows of a field spawn sinister warriors.

Fate. Kirill sensed a new meaning of the word. He felt that Balthasar's essentially cruel apostolic dream, which arose not from God's will but from the power of temptation, the seductive images of prophets of the past, the dream of conquering and transforming a barbaric country, had elicited an equally powerful response from the place, which did not reject Balthasar's dream but conquered him, made him part of its destiny.

The family fate, like a monstrous child of the marriages of heroes or gods with mysterious powers that gave rise to the Cyclops, Argus, Typhon, and others, came into the world out of those attempts to fertilize an apparent emptiness, a seemingly innocent womb.

Fate. An illusory monster to whom Balthasar unwittingly fed his children, grandchildren, great-grandchildren, and great-great-grandchildren. Fate that had historically appeared in images of a multiheaded German Hydra, encircling Russia, drinking its pure national blood, stealing its capital; in images of the fascist Hydra, sending in spies to penetrate the Soviet Land, poison wells, suss out the black hearts of traitors, and weave nets of treachery and lies.

Fate.

Standing at the entrance of the old university building and looking at the bas-relief over the gates—a plump infant playing and holding a skull while an hourglass counted the minutes over his head—Kirill thought: wasn't he like that infant, insouciantly playing with the bones of the dead while a clock counted out the time allotted him? Was his attempt to restore the past a dangerous chimera?

Just work, Kirill told himself. Write the book. You're not trapped, the whole world is open to you. Unlike your ancestors, you can always leave, change countries, switch your life, your biography. You are not in the identity trap. There won't be any tragedies.

He turned around and went to the train station.

***

*B*ack in Moscow, Kirill headed for the German Cemetery and Balthasar's grave with a new feeling he couldn't recognize. Now he was the only one in the world who possessed the secret of the zealous apostle's heart. Kirill thought that he had violated the peace of the grave, broken the seals; Balthasar had wanted to take certain things with him to the grave and had not told them even to his children, yet Kirill had learned his secret.

The plane took three hours to cover the distance it took Balthasar three weeks to travel. He had come to Russia with his younger brother, Andreas.

Balthasar started a correspondence while still in Germany with old Prince Uryatinsky—probably someone from the Zerbst court connected the young doctor with the high official. Kirill assumed that in Balthasar's plan Uryatinsky was the first step leading to the throne; the young ambitious prophet hoped to be presented soon to the emperor so that he could astound the sovereign with the marvels of homeopathy and lay the foundations for the empire's homeopathic baptism.

Old Loder had been waiting for Balthasar in Moscow. Christian Ivanovich corresponded with Tsar Nicholas I, the younger brother of his former patient Tsar Alexander. Balthasar had probably wanted to set up a homeopathic hospital on Uraytinsky's estate, present the fruits of his work there first to the prince and to Loder, and then, with their intercession, to the tsar.

In his letters, Balthasar, like a clever salesman, hinted that a remedy was found in Germany that might bring eternal youth, and homeopathy was already healing ailments that did not respond to the bloody, butcher-like practice of allopathy. Apparently, Balthasar did not want to explain the essence of the homeopathic method, figuring that the aging aristocrat would be more easily tempted by the glitter of fake beads.

Perhaps Loder, who had lived in Russia for a long time, would have warned Balthasar about Uryatinsky, perhaps he had done so in his letters; but Balthasar was unable to meet his father's old mentor—there was a cholera epidemic in Moscow, and he was detained at the cordon sanitaire, not allowed into the city.

Loder died two years later.

Kirill visited Loder's grave, also at the German Cemetery— where else could he have been buried? The old monument must have fallen apart, and it was replaced in the Soviet era, an ugly granite slab with LODER C. I.—as if part of some bureaucratic list of pensions or awards.

The graves of Loder and Balthasar were not far apart—the cemetery was much smaller in those days. Kirill thought about how many disasters could have been averted if only they had met, instead of being separated by the epidemic.

The paths of Balthasar and Andreas diverged at the cordon, and little was known about Andreas: whether he remained in Russia or went back to Germany. Kirill, enthralled with Balthasar, did not think about the younger brother, remembering only that according to the family tree, he died young leaving little trace.

Balthasar was forced to go to Uryatinsky's estate; the cholera left him no choice.

In his diaries, Great-Grandfather Arseny, the military doctor, sometimes quoted Balthasar's notes, left for posterity and lost or destroyed, probably, during the Civil War. He repeated Balthasar's handwritten line, "For seven years I worked, living on the estate of my benefactor, Prince Uryatinsky."

Arseny had paid attention to the obvious emptiness of those lines that encapsulated seven years in fourteen words. Or rather, great-grandfather simply did not know who in fact Prince Uryatinsky was: the grandee's descendants expended a lot of effort to hush up the rumors about him, to clean up the heritage and family name, and to get back their career positions.

Kirill would have missed the name, too, would have considered the first seven years of Balthasar's sojourn lost time, if not for the strange speed of the metamorphosis that followed: from apostle to ordinary man.

Within those seven years from 1830 to 1837 lay a mystery. Kirill went after it, for the history of the family came out of it; the mystery seemed to grow a twisted joint into the outline of each subsequent generation.

Kirill thought about the first time he visited Uryatinsky's former estate. It had been nationalized after the revolution, some of the outbuildings were torn down. Then the estate suffered in the war: in 1941, the Soviets defended themselves behind the thick brick walls, and in 1943, it was the German infantry, and the attackers tried to knock down the walls with artillery. The estate was rebuilt as a sanatorium. In the nineties, the short-lived Soviet additions began falling apart. The abandoned park was so overgrown with invasive alders that it seemed trees grew not from seeds but raindrops. In the midst of that forest, anxious and gray, the remains of the estate buildings rose like boulders of alien matter tossed there by a titan.

Descended from Tatar emirs who switched to serving Russia after Kazan was taken—the family went back to Siberia, to the nomads who had served Genghis Khan—Prince Uryatinsky, a guards officer and brief favorite of Catherine the Great in her late years—the princess from Anhalt-Zerbst—was a zealous Germanophile in his youth. He built his estate—the land a gift from his royal mistress—in the style of a medieval German castle; he even had the stones transported a thousand versts from German lands so he could have granite, and not limestone.

And now, over two centuries later, in the midst of desolation and squalor, in the midst of thick undergrowth, huddled the remains of his handmade Germany. The guard tower at the gate was square, with rectangular crenellations. Another building, with a grotto in its foundation and an encircling staircase, was the Tower of Solitude, as Uryatinsky named it. Embrasures on the facades, simple capitals, oriel windows as graceful as a lady's snuffbox placed on rough granite walls, ornamental gypsum vases and horns of plenty, sculptures of maidens and gods, of which only the lower half remained—a crazy mix of styles, everything that Uryatinsky seemed to have stolen from Germany, torn out of context like a marauder, combined according to his intuition and whimsy, and placed on swampy land fed by spring floods.

Even if Kirill had not known Uryatinsky's fate, it would have been uncomfortable, creepy to be in the midst of the ruins of someone's mad dream, among the remains of eccentricity of such scale that it ceased being eccentricity and took on the majesty of utopia. But Kirill did know Uryatinsky's fate, of course, and so he had goose bumps. He imagined traps in the mounds of brick overgrown with grass, in the darkness of the cellar windows, in the holes of the collapsed roofs, in the grass. He imagined being trapped here forever, as Balthasar almost was.

Kirill had seen one of Uryatinsky's letters to Balthasar in the medical archives, in which he discussed the conditions for the doctor's service. He was amazed by the handwriting—Kirill would have called it the handwriting of a fencer—light, healthy-looking, expressing something wholesome and open in the author. The handwriting must have attracted Balthasar; he imagined an enlightened grandee, close to Catherine the Great; a great and wise old man—Uryatinsky was seventy when Balthasar arrived in Russia—a patron of sciences, the one who would be the first to bow to the radiance of Homeopathy.

Kirill would have believed the handwriting himself, if he had not known who Uryatkinsky was, child of the Golden Age of Catherine in the reign of Alexander and Nicholas I—a shard of a former era, sent into eternal disgrace for the affair that took place in the Mikhailovsky Castle in spring 1801, a wealthy man locked up in his estate, vanished from the eyes of the world, ruler of his swampy, faraway land.

Uryatinsky made his fortune off Germans.

He hired recruiters for settlers, people who encouraged families in Germany to move to the Russian Empire.

Experienced farmers and craftsmen were needed—saddlers, smiths, coopers, millers, winemakers, stonemasons, and others. Uryatinsky's recruiters brought in the poor, the feeble and aged, and the hopelessly ill. And they robbed them, paying them a tiny fraction of what had been promised. Uryatinsky had his people in the guardianship offices in charge of foreign settlers, in the government chancellery, and the millions budgeted every year for travel expenses, food, and housing for the new settlers went to him—the aid meant for colonies of immigrants.

Catherine's senior favorites grew rich on military orders, on the navy, factories, timber, and grain. The junior Uryatinsky, inconspicuous, with no decisive influence, dipped his hand in the treasury from the other side: probably every German settler in the Russian Empire brought him income. Over the decades, he accumulated a fortune.

Uryatinsky had his agents in the German royal courts. He sent expensive gifts.

He also brought in various things to amuse the court and the empress, who was jaded by so much entertainment, demanding new diversions every day. Uryatinsky's people were not above manipulating children, maiming them, so they'd grow up to be dwarves or hunchbacks; he imported Arabs and wild savages from foreign lands, magicians, sword swallowers, fire eaters, fortunetellers, musicians, prognosticators, astrologists, actors, chess masters, healers, architects, tutors, chefs, priestesses of love, jesters, dwarves and giants, freaks of all sorts, six-fingered men, bearded women, children with rudimentary tails, hermaphrodites. But most of sly Uryatinsky's money was made on ordinary Germans—kopeck by kopeck, ruble by ruble; he robbed them when they arrived, trapped them in debt, and placed cunning bribe-takers in the colonial offices.

Alexander, when he declared Uryatinsky in disgrace, did not deprive him of his wealth. That was when a German castle arose in the forest, for Uryatinsky had become obsessed with Germans and felt—and apparently Alexander took this as a sign of impending madness—that the whole population of Russia ought to be replaced by Germans. As a teenager, Uryatinsky had lived through the Pugachev siege of Kazan, he saw the wild army of rebels—a mix of Cossacks, peasants, and Bashkirs. That is probably why he retained a lifelong fear of popular movements, and *strengthened* the banks of the Volga with Germans, like introducing plants with roots that could hold the soil filled with rebellion—without forgetting about his pocket.

Uryatinsky never dealt with his recruiters directly, his name was never mentioned in colonial affairs. There were times when he executed Catherine's diplomatic assignments, and so in

Europe he was known as a grandee from an enlightened monarch, one who controlled an enormous empire.

After his fall from grace in 1801, Uryatinsky did not travel anymore to Germany, in fact did not leave his estate. For three decades he sat in his retreat, like the fat stub of a heavy candle. Even the French in 1812 did not reach the estate, not a single cavalry patrol. Having outlived his enemies and friends, and remaining spiritually and mentally in the eighteenth century—not having the seen the nineteenth, hidden away in his forest—Uryatinsky turned the estate into a simulacrum of the empress's court, as he remembered it. This was where trade in living goods came in handy.

In a secret drawer of his desk, the prince kept the gifts of Catherine's brief benevolence—an emerald ring and a diamond-encrusted snuffbox. Uryatinsky gradually forgot that the benevolence had been fleeting, came to remember himself as being favored longer than others, and eventually, as being favored alone.

He filled his gloomy castle with dwarves and freaks and installed a serf troupe of acrobats. In his seclusion, in the forest, his Tatar blood spoke. He procured mares so as to have mare's milk—part of some cure—called in shamans and sorcerers—pretenders, in fact, who claimed to be from the depths of Siberia. The old man was ailing, his potency was gone, and messengers of the old voluptuary galloped down distant roads and European tracts seeking out rare roots and mixtures that could return the desire of the flesh. At his "court," treatments were offered by old women, herbalists, defrocked monks, and self-styled healers—and he would not let anyone leave. He blocked the roads.

Uryatinsky forgot his Germanness, it came off like polish. The prince lived like a khan, rubbing himself with stinking badger fur, drinking a magical decoction of cemetery herbs, and listening to the mutterings of the stargazer who flattered him and foretold the removal of the disgrace upon him. Then he had the stargazer punished, for flattery, ordering him to be left naked in the swamp as dinner for midges and mosquitoes.

The idea of eternal life, power over body and decrepitude, settled in Uryatinsky's mind, gnawed at him on stormy nights, in the heat of stoked stoves, in the belly of greasy furs. Uryatinsky rejected the diligence of youth, the acquired German respect for gold; others sought alchemists to turn lead into precious metal, but he, on the contrary, wanted to turn gold into a new substance, something more precious than earthly materiality, into a medicine that returned youth. He gave an outbuilding to some crooks, tramps who had allegedly been kicked out of universities by rigid professors, and paid them generously, eagerly listening to their fairy tales about original elements, fiery salamanders, and spirits of the earth.

Imagine the effect of Balthasar's unexpected letter. He wrote of "eternal life" and "overcoming matter" in the idealistic sense, wishing to delineate the boundaries, the horizons of homeopathy. But Uryatinsky read the letter literally. He latched on to Balthasar—hence the generous invitation, the readiness to expend whatever necessary, to give the doctor a hospital. Uryatinsky seemed to be getting words from the past, a direct indication from the Almighty on the path to take—and he believed in the German homeopath, not at all the way Balthasar had expected, but with a mad, dark faith. If Balthasar had demanded live sacrifices, Uryatinsky would have put his serfs under the knife without a second thought.

An apostle had appeared, a true apostle among a thousand false ones that he himself had brought from the German kingdoms and principalities. To him, who had appropriated the German spirit, who had spent so many years sifting sand in search of diamonds! Of course, Uryatinsky did not chase away his witches and sorcerers, for they—impotent and fake—nevertheless constituted his entourage, a platoon of lower creatures, like kobolds, who should tremble and fall to the ground encountering the arrival of the new Faust.

Balthasar, naive Balthasar, read Uryatinsky's letter, written in the clear hand of *a man of the sword*, as a confirmation of his own thoughts, a sign of the realness of his dreams. He went to the marvelous prince.

Kirill, standing amid the ruins, pictured Balthasar's arrival. And what he suffered over seven years of incarceration here.

Gray alders, swamp trees, loved the rust of water. Unyielding bricks that still remembered the flame of the firing kiln: "For seven years I worked, living on the estate of my benefactor, Prince Uryatinsky."

His benefactor.

Kirill did not understand at first why Balthasar had compressed seven years of life into two lines and never wrote or told anything more; he maintained the secret as if it were the secret of the confessional.

Kirill had found what was possible about Balthasar's life at Uryatinsky's estate: the prince's sponger, archivist and librarian, left extremely curious notes. His heirs bought them for a major sum and the memoirs were brought to Europe, where they lay in émigré archives; a young researcher prepared them for publication and thus led Kirill to them.

Balthasar, of course, existed on the periphery of the notes; nevertheless, there were things to discover. How Balthasar, learning that there would be no hospital nor presentation to the emperor but only the search for eternal life for a half-crazed old man, tried to escape; the second time, the prince attached a servant to him, an escaped convict, a murderer, who'd strangled one of the prince's biggest wolfhounds on a bet; how Balthasar refused to do something and the prince had him locked up in the Tower of Solitude, ordering no food to be brought to him, bringing Balthasar to a starvation faint, and the convict—who had developed a strange respect for his subject—fed him by pouring broth through a copper funnel; how Balthasar got caught up in the prince's madness, and together they made homeopathic mixtures; how Balthasar cured the prince's gout, which made the prince imagine that the clever German knew much more than he was willing to share and had him strung by his arms; how he changed his mind, hearing the twisted joints crunch, and wrapped exhausted Balthasar in his fur coat; how he married him off, mockingly, to the German governess, a young girl imported to care for the prince's bastards, and the priest, who was too afraid to refuse, performed the marriage rite, even though both were of a different faith; and even though the marriage was illegal, it was still before God, you couldn't just refuse, you couldn't get unmarried.

Then a new physician appeared, who claimed that he could heal with electricity and built bizarre machines to catch lightning; the prince, disillusioned by homeopathy, exiled Balthasar to a distant building and made him work as an apothecary and treat the local servants.

The eccentric obsessed with lightning taught that everything in the human body was moved by electricity, that it was the essence of life, and for rejuvenation the supply had to be refilled; it had to be natural, original, as he called it, electricity reaped from the swollen storm clouds—the eccentric had a streak of the poetic about him. No sooner did a storm threaten than he went out to the meadow, set up his machine—flasks, coils, iron rod—and waited in vain for lightning to strike the rod. Prince Uryatinsky stood at a distance beneath an umbrella, impatiently staring at the sky.

The eccentric almost achieved his goal. Ball lightning floated onto the meadow, circled the machine, danced on the tip of the rod, and then slowly sank; the lightning catcher touched it—and burned to death. Balthasar was on the meadow. Uryatinsky had invited him to see the new, true science of life and death, and Balthasar saw the fiery sphere flying in the twilight, saw the electricity healer burst into flames and turn to ashes.

Soon after, Prince Uryatinsky died. The notes contained the subtlest hint, in intonation only, that the prince had been poisoned. The archivist named no names, made no accusations—and certainly the relatives did not—the immensely rich prince died with universal accord, peacefully in his bed, for his earthly term had come to an end and God had called him.

However, interestingly, Kirill learned from his visits to the Uryatinsky estate and the neighboring villages that to this day the local old men, who were born in the thirties, before the war—no one older was left—knew the legend of a German doctor who had poisoned Count Kozelsky, owner of the estate, in 1917, and vanished with a fortune.

The Uryatinsky family did sell the estate to the Kozelskys in the middle of the nineteenth century. But the count never had a German doctor; Kirill had established that absolutely. The count had not been poisoned but had very prudently departed in the revolutionary spring for France, keeping his life and his savings. It seemed the old story that took place in 1837 was transplanted into new circumstances and retold.

There was no proof, but Kirill sensed that he was not mistaken; Balthasar realized he would never escape the estate that had become a prison unless Uryatinsky died. However much the prince complained about his health, he had no intention of leaving this world, Balthasar could diagnose that.

Balthasar avenged his imprisonment and his murdered

apostolic dream. Did Balthasar give the prince poison himself or did he merely supply it to somebody else? Or did he simply refuse to treat the prince, poisoned by another hand, not Balthasar's? Kirill did not know. Maybe Balthasar had nothing to do with it all, and the servants fingered him to avoid blame themselves?

But then why didn't Balthasar return to Germany? Was it because he didn't want to return to his allopath father, the prodigal son admitting defeat? One would think that after seven years in prison he'd lost his pride and would have wanted to return home.

Instead, Balthasar gave up homeopathy and took a job as physician in the Widows' Home in Moscow, where the widows and children of poor state officials lived out their lives; the post probably didn't require patronage to obtain. He served there for the rest of his long life, until 1883.

At first Kirill thought that Balthasar was trying to atone for his sin, intentional or not, by serving widows and orphans—that he decided to return to traditional medicine because homeopathy, or rather his dream of converting nations to the homeopathic faith, had taken him too far literally and figuratively.

But he could have helped the weak in Leipzig just as well. There must have been another circumstance that prevented Balthasar's departure, that made it impossible to consider.

Debts? A wife from a lower social order, married under duress against church canon? Fear of exposure and accusation as Uryatinsky's killer? But if he had feared accusations, he would have tried to leave.

Kirill went over these questions, focusing on Balthasar. And suddenly he realized it was Andreas, his younger brother! All Kirill remembered about him was that he had no children: on the family tree, he was a branch that bore no fruit.

Andreas! Kirill found him in the genealogy chart he'd posted on his wall: Thomas Benjamin, wife Charlotte, son Balthasar ... son Andreas. 1817–1837. He had served in the Naval Corps.

1837. Kirill flipped through his papers feverishly. Uryatinsky died—he couldn't say "was killed"—in fall 1837, in late November. Andreas—another look at the tree—Andreas died in February 1837. At the age of twenty.

Kirill hadn't paid close attention and was under the impression Andreas had died after retiring from the Naval Corps. Why had he died so young?

Had he even wanted to go to Russia? How did Balthasar tempt him? Or had he been sent by relatives with their own goals? That was more likely. Kirill studied the genealogical tree closely. Clergymen. Physicians. Officials. No one seemed to have anything to do with the sea. Probably most of them had never even seen the sea. Then how did Andreas end up in the Naval Corps? Through patronage from someone originally from Zerbst?

Then it hit him. Some German, a member of the Big Family, serving in the Naval Corps, offered to take Andreas, because he wanted to build his own clan of loyals. He needed his own children, not tied to anyone in Russia who would be obligated to him for their careers. Andreas was given to him, that unknown benefactor, and sentenced to the sea; he was a boy, he made no decisions on his own. Balthasar had simply accompanied him to Russia, as his traveling companion.

He studied at the Corps for five years. They took him despite the fact that Andreas most likely did not speak Russian. That meant his patron was very influential. Who was he? Did it matter?

Kirill wrote to the naval archives. A month later he got an email with a brief summary.

Andreas Schwerdt. Graduated as midshipman. Assigned to the sloop *Grozyashchy*, a military transport ship, bound for a circumnavigating voyage. He did not return. Died. That was all.

Kirill called a naval historian recommended to him.

"A circumnavigation? Right after graduation?" the historian asked. "Strange. You can't imagine how hard it was to get on any ship going around the world. Even the leakiest miserable longboat."

"Why?" Kirill knew little about the navy and had never thought about how the crews were assembled for such expeditions; he thought they simply sent a group of staff officers and sailors, with a sprinkling of scientists and diplomats.

"My dear sir," said the naval historian, laughing at Kirill's ignorance, forgivable in a "general historian" without a specialty. "Participation in circumnavigation was a most important factor in career growth. People came to blows over it, believe me. Admirals pushed for their protégés. Once you've been around the marble"—Kirill had not expected him to use the word—"you have a promotion out of turn. It speeds up the years of service for orders and pension. Like a trip in a time machine. Some officers got higher up on the career ladder after two or three circumnavigations that others couldn't manage over fifteen or twenty years of service."

"Thank you," Kirill said sincerely. "Thanks."

"Why are you interested in this?" the Seaman asked. Kirill knew the man was a retired captain, had seen action, served on warships. Kirill had unconsciously given him the nickname "the Seaman." "I thought you dealt with the twentieth century? I read your work on the Caribbean crisis. Well, from our naval point of view, the navy was deeply involved."

Kirill had not intended to share the details of his research and Andreas's life seemed secondary to Balthasar's. But suddenly he felt ready to take the risk; he felt there was an important detail to learn.

"I'm writing a book about a German family," Kirill said. "I'm interested in midshipman Andreas Schwerdt, on the *Grozyash-chy*. He died in the Marquesas Islands."

"It's a famous incident," the Seaman said. "Well, for us naval types. But not written about."

Kirill asked to hear about it.

"Gladly, with pleasure." He expected the Seaman to make him wait while he lit a pipe, then the thump of a peg leg on the floor, or the prattle of a parrot in the background.

"It was extremely rare. We're not the English or the French, who sailed those seas much more," he began. "It happened to them more than once. But for the Russian Imperial Navy it was extraordinary. Extra-or-di-na-ry!" He pronounced it both with edification and thrill. "The first and only. For an officer of the Russian Imperial Navy—"

"What happened to him?" Kirill asked impatiently.

"He was eaten," the Seaman said. "Eaten."

Kirill shuddered. The horrible word *eaten*, conjuring up corpses, the freezing cold of the Leningrad blockade, the famine of the 1930s; you're eaten, and where is your soul, is it in the other world, will it be resurrected?

An image appeared in his mind, a tiny ship, wracked by a storm, carried by the winds in the expanses of the Pacific Ocean. Food supplies gone, no water, and the mummy-like men crawl around the deck, sharpening their knives—sailors and officers no more, they were only survivors and dead men.

"It's astonishing, yes. The emperor decreed that the incident be kept secret, so as not to impinge upon naval honor," the Seaman said, clearly quoting the monarch's resolution. "The papers were hidden in the archives and the crew reassigned to other ships."

"The crew, the crew ate him," thought Kirill, horrified. Andreas, Andreas, the sacrificial lamb, sweet boy sent to his death by his ambitious relatives!

"Savages," the Seaman said.

"Savages," Kirill echoed softly, thinking his own thoughts.

"No, you don't understand," the Seaman insisted, sensing his mood. "Real savages. Cannibals. A local tribe. Natives."

A new whirlwind of images: palm trees, huts made of palm branches, tanned, naked bodies, spears, bone necklaces, white-clay face paint, smoke, blue smoke from a stone firepit, texture and weight of those head-crushing stones, which would leave you in blessed unconsciousness while they sharpened a fresh skewer, long and smeared with rancid, slippery fat ...

"The sloop set sail for Kamchatka," the Seaman said.

"Kamchatka. Transport. No cannons. They were running out of fresh water. The commander decided to land on an island. There was a charted bay there. It had a dozen names, each country's navy called it their own way.

"The islanders welcomed the sailors kindly. Too kindly. Promised water, fruit, fresh pork. But they wanted gunpowder and rifles in return. They wouldn't take anything else in exchange. The captain grew angry and ordered the arrest of the priest who came for negotiations. They made the priest drink rum and gave him a pistol. The priest promised to give them food. In the morning they took a boat to the island—the priest, Midshipman Schwerdt, the interpreter, and ten sailors. Schwerdt had been instructed not to land onshore but to wait in the water until the natives brought pigs and caskets of food. Apparently, the tide was strong and the midshipman ordered them to disembark. The sailors had rifles. A crowd of natives appeared. The interpreter said there were no women among them and that was a bad sign, but the midshipman ordered them to wait until the natives brought the promised supplies; he probably wanted to prove himself to the authorities."

Midshipman. Kirill replaced the title with the name—Andreas.

"The natives suddenly attacked the crew. With knives and spears they'd hidden amongst themselves. The midshipman shouted, 'Save yourselves!' The sailors used their rifles, but there were too many attackers. The boat was on the sand. The sailors jumped into the water to swim to the ship. The midshipman remained on the shore, wounded.

"First the sloop commander sent a big boat to rescue him, thirty armed sailors. But they were fired on heavily from shore. It was later learned that a French corvette had also been ambushed and the savages captured their rifles." The Seaman slowed down, then stopped. "While they turned around the sloop, loaded their weapons with buckshot, and organized a storming group—"

The Seaman stopped and Kirill realized that he was living through what he was relating, but as a cruiser officer—someone who had the right to send people to their death. He must have been more upset by the incompetent commander and the unnecessary losses.

"The buckshot knocked the natives out of the scrub. They brought a couple of the cannons onshore, slashed their way through the jungle." Here the Seaman's voice grew stronger, as if he were in charge of the landing. "But it was too late. They found what was left of the midshipman in the village. And scraps of his uniform. The savages had taken the epaulettes and buttons with them."

Kirill pictured the bloody scraps and felt nauseated. The Seaman's voice continued hypnotically. "There were reports that many years later those buttons were found among aboriginal rulers. Some had them in necklaces, others used them as earrings—that meant they revered the midshipman, considered him a worthy sacrifice, a great warrior. … And yes," the Seaman added with embarrassment, "the body was discovered, mutilated. With undoubted traces of cannibalism. And without the head."

Without the head. The headless horseman.

"The commander considered what was to be done with the remains. They could have buried him at sea, as tradition would dictate. But either he wanted to or was required to keep the body for the investigation. They marinated it. Stuck it in a brine barrel. He was buried on Kamchatka, their port. Without his head. It was all hushed up. But rumors spread, of course. Especially among the sailors. There was a researcher who worked with naval folklore. He noted that the legend of the Marinated Midshipman was known even among the crews of Rozhdestvensky's Baltic Squadron, on the eve of Tsushima, seventy years later."

"The Marinated Midshipman?"

"Yes. The Marinated Midshipman. The headless dead officer who lives in a barrel of brine. Don't ever open that barrel. If you do, the Marinated Midshipman will get out. And kill everyone. Take his revenge for being left to the savages. He'll eat you alive. But it's just folklore, inconsistent, a fairy-tale narrative. How can he eat them if he has no head? And therefore, no mouth or teeth?"

"Did the legend reflect the fact that he was a German?"

"No, not at all. Just the Marinated Midshipman. A universal, Russified one."

Kirill stared ahead stupidly. He made an awkward farewell, rushed the conversation to an end, then prepared some Turkish coffee for himself, which he didn't drink.

Andreas … During the years Balthasar was at Uryatinsky's estate, he had been at the Naval Corps Academy. Did the brothers correspond? Did Prince Uryatinsky allow Balthasar to write letters? Probably not. That meant that Balthasar had simply vanished for the German relatives, too—they thought he had broken all ties with the family, and Andreas, who probably got mail from home, must have known that Balthasar did not write to his parents; he had a believable explanation for his big brother's silence.

Balthasar left the estate after the prince's death, arrived in Moscow, and … by then the sloop had landed on Kamchatka, and the courier with the report had traveled through Siberia to St. Petersburg. For all that time, from February to November, the death of Andreas did not exist as an event. Only the crew knew, and then the military courier. And possibly not even the courier—it was just one report among all the others he was carrying.

Kirill imagined how long—months and months—the letter had traveled along muddy roads, and Andreas Schwerdt was still alive for all who loved him. Death had the shape of an envelope with a wax seal, traveled inside it, deferred until the envelope was opened. The courier carried those deaths—surely Andreas was not the only deceased—and disciplinary issues, recommendations for awards, reports on discovered lands and skirmishes with local tribes, carried them from one end of the world to the other, like a weak, nervous impulse slowly moving up the spinal cord of the dinosaur empire, from the serrated tail of Kamchatka to the head in St. Petersburg, for everything finally happened there, in the head, while the expanse of the periphery was immersed in the heavy, murky sleep of semi-existence.

Balthasar was free of Uryatinsky, but fate took away his younger brother and kept the death in the wings, like a good playwright. Balthasar was punished ahead of time. The manner of Andreas's death, being eaten by cannibals, was moral revenge.

Balthasar saw God's threatening face in all the features of the world, thought Kirill. He felt God's gaze upon him. His life no longer belonged to him, it was all about expiation. That was why he worked furiously at the Widows' House, why he lived with a wife forced upon him and may have even come to love her—or forced himself to love her; that was why he could not return to his father—Balthasar knew why Andreas had died, who bore the cross, whose fault it was.

He remained alone, beyond the network of the Big Family, the clan.

Alone.

***

*B*althasar had seven daughters: Anna-Sophia, Charlotte, Fredericka, Agnes, Gertrude, Ulrika, and Paulina—and one son, Andreas. The last child, a late child, the long-awaited boy.

Kirill regarded the family portrait. The eldest, Anna-Sophia, was already married, Andreas—still an infant. He slept in a cradle at the knee of father and mother in the center of the photograph; he was there, though not really present, not there for history and its Cyclopean eye, selecting victims. Kirill shuddered at the photo's predetermination: the child in the cradle was the only who would live to see the revolution of 1917. Kirill could explain it with rational reasons, the average lifespan and so on, but he couldn't shake the feeling that the shutter had functioned like a guillotine blade.

Kirill looked at the genealogical tree branching with dozens of lives. Eight children. Nothing unusual for those days. But it seemed to him that the *apostle* Balthasar had spent himself on children, had become a graphomaniac of fate, had poured out his gift, intended for miracles and exploits, as semen into the womb of his uncomplaining wife, striving to expand, to capture dark expanses; but he could only reproduce himself, hoping that there would be one among the copies of destiny that would have a spark and revive the apostolic dream.

But there were only daughters, women who would join their husbands' families, transmuted into a new line of existence. Nor could Balthasar, a man of his age, believe that a woman could realize his apostolic fervor; the faces, figures, and images of the daughters revealed his growing disillusionment in his ability to engender a true heir.

From stately Anna-Sophia, a maiden with a cold face and regal demeanor, a blond princess, to the mousy Paulina, who looked like a servant girl the master and mistress invited into the parlor out of the goodness of their hearts. Anna-Sophia's dress does not follow her figure but an internal outline of aloof dignity, as if the fabric could feel the emanations of aristocracy; Paulina's dress, made by the same dressmaker, merely covers her body. Andreas sleeps in the cradle, a delicate child, fortune's darling, a random spark that flickered over the fire.

Anna-Sophia became a governess in a wealthy landowning family and married the older son and heir; she converted to Orthodoxy and became Anna Preobrazhenskaya, mistress of a mansion with a winter garden, and died in 1914, learning that her grandson, son of her only daughter, had died in his first battle near Gumbinen.

Charlotte, who married a physician sent in 1875 to the Khanate of Kokand, to the ruler Khudoyar Khan, an ally of the Empire, died with him on the journey at the hands of rebels.

Fredericka, his favorite daughter, was most like a boy in character—and perhaps Balthasar had expected things from her. She must have felt the weight of her father's expectations, chose the most unremarkable life for herself, marrying a music teacher, a Pole, and moving to Warsaw with him; contact with her ended in 1915 when German troops entered the city.

Agnes, who became Agniya in the Orthodox Church, chose an ambitious husband, an official in the Ministry of Internal Affairs, and died with him when Socialist Revolutionary assassins threw a bomb at the wrong carriage—the official had bought one just like the one owned by a colonel of the gendarmes reviled for his cruelty in suppressing the revolution in 1905; they were neighbors and the envious counselor wanted the same luxury.

Gertrude was a loss. Judging by Balthasar's descriptions, she had early cancer, he did not diagnose it in time, he tried every method he knew and then returned to homeopathy—dusting off the old altar, burning incense for a rejected god—but in vain; neither the mixtures made by allopathic doctors nor the remedies of homeopathy could return life to the dying girl. Balthasar demeaned himself—perhaps he had recalled the Uryatinsky estate and the mix of healers gathered there—and called in a famous old woman who knew how to pray before icons and heal the soul of the sick, but even she was powerless; either she mocked the haughty German doctor who had disdained her before or she told him the truth—the candle was flickering and there was no saving that soul.

Ulrika was the wife of two husbands, a fugitive, a subject of two sovereigns. Had she been born a few decades later, she would have been an emancipated lady, but in those days she exhausted herself fighting conventions, battled for a divorce, exciting men's strife, which became woven into the tapestry of world conflagrations right up to the slaughterhouse known as the Battle of Jutland, where the battle cruiser *Seydlitz* of the Imperial German Navy, on which her son from her first marriage was an artilleryman, sank the *Queen Mary* of the British Navy, on which her son from her second marriage died.

Paulina—Pavla in Orthodoxy—was the quiet daughter, a

tiny woman who never knew adulthood and never separated from her parents, her family. She was the sister of all the sisters, the connecting link, for icy Anna-Sophia and mannered Agnes and Ulrika, who avoided them all; she was the spirit of sisterhood, the pin holding the hair of her older sisters, the thin silver clasp on a necklace of heavy agate beads. Silver lock, silver ring, wife of a priest from Ryazan—Anna-Sophia arranged the marriage, happily condescending to her sister—and she put up with her brutal husband, the beatings, but when he joined the far-right nationalist Union of the Russian People, she performed a delicate suicide, going on a boat ride on the Oka River, where her boat was flipped over by a wave from a passing steamer. Pavla did not know how to swim, and drowned, leaving no children. She was barren, which is why her husband beat her, and she died in the watery element that would take Ulrika's sons as well as Ulrika, who had purchased a ticket on the *Lusitania* for her voyage back from New York.

The only boy, Andreas: named in honor of Balthasar's brother, eaten by cannibals; brought as an exculpatory gift for Andreas the Marinated Midshipman; given to pay back fate. But fate did not accept the sacrifice; Balthasar's intention was too obvious and simple: substitute one life for another, dedicate his son to his brother's memory.

Balthasar feared that the boy would die in infancy. He imagined danger everywhere—in the shallows of the river, in low railings, in narrow alleys from which a carriage could come barreling out. But Andreas grew clear and straight, without the desire common to so many children to test the borders of life, to understand what is death.

He studied easily and surpassed his peers. He could count very well, his penmanship was diligent, and he had a talent for drawing—a lady living at the Widows' Home, who had studied painting with an Italian teacher in her youth, taught Andreas oil and watercolor; but he was even better at draftsmanship, for abstract figures animated his mind more than concrete objects. In fact, he was animated and excited by objects born of engineering genius: fortresses, dams, sluices, bastions, aqueducts, and especially railroad and bridges.

As if he sensed his "in-between" position, being German by blood and Russian by birth, Andreas loved railroads, the state they produced of being in transit, of not belonging to a specific place.

Not far from the Widows' Home lay the Moskva River. He spent entire days on its banks as an adolescent, watching the construction of the Borodino Bridge. Before there was only a wooden crossing subject to high tides, a crossing used by Napoleon's soldiers in 1812. Now a bridge was being erected, named for the great battle that marked the bloody confrontation between East and West. It was being built by Russian Germans, the railroad engineer Ivan Rerberg and the colonel-engineer Amand Struve, the future master of bridges who conquered the Oka, Dnepr, and Neva rivers, the creator of the Liteiny and Palace bridges in the capital, in St. Petersburg, the future owner of the Kolomna Locomotive Works that made the best Russian steam engines.

It was not known whether Balthasar Schwerdt had known Rerberg and Struve, and whether he could have introduced his son to them. On the one hand, the doctor of the Widows' Home was too insignificant to have connections to such great men. On the other hand, Anna-Sophia had married, entered high society, and even though she was not on equal footing with her new family, which did not care much for poor relations, she could have introduced her father or brother to the famous builders.

In any case, Andreas walked from the Widows' Home—this was in his notes—along the grassy banks, past vegetable gardens, grazing goats and cows, suburban cottages and houses, to the Dorogomilovsky Ford, where stone buttresses covered in scaffolding rose from the river floor and riveted metal trusses reached out toward each other in musical curvatures from the banks, opening a new road from the West, unlocking the river defense of Moscow; he walked and watched how quickly—in the course of a year—the bridge was built, embodying, materializing someone else's engineering thought.

Kirill, thinking about Andreas, walked along the same places, by the new Borodino Bridge. The family's fate converged there. In the nineteenth century, Andreas walked along the rolling hills. Just under a hundred years later, Kirill's grandmother and mother, back from evacuation near Engels, had moved into a house on the opposite bank.

His mother had told him about the evacuation: the train traveled for a month and the food they had brought with them had run out. You couldn't even get boiling water at the stations. They arrived and were taken to a kolkhoz. Later the only thing she remembered was a brick cellar where the smell of smoked meat was so strong you could cut it with a knife and eat it; there were cramped rows of hanging hams and sausages—the spirit of gluttony seemed to run through them, forcing the sausages to bend into rings and the hams to ooze aromatic juices. His mother had never seen so much meat. She fainted.

She had not been told where they were or why there were supplies here. She decided that the children and their mothers had been brought to Communism, the long-awaited Land of Abundance, which she had seen depicted in paintings and frescoes in the Moscow Metro.

Communism did exist, she decided. It was hidden for now, it wasn't for everyone yet, only the little ones. The Germans were attacking, and the children were hidden in Communism, revealed before its time, half-ready, not strong enough to fit in everyone.

She did not wonder who had prepared the marvelous food. Who had lived in the empty houses where they were brought. She thought that was how it should be: servants, builders created the oasis of Communism and went off to build the next one.

Many years later, she was sent to Engels on business. She decided to find the place they had lived when evacuated there. She learned that in August 1941 the Volga Germans had been exiled to Kazakhstan, given twenty-four hours, allowed only one bag each. So the Russian evacuees were moved into houses where the stoves were still warm.

The German hams saved Grandmother and Mother from starvation. When they returned to Moscow, other people had been registered to live in their room in the communal flat. So they huddled in the barracks near the train station. Nearby, at the Borodino Bridge, German prisoners of war were building a new structure. The prisoners worked so quickly and neatly that no one could believe they were real Germans. The propaganda taught that Germans were only capable of death, destruction, and devastation. These men were building as if they were going to live there, as if there were no war and death but only masonry, mortar, trowel, plumb line, and bricks.

They were given a room in that building. Kirill's mother wept, not wanting to leave the barracks: she couldn't understand how people could live in a house built by the fascists. She became accustomed to it, eventually was proud of their new place: as if the house were special, better, even slightly magical.

***

*T*he new Borodino Bridge extended to the Stalinist skyscraper that housed the Ministry of Foreign Affairs, a stone cliff like a gigantic palm raised to fend off people coming from the West.

The enormous building glowed with square windows, radiating a faceless, hive-like will, repulsing all arrivals.

Kirill wondered whether Andreas would have understood the fears of the girl who would become the wife of his great-grandson. Did anything of Andreas remain, in today's Russia? Of his dream of roads and bridges?

Andreas entered the Railroad Engineering Corps Institute in St. Petersburg—and it may have involved the patronage of one of his father's widowed patients. He graduated first in his class and was given a job at the Ministry of Railways, with a small civilian rank, but he hoped to avoid a clerical career.

Kirill's great-grandfather Arseny wrote that in the fall of 1917, as he went through the attic of the estate, he found some of Balthasar's homeopathic tubes with residue still on them, and a packet of his father's blueprints made as a youth—a bridge over the Volga, a bridge over the Ob, over the Yenisei, over the Amur. The Trans-Siberian Railway was slowly moving east, and ambitious Andreas dreamed that soon he would be laying the road through swamps and crevasses, drafting huge expanses of bridges. For now, he repaired other people's bridges, proposing only corrections in the construction. But he seemed to believe that the railroad itself was a *path*, and it would reward his loyalty.

And it was thanks to the railroad that Andreas met his wife and settled his destiny—although perhaps not as he had wanted.

Two oncoming trains were stuck at a way station near Kaluga, waiting for the tracks to be cleared of snow. A blizzard was followed by hard frost, and the wet snow turned to ice, and the mounds across the rails froze the switches.

Usually, only mail or freight trains stopped there.

Ten hours later the passengers had eaten everything they had brought with them and everything the stationmaster could offer. Someone was ill and needed a doctor, the children were chilled by the drafts, the stoves in the compartments were running out of fuel, the toilets stank, and the telegraph brought news that the cleaning brigades were overwhelmed and it would take at least another day to reach them.

No one working at the way station took on responsibility for that island in the midst of the frozen forest. The stationmaster and telegraph operator had never seen so many people in their lives, and realizing they'd be subject to the thunder and lightning of the angry passengers, they endeavored not to leave their office. The steam engine team was busy with their own problems—they decided to stop stoking the fire, the pump house was frozen …

It was Christmas Eve. People were traveling from Moscow to the provinces to visit relatives on their estates and from the provinces to Moscow. Mothers with children, old ladies with companions, retired military men, pensioned officials—people who could not host their own receptions and parties and form the bulk of guests at those given by others, the flowing collection of semi-familiar faces that move from one living room to the next.

Bundles with candies and presents, suitcases with gowns and ironed uniforms, a freshly killed bird, jams and pickles in baskets, delicacies from the capital, bottles of wine and champagne wrapped in straw—there was everything on these trains except a person who could deal with the coming catastrophe.

The smoothly functioning machine broke down, and rank and title meant nothing in the face of mounds of snow. The high-placed old men complained of gout, the former officers recalled the Turkish war, the retired officials grumbled about the new governor. Everyone waited for someone to propose something. Hysterical notes began to sound in conversation, ladies got into arguments over the filth in the toilet, a former gendarme official threatened to shoot the chief of the cleaning brigade as soon as he got there. An elderly senator demanded a telegram be sent immediately to Moscow, certain that the drifts had not been cleared simply because they did not know he was here.

Night drew closer. The temperature dropped. A teenager, garrulous and inventive, brought the news that he had seen a wolf pack at the edge of the neighboring woods.

Here Andreas's talent showed itself in full. Normally, he lived like a sleepy god, a favorite of fortune, whose life was a chain of small successes and friendly smiles from the universe, who did not labor, for labor is mastery, but merely performed magic as light as a joke.

The bridges of other engineers were heavy while still on paper, for the designers were struggling with matter, fighting the laws of resistance. Andreas's bridges, however, had an instantaneous aspect, like lightning, and were whole, like a beautiful rhyme joining two shores of meaning.

However, when life turned against Andreas, setting out battalions and regiments of unpleasantness, another Schwerdt awoke in him, who took strength from adversity.

The infants were moved to the stationmaster's house. The guard was sent on a sled to the nearest village for food. The remaining provisions were requisitioned from the baggage cars and someone's cook was set to making hot soup. They opened up suitcases and shared extra clothes. A physician traveling to Vyazma examined the patients with chills and handed out medicines. The toilets were cleaned out, the pump house repaired. The guard came back with bread, meat, pots, and a load of firewood. By morning an engine came from Moscow, pushing a snowplow.

Kirill wondered: did Andreas know that he was being observed? Did he guess it only later? The family legend held that Andreas had no idea he was being watched. Kirill, on the contrary, was sure the opposite was true, and that Andreas endeavored to show what he could do.

There was a parlor car that had been tacked on to the end of the Moscow-bound train. It belonged to Gustav Schmidt, the steel magnate, whose factories made rails, and who owned shares in several railroad companies. This particular branch they were stuck on was not his, so he could not order the staff around. He was probably interested in seeing how his competitors' people handled (or rather, failed to handle) the situation, and he likely drew conclusions about necessary clearing technology, organizing way stations, and heating railroad cars.

Schmidt was an engineer. He saw Russia not only as a potential market but also as a huge unorganized space, with great natural resources that had to be exploited. However, his personal technical talent (unlike his entrepreneurial perspicacity) was embarrassingly small: he had tried various engineering fields, but the only things he could design were pumps.

His enemies joked that Schmidt pumped money. He expanded production and took on steel making, railroads, and obtained commissions from the government for sapper equipment for the army. He dreamed of attaining the big prize—total participation in military production: building artillery plants, gunpowder and shell factories, defense manufacturing. Not many people were allowed in; Schmidt still had to make his way into that market, shouldering aside other manufacturers and suppliers.

Schmidt, according to family legend, watched Andreas, the improvised station commandant, avert disaster. Later, when the tracks were cleared, he invited Andreas to continue the journey to Moscow in his car.

Engineer met engineer, Schmidt met Schwerdt. And Schwerdt met Gustav's daughter, the nineteen-year-old Lieschen (her mother died in childbirth and Gustav did not remarry).

Here the family narrative grew incredibly saccharine. Kirill made a face, he couldn't abide the sentimental meeting on the snowy way station, two trains, a sudden meeting, turning into love at first sight. He grimaced but asked himself: what if people lived like that, loved like that, tied their lives together like that— as if in a cloyingly sweet picture on a candy box?

But he sensed that this was the official biography, the edifying story. Perhaps Andreas fell in love. Perhaps Lieschen did. Perhaps it was mutual. But would Gustav Schmidt, a wealthy man whose daughter would have had her pick of husbands, have given his only heir to an impoverished engineer?

The story appeared to be one in which the wise father did not interfere in the young people's happiness. But it didn't make sense to Kirill: why would Gustav have chosen this unknown, unproven young man, of unimpressive background? Andreas never achieved anything significant after his marriage; had Gustav's confidence in him been misplaced?

Then Kirill understood. Andreas never built anything because Gustav demanded a price for his daughter's hand—a terrible price. Gustav saw what others did not—Andreas's talent was not only great but universal, plastic, and the young man did not comprehend his own powers. He did not realize that he could have founded a scientific school or become a genius of construction, an inventor of engineering methods, could have built something comparable in scope to the Suez Canal.

Andreas needed a lonely personal path to realize his talent and abilities. Schmidt deprived him of that path, sensing future greatness. A refusal of his daughter's hand would have forced Andreas to taste fortifying bitterness, to mature and concentrate on his calling. Instead, he achieved happiness, a career, and a loving wife. Schmidt installed him, like a battery, in his company's mechanism, and Andreas, a captive, like his father at Uryatinsky's

estate but unaware of captivity, began fueling Schmidt's growing industrial empire with his talent, serving his father-in-law's
ambition: to obtain the profitable military contracts, to become
part of the military-industrial elite.

With great foresight, Schmidt insisted in 1882 that Andreas
become a citizen of the Russian Empire: he, his sisters, and his
father, Balthasar, had formally remained citizens of Saxony. Gustav had Prussian citizenship and did not wish to give it up. There
were interests that kept him in Prussia, that required him to be
a citizen there and a foreigner in Russia, Kirill posited—probably inheritance, shares of bank capital, or the hope for Prussian
nobility; Kirill could not determine what it had been.

But he wanted his daughter and her husband, whom he
considered as a son, to set roots in their new homeland. When
their son was born, Arseny Schwerdt, Kirill's great-grandfather,
Gustav made Andreas a full partner and increased his share of
the company. In exchange, so to speak, Andreas and Lieschen
became Andrei Yulievich and Elizaveta Gustavovna and applied
for Russian citizenship. There was talk of conversion to Orthodoxy, but Andreas, gentle and pliant, refused, as if the Protestant
faith had been part of his practical and rational engineering
understanding of the world.

Schmidt gave the newlyweds an estate near Serpukhov. He
seemed to have chosen the place with long-range plans, not only
for the beauty of the floodplain meadows and the views of the Oka
River: the neighbors were wealthy gentry and Schmidt had been
thinking of future spouses for his grandchildren. Importantly, all
the neighbors were Russian: one count, one artillery general, one
widowed princess in whom Kirill suspected Gustav had an interest; sedate and quality society that the young couple should join.

Andreas moved his elderly father and mother to the estate.
Balthasar had not wanted to leave Moscow—life far from the

city would have reminded him of his imprisonment in Uryatinsky's swampy fortress—but his son and daughter-in-law insisted. He moved, lived through the first winter, and died in the spring, a cold spring, having caught cold in his greenhouse, tending to his medicinal herbs.

In the March cold, over the icy roads, they brought the body to Moscow. Andreas bought land in the Heterodox Cemetery and paid a mason to create the limestone monument Kirill had known as a child. And so Balthasar Schwerdt moved to Russia forever, became part of its soil. But he lay surrounded by other newcomers: Napoleon's soldiers who died of wounds, English merchants who perished on their travels, European nobles who had come to work at the invitation of Peter the Great. A Moscow medical journal published an obituary, but in German, because all the physicians who read it were German or understood German.

One would think that Balthasar's death cast a shadow on the estate, on their new home. But in fact, the death aided Schmidt's plans. Over the year Balthasar lived in Pushcha—which was the estate's name—he became a kind friend of all the neighbors; he treated the progeny of the count and general, he treated the widowed princess—and he treated the peasants. Another would not be forgiven such mixing of social strata, but in his late years Balthasar seemed to have regained his apostolic fervor. He was meek but firm and unbending in his treatments, as if giving bits of his life to others; he fought death with no distinction between the son of a landowner and the child of a poor woman; another would not be forgiven, but he was, because he was the Doctor who knew everyone's ills and woes and brought the light of hope into the long night of suffering.

Thanks to the brief but glorious memory that Balthasar left behind, his son with his wife were welcomed into the local circle; the death of Balthasar, the kind doctor, opened doors for them. And most importantly, it preordained the fate of Arseny Schwerdt, the amiable grandson who barely remembered his grandfather.

**

*A*ccording to Arseny, his parents brought him to Pushcha every summer. The attic was where Balthasar's medical things were kept: instruments, books, and crates of vials, retorts, test tubes, homeopathic items that Balthasar took with him everywhere, unable to give them up.

Science, including medicine, was developing rapidly in those years. Arseny, who was allowed to play in the attic, decided at a young age that his grandfather was a magician—otherwise, why did he have those bizarre and mysterious vials, substances, and books in Latin? As Arseny wrote, he did not share his theory with anyone because he believed the grown-ups were deceiving him when they said his grandfather had been a doctor. He heard the local peasants talking about the good doctor and exaggerating the results of his treatments, but he did not know that the exaggeration was a naive desire to repay kindness with kindness, to say a good word to intercede in the next world, and took the stories as the plain truth. He stayed in the attic, making up his own explanations for the narrow-necked bottles and colorless powders, the disintegrating pills, evaporating tinctures, and desiccated manuscripts with puzzling drawings and symbols; he imagined himself his grandfather's heir, not suspecting that the adults considered his treasure trove mere rubbish and viewed his pastime with amusement.

His parents thought that Arseny loved the freedom of rural life and proximity of nature, while he simply missed the dusty attic; he learned to hide his desire because he sensed that it would not please his parents and certainly not his grandfather, Iron Gustav. That's what he called him in his notes, repeating the family and social nickname, the master of steel who took the boy to his plants, revealing his passion, pouring molten metal from cauldrons that cooled into pig iron, iron beams, copper bars, bronze pipes, the mechanical hammers falling from on high in heavy blows.

Only Clothilde, Grandmother Clothilde, Balthasar's widow, was Arseny's confidant—she was lost without her husband among the new wealthy and highborn relatives, removed from her married daughters.

Forced into marriage with Balthasar, she seemed to understand him better than he had himself. She bore children uncomplainingly, and she lived uncomplainingly in semi-impoverishment on the small income of the doctor of the Widows' Home—and shared Balthasar with everyone, accepting his coolness toward her; she learned to bind wounds, compound mixtures, listen to the febrile breathing of patients, apply compresses, and compassionately see patients off to the other side.

Balthasar left, but she continued treating the peasants, intuitively, like a healer—and she perpetuated his fame, and they began calling her the Good Lady; she was best with children's ailments. She wasn't very good with adults, sometimes her treatments helped, sometimes not, but she diagnosed children flawlessly, as if she had gotten a small bit of Balthasar's medical gift.

But she, too, died. She went to help the forest ranger's wife, who lived on the other side of the Oka. The ranger's wife was having a baby and her oldest son came on skis to get her. They made it across the river, she delivered the baby, but on the return trip the horse fell through the ice. Clothilde saved herself and pulled out the driver, but she froze in the icy river wind, covered with a crust of ice before the rescuers reached her. They wrapped her in furs and woven mats and drove her to the estate as fast as the horses could carry them, but when they unwrapped the fur cocoon, the Good Lady was dead, the driver was alive, but she was dead, her heart could not take the wild, whipping Oka winds.

Grandmother Clo, Arseny had called her: Grandmother Clo. That is how she entered his life—part of a name, a fragment of life: Grandmother Clo. He wrote that he remembered the train from Moscow, the gallop through fields, the empty hall, the table piled with juniper branches, the grand piano as hefty as an elephant, in a white cover, the light of dozens of candles, and the small, childlike face on the small satin pillow of the coffin. She seemed to be his age, a young girl who aged in an instant but had never known old age. Everyone she had treated was allowed into the hall, and women wept, pronouncing her name in their way, Kolotildushka; he kissed her cold forehead and knew that he would always remember the juniper and the resiny wrinkled berries, the futile weeping.

Iron Gustav did not come, he was traveling far away, and Arseny was grateful for the unintended delay. Things would have gone differently with him there; Gustav would have brought splendor and violated the severity of death. Quite probably he would have interfered in the fine fabric of predestination, his strength would have interrupted the gentle guidance that Clothilde had left, would have won the remote battle for their grandson's future; but Gustav was not there, and so the boy Arseny's story and future began.

Andreas was an inspired but hopeless hunter. He acquired hunting dogs at Pushcha, hired a kennel master, even though he couldn't even hit a heavy autumn duck.

Iron Gustav methodically built upon his artillery production, elaborating new methods for tempering cannon barrels, while Andreas shot into the sky the excesses of his talent not needed by his father-in-law's industrial empire. Gustav probably required only a tenth or fifteenth of his gift, and the remaining forces tormented Andreas; the talents sought escape through whims and eccentric habits.

With the birth of his son—Oh! the baton of the unfulfilled, passed on to children—Andreas with Gustav's sympathetic agreement decided to teach him to be an engineer. He invented and had built a toy that was unprecedented—a precursor of constructors, a toy railroad, in which the engines and cars could be taken apart and most importantly, with trusses and spans to make bridges. Arseny remained indifferent to his father's idea, but Andreas was caught up in it, he started production, opened a store. He masked his seriousness at the endeavor but he perfected the game, devising a kit in a wooden box that contained a miniature model landscape made of wood and stone so that you could play railway engineer laying a road. Losing all sense of scale, he covered the table with toy steam engines, commensurate with his inner life.

Arseny tried to stay near the dog kennels. His first teacher in doctoring was the old hunter in charge of the dogs. Arseny recalled that as a child he imagined he could resurrect Grandmother Clothilde, who had not died completely, even though he had seen her lifeless body. He did not seek an answer to resurrection in church but in the pagan, spiritual attention to nature. He felt everything was connected—berry and cloud, river and sand, star and dew. He imagined the thin, flickering connections hidden by the fog of imagery; he studied animals—wild birds, fish, his father's dogs—not like a scientist but as a young pagan sensing kinship with all living things. He attended church without conviction, marking time; his temple was the attic with Balthasar's flasks—as if they were the sandals and sword left under the rock for Theseus.

Once, Arseny's father took him on a trip to a factory under construction. When they got there, they learned the cattle in the region had anthrax; the local authorities were hiding the epidemic because it was the eve of the fairs and large herds had already been sent to be sold—maybe infected, maybe not.

Andreas worried that the peasants brought on to help dig the foundation pit would get sick; telegrams flew to the provincial capital and to St. Petersburg, and doctors and veterinarians arrived.

Arseny stayed with his father. Andreas had probably wanted to give his son a lesson on managing people and situations. But Arseny saw something else: the horrible similarity of death in the eyes of cows and humans; death's indiscriminate power, prepared to poison water sources and extinguish nascent life inside of seeds. He saw the funeral bonfires, the grave pits covered in lime, the endless rows of carts with firewood to keep the fire burning; he saw the clouds of ashes blocking the sky and he saw—he felt—the invisible paths that death travels, breaking out in carbuncles on the skin.

In the face of that death even Balthasar's *imagined* magic, the flasks and powders in the attic, was impotent. Arseny, without rejecting Balthasar's legacy, no longer interpreted it literally but as a sign, a pointing finger; he grew up in two weeks. Back home, Iron Gustav thought the boy appreciated his father's lessons, had listened to his instructions, and was ready to accept the family destiny—but this was a false impression.

Iron Gustav, with his sense of humor, asked the boy to take any volume of the *Brockhaus and Efron Encyclopedia* from the shelf and open it to any page; his future would be indicated by the article his finger found. Arseny almost landed on Metallurgy but pointed to Microscope. Gustav interpreted it his way, that is, he would study metals. Arseny interpreted it differently. Gustav gave him the best microscope, with iron legs strong enough to keep the slides in place, probably better than most university medical laboratories had, and Arseny went off into the microscopic world, lost to the larger world for several years except for the summer months in Pushcha, which were devoted to communicating with the natural spirits, animals, and plants.

Both Iron Gustav and Andreas overlooked Arseny, for they were involved in secret negotiations with the Director of State Railways Sergei Witte, or, more likely, with his negotiators, for Witte was buying up private railroads for state use. When it became clear what the only male scion of the line cared about, it was too late to argue or change him: Arseny had developed a subdued but firm personality, confident in its foundations, and unswerving in changing circumstances; his character would allow him to survive two wars, protect him from a curved blade, a knife in a boot, a waxed garrote, shrapnel, bullets, and fragments in order to bring him inexorably to the torture chamber of 1937.

Kirill was fascinated by this temporal *suitability* of personalities, their suitability to the era: the fact that a character trait could mean salvation in one time period yet be fatal in another. He thought about his own personality—what was it? Apparently, it was that of a rescuer: Kirill had inherited his grandmother's and his parents' gentleness, preference for solitude, fear of getting entangled in relationships, and ability to preserve his inner dignity without making a show of things.

Arseny, however, did not think about self-preservation. Wounded by death and turning it into his eternal enemy, he became somewhat soldierly. Balthasar had been doctor and apostle, while Arseny grew up to be doctor and warrior; the two concepts were connected in the name of the institution he chose to attend: the Imperial Military Medical Academy in St. Petersburg.

At first Kirill thought that in an effort to free himself from the protection and care of father and grandfather, Arseny chose to study at government expense and far from home, from Moscow. Then he realized that Arseny wanted to obligate himself to the Emperor by his officer's oath, putting blood and family ties second, subordinating himself to the will of the state rather than the will of his parents.

Arseny told his father and Gustav his plan ahead of time. He could have kept silent until the last moment, since he knew they would not approve. But Arseny seemed not to fear his father's pressure, his grandfather's wrath, even welcomed them as a test of the certainty of his decision. He got his trial in full measure: Gustav, deceived in his expectations, threatened to cut him out of his will and insisted he would punish the stubborn boy. But his father seemed to understand his son's character. While medicine for Gustav was a secondary occupation, useful but not important, Andreas remembered his father, Balthasar—and unexpectedly took his son's side and even found a good explanation for Gustav: he had calculated how many steel surgical instruments the army ordered every year and what profit they could make if they entered the market.

Gustav had a very vague understanding of the connection between Arseny's education and the potential order for surgical instruments, which his factories did not manufacture, but he saw that the father supported his son. Grudgingly, he retreated, even though he long harbored the hope of returning his grandson to engineering, calculating that the anatomical theater (he himself was not a coward but had a panicky reaction to corpses) would deter Arseny from taking up medicine.

Arseny had no interest in surgery. "A surgeon heals dozens, an epidemiologist saves tens of thousands," he wrote in a letter to his third cousin, the grandson of his great-aunt Anna Sophia. The letter was intended to convince the cousin to study alongside him, and it worked. As a consequence, the young man was killed in one of the first battles of the war, in Eastern Prussia.

War epidemiology as a discipline didn't really exist then, so Arseny studied military surgery but at the same time studied privately with civilian professors, with doctors who had practiced in Central Asia during army campaigns, and defended his dissertation on malaria, a disease that tormented the Caucasus Corps of the Russian Army in the nineteenth century.

He was one of the top graduates in 1903. His dissertation was published by the Academy; by then border clashes with the Japanese were growing in frequency in Manchuria. The day the Academy hailed its graduates, the Trans-Siberian Railway opened in both directions, and additional Russian forces journeyed, albeit slowly, to the Far East. Arseny asked to join the active army but was held on at the Academy for scientific work.

Iron Gustav—even though Arseny did not write about this—with his new connections in the military must have known about the coming war, for Russian intelligence reported clearly on the Japanese preparations. The old magnate had profited on the construction of the Trans-Siberian and was greedy for new orders, sensing what the war would bring.

The rift between Gustav and Arseny deepened: The Trans-Siberian Railway was built by convicts or recruited workers, whose lives were little better than those of convicts. Russia wasn't buying the needed construction machinery fast enough, so the branches were built by hand, with pick, axe, and wheelbarrow. Iron Gustav approved of this policy, deeming convicts human rubbish, good for dying while hammering ties into the permafrost.

Arseny studied the art of surgery on soldiers, the peasants of yesterday. He knew that his patients would be transported in railroad cars along tracks spattered in sweat and blood, paid for by death, sent by railroad to their slaughter. The industrial mechanism consuming human lives disgusted him, and even more disgusting was Gustav's enthusiasm for it and the treasure he reaped from it. Slowly Arseny came to the conclusion that the worst illnesses, the worst epidemics are not rooted in nature but in the social structure. It's not clear if he'd already read socialist literature, but he was ready to accept socialist ideas.

***

*A*rseny worked only a few months at the Academy. In the winter of 1904, Japan attacked Port Arthur and the Russo-Japanese War began. By April a squadron was being formed in St. Petersburg to bring support for the ironclads blockaded in Port Arthur. Arseny had already asked several times to join the troops, but he was rebuffed each time—Arseny assumed that Gustav had a hand in it; he had his own ideas of honor—rooted in business—and wanted to protect his grandson from battle.

The squadron was put together in great haste, and construction of some ships had to be completed en route. They had a shortage of weapons, iron cladding, workers, experienced sailors and officers, and physicians. Especially physicians familiar with the tropics and tropical diseases.

Some wheels turned in the military and naval mechanisms—perhaps someone saw the brochure on malaria—and Arseny was sent to the navy, to the command of the Second Pacific Squadron.

Arseny Schwerdt was assigned to the *Prince Suvorov*, the flagship of Vice-Admiral Rozhdestvensky; Kirill did not, and could not, know whether the battleship's captain, a German, Commander Ignatius, had a hand in this. The battleship, even though it had been put to water two years prior, was still under construction by the wharf wall; Arseny lived in the city for now.

The new battleship could not travel through the shallow Suez Canal—nor would the British have allowed it—so they had to go around Africa. No one in the Russian fleet had ever taken a squadron this large on such a distance—23,000 kilometers. None of the ship's doctors knew precisely and exhaustively what medicines would be needed on the voyage, what kind of illnesses could affect the combat capability of the already weakened squadron, for the sailors were all on their second term of service. The doctors prepared for the unknown, collecting reference books, refreshing their memories of foreign fevers and varieties of plague, and questioning the few who had taken long voyages in the tropics; in effect, the coming battle with the Japanese Navy, the slaughterhouse promising many deaths, took second place for the medics to the numerous unknown threats along the way. Admiral Rozhdestvensky, known for his harsh temper, would take it out on the doctors if the sailors succumbed to mass illness.

Finally, in late September, the squadron left port. Kirill knew that Arseny wrote home, but his letters from the rare ports where the ships stopped—the British tried to keep the squadron from being supplied with coal—were not saved. So Kirill reconstructed what his great-grandfather had experienced from books, memoirs and letters of seamen who had served on the *Prince Suvorov* and other ships.

The Dogger Bank Incident: the Russian ships fired on British fishing trawlers, taking them for Japanese torpedo boats in the dark. It didn't make sense for Japanese vessels to be in British waters, but nerves were frayed, intelligence had reported on the possibility of gunners and diversions. Kirill read a report of the event: hundreds of shells were fired, they hit their own ships, a Russian priest was killed on a warship. The English press called Rozhdestvensky's squadron a "fleet of lunatics"—the first omen. Kirill tried to understand what the men were feeling, why they were so easily deceived, taking fishing boats for warships—and he sensed the fatal premonition of seamen who wanted their fate to come as soon as possible.

The first madness appeared still in the Atlantic. Collapse of discipline. Breakdowns on the ships.

Then came the second evil omen, whose meaning was clear to Kirill, seeing it a century later.

The squadron anchored in Angra Pequena, off the coast of modern-day Namibia. They restocked supplies, made repairs. A few kilometers away was Shark Island. A few months later the German expeditionary corps was to create a camp for imprisoned rebels of the Herero tribe—the first concentration camp of the twentieth century. Several thousand people would die on the bare rocks of the island, guarded by sharks, better than any barbed wire. The Germans were fighting with the Herero, forcing the tribe into the barren desert; they already had prisoners in barracks in Angra Pequena doing forced labor.

"They saw evil but did not recognize it," Kirill said to himself. "They saw evil in its infancy, just testing itself, not in full strength, but they did not destroy it."

Kirill re-read the letters of a lieutenant who had served on the *Prince Suvorov*.

"I am writing from Angra Pequena. […] A ship arrived today with German troops. It turns out the English had armed a militant border tribe of blacks and sent them against the Germans. What can you say, what fine neighbors! The poor Germans just barely dealt with the Herero, and now there's another unpleasantness.

"We stayed in Gabon until 18 November. [...] Our officers bought a lot of parrots, gray with red tails, onshore; some are completely tame.

"On the 19th we celebrated crossing the equator, an old naval tradition. Neptune appeared onboard with his wife and a huge entourage of all sorts of devils to question the commander for the reason of our appearance on the equator, and he collected a huge tribute in the form of drinks from the gentlemen officers. After which, everyone who had not crossed the equator before was sprayed by the fire hoses and bathed in a huge tub fashioned out of a tarpaulin. Then Neptune gave us a free pass, promised beneficial winds and untaxed fishing rights. The celebration was very nice."

Kirill read it over and over.

"Tribe of blacks" ... "The poor Germans just barely dealt with the Herero" ... the parrots, the Neptune ceremony.

They were blind.

Kirill thought that if any of the sailors and officers had understood what was happening, had felt sympathy for the poor tribe doomed to death, then perhaps the fate of the squadron, also sent to its death, would have been different. But no hearts trembled, and the squadron was doomed.

Kirill thought about Arseny: what had he felt? He, whose sons and daughters would die at the hands of German soldiers, or at least because of them? Who would be starved to death in Leningrad? What had he thought looking at the hills of Namibia? Did he pay attention to the intermittent news from shore?

Kirill felt that the answer was no. Arseny was busy doctoring.

Kirill thought about the difficulty of recognizing a new evil. It does not have a name yet. It is judged in terms of the previous cruel age: to them, it had been the decimation of a tribe of blacks, with no intimation of the future.

Yet inside the familiar evil, which was considered inevitable or justified, the seeds of a new evil were growing. The seeds were there, but growing conditions were not yet ideal; the evils were not highly visible, would be considered excesses at best, abuse of authority, arbitrary command. The seeds would not grow everywhere at once; the old world could not accept a new evil because it had its own, commensurate to the era. But the new evil would travel, restlessly, relentlessly, seeking a place for itself.

Angra Pequena. A password that allowed entry to the back door of history, an unnoticeable door leading straight to a slaughterhouse that would occupy the entire world; Angra Pequena—had his great-grandfather remembered it?

Kirill thought that the answer would also be no.

By the time they reached the Cape of Good Hope, there were dozens of men on the ships who had lost their minds. The tropical diseases the doctors had so feared had bypassed the squadron, but madness took its toll. At first they locked officers in their cabins, and they kept the lower ranks and sailors in the infirmaries. Arseny, who was an outsider assigned to them, was sent to keep an eye on the madmen—they didn't have any specialists in psychiatric illnesses in the fleet; at each stop they loaded the patients on the hospital ship.

No one could treat the madmen; they had no knowledge and no medicines. Arseny followed his patients down the roads of their madness. The madness was of one kind: they were waiting for the Japanese fleet, which allegedly was traveling a parallel course. The crazed signal man constantly saw smoke on the horizon; the crazed admiralty messenger kept waking the chief with imaginary reports from the bridge; the crazed stoker did not want to shovel coal into the boiler, since that would only accelerate the fatal meeting with the Japanese; the crazed gunner could not shoot during training exercises, he was certain that the shell would explode in the barrel; the crazed telegraph operator received radiograms from the Japanese asking them to surrender.

Arseny later told his wife, and she wrote in her diary, that he had not been sure of his own mind. He imagined low Japanese torpedo boats flying on the crests of waves, and he wanted the waves to cease and the propellers to rest so that the ships would not hurry to battle. When St. Elmo's fire flashed on the masts of the flagship right near Madagascar, ghostly jelly torches, Arseny, who did not know what they were, thought that the Japanese were attacking with a new weapon. St. Elmo's fire was considered a good omen, but so deep-seated were the bad premonitions that this time the phenomenon was taken as a foretelling of death. Only the crazed artillery officer showed his good side, insisting that it was only electricity, and laughed and laughed, as if he had come up with a great joke.

At last, the squadron dropped anchor at Madagascar. They intended to send all the madmen home to Russia in an auxiliary battleship through the Suez Canal. Arseny—who later admitted this to his wife—secretly hoped he would be sent to accompany them and that his expedition would be over. However, the gears in staff bureaucracy turned again, and other doctors were sent to Russia. Arseny fell sick in Madagascar. Nowadays it would be called a psychosomatic fever, a psychogenic rash, but then they suspected an unknown infection and the ailing doctor was removed from the flagship to protect the commander from contagion.

Commander Ignatius wanted to keep Arseny on the *Prince Suvorov*, knowing what the battle would entail and how important every doctor on board would be. But the order was clear, and Arseny was given the choice of two ships: *Borodino*, the sister ship of *Prince Suvorov*, and the armor-piercing cruiser *Emerald*, which came from Kronstadt and had caught up with the squadron.

Russian roulette, life and death. Ironclad battleships had strength and power, twelve-gauge guns, but they led the charge. Cruisers were unarmored tins, but they had maneuverability and speed.

Arseny chose *Borodino*. First, he had already grown accustomed to being on a battleship. Second, he had a superstitious belief in the protective power of the name. But *Emerald*'s captain, Baron Ferzen, another German like Ignatius, had noticed Kirill and used behind-the-scenes diplomacy to get the physician for himself, thinking like the commander of *Prince Suvorov*: an additional doctor was a good thing in the squadron battle with the Japanese.

Emerald, Emerald.

Kirill pulled out the narrow drawer at the top left of the old desk. Inside, if you squeezed your hand into it—it was intended for a narrow woman's hand, but Kirill's hands were narrow, his family thought he might be a pianist—in the far corner there was a tab, apparently sticking out by accident. If you pulled on it, a small door, camouflaged as a carved wooden wreath, would open on invisible hinges. If you put your hand in there, you would feel a cold weight, like a coiled stone snake, sleeping in the dark of the hidden recess.

When you took it out, you must not forget to open the drapes to let the sunlight pour into the room, a lot of light was needed because jewels kept locked up for decades absorb the dark and it had to be washed away, chased from the faceted crystals.

Yes, this July light was good, albeit too thick; the sunshine of May or even April would be better, thin, colorless, still dispassionate, sinless as a child's kiss, not filled with the power of sun rising in summer's zenith. But July sunshine would do, viscous, self-intoxicated, as overripe as two-year-old honey. It would chase away shadows, feed the crystals with its willful radiance, and the heavy, unyielding emeralds, the hidden stones of the Urals, captured in the silver manacles of a necklace, would glow in his hand.

The cruiser *Emerald* survived the hell of Tsushima, where almost the entire squadron perished, broke through to Vladivostok, foundered on the rocks near the harbor, and was blown up on the orders of its commander, Baron Ferzen. *Prince Suvorov* perished, *Borodino* turned over, taking the entire crew except one sailor, while the minuscule cruiser, defenseless in the battle of line forces, survived.

When his mother learned Andreas was saved, she ordered an emerald necklace, of the best stones that could be found, for her future daughter-in-law, whoever that might be. Perhaps the jewelers, knowing why the necklace was commissioned, went through all their old trunks to find stones from Peter the Great's time, and a great marvel was born.

A special stone is in the center, an emerald of tender grass green and incredible size, like grass mowed at dawn, before sunrise; like its juice, innocent and sweet. To the left and right, in both directions, are large stones of various shades of green: from bright, changeable foliage resembling the glossiness of apple leaves to the thick green, falling into blue, of juniper, to crystals seemingly created from the waters of the ocean depths, where lies the *Prince Suvorov*, on its side, with gaping holes, the battle flagship.

The stones are held together by a fine chain, a silver chain; prongs hold each crystal as with the fine hands of ants—not spiders—and each link of the silver chain seems to be born of the previous one.

Kirill knew that Grandmother Karolina considered the necklace more than a family heirloom; it was a talisman and charm. In 1941 the necklace remained in her house in Moscow while the family gathered in Leningrad; she survived, the rest died.

Was the necklace a charm? wondered Kirill. Perhaps its power was exhausted, and now it was nothing but a beautiful piece of jewelry. He hoped that was the case; it was as if the joy over the salvation of a son where many others died—where the sea bottom was sown with dead ships—and elation, pride, and fervent prayers of gratitude had all imbued the necklace with an egotistical and spiteful nature that would protect only the chosen one and perhaps repel the rest.

Kirill lifted the necklace to the light; the faceted crystals glowed peacefully, tenderly. He put it back in the secret compartment.

Arseny was spared. Perhaps it was the protection of the Marinated Midshipman who had been eaten by cannibals when he was younger than Arseny. Arseny's patronymic was Andreyevich, and the Russian squadron sailed under St. Andrew's flag—the blue saltire on white background, the Ensign of the Russian Navy, protected by the apostle who had been crucified on a diagonal cross. Arseny was also protected by the martyr Andreas, who did not become an admiral, the family sacrificial lamb who had suffered at the hands of pagans.

The *Emerald* proved itself to be more than steadfast. After the battle it broke through to Vladivostok, its speed saving it from enemy torpedoes; it had few wounded and even fewer dead—a lucky ship, led by a lucky star. The fact that the cruiser foundered on rocks after having avoided the Japanese and was blown up on May 19—the commander was later tried and acquitted—was the required portion of failure for an astonishing success: being surrounded by battleships, being asked to surrender, seeing the

remains of the Russian squadron surre__
ing through the line of Japanese sh__

Thus Arseny ended up in V__
cian at disposal from a drowned cr__
crewmember of that ship; temporarily __
the squadron that no longer existed, for it la__
although it existed still as a unit on paper; assi__
but considered part of the army—a headache for__
bureaucrat who was supposed to decide what to do__
"gift." Arseny must have requested a move to the frontlin__
the war that he had almost missed; he was assigned to the eva__
uation hospital.

There were no major land battles after the defeat of the fleet, and therefore, not many heavy losses. The frontlines did not change, it became a war of attrition. However, Arseny still managed to find adventures. One night he traveled with two Cossacks right past the town they were aiming for and rode into a village taken by the Japanese. One Cossack was shot to death, the second one was wounded and fell off a cliff on his horse, while the doctor—even though Arseny thought he was pretty good with his saber—was knocked out of his saddle and taken prisoner.

None of the ten Japanese soldiers or their leader spoke a word of Russian—it must have been a new unit recently arrived from Japan. They tied him up and left him in the shed where the soldiers slept in shifts. Arseny had studied a conversational guide to Japanese during their sea voyage, but he was too agitated to understand what they said, the words did not resemble the transliterations he had learned; he might as well have studied Chinese instead of Japanese.

Arseny described his alienation in his diary; he could not understand even the gestures, even the emotions, he felt he had

mong opposite, contrary people, where everything was
erse of what he knew. Arseny could not find a hint as to
was going on; the shed, the soldiers, the lamp, the rifles in
orner, the horses—everything was alien, not as it should be,
he could not understand how these things interacted, what
tentions were hidden in objects and people.

Had he been in their place, he would have assigned two soldiers to convoy the prisoner behind the lines. But the Japanese
sergeant did not seem to be interested in him; he imprisoned
him by accident and just left him, like an unneeded object.

Arseny thought he was in a strange trap; he prepared himself
for torture, feared it, but in the end no one laid a finger on him,
they just left him alone, as if the ten Japanese soldiers were also
prisoners of someone powerful and invisible.

The doctor was freed in the morning. The wounded Cossack
survived, reached the Russian sentinel group, and they quietly
took the Japanese sentries with knives and killed all the sleeping
soldiers; only their sergeant sensed something was wrong and
grabbed his pistol, and they shot him instead of taking him prisoner as they had intended.

The Cossacks had not hoped to find the doctor in good
health and so they were very happy. The Japs hadn't had time to
have their fun. But a day later everything changed. Perhaps in
revenge for the slaughtered outpost, perhaps not, the Japanese
attacked the Russian positions—the hidden positions situated
on the other side of the slopes, which meant that the Japanese
could not have seen them with binoculars.

And they struck successfully, they destroyed a half unit, and
the battalion commander was killed, a direct hit.

Spymania flourished in the army by then. They said that
bribed generals had given up Port Arthur, that factories made
useless weapons, that all Koreans, cattle drivers, peasants, and

porters were infiltrators and that's why the fleet was destroyed.

It's not known if anyone gave the Japanese artillery a map of the Russian positions. Perhaps the god of war was on their side that time. But the Cossacks, remembering that the doctor came out of imprisonment without a single bruise, began whispering that Arseny had revealed their location. Pretty soon a story was circulating in which the doctor's hands were untied and he was chatting in Japanese with the officer when the soldiers burst into the shed.

No one might have believed the Cossacks, who were known babblers and braggarts, but ... But Arseny was a stranger in the regiment who had arrived recently and had not had a chance to make any friends. And where had he come from? Some sunken cruiser, whose existence nobody even had proof of. And then the name, Schwerdt: a German, you could see he was German, he was young and not yet polished by life.

You couldn't say they believed the accusation, but the command came to the conclusion that Arseny should be transferred somewhere, and in a such a manner that no new rumors would arise in the upper echelons that would possibly implicate the commanders in protecting a spy.

He experienced the event with a cheerful soberness, as if everything that had come before—crossing three oceans, the battle, the anxious night, the refusal to surrender, the breakthrough—was a game in which he did not quite understand what could happen to a person. But get lost in the dark—and now prove that the Japanese didn't know Russian or ask him about anything; you're on the brink of such destruction, such despair, that simple death seems like a desired reprieve.

Arseny must have told one of the military medical bosses what he had been forced to do during the voyage. They sent him to the mobile hospitals at the front.

These hospitals had too many soldiers who had lost their minds. The military doctors knew and were prepared for the fact that a given number of people who had been in battle, under gunfire, would lose their minds. But there were ten times, a hundred times more madmen than predicted by medical science and the experience of old physicians who had seen the Russo-Turkish war of the 1880s. Something had to be done with the madmen—gather them, treat them—they were no longer a statistical error, they had become a phenomenon. Does it need to be said how relieved they were when Arseny Schwerdt mentioned that he had taken care of the madmen of the Second Pacific Ocean Squadron?

This was a new war, Kirill thought; that was the point. It was the first war of the twentieth century, a new industry of death. The old tactics—advancing on foot, in columns, en masse—and the new technology: long-range artillery, fast artillery, large-caliber artillery, mines, machine guns, multicharged rifles, barbed wire. But the people were still from the old era, belonging to that past that seemed unhurried, even charitable somehow: peasants who understood death in hand-to-hand combat, a sword fight, a shootout in a field, not in the form of an eleven-inch howitzer shell that could send a unit into oblivion or a machine gun volley that could knock down a row of men—that kind of harvesting was beyond their understanding.

Arseny was given orders to collect all the mentally ill into one train and take them to Central Russia. Peace was concluded with Japan, troops were heading home, but he was stuck in the Far East. The top brass wanted the crazy soldiers in one train, not traveling in parts; perhaps the officers were confusing madmen with revolutionaries, dangerous freethinkers, and wanted the extra precaution. Revolutionary outbursts continued throughout the country, soldiers and sailors were rebelling in Vladivostok, railroads were on strike, while Arseny and his assistants organized the train in Harbin, gradually learning to recognize the rare fakers, distinguish illnesses, and improvise diagnoses.

The train set off only in January, after the government forces suppressed all rebellions; they moved in the direction of the Baikal region, where the punitive units of General Meller-Za-komelsky and General Rennenkampf had just passed.

Kirill imagined what they had traveled through. Arseny did not mention it at all. First the rebels had pillaged and burned, then the punitive troops hanged and shot the rebels, as well as "suspicious" types, anyone who got in their way. And this was normal, healthy, state-approved behavior. And the train carried men considered to be crazy because they heard voices or thought themselves to be someone else.

The coming madness of wars and revolutions was revealed to Arseny, thought Kirill. And unlike the sign of Angra Pequena, this message Doctor Schwerdt understood.

It took the train two months to reach its destination, Ryazan. In Harbin the doctor had lived apart from the patients, in a rented apartment. But the train had so little space—they had to wrest each car from the stingy quartermasters—that all he could have was a narrow compartment, which he shared with a colleague.

Day and night he made the rounds of the train cars—many of the patients were also wounded, some heavily. And he was permeated, permeated, permeated with delirium screamed during fitful sleep, whispered to a comrade, spoken into space. People seemed to be torn open by shrapnel, turned inside out by explosions, and they were trying to comprehend the world with tools of intellect. Gradually, in order to distance himself and keep from going crazy, Arseny began describing the most acute or unusual cases, seeking a rational seed in the madness, elements of common visions that infect, so to speak, a healthy mind as well, but which flare up in the madman's brain as blinding, all-explaining hypotheses and become obsessive faith.

Arseny's notes did not survive, he turned them over to the doctors who would be treating the mentally ill in Ryazan, but some things could be restored from his diaries.

"They'd fought the Japanese and searched for Japanese spies in every corner. The soldiers whispered openly that 'their excellencies had sold themselves to the macaques.' But there are no Japanese in the soldiers' delirium. None. They are too far, too alien. There are cannons. There are attacks. There are wounds. There are enemies. But no Japanese. What's interesting is that the enemies are not foreign, they are Russians. Rebels. Students. Rich men. Officers. Revolutionaries. Generals. Courtiers. The Empress. Stessel. Kuropatkin. The Emperor. Usurer kikes. Ordinary kikes. And Germans. The soldiers are diseased with the enemy. Everyone has his own, but they all have one."

Arseny began paying attention to the phantasmagorical Germans that existed in the soldiers' delirium. He was tempted to look into the crooked mirror and see himself, Arseny Schwerdt, to plunge into the murky soothsaying of a crazed Pythia and hear vague prophesies of destiny and fate.

One soldier, upon learning that the doctor was German, kept insisting that he grow back his lost leg. He was certain that the Germans knew the secret of such treatments but hid it from Orthodox people. Another thought that the German doctor was there to kill the wounded, a third that the whole war was started by Germans to make money and to have as many Russian men killed as possible. A fourth, who had been orderly to a German lieutenant, who was wounded and died in his arms, believed that he himself had become German; he recounted waking up one morning and he seemed to be himself, yet everything Russian was alien, and his boots smelled of a foreign pitch he didn't like, and the cavalry horses made foreign noises with their horseshoes; he said that he couldn't bear to live this way, everything nauseated him, and he asked if there was a way to become Russian again, otherwise he would kill himself.

The war had been in the Far East, but the soldiers who had lost their minds saw the enemies they had brought with them in the trunks of their mind from Central Russia. Kirill was most interested in Arseny's aperçu: there were no Japanese in their delirium. But there were Germans.

Kirill began wondering why. "The Japanese are too alien, too distant," Arseny had written. Kirill added: the Germans were no longer alien or distant. There was a reason why the cemetery in Moscow for the non-Russian Orthodox, where people of all faiths were buried, was simply called the German Cemetery by locals. That is, a German was both a German and also the Russian image of a foreigner in general.

For a German is not just an enemy, thought Kirill. For all the talk by Russophiles of the dominance of Germans in Russia, the German was somebody close, almost one of us, and at the same time a foreigner. This contradiction between familiarity and the presumed abyss of differentness inside the German is horrifying: you are open to your alien, he reads you like a book, he knows all your secrets and weak spots, all the levers of the national character; you are absolutely defenseless before an enemy like that.

Alien as one of us, our alien. And, thought Kirill, first there must be a consensus of acceptance and assimilation, before the pendulum of troubled national feelings swings to the other side, to rejection and refusal.

There are alien aliens, too, Kirill continued his thoughts. They appear in movies, slimy creatures that spill out of the human body, out of the healthy body of the nation, he added ironically. Nazi movies, in fact, except the action has been transplanted into space. A marvelous projection of social anxiety.

Our alien. Name: Arseny. Patronymic: Andreyevich, but surname Schwerdt. And a soldier asks you, magician-German, to grow back his amputated leg, and swears and curses at you, you-German, for keeping your medical secrets.

That was the mirror into which Arseny looked; that's what he saw there.

Two months of travel brought the train to Ryazan. There, far from the two capital cities, in the provinces, the patients were examined by a commission that included police officials. They were assigned to various hospitals or simply decommissioned and sent home if they weren't violent, because they didn't know what to do with them. Arseny was proposed for the order of Saint Anna Fourth Class, the most minor in the long hierarchy of military awards. But the proposal was recalled: that was the effect of his one-day Japanese imprisonment and the negative review of the regimental commander, who believed the rumors and suspected that the doctor caused the death of his men; he did not write that openly, but a hint was more than enough. Arseny didn't care: the war was over, and orders can be handed out to others.

***

*G*iven a long leave, Arseny went home, to the estate, to Push-cha; even though he later rented apartments in Moscow, in his diaries Pushcha was the only place he called home.

They were making trouble in the region. The eruptions of the first revolution were not as intense around Moscow as in the distant provinces, but still, the neighboring estates had suffered. Supplies were ransacked in some, horses stolen in others, and the neighboring general demanded a half squadron of dragoons to protect his property. But the marauders did not touch Pushcha— the fame of the Good Doctor and Good Lady protected the old place. Arseny followed in his grandfather's footsteps and began treating the peasants, increasing the family's good reputation.

One night a wounded man was brought in a sleigh: a sword had sliced through his arm to the bone. Arseny knew the muzhik from the fishing village at the Oka River; it was said he used to be a brigand, then supplied Nizhny Novgorod merchants with barge haulers, a business that died out when steamboats came in. He worked as a lightkeeper, sailing at night to light the beacons, and on long summer days rowed vacationers along the Oka's indolent channels, and he fished a bit, bringing enormous catfish, the black denizens of river depths, packed under thick burdock leaves to protect them from the sun, to sell at Pushcha. And now he lay delirious before Arseny, the wound was infected, and Arseny understood that the dragoons must have caught him thieving and chased him through the woods, wounded him but did not catch him, he got away, knowing the ravines and cuts in the forest, or perhaps by water, for fishermen had small boats hidden away, whether for some illegal trade or simply because their brigand blood enjoyed it.

Arseny knew that if the dragoons found the wounded man in his house, if he didn't report him to the police, they probably wouldn't arrest him, his relatives Gustav and Andreas would intervene, but he would be fired from his military service. Arseny might have reported him if he had not led the train of madmen, if he had not seen the Cossacks from the punitive units fighting and running men through with their sabers, if he had not been imbued with profound sympathy for the rebels.

He did not give him up. He hid the fugitive, cleaned and sewed up his wound. He knew that the beacon keeper could not go home, that the dragoons were waiting in his village. He gave him money for the road, and the beacon keeper floated away on the Oka, helped by his river brothers to Nizhny Novgorod, where thousands of people lived and where you could vanish without a trace.

Arseny must have thought this would be a unique event. But nocturnal guests trampled the path to his house in the twilight. Arseny did not write how many times they came to him, how many times frothing horses flew into his yard, but Kirill sensed that it more than a time or two—there were ambushes all around, searching for real and imaginary rebels, the general whose greenhouses of roses had been shattered was furious.

Did they threaten to give Arseny to the authorities? Did they try to buy him off? Or did he willingly receive the nighttime visitors from the unknown revolutionary force that burst out occasionally in crimson smoky explosions beyond the forest?

Kirill thought that Arseny had been firm: he opened the doors himself, no one forced him. That was the form Balthasar's apostolic fervor had taken in him: in the socialist idea he saw the medicine for everyone that Balthasar had sought in homeopathy.

Arseny Schwerdt underwent a deep transformation that summer. To complete it, fate gave Arseny two more meetings.

In late spring, the Oka thieves' transport brought a new guest to Pushcha. They must have learned about the strange doctor and checked him out, or perhaps there was no other choice. They brought the man Arseny called Comrade Aristarkh, no other name. He was a Socialist Revolutionary, one of the underground leaders of the December uprising in Moscow. He had been wounded and could not flee with the others; he stayed in safe houses until it became too dangerous: the police were combing the city, the gendarmes were finding all the revolutionary hideouts.

This was a big shot coming to Arseny. Apparently he was accompanied by two or three bodyguards.

The Bolsheviks later took credit for the Moscow uprising. In fact it was headed by the Socialist Revolutionaries, the SRs. Who Comrade Aristarkh actually was, how many names he used as indicated in the gendarme search warrant, Kirill did not learn right away; to begin he simply imagined a man without any special features, a professional at disguise, capable of appearing to be an agronomist, a merchant, even a private detective.

Arseny hid and healed Comrade Aristarkh—perhaps this time against his will. No one knows what the two men discussed—Arseny wrote laconic notations: "went to the barn," "went to the barn again," "was in the barn," where given Arseny's ignorance of farm life, he had no reason to go. The barn was the hiding place. Then Aristarkh vanished, to return more than once, for he was indebted to the doctor in Pushcha who saved his life and health, the doctor whose relatives included the factory owner Gustav Schmidt and Andreas Schwerdt.

In those same months, Arseny met his future wife.

What secrets can a night moth tell a butterfly? Kirill repeated the old poem as he thought about their meeting. The night moth circled under the barn eaves, among the smells of straw, caked blood, and medicine. The daytime butterfly fluttered above sunny roads, meadows where church belfries look down at the sea of growing wheat.

A boy from Pushcha was sent to neighboring Nikolskoe, to the bell tower to collect pigeon manure to fertilize Grandmother Clothilde's black roses, which had to be sprayed with special tinctures of iron filings for them to keep their color; the roses were the envy of the general whose dragoons had wounded the lightkeeper.

The black roses, Clothilde's late sentimentality—the boy slipped, overcome by the stink at the top, fell down the ladder, broke his arm, hurt his shoulder. Arseny came for the boy in a wagon—and met the priest's niece, visiting for the summer.

As Arseny wrote, Iron Gustav in his late years had a ready list of suitable brides for his grandson; the old man approached marriage with the ruthlessness of a horse breeder. Not having completely forgiven Arseny for the mediocrity of his chosen field, the meaninglessness of a career in service, Gustav decided to find Arseny a wife who could straighten out his eccentric character and return his grandson into the family bosom. Iron Gustav was cynical and stubborn, sending photographs of candidates with a description of their dowries—shares, estates, and so on—there were aristocrats and daughters of wealthy merchants among them. Arseny seemed to feel that marriage with any of these women would be too big, like a suit coat the wrong size; as if he could foresee the future, he looked not for social success but human reliability, loyalty, steadfastness—good qualities in a soldier.

He found them in the priest's niece, the fifth or sixth daughter of a clergyman who served a church in Vladimir but had been born in the far reaches near Murom, where the occasional pagan hermit could be found, worshipping stone circles laid out on sandy shoals in the swamps.

Arseny recognized Sophia's nature. Some things are so simple, yet amazing in the crude rationality of their form, created not to serve craftsmen who have hundreds of special sophisticated instruments for every project but poor men or soldiers: an army knife, a sapper's shovel. Objects for bivouacs, travel, escape, bad times.

Had Sophia lived in times of plenty, she might have never learned the truth of her character, for she would not have needed it all, and she might have taken up some charitable nonsense, revolutionary, religious, or social. But these causes would have been only manifestations of her strength, unrelated to an idea or faith, just her pure and natural talent for order, for keeping the world from spinning out of control. In an era of chaos and catastrophic change, people like that become islands, a raft for the shipwrecked, for those who are carried away in the whirlpool and seek to create a new meaning out of the fragments of their lives.

Iron Gustav furiously threatened to disinherit his grandson; he had negotiated the hand of the daughter of a second-rate lady-in-waiting to the empress for him. However, once again Andreas took his son's side and gave his blessing, and Gustav arrived in Pushcha, certain that he could still stop the wedding.

However, Sophia got to the old man. Just as he had seen a source of energy and propulsive power in Andreas, he saw a raw, reliable, steel support in her. Gustav must have viewed family as a monstrous mechanism in which people had merged with factories and formed a whole—and there was a place for Sophia's support in it.

"She will withstand a lot," said Iron Gustav. His decree— "She has no money but she is priceless"—spoken at an industrial reception, became a familial bon mot. There was one more thing: he never again insisted that Arseny retire and take up the family business.

Gustav stopped criticizing Arseny's life and began improving it secretly. Arseny guessed that Iron Gustav had organized his transfer to the Moscow Military Hospital, aided his easy separation from the Navy—in those days correspondence between the Admiralty and the Military Ministry took years—and assured that Arseny would work in a laboratory on the prevention of epidemics in the army, a topic Arseny had selected back in college.

Perhaps Arseny achieved all that himself, with the shadow of Iron Gustav behind him. The old man had made it into the circles of military industrialists, established a complete cycle of artillery production near Kiev—gunpowder, shell casings, gun barrels and carriages, scopes—and began campaigning on behalf of General Sukhomlinov, the governor general of Kiev, Volyn, and Podolsk. Sukhomlinov had his own party, he was expected to become a military minister. Gustav tried to establish his plants closer to the western border, since he also traded with Europe, and Sukhomlinov helped him a lot during the revolution of 1905, when factories and railroads were on strike.

It was enough to be Gustav Schmidt's grandson for doors to open for you. Arseny was not a classic protégé, spending much more time looking into his microscope at Koch's bacteria and spirochetes than into the eyes of his bosses—typhus and tuberculosis, tuberculosis and typhus were his main enemies, for he remembered how they had killed as many soldiers in the Russian camp hospitals in Manchuria as Japanese bullets did in the battlefields.

Naturally, Arseny perceived the Two Ts, as Kirill called the two diseases, within the context of the socialist idea: as the consequence of the oppressed state of workers, the scum of the old, rotted world, the symbol of the moral filth. Looking into the bronze oculars, what he saw on the slide were not bacteria but class enemies—as Arseny later wrote bitterly, when he himself was considered a class enemy, the carrier of filth, the poisoner of society's health.

***

Kirill liked coming here, to the quiet side street near the Garden Ring. The grim hulk of the Stalinist skyscraper housing the Ministry of Foreign Affairs loomed over it, but the lane itself breathed a different air, specifically Moscow air, gray like sparrows and pussy willows, myopic, better at transmitting the shuffle of an old man's shoes than the ring of coin. The house built in 1910 by a famous architect for Andreas and Iron Gustav, a two-story mansion in the Moscow Moderne style, still stood at the old address, even though the lane's name had changed three times.

The mansion now belonged to one of the shadow structures of the Ministry of Foreign Affairs. Kirill kept trying to guess what was there—intelligence? A semi-official business? He had not been allowed inside even with a letter of recommendation from the city cultural department. He looked at the tile roof, the wrought-iron bars on the balconies, the mosaic panels, and the old round windows like portholes; there was no connection between him and the house, he had grown up in an essentially different country and couldn't imagine himself living inside it.

The biggest panel, over the main entrance, depicted a fish: a burbot swimming among water weeds on a river or lake bottom. The weeds floated in long ribbons, stems with orange flowers resembling gerberas; the burbot was winding its way, pink mouth open, eyes raised as if in prayer to the God of fish, pastor of schools and shoals, Father of cod, Lord of sperm whales and sharks. Next to it and a bit lower, strode a lobster sheathed in armor, antennae raised militantly.

When Grandmother Karolina taught Kirill how to draw, she often depicted the underwater world, accompanying her drawing with a poem that Kirill thought was for children:

Leeches and crayfish crawl through the silt,
The water hides many terrors …
The pike—the crocodile's younger sister—
Stands dead by the shore.

Crayfish, burbots, pikes, sea grasses with unknown orange flowers appeared in her drawings. Kirill was delighted by land beauty transferred underwater, and he quickly picked up the game and added roses and dandelions. He never wondered why Grandmother was so devoted to this subject, why she never drew the mushroom forest at the dacha, or a city park, but only the strange underwater realm inaccessible to the living.

The first time he saw the mansion, Kirill understood why. The mosaic over the door remained a secret sign for his grandmother, marking the blocked entrance to the past.

The fish, an ancient Christian symbol, what did it mean? A tribute to Andreas the seaman eaten by savages? A dedication to Arseny, who suffered at Tsushima and watched his comrades drown? Or was it just a vague sign, foretelling the coming flood that would be survived only by Noah in a house with porthole windows? Whatever it was, his grandmother never took Kirill to the house but continued to draw the picture with him that he would easily recognize if he ever found himself in that lane.

After his first visit there, Kirill naturally remembered the poem. Driving home he wondered who wrote it. He guessed it was Kornei Chukovsky; the intonation was magical, specially created for a grandmother to read aloud while knitting or playing a game.

But it was Boris Kornilov. A poet arrested in 1937 for being a Trotskyite and shot dead in 1938. Kirill recalled the thin book of his poems on Grandmother's shelf. He picked it up: "Serafima," a bitter poem about love in which the childlike quatrain was embedded.

… Both he and she smelled of mint,
he says goodbye at the far window,
and his crumpled jacket of prewar thin fabric
is soaked by dew.

Kirill closed the book. Kornilov, a Leningrader accused of kulak leanings, was an acquaintance of Grandmother's sister Antonina, Tonya. The book's pages radiated unrequited love, a lonely emotion. Had Grandmother been in love with Kornilov? But her unknown love was called Arkady. Maybe Tonya, a resident of Leningrad, was in love with him. And Grandmother, by repeating the lines that corresponded with the river mosaic, was memorializing Tonya, who had no grave or marker.

Could they have foreseen it all, being inside the light-filled house—Kekushev the architect had designed enormous arched windows—on Christmas or Easter? Kirill knew it was a meaningless question, but still he kept returning to it. He went there, to that quiet lane, to imagine the few happy years that preceded World War I. Nothing came to mind except candles, white curtains, a set table, food, gowns and frockcoats, wrapped presents. Happiness does not remain in history, it does not form its substance, thought Kirill. It's not just the same, to follow Tolstoy's formulation, it means nothing on the big scale of fate, it can't be used to atone, justify, or save anyone, it is like counterfeit money. It draws a blank in memory.

Kirill had hoped to find the key to those days in the family album that his grandmother had saved. Of course, Kirill wasn't sure that she had saved all the cards; this must be a reduced, censored selection, while the compromising correspondence was burned in the twenties or thirties.

The postcards had adorable poodles mischievously looking at the camera; gentle kittens with bows; a sleeping chubby-cheeked girl hugging a toy soldier; pastoral children dancing around a lamb; another card showed a pair of kissing children, a pair of kissing lambs, bunnies cuddling, and two floating butterflies in a beautiful outdoor setting. Happy Name Day ... Happy Birthday ... Christ Is Risen ... Kisses ... Love ... Love ... Dear ...

And it was all so lovely, so touching, that it was impossible to believe that a few years later, a few months later these same people would pick up weapons and go off to annihilate people just like them, with the same puppies and kitties, buds and flowers—using the slash of a saber to cut down to the saddle and tear through all the layers of flesh.

Kirill wondered if his great-grandfather Arseny really was given to this sort of sentimentality. Had he been sincere when he sent all these family messages with curlyhaired girls and adorable angels? Kirill could not feel these emotions, they were as outdated and obsolete as crinolines and dyed mustaches and gramophones, so he could not imagine himself in Arseny's place. But Kirill sensed that his great-grandfather fulfilled the family and social rituals out of duty; his feelings sought other symbols, only nascent then.

* * *

*S*pring 1912. April. A brief entry in Arseny's diary. He had stopped keeping a diary and used it as a notebook for medical notations. Before Arseny had written either in Russian or German. His German was grammatically ideal; he made occasional mistakes in Russian, but they were the kind a person who is fluent in the language would make, sensing the contradictions between grammar and natural speech.

If he needed distance to regard something critically, he wrote in German; if it was with approval and acceptance, he wrote in Russian. When he used borrowed words, like *landshaft* or *mikstura*, he wrote them in German as *Landschaft* and *Mixtur*, creating the impression than he meant German landscapes and mixtures; in language he appeared as a dual, divided man who could change masks, becoming Russian or German, valuing that vagueness, the ability to roll from one identity into another.

Now both languages were replaced by illegible Latin (even his handwriting had changed). Arseny seemed to have moved away from reality, hiding in an ancient language, in medical scribbles that only a colleague could decipher.

Latin, the secret writing of Latin, in which Kirill recognized only the most common words, even though he had studied it at the university.

And then—an entry in German: Father visited. He asked about the symptoms and consequences of being poisoned by spoiled meat. And four—four!—exclamation points in the margins, underlined twice.

There weren't four exclamation points in total in all the rest of his diary pages. Arseny wrote not without feeling but without intonation; he wrote as he lived: smoothly, without splashes. When an earthquake destroyed Messina in 1908 and a Russian squadron anchored in the harbor saved thousands of Italians, Arseny, a naval doctor in the past, noted the event in his diary and added a single exclamation point.

And here there were four. And spoiled meat.

Kirill imagined spring 1912. The broken ice on the Moskva River, the drip-drops, sunshine; the smells bursting in after the winter freeze of tar, manure, smoke, warming soil; the freshness of space, the renewed emptiness, the space available for the clouds and storms of the coming summer. Where did the stink of spoiled meat fit in, which Kirill imagined clearly after reading the words?

He understood why he imagined the smell so easily, so powerfully.

Russian history of the start of the century, from the revolution of 1905 to the revolution of 1917, stank of spoiled meat, as if the rotting corpse of the empire exuded the rankness; social life decayed, turning into something disgusting, indigestible, inedible, and contemporaries could sense it in the air of the times.

Spoiled, maggot-infested meat was one of the key images of the two revolutions captured in Soviet culture: the image of tsarism that could no longer be tolerated, swallowed, it was the end of patience.

Kirill recalled Eisenstein's film *The Battleship Potemkin*. Part one, "Men and Maggots." In the first scene the old-regime boatswain rouses sleeping sailors, awakening them for revolutionary consciousness. In the third or fourth scene the sailors meet at the hanging beef carcasses intended for their pot. The carcasses stink, even the black-and-white film transmits the stifling, viscous odor of decay. The ship's doctor examines the meat with his pince-nez—the magnifying glass shows white maggots. But the doctor and officers do not see the maggots, do not smell the rot, because they belong to the old times, they themselves are rotten to the bone, crawling with maggots.

The crew refuses to eat and starts a rebellion. A red flag is raised over the battleship—Kirill remembered the film from his childhood.

A second image, a second plot—an echo of *Potemkin*—is the execution at the Lena mines. A rebellion at the gold mines in Siberia. On the command of the gendarme captain, soldiers opened fire on striking workers, killing several hundred people.

The event stunned the country, opening the doors for a second revolution. The investigation gave a start to the political career of the lawyer Kerensky, future chairman of the Provisional Government. The rebellion had started over rotten meat in the canteen cauldron. People worked in horrible conditions, lived in barracks on permafrost, laboring twelve hours a day, bearing what is impossible to bear—but they rebelled over maggoty meat.

Kirill could not recall when exactly the Lena executions took place. Before World War I for sure, before the war. He turned not to the Internet but the *Great Soviet Encyclopedia*, just to show off. And read: April 1912.

Kirill, with a foreboding of what he would find, looked for information on the owners. Lena Gold Fields, Lenzoloto, Russian capital, British capital, shares sold on the stock market, a struggle for control over the mines. There were two or three half-familiar names on the board of directors—Kirill had encountered them in descriptions of parties at the Schmidt-Schwerdt house. Nothing more, but now Kirill was certain that Iron Gustav had been among the Russian shareholders, acting through intermediaries.

So, Andreas and Gustav were trying to find out if food poisoning from rotten meat was so serious that people were prepared to take on the gendarmes. They didn't understand, they didn't feel the wave of outrage rising in the people, thought Kirill. Arseny did. The four exclamation points were not about the execution per se but the stupidity and blindness of his grandfather and father.

Gustav and Andreas were on the government side. On the side of the minister of the interior who announced from the Duma that the gendarmes' use of weapons was correct. "That's how it was, that's how it is, and that's how it will be!" If only they had known how it would be. Arseny had already betrayed his family, he was already red, while remaining a Russian German.

In the meantime, Iron Gustav had obtained large military commissions. Arseny and Sophia had babies, and the widower Gustav pictured the growing family's future. The old man had a second wind, although he was unlikely to care deeply for children; they were primarily heirs, expressions of family, little adults, three-year-old brides, five-year-old managers of shareholders.

The children appeared one after another, increasing the number of birthdays, name days, presents under the Christmas tree, rocking horses with manes of real horse hair, the changing faces of dolls, toy train sets, magic lamps, the saccharine postcards that Kirill would later find in the album. Gustav was seeking to tie the family together with threads of amity, laying the foundation of future amicable relations, but because he was Gustav, it was all heavy-handed and oppressive.

Perhaps if Arseny had not had six children, Gustav would have behaved differently in commercial enterprises and the family's future would have been different. But apparently he wanted to prove something to fate; his business sense did not fail him, but his sense of proportion did. He lost the ability to differentiate between family and family business, he planned to give each grandchild an enormous fortune—even though he was rich as it was; he openly took on the top men in the war ministry, creating dangerous enemies who started spreading rumors: a German is supplying the army, that's potential sabotage! Of course, such charges surprised no one, industrialists often created such intrigues, sending letters to the police, Senate, and Ministry of Justice that "revealed" their rivals' ties with Germany or Austro-Hungary. But in the summer of 1914 the risk of such charges grew exponentially in a flash: war broke out.

Kirill vowed not to try to imagine how the family members responded to the news of war. He had an answer: Arseny never again wrote in German in his journal. The old book, only half full, was put on a shelf. The new one, started in August, had only Russian and Latin; soon the Latin vanished—he must have subconsciously prepared himself for being searched someday, and an illiterate military investigator or policeman would suspect the incomprehensible Latin words to contain treason, spy secrets.

Arseny, who had dealt with counterintelligence after his brief imprisonment by the Japanese, saw further than Iron Gustav and Andreas, who realized that their position was shakier yet still felt protected by their status, money, and most importantly, connections, highly useful connections.

Iron Gustav swallowed his pride and applied to the Highest Name with a request for citizenship for himself, Andreas, and other family members who needed it. The request was granted, but not as easily as Gustav had expected.

The newly minted Russian citizen welcomed the war—but was he sincere? Iron Gustav was counting on the war strengthening his positions, for he would demonstrate the superiority of his shells and cannons and of course would enrich the family—so thought Arseny, who did not like his grandfather's enthusiasm and the patriotic meetings he organized at his factories and the large amount of money he contributed to the court's charities, a bow to royal patronage.

But Kirill thought otherwise. Looking at the past from the future, he felt that both Gustav and Andreas sensed the danger in being German. All of Schmidt's companies changed their signboards, choosing indefinite and neutral names like Sunrise or Dawn. It was ironic that those names survived the revolution and remained in the USSR, in harmony with the new mood. St. Petersburg was renamed Petrograd on August 18, and couldn't Iron Gustav take the obvious hint, Kirill asked himself, and immediately answered: no. Gustav and Andreas felt that they had already gone too far, been too aggressive in the marketplace, had stepped on too many toes, had stressed the Germanness of their machines, mechanisms, and weapons intending to signify their unsurpassed quality, and were now afraid that their competitors would take advantage of the situation.

Arseny, who was still working at the Moscow Imperial

Military Hospital, was not bothered in the first months of the war—the general opinion of all sides of the conflict was that the war would end by Christmas; the commanders thought the present staff could handle the flow of wounded.

Therefore Arseny spent the fall in Moscow. His father and grandfather had separated themselves from the rest of the family, taking on the cares and fears of wartime. Previously, the household had been held together by their participation, in the daily breakfasts, lunches, dinners, evening conversations by the fireplace, the numerous small ceremonies, and mostly by the very presence of elders who found time to be interested even in the affairs of the children, to teach them German—elders who did not seem like old men. Even though Gustav was in his eighties and Andreas approaching sixty, they both seemed impervious to old age: like pagan gods, they held the capitalist horn of plenty that spewed out machines that produced machines.

For the two titans, the war was a purely commercial issue for now. The others knew war only from the newspapers, from rumors, from the whispers behind their back: Germans. Only Arseny had encountered real war: in the hospital where they received individuals, then dozens, then hundreds of wounded men. Interestingly, Doctor Schwerdt was never rebuked for his German nationality. There were several other German doctors at the hospital and they were looked at askance, but in Arseny they saw first and foremost a physician. The other German doctors spoke Russian without an accent and had lived their entire lives in Russia; many had been at the hospital longer than Arseny and had received deserved glory—yet they were instinctively and instantly perceived as being alien while Arseny was one of our own. Why? After all, Arseny was much more likely to be a scapegoat out of envy alone, for everyone knew that his grandfather and father were German industrialists, wealthy men.

They probably felt something at the hospital that Arseny may not have felt: his definitive separation from the family and his switch to Russian citizenship not in terms of civil status but in the sense of readily desiring to share the fate of his new homeland; or they sensed that Arseny was far from the reality of life, he was a fool and a saint fixated on bacteria and infectious diseases, a man seriously fighting death—a very recognizable Russian type.

The wounded began appearing. It turned out that Arseny with his modest military experience had things to teach his academic colleagues. They—despite having worked in a military hospital—did not understand that wounded soldiers were not ordinary patients; the war was still living inside them, and they needed special care.

Gustav and Andreas were worried about maintaining and increasing the production of cannons. At the hospital, Arseny saw soldiers with their legs blown off, doomed cripples, an eternal burden to peasant families. And even though Gustav's factories manufactured Russian cannons and the soldiers had been wounded by German ones, a switch took place in Arseny's mind: he felt that weapons made by Schmidt and Schwerdt were the ones that had disfigured his patients.

Interestingly, Arseny did not talk about treating the wounded. He had gone underground, apparently realizing that he would not find a common language with his grandfather and father. They considered the death of soldiers inevitable, while he rebelled against that inevitability; also, Arseny discovered something new in the soldiers that he had not seen in the Japanese war and which he barely understood.

Arseny had expected that there would be many men who had lost their minds, as there had been in 1905, but it was different this time.

He's mad but he is healthy, wrote Arseny about a soldier who talked about the treason of the empress—a German. Mad because he reduced all catastrophes to the evil will of Alexandra Fedorovna, and insisted on it until he became delirious. And healthy, because the decay of the Russian state had a reached a point where it was easy to see evil intentions, a conspiracy—certainly the authorities would not allow such chaos and disarray without secret reasons.

The slag, the fallout of the mind that had once gone into the exhaust pipe of pure madness and self-destruction, Arseny thought, was now differently transformed: into deferred aggression directed outward. The soldiers in the trainload of madmen that Arseny led from Vladivostok in 1906 were essentially harmless in their crazy fantasies. Now, when delirium and darkness of the mind became the norm, madness had become dangerously realistic and bitter; the soldiers felt that traitors had dug in behind their backs, their own people turned alien. Of course, this had existed during the Japanese campaign, but in a weaker, diluted form—and now it had thickened, strengthened, and was contagious like an infection. The soldier who went on about the empress replied to the nurse who told him not to blacken the monarch's name: "I have no goodness in me for any living thing." And Arseny wrote that in those words he heard a note of madness and at the same time a frank admission of a sober and wise man.

Arseny may have befriended that soldier, his name was Petr Nezabudkin (from the word *forget-me-not*), a good, Dosto-evskian name for one obsessed. They had wanted to turn him in, but Arseny protected him, explaining that a soldier after being wounded is not himself and repeats stupid rumors, but when he is healed he will be ashamed. The hospital gendarme believed Arseny: he knew that Schwerdt had treated crazy people back in the Japanese war.

Nezabudkin thanked him in his own way: he introduced him to several soldiers who formed a "circle." One of the guards at the hospital, from Moscow, was a Bolshevik agitator and brought leaflets for the trusted patients to read, knowing that the soldiers would be sent back to the troops after they had convalesced.

They hunted the hospital Bolshevik. The gendarmes set ambushes at fence holes and searched carts carrying firewood. The agitator was eventually arrested with a pile of leaflets; Nezabudkin may have felt out the doctor, an officer: would he agree to be the new courier? Kirill did not know whether Arseny agreed or not. One thing was clear: the wounded soldiers considered Arseny a defender, and that reputation was passed along the "soldiers' telegraph" to the front, when in December Arseny was called to head the evacuation hospital.

Naturally, Gustav and Andreas expected Sophia and the children to stay with them in the Moscow house, with nannies and a governess. But Arseny decided otherwise. He sent the children to stay with distant relatives in various cities, and took his wife and his eldest daughter, Karolina, with him. Why did he do that? If he cared about the children, it would have been better to leave them in a home that had every luxury, with a loving grandfather and great-grandfather; it was a ticklish moment, fraught with old men's injuries and jealousy.

The only thing Kirill understood was that Arseny wanted his sons and daughters to grow up primarily as his children and not as the grandchildren of Andreas and the great-grandchildren of Gustav; he was afraid to entrust their fate to the willful old men, sensed that they could spoil the children with unbridled adoration, indulgence of their whims, and expensive gifts.

Or perhaps Arseny foresaw the future and guessed that the

mansion once full of light and voices would be plunged into grim silence that the children could not dispel, and they would have to live in it, anxious and echoing; the once hospitable house would become a lonely citadel where Gustav and Andreas, like gods of a lost time, would have long conversations about the new times, their shameful impotence, and how to save themselves and everything they had built up over a long prosperous era.

***

Kirill imagined that conversation easily. It probably took place in the study on the second floor, where the wide window faced south. Kirill saw the heavy old bog-oak furniture, with carvings—perhaps Gustav had brought it from Germany—furniture that remained in a state of bewilderment: if the owner wanted to open a door or pull out a drawer, the hinges would creak or the key would stick. No, furniture did not have reason or will, but the entire life of the house, formerly fed by the energy of Iron Gustav, now seemed out of sorts, frozen in frightened anticipation.

A late evening that lasted for years. The drapes tightly drawn. The house quiet, residents and servants sleeping. As though a carriage or automobile would pull up at any moment and the doorbell would ring.

August. August 1914. It must still have been hot in town, dogs barked in increasing clusters along fences in the suburbs, and boys angled in the river for fish rising to catch dragonflies and butterflies exhausted by the lean summer air. On the main thoroughfares the tramways were late more often, bearing nocturnal passengers into the dark, into the unlit outskirts. From there, from the outskirts, came the wind, carrying voices caught in the forests and fields, overheard by village windows:

the keening wail, the blank verse of recitative farewell—women seeing off sons, husbands, and brothers with ancient words, nameless, powerful in chorus, and in impersonal grief; the women sobbing in unity, like an enormous belly expelling the sound; they bore children in pain and would see them off to death in pain, giving away the flesh of their flesh to the evil of killing, to die in foreign lands.

Shadows, contorted by whispering crosswinds, dance on the walls, bitter voices pound the windows, but Andreas and Gustav do not hear. Night, black as oil, drips from their black coats. The dull light of lamps shines on the blades of ancient daggers, sabers, and swords hanging on the wall like a multibeamed star. The two masters of steel regret for the first time that they had hung the blades here, the cold night sun of weapons rises over their heads, the blades are raised over their necks.

Kirill sees Gustav and Andreas in their house, but he cannot hear what they are saying—an invisible, incorporeal wind tears the words from their lips and crumples them, carries them through the walls. But Kirill knows what they are talking about. The announcement from the Ministry of Internal Affairs. All German citizens ages eighteen to forty-five are considered military prisoners and will be sent into exile—at their own expense. Yes, Gustav and Andreas are older. They are now citizens of the Russian Empire. The blade flashed close to their heads, they felt the swish. Danger. What next?

Messengers gallop along the nocturnal fields, illuminated by indolent bolts of lightning, heading for the army of people, horses, and forage. The first scouting missions are now on foreign soil. Somewhere in the night of East Prussia, Gustav's cannons are moving, his artillery carts are rolling, his pumps and boilers are working, his armor is protecting sailors on military ships, dreadnaughts and cruisers; military trains rush from every corner of the country along his rails. But all this is separate from Gustav, it cannot be credited to him, for now he is a pariah, a leper, and the barefoot newspaper boy shouts his name with cheerful hatred.

Gustav and Andreas know that various clubs and societies are expelling Germans. The newspapers are full of stories about coming deportations and arrests, about turning confiscated property over to military hospitals. The public mood is bravura for now, reports coming in about the victory near Gumbinnen and German troops retreating deep into Eastern Prussia, and it might seem that the patriotic fervor will soon dim, by Christmas the troops will return to the winter quarters, and peace will be signed.

However, while Gustav retained some illusions, still hoped that his good name would be protected from attacks and the quality of his products would lead to an uptick in orders, Andreas, who had a limited understanding of military things and avoided politics, had an engineer's sense of harmony, and felt that the old construction of the world was reaching the end of its tensile strength; war was only a valve through which the demons of the future would burst into the world, and that valve could no longer be shut.

The monsters of the coming world appeared to Andreas as new technology that the war would create: gigantic cannons, armored trains, floating fortresses with hundreds of weapons, monster zeppelins carrying firebombs. A few of Andreas's sketches survived, hidden behind the postcards in the album. Kirill was stunned by the four horsemen in bolted armor and gas masks riding mechanical horses, but Kirill did not feel the artist's confusion, as you do in Dürer's *Four Horsemen*; he then realized that Andreas was not afraid of the future, guessing that as a man of the old era he would not live in the new one, and all his concern was for his descendants.

The balance of rights and will between Gustav and Andreas invisibly shifted in the latter's favor; Gustav was still head of the company, but Andreas spoke more in their evening conversations, while Gustav listened.

September 1913. The Russians lost the battle at Tannenberg, which destroyed General Rennekampf's First Army, whose punitive forces Arseny had seen during the first revolution, when he delivered the soldiers who had lost their minds from the Far East to Ryazan. Now once again, trains carried a horrible harvest of wounded men instead of grain, and people talked about German generals at the head of the Russian army: was there treachery?

Once again the two stood; at sunset the sun turned red, like a bandage on a wound, and now night was black like the inside of a rifle barrel. Their factories were still working, melting steel, laying tracks; the lathes still turned, the freight was shipped, the bookkeepers counted money—but the former confidence and drive was gone, evening moved through inertia, which was slowing down. Some contractors had declined work, state officials were no longer as pleasant, rivals stole their contracts, and their shares were falling; innumerable herds of lathes, machines, and mechanical leviathans were sweating the oily fear of metal.

Gustav and Andreas knew they should flee—but they were unable to abandon their profits. And where would they run? In Germany and Austro-Hungary, they were Russians; in the Triple Entente countries, they were Germans. Should they go to neutral Sweden or America? They carefully felt out the possibility of selling their enterprises. But they were offered ridiculous, insulting prices; they decide to hold.

December. Soon there would be Christmas balls and masquerades. Two-thirds fewer invitations than last year. The family was upset, but Gustav and Andreas were happy. Their life in the last month was like a vicious masquerade: almost no one openly revealed hostility, some were sympathetic, some were compassionate, still others offered help, vaguely hinting at interceding with the emperor, still others wanted to join the business, but it was all a game of masks and they could believe no one.

And suddenly, the masks came off: The Society of 1914 was established in Petrograd; patriotic bankers and industrialists united to lobby for the interests of national capital. Gustav and Andreas were not invited. However, they think it will be easier now: there was a tangible foe, acting with understandable methods, and they will be able to handle him.

The cold sun of ancient blades shines off the wall; the blades have awakened, the ring of sabers can be heard from distant fields; Kirill imagines that a century later he can hear the silence of the damask steel, feel the grim weight of dozens of blades, swords of Damocles, hanging over the heads of the old men.

It was an evil hour when Gustav came up with the idea to collect swords, to create a metal sun on his study wall, an otherworldly sun, shedding spectral light on the night that befell the family in August 1914.

Gustav, thought Kirill, was collecting an herbarium of coats of arms—having none of his own—the stingy slow- and long-lived souls of weapons: as vestiges of ancient catastrophes, witness of familial collapses; as proof that the true strength of an ancestral line lies not in a martial spirit, not in bravery but in the intelligence and knowhow of the bourgeois entrepreneur who values contemporary life.

And now, thought Kirill, the blades were mocking Gustav because his weapons—bank accounts, shares, capital—could not protect him, and he had no others.

Rumors, whose reliability Kirill could not establish, said that Gustav had bought a special sword from Schliemann himself after his excavations in Troy; perhaps there were secret connections between the two Germans who had come to Russia in the middle of the nineteenth century and made their fortunes, but Kirill could not part that curtain.

The image of the Trojan sword did not leave Kirill.

He often thought of the First World War as the Trojan War of the new times. In the *Iliad*, everyone was called upon to fight; the war divided the universe into two battling sides, from the heights of Olympus to the depths of Poseidon's ocean and the gloomy underground of Hades. No one remained neutral, neither men nor gods. War engulfed the entire world, and then spat it out changed, so changed that it took Ulysses twenty years to find his way home: the former topography, the old roads were lost.

In Homer's world, only men bearing arms had the power to act, to change fate. The Trojan sword reminded Gustav that today only warriors and not merchants could save the world; no one else could avert the threat.

The threat was great. Leafing through the government anti-German documents, Kirill saw the birth of totalitarianism in Russia—before the Bolsheviks came to power. He saw how a repressive state arose, how the public was willing to praise terror, keep looking for "aliens," turncoats, agents of evil who were the cause of the all the country's ills: there wasn't enough bread and the kerosene lamps blew up.

If not for the history of spymania in the last years of the empire, it was not clear why people in the Stalin era slid so easily into the madness of mutual denunciations, approving mass arrests and demanding bigger and more frequent executions of "enemies of the people."

But the citizens had already been exposed to state propaganda that blamed defeat in the war and lack of weapons on German agents who had penetrated headquarters, given away secrets to the enemy, and sabotaged production. The power of that exposure was so great that ten years later, when the first show trial began, the "Shakhty case," prosecution of "saboteurs" in the coal industry, people readily "remembered" the picture of a world filled with traitors, and they believed it again.

Andreas and Gustav finally found a warrior, a man of war, who could protect the family. Kirill loved this plotline more than all the others in his future book. His great-grandfather Arseny didn't know it, Grandmother Karolina didn't, his father didn't. Gustav and Andreas kept it from the younger generation—but Kirill figured it out, calculated from the details, from the brief journal notations.

The end of January 1915. Once again the house, the night, and the black wind brings the smell of burning and gunpowder; the house does not smell of oven smoke but the stench of the trenches. Gustav and Andreas are reading the draft documents they bought at great expense that the emperor would be signing in the next few days, and each paragraph squeezes and compresses Gustav and Andreas, reducing them to the size of the bronze soldiers on the desk guarding the inkwell.

But Kirill is reading the documents published in a book and feels what the two old men had felt at home: the horror of doom.

The first document: "On landowner and land use in the Russian State by Austrian, Hungarian, German, and Turkish citizens." They had escaped that bullet; Gustav was a Russian citizen by then.

The two read as if watching beaters rounding up the prey in a hunt on a distant hill.

"Acquiring property by any means is forbidden ... This rule does not extend to renting apartments. ... The ban extends to societies if enemy citizens are shareholders ... In joint-stock companies that have the right to acquire real estate, people with

German citizenship are not allowed to be chairmen or members of the board ... assignees ... agents ... technicians ... clerks ... or any workers. Real estate in the provinces can be confiscated ... Special lists of names ... Complaints within a month."

Even the orders of 1937 introducing execution quotas in the regions—how many people must be killed in a certain period— did not shock Kirill as much as this paper. He saw the succession of evil, for which tsarism or communism were mere stand-ins.

Of course, Kirill did not consider this a specifically Russian phenomenon. He recalled the memoirs of the chief of German intelligence Walter Nicolai, who described the fear of espionage in the early months of the war: rumors about cars filled with gold to bribe German generals, of telephone cables leading to France for espionage purposes. The Russians persecuted Germans for half a century. Germans under the Nazis destroyed Jews. Americans put Japanese in concentration camps during World War II—everyone had his Other. Kirill was interested in how the same archetypical evil reacts to the local soil, what monstrous variations develop through the peculiarities of national fears, what forces bring defeat or victory, national catastrophes or triumphs.

Kirill observed through the fates of Gustav and Andreas how the fear of Germany grew, embodied by events, both real ones— defeat in war—and those invented by propaganda—German colonists burning wheat and knocking down telegraph poles—a fear that would remain deep in the subconscious of the residents of the USSR. Kirill thought that the victory in 1945 gave rise to such profound feelings because they had conquered fear, which was much older than the war itself, but they had conquered only one concrete fear, which did not make them fearless and left them Stalin's slaves.

A second document: the decision of the Council of Ministers

to limit land ownership and use by Russian Germans. His Imperial Majesty personally wrote: BE IT THUS.

Be it thus …

Two at the desk, Gustav and Andreas. The inky night spills over the floor, rapidly rising, like floodwaters, the two are drowning in it, while on the surface the tubby inkwell bobs like an ancient ship. Somewhere outside, far away, at a printing press the typesetter is composing lead letters into a text that will be spat out by the printers: "It is no longer permitted to conclude any act of acquisition of the right to property, the right to own and use real estate … The ban extends to individuals of Austrian, Hungarian, and German descent … Paragraph d) who became Russian citizens after 1 January 1880, as well as societies whose membership includes any of the above-listed individuals."

The bullet hit its mark. Andreas had become a Russian citizen in 1882, Gustav, his father-in-law had insisted on it, but it was too late, too late! He should have done it two years earlier! Gustav had only recently become a citizen.

It was a terrifying game of cat-and-mouse, of Battleship: A-2, miss; G-6, wounded; D-7, killed. The printing presses rolled again, spitting out new pages; in the Baltic Sea, Russian destroyers see the smoke of German squadrons on the horizon.

"In the western and southern border regions … seize all real estate by voluntary agreements … Including the entire territory of the Crimean Peninsula … Along the entire state border."

Gustav had moved his manufacturing closer to Europe so that he could sell to two markets more conveniently—and now his lands were subject to being taken within a year.

And suddenly, lines that saved some people.

"3. These rules do not apply 1) to people who can certify one of the conditions below: 1) being Russian Orthodox from birth or being converted before 1 January 1914."

Oh those parentheses, the usual punctuation points regulating the flow of speech—suddenly becoming guards, supervisors, deciding who will die, who will live. Oh grammar itself, with its rules, its rational construction seeming to reflect impartially the construction of life—suddenly becoming the conductor of evil will, will that uses what is already there in language: negation, the imperative mood, the bureaucratic sticky routine, neutral verbs like "extend" and "certify" now no longer neutral but threatening and demanding.

Kirill had a feel for language, he liked written speech, he liked the strictness of legal definitions. But here, for the first time, he sensed how language separates itself from a person, becoming the voice of an institution, the letters donning police uniforms, growing in false significance, becoming dangerously bigger than people.

Conversion to Orthodoxy was the loophole for the weak. Far-sighted Gustav had insisted on it back in 1882, but Andreas refused—another saving thread snapped off. What did they say to each other, the two old men in a shaky house that had seemed so solid? Did they have regrets?

The machines keep printing:

"c) One's participation or the participation of a descendant or ancestor on the male line in military action of the Russian army or Russian navy against an enemy in the rank of officer or as a volunteer, or belonging (self or one of the listed persons) to the number of people who were awarded for military excellence during action of the army or navy, or the death of a descendant or ancestor in the field of battle."

A warrior. That's why Gustav and Andreas needed a warrior. One who paid with wounds or death for the right to be considered a loyal citizen, one who alone saves dozens of people: cousins, sisters, aunts, grandparents.

This was something like the recent wedding of the Swedish princess, thought Kirill. The commoner fiancé was brought into the narthex of the cathedral, the doors were closed, and a miracle occurred, for when he came out to join his bride, his blood was deemed royal. Just like a German who fought under the Russian banner and shed blood for Russia magically became a Russian.

Probably they first thought of Arseny. He had not received any awards, but he was an officer in the Battle of Tsushima, then served in the active navy, was in combat. Without telling him, not wanting Arseny to feel that he was expiating imaginary sins, they sent documents to the government regarding paragraph 1.c.3 of the decision of the Council of Ministers requesting the immediate exemption from the confiscation lists. It is likely Gustav asked his patron Sukhomlinov to intercede and assumed things would be settled quickly.

The reply did come quickly. However, it was not what Gustav and Andreas were expecting. It was an expansive document of a dozen pages that said few things if one wrung out the legalese.

The person of Arseny Schwerdt, medical officer, raised questions among the high commission. Arseny was perfectly fine for heading an ordinary frontline hospital and his superiors were satisfied with his service. However, as a living indulgence, a forgiveness of the sins of origin for Gustav and Andreas, Arseny was examined with special attention in other spheres as well. And in those spheres, there was the opinion that Arseny Schwerdt could not be counted as an example of atonement because "in not fully clear circumstances" he spent the night in Japanese prison and subsequently had a reprimand from the regimental commander, "which served as the reason for removing him from the list for a military award."

Another heavy stone on the scales was the fact that the colonel who had suspected Arseny of treason nine years earlier had grown significantly in rank and was now a general of the Imperial Retinue. Even worse, he was in the enemy camp against Sukhomlinov, the connection between Gustav and the minister of war was no secret from him, and when asked once again about the circumstances of the affair long ago, the newly appointed general vengefully repeated his suspicions, adding new ones: Arseny Schwerdt was definitely a traitor and escaped punishment only thanks to the minister's patronage.

Of course, there was a second opinion: Arseny Schwerdt was an educated officer, the charges were nonsense and intrigues, and therefore the request should be granted immediately. But that was the second opinion and bureaucratically less weighty, so the petitioners were informed that their case would be examined by an ad hoc commission when the Council of Ministers promulgated the legal interpretations for the liquidation legislation.

The reply did not offer much hope. Actively pursuing their position and demanding justice meant drawing more attention to Arseny, and that attention could destroy him, ruin his career, poison his life. Gustav and Andreas knew that they wanted to take away their company, and if Arseny became an obstacle, they would simply trample him in the mud.

The night outside the walls was as black as the ocean abyss. The mansion with palms growing in the rooftop hothouse was like a tropical island sticking out of the water. Candle flames flickered on the lower floors like glowing bottom fish darting in the deep. A tugboat tooted out on the Moskva River and it seemed like an ocean liner releasing steam from overheated boilers, the ship lost under foreign skies where savages as alien as people living on stars celebrate their rituals.

Who suggested this, Andreas or Gustav? Gustav, thought Kirill. Andreas would not have wanted to upset the memory of the long-ago Andreas. But Gustav won, and the Marinated

Midshipman was taken out of the barrel of oblivion, dressed in his torn uniform, a naval officer's sword placed in his hand, and the headless cadaver was sent out to war.

A new letter went to the commission: an ancestor, Midshipman Andreas Schwerdt, died during military action between the Russian Navy and indigenous foes, he died on the battlefield, weapon in hand, and the savages violated his body. Therefore, in accordance with paragraph 1.c.3, the Schwerdt family has the right to retain their property.

Clever Gustav! He must have known that the commission would be in a bind when it came to a cannibalized midshipman, a ghost from many years ago; they would have to get the archives, gather a council on whether a random fight with savages was to be considered "military action," whether aborigines with stone axes, spears, and a dozen stolen rifles could be considered "foes," and the sand on the beach where the sloop from *Grozyashchy* landed on a battlefield. But that was what he wanted: to drag things out, complicate them, and in the meantime Minister Sukhomlinov would step in (Gustav was preparing an additional gift for him), and the family would be saved.

Even the high-ranking general who persecuted Arseny could not accuse the Marinated Midshipman of anything; the grim and terrible ghost of the eaten seaman could affect the most hardened conscience; how can you eat, how can you drink post-prandial Madeira picturing death on a spit? Like a shadow rising from the grave for the sake of posthumous justice, the headless midshipman wandered the ministry offices and no one dared to refuse the mournful petitioner, permeated with the quartermaster's strong brine; the case seemed to be going in the Schwerdts' favor.

Gustav, Gustav! He did not know that the foe had been released, hunting his ghost.

In December 1914 the Russian counterintelligence arrested Lieutenant Kolakovsky. Kolakovsky had been imprisoned by the Germans, and now was back on Russian territory. He was suspected of treason. To save himself, Kolakovsky, a liar and a Cagliostro, invented an alibi: as a prisoner he agreed to become a German spy, but only in order to learn German secrets and pass them along to Russia. The Germans, Kolakovsky maintained, believed him and revealed their espionage organization to him.

On Kolokovsky's denunciation, Colonel Myasoedov, Sukhomlinov's protégé and confidant, was arrested. The net would be cast widely: Myasoedov's family, his mistress, and his business partners would be arrested; the counterintelligence agents would come for the owner of the station café where Myasoedov ate, for the wine merchant who supplied his liquor, for the music teacher who lived in the same rental apartment as his mistress, for the owner of the typewriter on which he once typed something, for lawyers, well-diggers, hunting friends—for everyone who had a connection to Myasoedov.

Minister Sukhomlinov, under attack, would have no time for Gustav. Sukhomlinov would see that he was the real target, that they were trying to topple him using Myasoedov, and he would cut off all his former contacts.

Gustav, who had dealt with Myasoedov when he had been Sukhomlinov's confidential agent in Kharkov, hoped that no one would ever recall that connection. The only one who could protect the family from collapse would be the Marinated Midshipman, the ghost wandering the ministry corridors.

***

*K*irill understood that the Schwerdt family stood at the edge of a precipice as a result of the Myasoedov case. They were saved by the fact that the higher authorities demanded a swift sentencing, and counterintelligence did not have time to arrest everyone the colonel had known.

Kirill was amazed by the fascinating horror of Myasoedov's fate, the plot of his life and death; the colonel seemed to have been shown to Gustav, Andreas, and Arseny so they would understand something important about their future.

Myasoedov. Gendarme, served with the border guards along the border with East Prussia. Knew German well. Was personally presented to Emperor Wilhelm, hunted at his estate.

Myasoedov. Bon viveur, Don Juan, a man of dubious morals.

Myasoedov, who tried to organize a shipping line to bring immigrants to America by using his service connections. Corrupt.

Myasoedov, whose rivals—probably owners of another shipping company—used "their" police to falsely accuse him of aiding smugglers and revolutionaries.

Myasoedov, who as a consequence of these charges left the gendarme corps under a cloud, giving information during his trial that exposed the dirty methods of police work—thereby setting the police department against him forever.

Myasoedov, in retirement, befriended Sukhomlinov, who was then commander of the troops of the Kiev Military Okrug and the governor general, and became his fixer for dubious business dealings.

Myasoedov, who tried to return to the service many times and was always rejected—because Prime Minister Stolypin remembered his testimony against the police.

Myasoedov, restored after Stolypin's death by Sukhomlinov, by then Minister of War, as "officer for special assignments" at the ministry.

Myasoedov, who in 1912 was accused without evidence of

espionage by the leader of the Octobrists, an adventurer and duelist, former Duma chairman Guchkov, who needed to involve Sukhomlinov in a scandal, the better to remove him from his ministerial post.

Myasoedov, loyal to his protector and fired on the basis of Guchkov's charge.

Myasoedov, who tried at length to be taken into the army when the war broke. He was made a translator in intelligence. He served in the headquarters of the ill-starred 10th Army, which suffered a crushing defeat by the Germans.

Myasoedov, who was accused of treason by Lieutenant Kolakovsky when he made up his stories about the German conspiracy because he remembered the name from the newspaper articles about the "spy case" inspired by Guchkov.

Myasoedov.

Doomed to be the scapegoat.

Kirill used him as a model for an algorithm: how people become victims in history, which he called the "Myasoedov archetype."

Kirill wrote out the algorithm in a café at Stockholm's Arlanda Airport, watching border and customs officials in the café after their shifts, watching the crowd, sorting, classifying, attaching an invisible label to each.

You have to be a public figure, people must remember you when talk of your espionage comes up: oh, there were suspicions before, he was on a slippery slope! This lends a sense of recidivism to the event, serving like proof of guilt for the public and inspiring fury: You mean they knew about him long ago? Who was covering up for him? Treason! It's not an individual case, it's a system!

You must indulge in certain immoral behaviors that are shared by many, who delight in seeing them in others. Bribes, debauchery, weakness of character, falsehood, illegitimate children, debts, excesses: anything that demonstrates your ruin. This is not incontrovertible evidence of guilt, but it makes it psychologically believable.

You have to have an entourage of dubious repute. It may have formed reasonably, by virtue of fate, profession, interests, but the public will see that you are not worthy of trust on the principle of Tell me who your friends are and I'll tell you who you are.

You must have a powerful patron (Sukhomlinov) who can be compromised by compromising you. The end of this intrigue must (for the intriguers) justify the means, their scope, cost, vileness, and immorality.

You must have formidable enemies, acquired long ago, who by their action or inaction will support the attack on you (in Myasoedov's case it was the police department, which he had discredited by revealing certain facts).

You must have a personal torturer, an eagle for Prometheus (Guchkov), who sees an opportunity for fame and media capital in your case, an opportunity to promote his views on a number of social and political issues.

You must have a pile of circumstantial evidence against you, which essentially proves nothing and can be explained but which fires up the public's hunting instinct: catch him already, why is he still out there running and lying, catch him and kill him!

You must NOT have the opportunity to defend yourself properly: Myasoedov was court-martialed, the judges had orders to send him to the gallows.

You must have exhausted the limit of success and become the object of infernal irony. Everything must turn against you: people, things, circumstances. It's the reverse of your villainy: the fact that previously evil served you will now expose you.

The accusation must not be the start of your misadventures. You must already be mired in serious problems: personal, financial, social; be profoundly bewildered, disillusioned, exhausted; you must give up a few "life preservers" that might have helped later.

You must not be a fighter by nature. Not a wimp, but not a fighter. And you must not be attractive. You may be talented and gifted (colleagues spoke well of Myasoedov as an intelligence office), but you must not be interesting, charming, or sympathetic.

Your case must have some concrete evidence, real or invented. Myasoedov serves in the headquarters of the 10th Army, and it has been crushed! And they found documents in his possession describing the location of troops (even though he was supposed to have them as an officer in intelligence).

Society, which has felt a decline in patriotic hurrahs and which is disillusioned by failure, terrible defeats that seem inexplicable, should have embarked on an irrational search for spies and traitors.

If you add them all up, a fatal result is inevitable.

Kirill wrote down his conclusion on the reverse of his printed e-ticket. It was the standard, the lens, through which he regarded the biography of the Schwerdts, recognizing in it fragments of the deadly Myasoedov pattern of fate, the dull links of fate entwined in the chain of ordinary events. He did not turn that lens on himself, in part because he was certain that his fate was insignificant and in that sense insured against great misfortune and in part because in the depth of his heart he was afraid to see and recognize in his life the same dull and terrible links.

***

A German conspiracy.

Espionage.

All the newspapers wrote about it, soldiers whispered about it. Almost all the future Soviet generals and marshals served in World War I as soldiers, noncommissioned officers, captains, thought Kirill. That means they "knew" that Germans colonists were injuring horses, sending signals to the enemy. Teaching German was banned in the country, the newspapers attacked Germans, everyone witnessed the deportation of German citizens to Siberia, the robbery and confiscation of their property; the shadow of their future engulfed the Schwerdts, but Gustav and Andreas thought it was the shadow of the near future only, and that further down, there would be light.

Night, another night. It breathes like a dying horse, blood-flecked foam on its lips, blood flowing down the gutters; evil lights illuminate its fading eyes, the lights of fires reflected in broken store windows. Signs are torn down from apothecary shops and ateliers, bakeries and studios, the pharmacy bottles broken, pastries squashed, fabric thrown into the mud, and there are no police whistles, no police badges to be seen or heard—the Russian din rolls over in waves, dark and thick, drowning cries in German, cries of horror and pain. Janitors will come out in the morning to sweep away the glass, wash away the blood, but it is still night, smelling of rubbing alcohol and pharmacy lotions, carousing over Moscow, and the May lilacs are intoxicated by blood.

Two in the study on the second floor. The mansion's walls are sturdy, the armaments room has loaded rifles, but what are rifles against an elemental pogrom? Against the government?

Night follows night; Moscow cleaned itself up, glaziers replaced windows, the dead were buried at the German Cemetery. But now others storm houses and offices, men in the uniform of military counterintelligence, with search warrants. They're after traveling salesmen selling German agricultural equipment—for they allegedly spy on the harvest; they came to Singer to stop sales of sewing machines and the company was declared a threat to national security; June, lightning, and a telegram—Sukhomlinov's departure, the minister unofficially charged with aiding Germany.

But Gustav's factories are still working, still manufacturing tracks on which army trains travel; the commission is still studying their appeal and ancient admirals are still discussing the case of the Marinated Midshipman; the house is still standing, and the bolts are still strong.

A year of war. August 1915. New agencies are established—Special Councils. The most important of these: the Special Council for the Discussion and Unification of Measures on State Defense. The word "special" receives the meaning it will retain under the Bolsheviks: a symbol of the state's power over a citizen's property and life.

The chairman of the Special Council can sequester an enterprise; set general and individual requisitions; fire directors, managers, boards; pass resolutions on changing the character and volume of production; determine salaries.

The Schwerdt case got hung up, the government commission is unable to determine whether the death of the Marinated Midshipman can be an exemption for his descendants; the commission does not want to take a risk and awaits subsequent acts under the law, instructions; and thus a year passes.

Gustav is no longer Iron, but Decrepit Gustav, a ruin in which the outlines of his former strength can only be guessed. Andreas is no longer energetic and he is visited more frequently by thoughts of the other Andreas who was eaten by savages, of the mystical meaning of sharing a name.

His engineer's mind resisted false constructions, but the tendency toward mysticism of his father, Balthasar, appeared in his mature years and whispered something different. Andreas must have been confused, agitated by the Rasputin affair, the heir's hemophilic bleeding healed by the shaggy-haired Siberian elder: a reincarnation of Uryatinsky's estate, where Balthasar, the doctor, was incarcerated. Andreas secretly began looking for his sacrificial field, the opportunity to respond to the sacrifice of Andreas the sailor who had protected the family for several years now.

Gustav died in the night, in December. That day he had learned that the lands taken away from citizens of German origin would be bought by the Rural Land Bank, and the bank would set its own price. Gustav understood what was going to happen and what the newspapers would be writing about: the land purchases would be handled by influential people, landowners, ministers, and they would buy up the best for a song, using their connections in the bank; no one had yet touched land belong to the Schwerdts, they were still protected by the headless ghost, but Gustav got tired of waiting to be rescued and seemed to put out the flame of his own life.

Andreas became master of all the property. And he was immediately made an offer—the buyers didn't even wait for the traditional forty-day mourning period to pass—for the most valuable factories. Not directly, of course; Kirill guessed the intermediary might have been Prince Andronikov, an agent of the secret police who later became head of the Kronstadt Cheka and extorted money from his former society friends for permission to leave Soviet Russia—but at the time he was an intriguer, publisher of a patriotic newspaper, and inside the Rasputin circle.

Andreas was faced with an ultimatum. He did not have

the weight that Gustav did, and the connections he inherited
after Gustav's death saw a convenient moment to end those
ties. Many sent only flowers or telegrams to the old magnate's
funeral, without appearing in person, and some did not send
flowers or telegrams.

Kirill could imagine what was hinted at, what the veiled
threats were. The commission of General Batyushin was created
within the apparatus of military counterintelligence, and it was
subordinate to the chief of staff of the Supreme Commander.
"In fact, Batyushin was the dictator of Russia at that time,"
Kirill read in postrevolutionary memoirs. Batyushin's people,
according to the laws of wartime, had the right to search and
arrest anyone at all, and so they were raiders and blackmailers
threatening to charge people with state treason, a capital crime.
Working in parallel was the Special Committee Against German
Dominance, which studied the bylaws of companies to discover
suspicious investments.

Special Councils, Special Commissions, illegal punishment,
government violence—the Bolsheviks didn't invent anything,
thought Kirill. They created the Cheka along the fresh tracks
of their predecessors. A long war, defeat, and the threat of a
popular revolt had made the tsarist government ready to implement extreme measures as the norm, to implement paranoid
witch hunts, which the Soviet government adopted and which
returned again with the Chekist regime in Kirill's day.

Batyushin later joined the Whites, emigrated, died in
Belgium, and in 2004 was reburied in Moscow with the participation of the FSB. What a posthumous career, what a
legacy, thought Kirill. His closest colleague, Lieutenant General
Bonch-Bruevich, was the first tsarist general to work for the Reds,
for Stalin and Dzerzhinsky, heading the military bureau of the
Party; Bonch-Bruevich was the link between the generals of the

General Staff and the future creators of the October Revolution.

The VChK, the All-Russian Extraordinary Commission, commonly known as Cheka, founded right after the Bolsheviks seized power, was the direct descendant of the commission of Batyushin and Bonch. It was reborn many times, changing its name, growing new fangs to replace the ones grown dull: OGPU, NKVD, MGB, KGB, FSB … but the seeds of evil were sown in tsarist times. Andreas—Kirill caught his breath—Andreas was one of many who helped the evil grow, thinking they were doing good or at least choosing the lesser evil.

Andreas's factories and plants were not taken away in the first half of 1916. There were no documents, no hints of how this happened, but Kirill figured that Andreas paid off the right person, Rasputin or someone from his crowd, or maybe he came to terms with Batyushkin, bought him off. But sensing that these people would keep demanding more and more from him and that their promises were not to be believed, Andreas starting giving money for the revolution.

At first Aristarkh, Arseny's old acquaintance who was healed at the estate after the first revolution, made his presence known indirectly to Andreas. Kirill thought that the experienced underground fighter had learned long ago whose son Arseny was and what a rich family he therefore had in the palm of his hand, for if the case were revealed, Arseny would be in danger of punishment for hiding Aristarkh.

Aristrakh bided his time while Gustav was still alive. But now he turned up, probably learning from the papers that the old man who would have kicked him down the stairs had died.

Andreas was informed that the workers at the factory, who were working on a military commission that could not be delayed, were planning a strike, and representatives of the strike committee wanted to meet with the owner. Andreas realized that someone was staging the strike, but at first suspected competitors who wanted to ruin him and force the sale of his company—but it was the group headed by Aristarkh, extorting money for the Party coffers.

At first Andreas gave money reluctantly, to avoid the strike and cover up his son's old sin (he didn't write to Arseny about it), even though he was putting himself in their hands and they would come again, threatening to compromise him.

But then—and the "then" came very soon—he seemed to recognize his sacrificial field, his (not literal) repetition of the fate of the Marinated Midshipman Andreas.

He decided to sacrifice his wealth, good name, way of thinking, education, his entire life to make sure that their persecutors were punished, so that the Schwerdt family could stop being afraid of their name. There may have been a secret desire to take belated vengeance on Gustav for taking away his talent and using his gift for the profane business of enriching themselves.

Andreas saw salvation in the doctrine of the International, in the Marxist idea of classes. He started giving the fighters more and more money, turned a blind eye to the agitation at his factories. He must have expected on some level that his collaboration with the revolutionaries would be discovered, that he would be arrested, sentenced, perhaps executed, but that afterward, the revolution would punish his enemies.

Kirill suspected that things did not end with money. The revolutionaries could have used the warehouses of his companies, the accounts, they could have been put on the payroll so that they would have a legal right to travel around the country; Andreas must have had connections in neutral states, entry to the black market where things that were not allowed to be exported from warring states could be bought, old and secure contacts with customs, expediting offices, foreign banks, newspapermen, diplomats. The underground group could have used his import-export lines for smuggling and his accounts for bringing in money from abroad.

It's unlikely that Andreas expected his dream of revenge to come true so soon.

In the fall of 1916, the instructions came at last on how to interpret the law, and a commission started working on the case of Andreas the sailor. The instructions required evidence of "valiant behavior" on the part of one who died in combat; the gray naval officials considered whether the death of Midshipman Schwerdt was a manifestation of valor, studied documents, the ship's log, and reports on whether he had time to take out his weapon, and whether the concepts of valor and death by cannibalism were compatible.

A bit later the Council of Ministers decided to liquidate industrial enterprises on expropriated land, including the smallest ones with fewer than ten workers; the enterprises were either bought by the Land Bank or shut down, and it was looking as though the Marinated Midshipman would not save the Schwerdts and their holdings would go under the hammer.

In the winter of 1917 the railroads stopped. The blizzards that had once brought Andreas and his future wife together blocked the tracks. The rails, cars, and engines worn out over the three years of war were breaking down; the same thing was happening to Andreas's body. Never ill before, he began complaining of terrible headaches, he could not sleep, pacing in Gustav's study, where he had the sun of swords removed—he couldn't bear having blades over his head.

The February Revolution—the desired vengeance—found Andreas near death. The universal rejoicing touched him glancingly. He seemed to be ashamed of hurrying to join the underground instead of waiting for the events that now seemed inevitable, precipitated by the course of history. And also, Kirill thought, Andreas had peeked behind the scenes of the revolution and could see much sooner than others what he had financed, what future he had brought closer.

One of the earliest decrees of the Provisional Government repealed the repressive laws against citizens of German origin. Andreas could have taken a free breath.

But the same government, deciding to fulfill its allied obligations and continue the war, picked up the war's spymania. After the armed insurrection in July in Petrograd, detectives and investigators cast a wide net, trying to prove the connection between Bolsheviks and the German HQ; Aristarkh by then had quit the SR party and joined the Bolsheviks, and now Andreas's money was going to the coffers of Lenin's party.

Kirill read all the volumes of the case against the Bolsheviks, outstanding in number and degree of legal acrobatics; in the background, in secondary statements, the names of Andreas's companies flashed by. That meant he was back in the sights of counterintelligence, once again had made the wrong choice, and he must have expected to be arrested soon.

Andreas could have fled, he wasn't as stubborn as Gustav, but he was ill and he infected his wife, so to speak, who was emotionally dependent on him; she also began suffering migraines, was unable to get out of bed, and soon the most frequent visitors to the house were doctors. Some recommended neutral Switzerland for the waters, but all paths there went through warring countries and dangerous seas; others recommended the mineral waters and baths of Piatigorsk, but there was war in the Caucasus, too, Russian troops fighting yet again near Kars, and revolts exploding in the mountains.

So Andreas was there for the October Revolution. Not far from the house, on Krasnaya Presnya, skirmishes raged, people

SERGEI LEBEDEV

shooting cannons and rifles made by Gustav and Andreas; during those days when the city did not yet belong to anyone, furious requisitions ensued: reserve soldiers, deserters from the front, and street thugs wearing red ribbons robbed the houses of the bourgeoisie.

Andreas had paid a price not to be persecuted for his nationality—and he was robbed not as a German but as a rich pig, fully in accord with the doctrine he supported. For the first time the door of the mansion was broached by uninvited guests, for the first time he was defenseless in his own house. Desperately, Andreas met with Aristarkh, who held a post in the Moscow Cheka, and received a safe conduct pass from him: the note on Cheka stationery stated that the Schwerdt family actively helped the revolution and was under the protection of the agencies of revolutionary law and order.

He tried to show the note to the next band of robbers who broke down the door and stormed into the study—and was killed. The note did not stop the bandits. He tried to defend himself with what was at hand, he grabbed one of the swords that until recently had hung on the wall—and was stabbed with it, killed by his own weapon: a savage, ludicrous death, to be stabbed by an ancient blade in revolutionary Moscow.

***

Kirill knew the room where Andreas was killed. But generations of Soviet bureaucrats from the foreign ministry had not only taken over the walls and rooms, they had destroyed the very idea of former ownership of the building, made it part of a city suffering from amnesia. Even the death of his great-grandfather—in this house, on this street—was not subject to resurrection or emotional reconstruction, as if he had died in an

208

unreal world that had no connections with today's world. The connection—if there was any at all—was with Pushcha, the former estate given to Arseny for his wedding, the estate where he returned in early winter of 1917 after three years at war, missing his father, who had been killed in Moscow.

By Kirill's time, there was nothing left of the estate. The log house had been taken apart in the thirties, as Grandmother Karolina wrote, and moved to the nearest large village, to house the village council. After the war, the old council was razed, and then the land of the former estate was used for a dacha complex.

But the site of the estate had been so cleverly chosen—on the incline of a steep ravine holding a fast-flowing brook headed toward the Oka River—the landscape, as if it presupposed the presence of a house, caught the searching eye and was easily recognized from Grandmother's descriptions and the old photograph that Great-Grandfather Arseny made in the winter of 1917–1918. He had a Kodak, some glass plates remained, and he hurried to use them up, photographing the house and surroundings, as if he knew they would all be gone soon.

There must have been more photoplates, but Karolina saved only six: the house, the ravine, the birch grove, a horse by a haystack, the road that Arseny with wife and daughter took to come home in November 1917, and a photo of the three of them in front of the house.

Later, in Kirill's lifetime, the photos were transferred to paper and printed in large format. Grandmother spent hours in the evenings looking at them with a loupe, bringing up part of the photograph like the surface of the moon, covered in craters, canyons, and shadows, and Kirill used to think that she was studying the mysterious layer of silver, which captured, like coffee grounds, signs of the future, and trying to guess if the future of the house and its owners had already been preordained back then.

Kirill visited the former estate many times. In spring, the murky brook rushed down the ravine, and children came to build rafts; in summer, the old and untended apple trees of the garden, lost among the weed trees, showed themselves with red fruit; in fall and winter, when the branches were bare, the birch grove became transparent and the view opened all the way to the Oka. It created the false but pleasant sensation that you were in a safe spot, a place of peace, a sensation that slowed you down, invited mindfulness, the wisdom of expectation; every time he left, Kirill felt that he wanted to stay, to look in the distance, enjoy the tranquility of the valley—and understood even better the fateful winter of Great-Grandfather Arseny.

For three years Arseny's hospital moved along the front, following the advancing and retreating Russian armies. Of his six children, he brought only Karolina, the eldest; Gustav had chosen her name, and it was German; the following children had only Russian names.

His wife, Sophia, went with him as a nurse; she returned to the estate several times—most frequently in summer, during harvest, to oversee the work—and then went back to join her husband in the army.

The other children were sent off to relatives. The brothers Gleb and Boris to Vladimir, to the wife's family; the sisters Antonina and Ulyana to St. Petersburg, to the family of Gustav's cousin; the youngest, Mikhail, born in 1915, after the war had begun, was sent to Tsaritsyn. Distant relatives of the Schmidts lived there; they were descendants of German colonists who sold salt and horses and dealt with the Kalmyk tribes; the youngest child had stomach problems and the family pediatrician had prescribed treatment of koumiss, mare's milk.

For three years Arseny ran the frontline hospital. Kirill knew almost nothing about those years. The hospital documents were lost during the Civil War; Arseny's letters were probably destroyed later, out of fear that zealous NKVD investigators would find evidence against the former tsarist officer.

Only postcards—again, postcards—sent to the children on holidays, and their responses. But of course there wasn't a word about war: cupids and puppies, baskets of flowers and ribbons—only the postmarks allowed him to follow the hospital's journey, juxtapose it to geography and the chronology of battles.

A few of Sophia's letters survived; she wrote the bailiff managing the estate. The house was getting old, the outbuilding needed repairs, he had to buy a water-hauling carriage, the greenhouses lost windows in hail storms. The local men were at war, bringing in the harvest was difficult, but they were sent two prisoners of war, former soldiers of the Austrian army, Serbs by nationality: they worked hard, but the bailiff still considered them enemy agents and suspected them of evil intentions.

The bailiff, a distant relative of Sophia's hired at the request of family, had once been dutiful and obedient. Now—his health kept him out of the army—he felt he was the master of the place and handled money freely.

Arseny's notes at the front consisted of medical instructions and books. Even though he did not fight but healed, the war exhausted him. He saw the futility of treatment: soldiers were brought back wounded a second and third time. He did not see a way out: just movement toward the abyss; he was crushed by the horrible meaninglessness of any effort, the disappearance of all passion that could give meaning to today's suffering, find justification or at least explanation in the future.

Even his previous socialist fervor was gone. What was left was the certainty that things could not get worse. The only meaning in the field of meaninglessness was to end it—stop time, block the flying bullets in midair, withdraw the crossed swords.

Therefore, thought Kirill, Arseny heard the Bolshevik call for "peace without annexation and contribution" not as a tactical political move but a voice outside the political context, the voice of reason in the midst of unbridled madness.

Mentally exhausted, Arseny became slow in his actions; he no longer believed in man's ability to decide anything in his life and waited for instructions, suggestions, impulses from fate—an outside will that would spare him acting of his own volition.

Tied to the hospital, to the wounded, Arseny spent the spring and summer of 1917 without thinking. Russian money was still worth something, the borders were open to neutral countries, but Arseny did not undertake anything that Kirill's backward glance prescribed.

Kirill finally understood why not. Arseny had missed the moment when he could have safely sent his wife and daughter home. It was growing more dangerous for them to remain at the front, the soldiers, especially in the nearby rear, had stopped being an army—but it was even more dangerous to embark on the long voyage alone. Had Arseny been a different man, he would have come up with a fake illness or begged for an unscheduled leave—but he was simple-mindedly honest, and the honesty was fed by the passivity of his nature.

In late August, during Kornilov's advance, a lieutenant colonel bayonetted by soldiers raging against Kornilovism was brought in to the hospital. He was still alive, but died after a few hours of suffering. The notation about the officer torn apart by subordinates who had, as the regimental party committee, actually elected him as their commander, was the first diary entry in all the time he had been at war: Arseny had apparently separated himself from the army and felt himself to be an individual, a civilian.

Typhus broke out in one of the units. Arseny was ordered

to take the patients far to the hinterland, into quarantine. He risked infecting his family, but the risk paid off: marauders did not attack the typhus train, it was not stopped by various authorities and committees, self-appointed soldiers and sailors barricades. Protected by the deadly illness, Arseny was able to get his daughter and wife away from the collapsing, dispersing front.

✱✱✱

*T*hey arrived at the estate in early October. Kirill wondered why Arseny had not stopped in Moscow at his father's, in the big house, why did he go to the country? At first Kirill assumed that Arseny had put his family in quarantine to be sure they were not infected. The incubation period is about two weeks, and the onset of the disease is sudden—Kirill checked the medical encyclopedia; if Arseny were infected he could bring the disease into his father's house inadvertently.

But then Kirill realized that Arseny must have used that excuse because he wanted to hide from his father, the big city, the epoch, the world, and stay in the country where his trade as a doctor protected him better than any gun and where he could wait until the politicians decided who would be in charge.

An old servant woman and the two Serb prisoners of war lived at the estate; the bailiff ran away with the money from the harvest. This loss was insignificant for the family; Andreas was still wealthy and could give his son money. But the theft and flight were evil omens.

Not far from the estate in a clearing was a house with outbuildings, and the place was called Katya's Farm. It stood in an abandoned garden, inhabited by an old woman, a priest's widow, and her companion. Her sons had been wanting to move her to nearby Serpukhov, but she refused, saying she wanted to die where she had lived with her husband. She was a stingy old woman; when she was still strong enough she chased the village youths from her garden. Arseny remembered that they used to say she had a gold cross and money her husband had saved hidden in her cellar. They joked about it, just to harass the old woman, and the youths tried to climb in her windows to see if she ever accidentally indicated where the secret door was that led to the treasure.

The old woman and her companion were killed the day before Arseny arrived. He was called in to look at the body. The women had been tortured, their hands burned in an effort to get them to reveal the location of the treasure.

People had lived nearby for years, everyone knew the old woman was poor and had no golden crosses, they just gossiped out of malice. But now that the time of troubles was upon them, one of yesterday's kids tortured the old woman to death; either he came to believe the old stories or he was showing off.

Arseny was armed and did not need to fear an attack. But his fear was of something else: he sensed it was a time of tricks of mind and visions, phantasmagoric transformations, evil mirages through which the future near and distant could be glimpsed. What happened later merely confirmed Arseny's premonition.

***

Kirill put his grandmother's letter on top of his great-grandfather's diary; he was stunned by the realization that he was the only one who could read both texts; he was the third, he was the all-seeing.

She had written the letter in 1937, in the fall. She was in love, while all around people were being arrested, and the arrests moved closer. For some reason she had not sent the letter—most likely because the recipient had been arrested, removed from the world of the living. No address, no surname, only his name—Arkady; the ink was blurred by tears.

She was attempting to persuade her beloved to reciprocate, that she could protect him if their love was mutual. In order to prove her ability to be his amulet, she described an evening in the fall of 1917, when she was alone in an empty room of the estate.

Kirill checked the calendar: it was the last autumn storm of 1917. A late storm, when the skies are empty and weak, and there is no trouble in the air. Kirill imagined how it had happened, comparing the notes of his great-grandfather and his grand-mother's letter.

The storm was not too fierce: there was thunder beyond the woods, a flash in the distance, and then quiet. They were expecting rain, but not a drop fell. The evening light changed, lengthening the roads and widening the fields; then came twilight, which took on the stormy tension, diffuse, the power of electricity that had been unable to produce a lighting bolt. It was the kind of twilight that makes you think that someone would appear, walking from the field or driving down the main allée; you know that no one is expected but you watch standing on the veranda or resting your forehead on the window pane—will a stranger appear, will light flash from the lantern swinging in his hand?

Grandmother Karolina—just Lina back then—must have stood that way in the big room; it had been closed for the winter, so as not to heat more rooms than necessary. No one would disturb her there. She stood and waited; she had returned from the war with her father, the miracle had already happened, but she had a supply of expectation, believed in the return of her broth-ers and sisters; she had to live through the expectation, return it to the emptiness of the fields, the pull of the waxing and waning of the moon, dissolved in nature.

They found Lina by the window with an open pane. She was neither dead nor alive; the pulse was very weak, her eyes did not respond to light. She lay unconscious for three days, and then could not speak for another two weeks; she did not try, she did not make sounds or try to force her tongue to shape words; it was as if she were numb inside.

They said that there was a mad dog in the area, someone's escaped wolfhound, and that at night it approached houses, looking for people outside alone; it lived—allegedly—near Katya's Farm: one evil begat another.

Arseny wrote that when he found his daughter unconscious, his first thought was of the dog from Katya's Farm, that it had come to the window and frightened Lina; there was so much talk about the dog, it seemed so vicious, enormous, black, as it was described, a harbinger of catastrophe.

The next morning Arseny saddled a horse, took a hunting rifle and pistol, and galloped to Katya's Farm. It was muggy and gray, the rusty leaves rustled in the oaks. He was back from war, he had been in trenches during bayonet attacks, he had gone through artillery attacks; but he was afraid—he admitted in his notes—he kept imagining the mad eyes of the dog.

The farmhouse was boarded up; there were no fresh tracks, human or animal. Arseny felt that the dog had outsmarted him, hidden somewhere nearby. His old horse was more accustomed to yoke than saddle and his old rifle often misfired; Arseny began to think that the dog had lured him into a trap. Cursing, he galloped away, superstitiously not taking the same road that had brought him there.

At the edge of the field was a ditch where the villagers dumped dead cattle. Arseny rode past and saw a dog rummaging in the rotten carcasses. The dog that lived in Katya's Farm, a small black mongrel. He realized with shame and anger that this was the "mad dog" terrorizing the area.

He was so angry with himself that he dismounted, found a sturdy stick, got into the ditch, caught the dog, and beat it to death, burying it under a pile of leaves and rubbish.

Arseny expected his daughter's speech to return gradually, word by word. But the first snow fell, the whole yard was covered and the fields whitened—and Lina, as if awakening in another world, began to talk; Arseny noticed that she constructed her sentences differently, gone were her favorite childish words, her sentences were longer, the images clearer, as if she had grown up by several years. She did not remember what happened in that room. She went to the window and suddenly it was dark—that's what she said.

Arseny noticed that Lina went off on her own more, as if invisible chains connected her to someone or something; he wrote off the attack and illness as nervous exhaustion, explained them by the difficult trip from the front, everything that was not for children that Lina had seen.

In the letter to her vanished beloved, Grandmother Karolina described what she never told her father or grandson.

Kirill had never forgotten the summer storm of his childhood that smashed the apple trees, and his grandmother shutting all the windows in the house, checking the hinges and latches, and then freezing before the blurred and rainbow-like reflection of the candle in the sweaty window, fainting, and then whispering as the smelling salts brought her back: "Enough, don't, Father." Now Kirill knew the source of her fear and why it was so strong.

Lina stood in the room, feeling the storm gathering in the charged autumn air, filled with the warmth and damp of the last sunny days—half-hearted, straining, unable to let loose with thunder and lightning.

A light flickered in the yard—one of the household with a lantern, thought Lina, but remembered that they were running low on kerosene and the lantern was put away. What was it then? She drew close to the window and saw floating toward her an orangey yellow sphere with violet crackling veins, full of a beautiful and furious fire.

The ball delighted her—and terrified her; she couldn't move, her feet, her fingers, her tongue would not obey. She saw that it had come for her, that ball, and would kill her, because she, because, because, because—Lina feverishly went through all her sins, which had become manifold and towering, like night shadows in candlelight, but still not significant enough to explain the appearance of the golden burning ball.

The ball hesitated outside, and then, as if endowed with will and reason, flew in through the open pane and headed inside the house; it swayed, stopped, trembling, two meters above the floor, like a gigantic cyclopean eye searching for someone in a dark cave.

Lina guessed whose eye it was: God was looking at her, God who knew she did not believe in him enough, that she had been bored when her parents took her to church to pray for their escape from danger and for the speedy return of her brothers and sisters.

It was cold in church, she wanted to go home, where her little bed stood behind a screen in her parents' bedroom and which she had outgrown over the last three years, but into which she tried to fit, squeezing in and pulling up her elbows and knees, to fall asleep there and wake up back in the past, which she barely remembered, only the gold-painted shells of the walnuts that had decorated the last prewar Christmas tree.

God, whose presence Lina had not felt in church during

the boring service, was now looking at her, who had dared not to remember Him. She fainted, fell to the floor, and awakened to the smell of ammonia; God's eye had vanished, there was a strange draft carrying a cool heavenly freshness; the fiery sphere glowed before her, as if it had been branded on her eyes.

The ball lightning was a collective symbol of all the terrifying mirages of that autumn, a kiss from the future, a sign of who would survive, thought Kirill. If she had not lost the ability to speak, Lina would have told her father about the appearance of God: the flaming bush, the sphere of flowing fire that she saw on icons. But her power of speech was blessedly taken away, and the mystery remained unspoken.

Later, when it returned, she kept God to herself. God as a terrible miracle that gave her the knowledge that there are no safe days and places, no quiet harbors, that something wild and all-powerful is always near and ready to fall upon you with all its strength.

Of course, in her letter Grandmother Karolina talked about the ball lightning, a material phenomenon, and wrote the word *God* with a lowercase *G*. She was trying to persuade her beloved that any catastrophe could be faced, that there was no need to despair—but she contradicted herself, since she admitted that she seemed to have died in that room and that was why she now had the "powers" to live now, in 1937; she put powers in quotation marks, not indicating irony but otherworldliness.

Karolina's muteness and subsequent resurrection seemed to explain Arseny's inaction: he did not gather his children scattered in various cities. As part of the family history, the fact did not attract Kirill's attention at first; but then he, himself not yet a father, suddenly wondered how it was possible to have not seen your children for three years, and still to put things off.

Kirill imagined his great-grandfather: in the early weeks he restored order to the estate, treated the peasants, arranged deliveries of provisions for the moment and for the future. Arseny must not have understood for sure where to gather the children, at Pushcha or in the Moscow house, or maybe in St. Petersburg, where Antonina and Ulyana were living, closer to neutral Sweden, reachable by train via Finland, where they could all go ... But there was shooting on the street almost every day in Petrograd. In Vladimir, with his wife's family, out in the provinces with its strong traditions, where no revolution could reach? But how would the relatives react, and then what? In Tsaritsyn, where Mikhail was, at the Volga crossroads, where roads lead to Siberia or Asia or the Caucasus?

The children in different cities were like lighthouses promising different pictures of the future. Arseny, who after seeing the collapse of the army, the thousands of deserters and the hundreds of murdered officers, was unsure of how to proceed.

He could have gathered the children at the estate and decided later—but he wanted to avoid unnecessary trips on railroads held by soldiers fleeing from the front, and looked for the simplest routes.

The estate was not far from the city—in the olden days the mailman brought newspapers and telegrams—but now the news that reached them had aged along the way, creating an ephemeral world of echoing events that nevertheless still had real qualities here.

Kirill subconsciously expected the Bolshevik coup to affect all of Russia instantly, in one second, like a jolt of electricity; but rather vague news reached Pushcha only a week later.

However, and this was the most interesting thing for Kirill, the profound dramaturgy, like a drawing of great events, developed in the life of the family independently of the news they received or did not receive in their backwater.

Kirill discovered a stratum of great images that defined life, images in which people can see history—and they were not demonstrations, battles, the cannons of the *Aurora* aimed at the Winter Palace, but the quiet mysteries of daily life, crystals through which you can see the essence of events.

One day Arseny took his daughter with him to see a patient in a distant village. He did not want her to lose any nursing skills and he wanted the locals to remember her as a helper. On the way back, in deep twilight, they traveled along the floodplain of the Oka, past oxbow lakes rich in fish.

The river had not yet frozen, it was slush, the lakes were covered by the first ice, smooth, transparent as mica. In the evening dusk they saw lights ahead, illuminating the treetops, reflected in the ice, warm yellow fog penetrating the ice. Light snow was falling, a silvery rope tightening the space; smoky torches burned, their flames mixing with the thick steam of breath; and dark male figures slowly moved along the ice, some with wooden mallets, others with spears. Both father and daughter knew what they were seeing, but the figures were so strange, so like a dark procession of pagan Slavic gods, so unexpected was the fire in the night, so fresh were the rumors of robberies and arson, so malevolent were the spears and hammers that they stopped their horse; it seemed as if the countryside, exhausted by soldiering, had risen up against city and church.

Night ice fishing: the oxbow lake was famous for its burbot, a predatory fish that does not sleep in the winter. The burbot swims toward the light, the fisherman strikes the ice with a hammer, deafening the fish, and then breaks the ice with the gaff and pulls out the catch.

Finally recognizing the men from the nearest village, they rode over to the shore; Arseny probably expected them to offer him some fish as a sign of respect.

A thin ice had spread over the freezing water, October water. Above it, it was November, and the fishermen walked with spears and hammers scattering fans of predatory light; the chilled sheets of silence creaked, beards steamed, and they could hear quiet conversation, resounding sharply in the hunting night. Bam! The wooden hammer struck, the ice bent in a branching star, filled with the wild white milk of the blow, the gaff plunged down into the ringing slush—and the crazed burbot lay with its curved yellow belly on the ice, sprinkled with snow like sugar.

Splash! The gaff from November plunged down into October, the quiet of unmoving water, clear of silt, and the fish was instantly on the ice, thrown into the future, pierced by the spear's jagged teeth.

In the 1930s, Grandmother Karolina wrote about what she had seen and remembered during World War I, the Civil War, and later. But the fishermen on the thin ice, the winter flames beneath the icy skies, the blows of hammers, the splashes of spears, the death dances of the repulsively resilient fish, the bloody water spreading on the ice, the greedy jaws of the ice holes—this seemed to always stand before her eyes like a prophesy.

"Dear friend, even in this quiet house fever strikes me." Grandmother Karolina mentioned that when she read Alexander Blok's poem in the 1920s, she immediately thought of the fall of 1917 at the estate—as if Blok were writing about her and her feelings.

Kirill took down the blue volume of Blok's works, the third volume of eight, and found the poem in the index. An aspen leaf that had lost its crimson color slipped out of the open pages— Grandmother had liked such random bookmarks.

Dear friend, even in this quiet house
Fever strikes me!

I can't find a place in this quiet house
Near the peaceful fire!
Voices sing, the blizzard calls,
I fear this coziness …
Even behind your shoulders, my friend,
Someone's eyes are watching!
Behind your quiet shoulders
I hear the rustle of wings …
His glowing eyes strike at me
The angel of the storm—Azrael!

Kirill froze. The first time she read this poem, she could not have known how it would end. The angel of storms, Azrael, angel of death, conductor of souls, had looked at her with glowing eyes.

The fierce eyes of God floating in the twilight, the flaming ball lightning in the white room, unconsciousness, muteness, doom, solitude—and then less than ten years later, as if in a mirror, encountering a similar experience in Blok's work, as if the number of great images is limited, like the number of cards in a fortuneteller's deck, and in similar situations the same ones always appear.

Kirill recalled the gaze of the eye at the German Cemetery from a Masonic tombstone; he forbade himself to think along those lines, as if trying to avoid the rhymes of destinies.

***

I fear this coziness …

They closed up the big room. They covered the grand piano with white cloth, as they once did for funerals. It had gone out of tune over three years. The tuner used to come from town, but now he was gone, and the piano was no longer played; the lovely evenings for which it had been bought were no more, as well. The glazier was gone, too, and he was supposed to repair the windows for winter; sensing disaster ahead, people were leaving. Before, they would have found another one, but now it seemed craftsmen existed only in single numbers of each kind, and the material world was rapidly becoming depleted: you couldn't buy glass, kerosene, salt, soap, or nails, everything was being hoarded in case of need or in hope of profit.

It seemed Great-Grandfather Arseny was frightened by the impoverishment. He was a firm man, but firm in secure times when the order of things was not disturbed. And now even *things* seemed to be affected by human activity, in the revolutionary changing of masks, features, sides; they had stopped being what they seemed: kerosene only smelled like kerosene but was water, soap didn't lather, sugar had a chalky aftertaste, and forged banknotes appeared. Arseny spent more time on the second floor in the small room that had belonged to Balthasar. After his death it became a repository for unneeded or broken things; homeopathic flasks and ancient medical books still stood on the shelves, and the small copper-trimmed trunk that locked with a key held Balthasar's papers—letters, notes, medical tracts.

Lina would sneak up the creaky staircase; it was impossible to see in, so she listened to her father unlock the trunk, the papers rustling, the pen clinking against the inkwell. He sat there at the watershed of the year and era, like Balthasar in the Tower of Solitude, reading his grandfather's documents, making his own notations, in a country that no longer existed and was about to fall into the abyss, a country in which he was born because his ancestor had believed in a chimera, and that chimera, when mixed with the fraught soil, gave birth to a line of damaged destinies.

Her father never talked about what he did in the attic. Lina sensed that Sophia wanted to drag her husband out of his refuge and tie him to the present—but Arseny was inflexible.

Kirill thought he had the same stubborn strength to resist flight, demanding that the past you are escaping from must first be sorted and packed, so to speak, otherwise the anxiety over something forgotten, misunderstood, unclarified will not let you set out or will lead you in circles; you won't get through, you'll be snagged, you'll be stuck.

Lina considered her father's secret solitary work malevolent. At her age, she was more closely tied to her given name than to her German surname; she felt she was Lina rather than Karolina Schwerdt. Three years of war had taught her to see the enemy in Germans, and her German origins, which sometimes made her the butt of good-natured but unabashed jokes among the nurses and aides, had become the object of indignant rejection. She imagined that the surname Schwerdt meant nothing, it was just a collection of letters; Balthasar was as elusive as a ghost, and Iron Gustav and Andreas were Russians, because, illogically, she considered herself Russian, and she was their granddaughter and great-granddaughter.

Karolina later recalled that strangely, the family almost never spoke of the German relatives, the children and grandchildren of Balthasar's middle brother, Bertold, who had remained in Germany. One of Andreas's sisters corresponded with him, even went to visit. But Andreas was not close to him, limiting their contact to holiday greetings and presents. Perhaps that had been Iron Gustav's wish, to avoid having parasitic German relatives, but it's more likely that Andreas continued to bear the cross of his father, who had considered himself guilty of the death of his younger brother, Andreas the Marinated Midshipman.

But all that was before World War I. The war cut off all ties, and boundaries of love and hatred were very clearly delineated. And now Lina, who was not quite sure what the mysterious German trunk contained, watched her father very closely, watching that he was not transformed, like a werewolf, into a German, by reading German words.

Arseny read Balthasar's texts aloud, recalled his childhood, in this very attic, the medicine vials that made him a doctor, and tried to understand who Balthasar really was, having come to Russia to proselytize homeopathy, plunging his descendants into the indeterminate, brittle world on the border of countries and cultures, a world born of his apostolic illusions—and what he, Arseny, should do now.

Lina only heard foreign speech, unfamiliar on her father's lips, because the German lessons had stopped during war. She was afraid that by uttering enemy words, her father would stop being her father and become *Herr Doktor*, as he was called by the German prisoner of war from an uhlan unit, wounded by a lance in a skirmish between patrols and brought to the Russian hospital. Lina recalled with astonished horror that her father accepted that form of address as the most natural thing, as if he truly was a malevolent *Herr Doktor* and not a physician. For Lina the words *Herr Doktor* did not mean "mister doctor" in another language, but were a vicious name for a murderer with a scalpel, a secret collaborator with that arrogant uhlan who, they say, cut down three Russian cavalrymen before being thrown off his horse with a lance.

So Lina kept watch by the door. Her father's profession, the foreign Latin, his absolute power over patients in beds—the power to decide whose leg is kept, whose arm is amputated, who can get up, who has to stay in a cast; the right to prescribe medicine, white, yellow, round, oval pills with incomprehensible names, three times a day before food, once a day on an empty stomach, six times a day with water, medicine about which the patient knew nothing, with strange names, the composition unknown, the action undefined—all that taken together seemed very suspicious to her.

When they dined together, father was father. But when he went off alone upstairs, Lina felt the stirrings of those suspicions that were not about her father specifically but about the white garb—alienating, repellent—of the physician, beneath which it is so easy to hide black intentions.

Lina's imagination might have wandered further if not for a belated message from Vladimir, where the brothers Gleb and Boris were living with Sophia's parents. Sophia's mother was gravely ill. The children had to be taken back, the mother had to be moved, too, because Sophia's brothers were at the front and her elderly father, a priest, could not take care of his wife.

Rumor had it that skirmishes continued in Moscow between the Junkers and the workers' units. So Arseny took a roundabout route, via Ryazan and Murom, via the swampy Meshchyora Lowlands, on a sledge. He did not like Sophia's mother, or any of the family in Vladimir, but he could not refuse.

Three weeks later Arseny was back, bringing his sons and paralyzed mother-in-law, managing to travel through three cities where they were arresting officials of the Provisional Government, seizing banks and post offices, handing out guns to workers, releasing peasants jailed for taking over estate lands, and adding red ribbons to the coats of soldiers from the reserves; officers avoided appearing in uniform on the streets, and inns passed along reports of robbed and murdered travelers.

Arseny knew that the illness was untreatable; the question was how long it would last. The important thing was that Sophia's mother had almost died on the road, and it was impossible to take her even to Moscow; she would not survive another trip. So the family found itself locked up at the estate, tied to the life and death of the grandmother from Vladimir.

She was given the room closer to the stove. She lay in bed, surrounded by pillows, beneath an ancient eiderdown. Her body seemed enormous, like a giant mound; even death could not take her all at once. Candles burned hot before the icon of the Mother of God brought from Vladimir.

Sophia's mother had lost her mind. On the brink of death, after three years of war and all the sermons and prayers for victory over the German invader, she thought that Arseny was a foreigner, a German—not her daughter's husband—and that the grandsons were Sophia's children from her real husband, a lieutenant from Vladimir who died in 1914; Arseny had a real, German name, he was a demon come to seduce Sophia. Lina was his servant, not his daughter, she could turn into a black raven, steal, spy, and cast spells.

Life at the estate now revolved around the deathbed.

When Arseny learned of his father's death and left for Moscow, armed with a pistol, the old woman begged her daughter to bring a real doctor, since the one who called himself Arseny was not a doctor but a poisoner. She had heard from old, wise people, church men, that German doctors were spreading the black death in provinces, poisoning wells, sickening cattle, infesting the area with poisonous flies, and that is why people, when they caught the flies, beat them to death and threw their bodies into the ravine for dogs to eat. The bread was bitter, the yeast was not as strong, the salt was weaker, the emperor was drugged with herbs and made to abdicate—all the fault of the Germans.

When Arseny returned after burying Andreas and leaving the mansion in the care of servants, he had to pretend he was not in the house, that Sophia had chased him out and was waiting for her true love to come back from war. That was when Lina stopped being suspicious of her father, her mental fever came to an end, because the old woman didn't want to see the black raven, either, so she had to disappear, flying out the window. Her brothers were younger, and they treated the old woman's fantasies as a grim game. Lina, who was not only older but had spent three years in wartime hospitals, in the midst of the delirium of the wounded, Lina was cured, as if she had been ill and developed an immunity to madness, which would save her in the future.

Even the murder of Andreas did not give Arseny the determination to act. Now it was totally unclear where there was danger, where there was none, who was protected, who would be punished. The thought that it was dangerous everywhere and no one was protected was too terrible to contemplate then.

Arseny hid behind his father's death, fencing himself off from his silently demanding wife who was prepared to stay with her mother if he would only take the children—as far away as possible. He eliminated that option, however, by lending a large sum of cash, which he found in Andreas's safe, to an old army friend who planned to make money supplying medicine from neutral countries. After a conversation with Andreas's trusted bailiff, Arseny learned that his father had given money "for the revolution," learned about Aristarkh and the safe conduct letter for the Schwerdt family; the letter had not saved Andreas, but Arseny found it among his papers and brought it with him to Pushcha—to calm Sophia down a bit.

The arrival of the new year, 1918, was missing from every text that Kirill had located. Apparently, Sophia had asked him to bring their daughters from Petrograd and their son from Tsaritsyn, but Arseny expected his mother-in-law to have less than two months to live (without telling his wife) and waited for the inevitable end that would allow him to leave.

Arseny went to Moscow to get the loan back, returning in disappointment: his friend said the money had been seized during a search. Arseny did not know if this was true or not; more than by the loss of money, he was shaken by the possibility of suspecting a friend known for his impeccable reputation, by the changes in people who turned out to be Januses.

He also brought the news that there would soon be a change in the calendar: the Bolsheviks were preparing a decree on switching to the Gregorian calendar.

Kirill, who could never remember to add or subtract days when converting from Old Style to New, at first thought that Lenin had given Great-Grandfather Arseny two weeks that did not exist in nature to extend his Fabian delay. Then he checked and saw that the change had tossed Arseny from January 31 right into February 14.

Knowing his great-grandfather's entire history, Kirill sensed that those lost days, the two weeks crossed out of the calendar by the Council of People's Commissars (there was an idea of bringing the calendars closer together by a day a year, but Lenin insisted on the leap), were fateful, key. Arseny would be short those two weeks in the future to complete his plans; they—and soon it would be expressed in space as well—were an expression in time of the geometry of the family fate.

The icy path tossed Arseny into the middle of February. On the eve of spring and sowing, representatives of the village council, recent deserters, appeared and demanded that the fields and barn, where the wounded Aristarkh had once hid, be turned over to common property and that the family move out of the manor house into an outbuilding; the library and grand piano would become property of the village club, which they would allegedly open at the estate.

Other families might have been kicked out onto the street.

But the old fame of the good doctor and Arseny's own medical service still provided a thin shield of protection to the family. But the village was swiftly turning Red, while Arseny was a gold-epaulette officer, and the people he had treated yesterday could come tomorrow to divide up his fields in accordance with the land decree and with their own understanding of what was fair.

However, Aristarkh's note slightly cooled the zeal of the expropriators and gave Arseny an understanding of how to proceed: color the family and adopt the victorious red, symbolically or practically. Arseny went to Moscow to see Aristarkh and returned a Red Army doctor with the right to preserve the house for his family—not the land, not the library, but at least there was a roof over their heads.

The new, Red Arseny became the man that Kirill had known since his adolescence, albeit spectrally—Grandmother Karolina had a photograph of him in her room, wearing an old-style Red Army cap with a red star on the band. In order to bring the children into the new reality, in a collapsing country that was losing its sense, you needed to have status, a magical artifact that opened doors and controlled chaos; that artifact was the uniform of the Red Army, recut from the imperial cloth.

Arseny received a lacuna of time. The Red Army as such did not yet exist, there was no unit where he was supposed to report, but the uniform existed, he had papers, and using them he brought his daughters from Petrograd and made sure that the fields of a Red Army family were plowed. Even the German surname, which sounded dangerous in the old country, seemed to have lost that effect in the new: *Comrade Schwerdt* meant something different than mister or excellency.

Kirill tried to figure out how sincere Arseny's metamorphosis was, how far he planned to travel on the Red path. As an adolescent, Kirill saw only the Red side, as if his great-grandfather had been born to exist only in 1918, with a red-starred cap on his head; now his vision had shifted to prerevolutionary times, and Kirill could not combine the two identities.

The red wave he had planned to ride by signing up for the army rose high. The Civil War, which began with skirmishes around Petrograd, engulfed more regions. The spring warmth allowed combat to spread, the Cossacks arose in the south, Germans invaded from Ukraine, the volunteer army of the Whites and Cossacks jointly attacked Tsaritsyn, which was soon besieged.

The cursed two missing weeks worked for the first time: Arseny had almost reached the city where Mikhail, their youngest son, was, but he was traveling on his own, without orders; the Whites surrounded Tsaritsyn, cutting off the roads, and he was forced to turn back.

He asked to join the troops defending Tsaritsyn, but reinforcements were being sent from other directions; but when they studied his papers, he was sent to run the hospital in the rear.

There was constant fighting around Tsaritsyn, the ring of Whites narrowed then expanded; communications were not working and it was impossible to find out if the relatives were alive, if his son was alive, inside the city. July, August, September, October, November, December, January—three long sieges, river battles on the Volga—the city turned, as did Leningrad later, into the next world that is reached by water, by river, along the narrow road of life, where not many are allowed to pass.

At the estate, under Sophia's watch, her mother faded. Arseny, in his hospital, located in a small provincial town, watched the new regime, which had ceded the best wheat-growing regions to the Whites, strengthen the requisition system it had inherited from the empire, introduce a monopoly on bread, and declare that anyone hiding grain and flour was an enemy of the people. A Food Requisition Detachment arose in order to squeeze supplies out of the villages; Arseny saw murdered requisition agents, peasants shot by the Reds in retaliation, and he must have understood whom he had decided to serve, what the red star meant on his cap. Former coworkers found ways of making their way south, to join the Whites and fight the Bolsheviks, but he had a family, his son was trapped in Tsaritsyn, and his dying mother-in-law could not be moved. He waited, he stopped keeping a journal, and lost himself in medicine; there was only one scene he recorded, which Grandmother Karolina found later and retold in a letter.

There was a distillery near the town. The mash was poured off into the pond at the edge of the town. The distillery attracted armed deserters, wandering soldiers, who took over empty houses; they bought or took alcohol, and drank, drank, drank, and drank … Pigs and other animals started frequenting the pond; they got drunk, too, and sprawled in the mud; once for a joke, someone tossed a worn overcoat on an intoxicated pig, which then ran around the streets, urged on by shots fired in the air.

The requisitions brought the distillery to a halt, there was no more grain or potatoes. The deserters remembered the pond with the mash, the murky substance that could be forced to yield a little more alcohol. So men and animals gathered at the stinking, foul puddle, deserters with pails stepped into the muck, sinking, while pigs slurped the mushy waters and ate intoxicating mud. A shot intended to chase the pigs from the pond winged a hog, the pigs panicked and ran into the deepest part of the pond, trampling two drunkards; another shot, another miss—the bullet struck a mash collector's shoulder; an answering shot—and now men and animals were embroiled, struggling in the sucking mud, passing out from the fumes; no way to tell the men from the animals.

Arseny, as a Red commander, could have thought that the Bolshevik regime existed to establish order and restrain dark passions. But he saw demons being driven out of swine and entering people, contrary to the biblical story; and he was no Red commander, anyway, his coloring was a pretense; the pendulum of his sympathies—if he paid any attention to sympathies—swung to the Whites.

Did he understand that while the White Army was winning victories, the victories of Bolsheviks were ripening in the future? Moreover, the current serious but not decisive victories of the Whites were the surety for the coming victories of the Reds who sat on military supplies from tsarist Russia, concentrated in the middle of the country, exchanging time and space for the opportunity to discipline and train its motley army.

Kirill assumed that this great-grandfather did not see that far, that he was convinced by the military success and massive attack of the White armies and the aid from allies in the Entente. After all, he knew some of the leaders of the White movement personally, had served under them in Galicia.

Also—and this idea, this image stunned Kirill when he realized—White Russia lived according to the old Julian calendar. When the Whites took a city, the newly appointed commandant immediately issued a decree turning back time.

Turning back time!

It was the first point of the leaflets pasted on fences: not bread, arms, order, establishments, trade, private property, agitation, system of government—all that came later, below—but time per se. And therefore when the Bolsheviks took the same city by storm, their first decree was the unfolding of time, replacing the Julian calendar with the Gregorian, throwing the residents two weeks into the future. There was a rigid, inexorable metaphysical quality, more terrible than extrajudicial executions, torture, and starvation, in the struggle of two calendars and two times, the White past and the Red future; this military, revolutionary power over time, habitually accessed by any Red regiment commander and any White staff captain made city commandant, cast the Civil War battles, modest in comparison to the recent World War, in the light of the War of the Titans, reducing people to grains of sand and permitting every sort of ruthlessness.

Arseny, having experienced that eerie leap from late January to mid-February, might have considered switching to the side of the Whites in order to return to the past, to get back the time that was unjustly taken from him.

Here a plot began that Grandmother Karolina never wrote about, she simply didn't know even though she took part in it; for her these were just work transfers for her father, new appointments, the topography of life. But Kirill juxtaposed all the circumstances and became convinced that Arseny was planning an escape, and a very elegant one: an escape without moving from the spot.

In January 1919, Sophia's mother died. The Whites still had Tsaritsyn under siege, and in accordance with the campaigns of the previous year, a new advance of White armies from the south could be expected in the spring or early summer.

Arseny called his wife and children to join him at the hospital; he sent an orderly to protect them on the journey. Sophia did not want to abandon the estate, which would certainly be plundered by the peasants, or Andreas's empty house in Moscow, in which they hoped to get a room or two from the new regime; but Arseny insisted, and she obeyed.

Then Arseny asked to be transferred closer to the front, to the city of Borisoglebsk, two hundred kilometers from Tsaritsyn. This was the sector of the front that the mounted Whites would traverse in the summer.

Grandmother Karolina was not surprised by her father's request for a transfer, noting only that he wanted to be closer to his son Mikhail, lost in Tsaritsyn, and perhaps hoped there would be an opportunity to get into the besieged city. Kirill compared military charts with their red and blue arrows, wrote down key dates, and figured out Arseny's secret plan: he had hoped that the Whites would take both Borisoglebsk and Tsaritsyn in the summer and the front would move in a solid line to the north; the family and the lost son would then be behind the White lines.

Kirill studied yet again the places where his great-grandfather's hospital had been stationed during World War I and calculated which units sent their wounded to the hospital, and it all came together: they were the infantry regiments and Cossack cavalry that later formed the foundation of the White Army.

So he really could have counted on meeting people he knew, who owed their lives to him, among the White officers; he could have hoped that he would not be accused of treason for serving in the Red Army—at that time both armies were made up of turncoats, who went back and forth in platoons, squadrons, battalions, regiments.

The idea almost worked; but again at the most crucial, most dangerous moment that curse of the two missing weeks went into effect. Because of arguments in the command, the White armies did not attack in concert; the right group headed for Tsaritsyn confused the Red battle order, while the left group of General Mamontov did not turn back to the front, broke through the defense lines, and went to storm the Red rear, bypassing the hotbeds of resistance and allowing the Reds to re-establish their positions.

Even worse, Arseny and his family left later than planned because of hassles with the appointment and documents. If they had been just a little earlier, he would have been able to reach the bottleneck where Mamontov would break through, he would be where there was a moveable but useable corridor for a week or so to the White side. But he was too late. The locomotive was gasping on second-rate coal, the train traveled slightly faster than a pedestrian, and as a result it intersected with the route of Mamontov's cavalry when it was returning from a raid in the Red rear guard.

Arseny must have thought he would make it to Borisoglebsk in time and then when the Whites took the city and set up a garrison, he would find some senior officers he knew. Kirill did not know if he planned to join the White Army or after finding Mikhail in Tsaritsyn, leave Russia, through the south, through Crimea. The world war was over and the sea routes to Europe previously closed by the Turkish fleet were now open.

But the army train on the road to Borisoglebsk met only a distant cavalry unit, a half squadron or squadron, sent to cover the rear of Mamontov's main column, retreating, going back— without senior officers, without firm command, just a hundred men on horseback.

There Arseny experienced the feeling that Kirill came to call the Borisoglebsk horror.

It was getting toward evening. The train stopped for minor repairs in the middle of the steppe. Suddenly a crowd of cavalry-men appeared from the dark side, from the east. Wearing shaggy hats and bearing spears, they seemed like visitors from the distant past when militant nomadic tribes followed this route to the West. The bright moon appeared from behind a cloud and he could see that the horsemen were dressed in stolen fur coats, men's and women's. Instead of horse blankets they had mud- and blood-spattered cuts of expensive cloth; gold and pearl icon covers, stolen from churches, sparkled in their saddlebags; the moonlight, the steam from the horses' nostrils, the pale faceted tips of the spears—it was a demonic host from hell, Mongols come to take the wooden cities of old Rus.

For one second Arseny, a physician, an officer, really believed that this wild mounted horde had been spewed from the steppe of the past. That was the moment of the Borisoglebsk horror, the infernal abyss, a hole in the spreading fabric of history through which the riders of the Russian Apocalypse came into this world.

The train started, the driver was in a hurry to move the train. With that, time seemed to start again, too, and the moment of the present returned. It was only then that Arseny realized he was seeing Mamontov's long-anticipated cavalry, the flying Cossack formation—rather, marauders, rapists, and killers into which the units he had once known had turned, who even in the past had no qualms about robbery or pogroms but had still obeyed their commanders.

The train picked up speed. The Cossacks shot at the receding train and then vanished in the dusk on their worn-out horses. So Arseny ended up in Red Borisoglebsk, commanding a hospital again. Tsaritsyn remained White and there was no way to reach it.

It might have been possible to try to join the Whites, there were guides who knew the hidden paths in the steppe, the dry creeks, the secret fords, the roundabout roads—but the Borisoglebsk horror, not so much fear for himself and his family as a swoon from the unexpected nearness of that terrible, underground Russia, where his grandfather Balthasar had come, without knowing it, the Russia of choleric revolts and the mad Prince Uryatinsky, frightened Arseny for good and deprived him of willpower; they needed to flee, but he could no longer run, the Borisoglebsk horror pursued him on ghost horses.

So his great-grandfather remained a Red: the uniform and cap grew into his body. He led the hospital diligently, accepted the loss of the estate, and seemed to forget his previous life completely. The family accepted it, too, except for the middle son, Gleb, who tried to run away from home, traveling with the peasants on a cart; the cart was stopped at a checkpoint in the outskirts, and one of the soldiers recognized the doctor's kid trying to pass as an orphan.

Gleb told his father that he wanted to get to the front to fight the Whites, but Grandmother Karolina, a perceptive sister, always believed that Gleb had lied to his father: he did want to go to the front, but to join the Whites, not the Reds.

The older brother, Boris—Gleb's rival—played war with him, pretending to be a Red cavalryman galloping on a broom, wearing a budyonovka hat while his father wasn't watching; that left the role of the White to Gleb, who was jealous of Boris, their father's favorite. He decided to join the Whites. That was a strange preface to what would happen twenty years later, during the next great—greater—war.

**

Kirill often thought about the 1917–1919 period in his great-grandfather's biography: afterward it was just empty time with no possibility—for Arseny—to change his fate.

Using Arseny as an example, he tried to understand the strategy of behavior in History writ large. He tried thinking and feeling not as a scholar but as a victim of history without strength and time to think, but forced to act—without those two weeks in reserve, panting for breath. His thoughts were scattered, abbreviated, and not forming a whole picture.

In the current of life, flowing among habitual circumstances, you don't feel that something is holding you back, that you are stuck. But the moment comes when you must act. You send your children to various cities. You think it'll be a few months, it turns out to be many years. You've rewritten their destinies in some details that you yourself do not know, the most intimate ones. As if different spells were cast over their cribs and now cannot be recalled. If they had not been dispersed, would they have been saved later?

Your mother-in-law is dying. Hidden conflict. You never liked her but you are a physician. You can't abandon her, your conscience won't let you.

You lent money to a friend, and it was seized during a search. Not fatal, but bad; the money could have solved something, but not anymore, it's in a soldier's pocket—or your friend's.

The estate had been a dream but it's become a burden. You lived with the burden, took care of it, but now you can't sell it and the village soviet is threatening to take it away, and you don't want to abandon it.

Reading, thinking, Kirill didn't need look at the details in order to see—like a psychic—the energy flow of history. He didn't have the needed metaphorical language to describe what he saw and felt, but he did formulate a few points for himself.

A great historical event creates a force field that shifts reality, bends the lines of destiny, tests life decisions and actions that in the ordinary course of things could work even if they were imprecise. All the hidden tension bursts onto the surface, all the mines and traps placed earlier, through carelessness or mindlessness, are set off. In some destinies these changes are imperceptible, in others they are enough to cause something unforeseen and destructive, or as the engineer Andreas would put it, the construction reaches its fatigue limit.

Thus a new, additional eventfulness that reproduces itself appears, acting as a catalyst.

The "mechanism" of events acquires new elements that can

function either as sand or as lubricant. The timing of events, previously generally even, separates, flowing at different speeds; one thing happens faster and easily, another more slowly and with great difficulty.

This additional eventfulness, reactively expanding, turns into an avalanche.

That's why a catastrophe cannot be explained rationally. You can see its basic dramatic lines, the main details, but not the whole, because the whole is subject to the tiniest of shifts, the loosening of seams, the weakening of all connecting elements.

The catastrophe does not destroy something solid, strong, congealed. People would already be forced to take unusual steps, to creep out from their usual holes and dens, for the stability of the structure has already been dangerously exhausted.

Otherwise it would be like the British formations at Waterloo—the order will withstand attack.

The uncertainty of the future, the daily tasks of survival force people to behave egotistically, focused on their inner circle, decreasing the general resource of solidarity and thereby opening the way for passionate minorities.

It is only at that moment that the minorities can provoke and develop events, sucking the disorganized masses into the narrow funnel of the future—of conflicting futures.

In that sense the division into Whites and Reds was provisional. They did not yet exist in 1917. But there were radically oriented groups who set events into motion, forcing everyone else to choose, to take sides.

Kirill returned to his thoughts about the generations of the family and their interrelationships.

How Balthasar had unwittingly created, like a demiurge, a world consisting of fractional people, of German and Russian halves, quarters, eighths. Superfluous, transitional, additional, not fully part of the protective context of tradition. The price of misfires, accidents, bad coincidences was very high in that world; in it, a ridiculous suspicion, a nasty rumor, a mean gaze had great power to control reality—because fractional people are more vulnerable than whole ones, it is much easier to present them as demons in the current political bestiary.

Grandmother Karolina and her brothers and sisters tried to break out of Balthasar's world, to use the chance offered by the early Soviet era, which had seemingly abolished the old imperial prejudices, proclaimed the coming International, created a new history in which, thanks to Aristarkh's letter, the Schwerdt family could find a place, as if on a train.

But no one succeeded in escaping; even Grandmother Karolina, who had survived, had paid such a price that it could hardly be called a salvation. Only one person avoided the common fate, but only because the capricious Schwerdt family fate played a joke on him: it took away his name, memory, and family, turning him into a true child of the era, protected by the absolute absence of a biography.

***

*G*reat-Grandfather Arseny traveled to Tsaritysn, which became Stalingrad in 1925, three or four more times. He learned that back in 1918 the Cheka had executed the family that had taken in Mikhail. It was rumored that they were killed not for their counterrevolutionary activity but for their valuables. Their big house in the suburbs was on the line of defense of first the Reds and then the Whites; only ashes and rubble remained of the street.

There was no hope of finding neighbors; some died during skirmishes, some were hanged by the Reds for being fat cats and class enemies, some by the Whites for feeding Bolshevik soldiers;

people scattered, moved away, sailed away, the men taken into the Red and White armies.

Arseny found only one physician colleague who had treated the head of the vanished family. The doctor told him that the boy had a wet nurse, a baptized Kalmyk woman, strong, born in the steppes, good on a horse: perhaps she managed to take the boy out of the city or hide him there?

At that time, the steppe was still in turmoil. The remains of the vanquished White armies and all kinds of gangs borne by the war were hiding out there; the Red Kalmyks killed White ones and vice versa; it was madness to poke your nose into the steppe without an armed platoon. Arseny started his search another way: he sent word with the commander of the Red Kalmyk squadron, who came into town for weapons, ammunition, and uniforms, that he was looking for a woman named Naikha, who had fed his son.

The steppe responded, the steppe as a whole, more ancient than the squabbles of the new age: along distant paths and caravan routes from the foothills of the Caucasus to the Volga, from the Caspian Sea to the desert, from the Volga delta where pirates, heirs of Stenka Razin, ruled among the thousands of islands, to the Cossack villages, where skeletons from the infamous Civil War battle known as the Ice March still lay in ravines and washes, the word traveled, passed from mouth to mouth, crossing borders of hospitality, and returned: the woman called Naikha who had worked in Tsaritsyn for the German colonists, was not among the living, she did not return from the city, and her remains were there and not in the steppe.

Arseny searched in orphanages for a boy who remembered the meaning of *Mutter* or *Vater*—they had spoken German at the colonists' house. He also had a photograph sent to him in late 1916, Misha in a shirt and sailor hat, but how do you recognize a two-year-old in a seven-year-old boy?

The orphanages had hundreds of children who had forgotten their names, who had gone through sieges on the frontlines, wounded, concussed. Even more children were homeless.

Mikhail was not found.

Later, after World War II, Grandmother Karolina had stopped thinking of Mikhail as being alive—his draft age put an end to that.

But Kirill still felt that Mikhail could be found. What Arseny failed to do in his time, he would manage decades later.

No one in the family except Karolina had survived World War II. It was not the war per se that killed them, but their German ancestry, an echo of the past in their destiny.

That was why Mikhail was important to Kirill, as a laboratory specimen showing how a man who does not know his fateful ancestry lives his life—and how fate treats one who does not know. Different from the ones who do know?

And also—although Kirill would not admit this out loud—he sensed that Mikhail had not starved to death as a child, did not perish during the sieges of Tsaritsyn, and had survived the war.

One day Kirill took the photo of Mikhail as a child and stared at it in steady candlelight with the drapes closed. Freeing his mind of extraneous thoughts, he thought about what had happened to the boy.

Essentially, Kirill was inventing his great-uncle. It was his favorite method of searching in places where the chains of information were torn and evidence destroyed; the accuracy of his artistic conjurings had often led him to true facts.

Could Arseny not have recognized his son at an orphanage? Kirill felt that the answer had to be no. That meant they had not met. Was Mikhail a homeless child? Yes, no? No. Had he been adopted? Likely. But by whom? Who could want to take on a child in a destroyed country? Who could afford to support him?

A military man. Kirill imagined the figure of a soldier.

An adoptive father.

Mikhail followed in his footsteps.

He graduated from officer school just before the war: aviation, artillery, tanks—no, infantry, ordinary infantry, a commander of a small platoon. Kirill was also certain that Mikhail, who had lost his first life in the siege of Tsaritsyn and found a new life in Stalingrad, obtaining a new identity in the city renamed in 1925, had participated in the Battle of Stalingrad, in the second siege, and there, in the fire, the personality and fate became totally his own.

Kirill traveled to Volgograd—the city had formerly been called Stalingrad—in the winter.

Of the three seasons of the battle, he could have chosen the stifling heat of August, when the Soviet troops in the territory between the Don and the Volga were rolling back toward Stalingrad, despite the command "Not a step back," and the first German bombers were getting through to the city neighborhoods, and the residents were digging ravines and trenches for external defense, which would help no one.

He could have picked the cold fogs of autumn, with the chilling wind from the Volga, the harvest of grapes and apples: the time when the Germans pushed the defenders of the city to the very banks of the river.

But he chose icy January with its blizzards blowing in from the Asiatic steppes, the January of being surrounded, dying, the rime-covered cellar walls, rats, cats, and ravens eaten by starving citizens, the January of gangrene, gingivitis, and the last planes to the south, in the direction of Millerovo—the final January of the Sixth Army.

The flight was delayed for two hours at first, then until evening, even though other Volga region airports were open. But

Kirill knew that in the winter Gumrak Airport, coincidentally, the last airport surrounded by Paulus, turns into the Bermuda Triangle—as if the battle had left its mark in time and climate; as if every winter sees a repeat of the mystery of being surrounded, cold death, and freezing fogs and fierce blizzards shut down the runways.

The passengers on the postponed flight moved to the café; only one man, thin and distant, remained at the counter. Kirill liked eavesdropping and listening in on dramatic moments in other people's lives; he pretended to be having trouble with his bag and listened.

The man was carrying a zinc-lined coffin with his father's body—this information was withheld from the other passengers out of superstition. Now he was worried where the coffin would be kept for the duration of the delay and if the baggage handlers would be around to reload the body when they took off. Kirill was not afraid to travel with a corpse, but he did note that he was flying to find a missing dead man, and a different dead man was traveling on the flight with him, as if the mocking gods had sent him a guide.

Kirill sat down at the café and had a beer, but the traveler in the zinc coffin did not leave his thoughts. The dead man had been in the military—the son was telling the airport personnel about some discount—and Kirill, feeling a playwright's thrill, called him the Officer. Something jangled softly in the son's bag, and Kirill realized they were medals that would be placed on velvet cushions carried behind the coffin.

Suddenly Kirill heard German spoken; he looked up and saw an elderly German at the next table talking to a heavyset blond, clearly Slavic, while pouring warm Sovetskoe champagne into their glasses; he poured with one hand, the other was missing. His sleeve was pinned to his side, in the Russian manner.

Kirill shuddered. As a child on May 8 he saw many elderly men with missing limbs, but this was the first time he ever saw a German invalid.

Kirill learned that the German was married to the Russian woman and they were traveling to visit her mother. In terms of his age, the one-armed man could not have been a soldier of the Wehrmacht. But here and now, inside the play Kirill was writing, he was, and Kirill called him the Invalid Soldier.

He needed a third dramatis persona.

Beneath a palm tree crookedly growing in its pot sat a priest: black cassock, gray beard, powerful wrestler's body. He seemed to have sat next to the sickly palm to be noticed, and Kirill happily wrote him down in his mental cast of characters: the Priest.

Invalid Soldier, Priest, and Officer, and the last was unknown to the two live passengers, only Kirill could see him. Who were they, what connected them? Different people or versions of the same?

Kirill knew that seeking an answer by staring at his fellow travelers would be pointless: they presented only a vague picture, the reflection of a reflection in a reflection, and only the future could decipher this puzzle and lay out the images in the right order. But he sensed that it would definitely be about Tsaritsyn/Stalingrad/Volgograd, about Mikhail and perhaps someone else whom he did not see the way the two men could not see the corpse in the coffin.

At nightfall the flight was delayed yet again and they were taken to a hotel; then after 1:00 a.m. they announced departure. The airline staff ran around to the rooms, shaking passengers out of bed, gathering everyone in the bar, where the hardiest were still drinking. The confusion of a hangover, the hoarse sick sky, the clouds as rumpled as bed sheets after an arrest, the orphaned streetlights, stinging rain, mounds of darkness—still waking up,

Kirill imagined that it was the wrong hotel, the wrong airport, the wrong sky, and they were going to fly somewhere wrong, to some other Volgograd.

They flew in thick clouds. There were occasional bumps, but nothing much. Irritated whispers broke out among the passengers: they should have set out earlier, what had the pilots waited for? Then the plane escaped the lower edges of the storm clouds, and Volgograd appeared beneath them: the red ribbon of lights along the dark Volga, which reflected nothing. Chains of streets, horizontal and vertical: the horizontal ones were the lines of the Soviet defense, the intersecting ones the lines of the German attack; Kirill knew the map by heart and it seemed to him now that the postwar planning of the city captured the simple geometry of mortal resistance.

The plane taxied a long time to the airport terminal. The lights on the wings flashed rhythmically; the light seemed to dissipate fruitlessly on the steppe. Looking closer, Kirill saw the sastrugi, the sculptural image of the blizzard's power. In the way that a lathe can cut grooves in metal, the fierce demons, the spirits of the air, somersaulting, flying up over the ground and falling down, twisting during the flight, had carved and chewed the mounds of snow along the runway.

Kirill was met by a former classmate, Maxim, who worked in the local department of culture; he knew everyone and everything in the archives, museums, and search departments. They were not friends, but the thread of liking one another from their student days was unbroken: they shared a weakness for poetics and metaphor instead of strict scholarship, and both were wounded by history—Maxim was looking for traces of his grandfather, who was taken prisoner of war in 1941 and died in the Stalags.

Maxim drove and talked about developments at the archives and the museum, Kirill listened with half an ear, looking at the road, the houses, the fields. The unclear dawn flickered, the car wallowed in potholes, avoided ruts, and they were enveloped in darkness, a gloomy illusion of the place itself.

He had the impression that through the Battle of Stalingrad something had happened to matter itself. Matter had been crushed and destroyed for so long and so persistently that its essential cohesion had been altered, and it no longer could retain its form. That is why the roads were like this, as if the dead were digging them up from below, and the winter fogs were so threatening—as if the evaporating snow were stealing another bit of the connectivity of matter, and reality thereby became more spectral and variable.

Maxim lived in an old Stalin-era house next to the Allée of Heroes, inherited by his wife; his own family would not have had such a place in the unspoken Stalingrad hierarchy, commensurate to rank, medals, and military lives.

Over tea, Kirill explained why he had come. He expected Maxim to send him to the city archives, but after hearing him out (Kirill had even described the strange fellow passengers on the plane), Maxim poured them some cognac and began talking.

"You know, I had a dream when I was a child in winter," Maxim said. "At the panorama, by the battle museum, there's a steep descent to the Volga. The stairs go down through a small tunnel. In December it's dark by three there. I was always uncomfortable walking past on my way home from school, as if it was some animal's den. In my dream ... I saw this bank as if in cross section, from the Volga. During the war it was riddled with foxholes, caves, the headquarters were inside the slope, and so were the people behind the lines, while the front was a hundred meters above, among the buildings. In my dream I saw a huge cave open from the Volga; dull campfires burned there and the distorted and self-enclosed space, like a Mobius strip, held all the houses, all the streets of the prewar city; all the residents of Stalingrad-Volgograd ended up there after they died, and they fought the Germans for eternity. And I knew that I would end up there."

Kirill said nothing. The cognac, with lemon slices sprinkled with sugar and coffee grounds, had relaxed him, but there was still a fixed point of intense, detective-like attention within him. Maxim stopped, as if weighing whether he could trust Kirill with what he was about to say, and continued.

"Do you know how many bombs and shells they are still digging out? The earth is still exploding, the military metal is only slightly covered over. The postwar city is above, the prewar one with its cellars is below. They touch sometimes. They meet. And then the sparks begin. The old capsules come alive. Truth surfaces."

When Kirill studied the history of the war, he paid attention to a special Stalingrad phenomenon. Not only did the big city allow the Soviet Army retreating over the steppe to grab on to the earth, hide beneath roofs, behind walls, in the depths of merchant cellars, amid factory workshops, behind brick chimneys, in blast furnaces, and stacks of rolled steel, it became a text: the soldiers wrote in blood, coal, paint, flame retardant on the walls; they left letters in cans, bottles, bullet casings, soap dishes, apothecary tubes, as if hope had returned and with it the grammatical category of future tense.

Beneath the walls of old buildings hastily plastered after the war, these writings still lived, the immortal messages lay in the ground. Kirill felt that if Mikhail had disappeared in any other city, he would have been lost with no hope of being found; but here time itself was riddled with mole tunnels, penetrating history, and therefore it was possible to get word of a person missing in action.

"Recently a German bank opened a branch here," Maxim said. "They picked a mansion and bought it. They began reconstruction, broke through to the cellar. Our rules here require calling in museum workers and the police. In the spring of 1943, when it got warm, how did they bury the dead? Tossed them into a cellar and walled them in. So ... the whole city is built on bones. But there was something else in this cellar. Green trunks, metal lined. Military trunks. German. In the corners. And in the middle of the room, a desk, on it a German field telephone, the wire leading out beneath the rubble. It's just there, inviting you to make a call. Our people and the German bankers, everyone's crowded in there, raising dust. They broke open a trunk, it's full of papers and shoulder patches. And each paper, each patch has the emblem of their bank, exactly. Turns out they were the accountants for the Sixth Army, paid the salaries. ... One of the German bosses turned gray and looked at the phone. As if it were a telephone to the other world. And you could call it.

"Our whole city is like that," Maxim said firmly. "You can actually call there."

***

A city where you can make a call to the other world.

The image captured Kirill's imagination. It was terrifyingly realistic: they won't hear you knocking or screaming, but you can call. As if somewhere on the outskirts, a single telephone booth has a phone that truly can connect worlds and eras; you can find it, the important thing is to know what number to dial and who to ask for from the otherworldly operator.

Kirill felt that this metaphor gave him a clear indication, albeit vague like all prophecies, of what he had to do.

Intoxicated by the freezing fog, the overwhelming darkness, and the low movement of the unfreezing Volga, he was prepared to believe that here he truly could make the call that would lead him to his great uncle. He rushed around the center of town, went into yards and entryways, the residents took him, wearing an expensive coat, for some kind of official, an inspector from above—that's how they put it: you must be from above—and tugged at his sleeve to tell him about leaky roofs and broken elevators, as if this miraculous emissary from unknown agencies could show up once and fix everything. Kirill only heard that he was from above, from the surface, the upper world, and desperately sought the entrance to the lower world, the buried one.

On his third day, when he was walking along Lenin Prospect toward the Fallen Soldiers Square, where the Eternal Flame burns in a bronze wreath beneath a granite obelisk bayonet, he heard a strange sound, either a distant volley of guns, or the leaden icy sky cracking open. A push, and he fell into a snow bank, someone on top of him, pressing him into the snow crust, and overhead shrapnel whistled, explosions rumbled, and shards pierced his coat.

It stopped. He stood, wiping blood from his brow—he had scratched it on the icy crust of the snow bank. Next to him a man shook snow from himself and rubbed his hurt knee, his savior, a man in a military winter camouflage jacket, and missing his earflap hat; steam rose from his sweating head.

The wide sidewalk—in the city center they were cleared—for the length of forty meters was covered with broken ice. Small bits of ice scratched the windshields of parked cars, struck shop windows, left white vaccination marks on tree trunks. Cones lay in the middle of the sidewalk, remains of large ice blocks, surrounded by rings of white ice powder, like gunpowder traces on fabric after a close-up shot.

It was only then that Kirill realized he had almost been killed, saved by the silly-looking chubby officer, a lieutenant colonel, still looking for his cap, even though it was by his feet; if not for him, the long cornice-shaped sheet of ice that fell nine stories from the roof would have battered him into bloody pieces.

"Welcome to Volgograd," the officer said in a cozy, professional sounding voice, now that he had found his hat. "Are you from St. Petersburg? I hear you use lasers to knock down icicles. Lasers! Here it's like this. If it warms up a little during the day, then watch out. We get two or three corpses every winter."

"Thank you," Kirill managed to say. "Thanks. You brought me back from the other world."

The colonel looked him over, chuckled, surprised by the high-flown language, and offered his hand.

"Kirill."

"Kirill," responded Kirill.

"Ah," said the colonel with interest. "So that's how it is. Namesakes. We have to drink to this."

"With great pleasure," Kirill said, hearing his stupidly lively voice.

Kirill had money, but the colonel led him to a dive not far from the Central Market, where they sold Praskoveysky cognac and Krasnodar wines by the glass. At the market they bought a holey cheese redolent of the steppe, basturma with red-pepper powder on the rind, a bunch of marinated wild leeks, plump with brine, and ducked into the alcoholic warmth, where the floor and tables were spotted with wine, where the red-eyed regulars turned their glasses, counting the facets, and the drunken radio sang, "Let's drink to us, let's drink to you, and to Siberia and the Spetsnaz!"

Later everything swam in the smoky mists of intoxication,

as if Kirill had been wrapped in a felt mat in order to suffocate him; they drank alone, then with someone else, and then just alone again. The colonel persisted in thinking Kirill was from St. Petersburg and explained that Stalingrad had suffered more than Leningrad; Kirill for some reason began talking about why he was there, and a circle of listeners formed around him. The colonel listened closely, covering his glass with his hat, and Kirill realized that his namesake was from the Eighth Guards Corps, who had been under General Rokhlin, and had fought in Chechnya, and for him Kirill's great-uncle officer lost by the family was like a brother, like his comrades who did not come back from the war.

Another shot of cognac and Kirill was going to ask for mercy; a blizzard was howling outside the window, a warm, very snowy blizzard, for a thaw had spread over the last few hours; unrecognized earlier, it had weakened the grip of the ice on the roof and sent the ice blocks flying. Suddenly the colonel grew tense and looked around, trying to hear a sound of warning in the loud but friendly conversations of the drinkers; he grabbed his coat and hat and dragged Kirill outside.

The soft snow muffled sounds, dispersing them, swallowing them, but even Kirill could hear something: a distant rumble, the screech of metal, the squeal of large metal gears; it seemed that behind the wall of the blizzard, carousing and erasing buildings, blinding streetlights, swirling snow to create avatars of pedestrians, consuming the neon letters in signs, an ancient power had appeared.

They came out of the blizzard with increasing din—tanks, old T-34s, their long narrow trunks raised. It was impossible to see if anyone was driving the tanks, if men in helmets stuck out from the hatches; there was only the yellow light of the head-lights, the coordinated movement, the blue-gray diesel smoke, and the design of the tracks in the snow. Kirill thought he had finally fallen into the well of time, for an invisible hand had removed all the cars, erased the pedestrians, and only the blinking yellow stop lights showed that this was still this world and not the next.

The tanks rode past, turned right onto the Square of Fallen Soldiers, to the department store, where Paulus and his staff were captured by the Soviet infantry in the basement.

The colonel grabbed his sleeve and dragged him down the sidewalk after the tanks. To the Eternal Flame, the flame of the Stalingrad hell, guarded, encircled by the ritual bronze wreath to keep it from escaping.

"Firebrands," whispered the colonel. "They were like firebrands. Then, at New Year's. I can't stand the sight of fire since then. I can't eat shashlik, I instantly see that. But, but ... once a year... I go far away. Alone. To the village where I was born. There's no village anymore, just three houses. I have a field there. When we were children we had a bonfire there when we pastured the horses. At the riverbank. A pure, good river. So there ... I gather branches. And have a fire. Just a fire. Alone under the sky. And I think I feel better."

The colonel stopped talking, staring into the mouth of the Eternal Flame. Kirill felt a cast-iron exhaustion; but through it came a vague image suggested by the colonel's words. The tanks moved on into the blizzard, as if they had never been there. The snow covered their tracks, and Kirill realized that this had been a rehearsal of the annual parade celebrating the end of the battle; the colonel had been remembering his winter storming of Grozny, his first battle, in the winter of 1994–1995, when the Chechen grenade throwers burned the tank columns that entered the city without cover.

Kirill looked at himself. He felt as if he had been in battle—the wound on his cheek from ice shrapnel and the joy, mixed with alcohol, coursing through his veins of his lucky brush with death.

Priest, Officer, and Invalid Soldier: Kirill thought the solution to his puzzle was closer.

* * *

*I*t was around three. Getting dark. The joyless winter sun hovered above the high bank, above the distant buildings of the city. A fine-grained drifting snow ran along the frozen sand sastrugi; white and beige sand was frozen in small waves. Whitecaps danced on the dark river.

Kirill gathered a pile of driftwood, branches and small logs, resembling smooth gray bones. One log still had some bast for kindling. The flames contorted the bast in fiery convulsions, a puff of smoke rose, and soon the teepee of driftwood was burning smokelessly, extending its bright and softly roaring tongue of flame to the darkening sky.

Long shadows of stumps and shrubs stretched along the frozen sand; the firelight expanded space, pushing the city to the north and the opposite bank even farther away, but bringing the forest closer and lowering the murky sky almost to his shoulders.

Kirill stood watching the flames; he liked fire, he liked solitary campfires at the edge of the world, but now didn't know what to do next, where to look: at the sky, water, sand, grove, where to seek signs. The icy wind augmented the fire, the crimson coals trembled, and the flames entwined the logs in a spiraling movement, throwing splashes of light to the south, north, east, and west, like a lighthouse.

Kirill had an acute sense of the forest's grimness. The gigantic poplars, willows, and oaks had grown on the fruitful river floodplains, contorted in burls, crowned with balls of mistletoe;

beneath them were thick, entangled bushes; the Creator had tested his pencil here, and all the curlicues and scribbles took on wooden flesh and became the broken lines of tree trunks.

He saw himself standing by the campfire on the bank with the eyes of the forest, the dark pupils of the grove. He realized the point of the fire was not to bring someone to him but that the light would make him visible to the secret inhabitants of the forests, the ghosts, and to those who wouldn't have to be next to him on this little island but could see him from afar. The fire was dying out, the winds tossed dead petals of gray ash onto the sand, and the last rays of the sunset vanished behind the city.

Kirill felt he had been noticed. He had made the call. There was a reason that he took a motorboat here, that he had chosen this island, Hungry Island as it was called, an enormous layer cake of river deposits cutting the Volga channel in half. The river had built it for centuries out its own deposits, washing it away and creating it anew, nibbling at the tumbling shores. In relation to the city—geographically—it was the bottom, collecting, absorbing everything the city disgorged, garbage, outflows; during the battle its slag precipitated here—blood, oil, ash, everything that the streams in the spring of 1943 washed out of the ruins, where stone, flesh, and iron were mixed. The island was a sponge, its soft silty layers were like tree rings, carrying the memory of cruel winters, fires, and volcanic eruptions.

Standing on the porous, pliant river terrain, ready to absorb and surrender everything under his feet, Kirill felt the gluttonous womb of silt, like the puffed up belly of a toad—you hardly had to press on it and out would seep jelly-like roe with black eyes, or digested insects, bleached butterflies, grasshoppers' bony rapiers, beetles' armor with a pale greenish glimmer, and the tiny flakes of mosquito wings.

He had pressed an answer out of the island of dead effluvium. The fire cast shadows, and the shadows led him to the past.

Maxim had promised to take him to the storerooms of the Museum of the Battle of Stalingrad. Kirill wasn't very interested in going; he hated the Soviet white tower of mourning, where on the lower floors, so dim that even camera flash couldn't dissipate the gloom, exhibits gathered dust—weapons, uniforms, leaflets, banners, maps. The lower floors held the profane world of objects, while upstairs, on seventh heaven, where the winding staircases led, a panoramic mural depicted the battle from first to last day, closing time in a circle. The main truth of memory was entrusted not to real objects but to the artist's brush, which had portrayed the locally honored saints of the battle, martyrs, heroes, whose names were given to new city streets.

However, Kirill always liked storerooms, special places for the stand-ins of history, the ones who didn't have the scope or the opportunity (a superior officer killed) to rise into leader and hero. They were places for ideas that did not conquer the world, weapons that did not have a worthy target, canvases that would have hung in the gallery if their mastery had not been surpassed by another artistic genius; in other words, they held all the draft work of the world, all its failures, everyone who was second, third, fourth, fifth, after Columbus. Knowing and accepting his secondariness, Kirill felt this milieu was his own, and it would be easy to orient himself in it and find the signs he needed.

Kirill wandered around the rooms, moving deeper into the dimly lit areas until he hit a dead end. Cardboard boxes were piled in the corner; an old ornamented candlestick and binoculars in a leather case stuck out of one, the handle of a dagger or short sword from another. A painting in a gold frame leaned against the wall, a hunting rifle, a camera on a tripod; a greatcoat and parade tunic with a colonel's insignia lay across the boxes; medals and orders glowed dully, they had not been polished in a long time: Red Banner, Red Star, the Order of Alexander Nevsky, the Order of Bogdan Khmelnitsky, the Order of the Patriotic War second class, the medal "For Taking Berlin," and others, postwar, anniversary, another two dozen or so.

"They bring this to us," said the museum curator. "When the veterans die. We find such interesting things! Recently the grandson of a general brought us an entire landing boat, German. He found it in his grandfather's garage. The generals were given individual parcels of land in the city, some of the houses are still standing."

"May I look at these things?" Kirill asked. He probably would not have been interested in the stolen inheritance of a dead soldier. But the handle of the dagger with a straight cross guard, cast hilt in the shape of a snarling wolf head, and dark faceted drops of garnets on the tips of the cross suddenly reminded him of Iron Gustav's collection of weapons, his sun burst of swords. Kirill could easily explain that the unknown colonel brought back a trophy camera, even the candlestick, as symbols of bourgeois plenty, but the medieval dagger did not fit the standard portrait, required additional personality traits that may have surprised the man himself and had not yet been figured out by Kirill.

"Well, these aren't official exhibits yet," the curator replied. "Look. I'll turn on the light."

A chain of bulbs flashed on the ceiling.

"Colonel Vladilen Ivanov," said the curator, glancing at the paper label glued to the box. "Fought in the Battle of Stalingrad."

But Kirill was not listening.

He was looking at the painting in the gold frame. The formal portrait of the colonel in the uniform that now lay before Kirill, with the same medals; it must have been done by a local artist, master of the genre, well-practiced on portraits of generals but deigning to work with lower ranks, who knew how to capture a face and give it the appropriate spirit of untiring valor. The face did not require retouching; it was the face of his great-grandfather Arseny Schwerdt, with a recognizable mixture of Balthasar, Andreas, and Iron Gustav: the high balding forehead, the short thick mustache, the combination of features that appeared in the photos of Gleb and Boris.

"A very interesting biography," the curator continued. "He lost his family in the Civil War, he was the son of the regiment. I knew him. He lived not far from here."

Trying to conceal his excitement, Kirill asked, "Could I learn more about this man? His face is so typical, a real soldier's face. A Russian face," he added, checking to see if he was the only one to know the secret.

"Russian, that's for sure," she replied, leaning over the painting. "A local Stalingrader," she repeated, strangely. "Vladilen Petrovich. Well, you know, Vladilen is a contraction of Vladimir Ilyich Lenin. Our journalists wrote about him several times. And he left an autobiography, too. His grandchildren were moving, sold the apartment, and donated all the things to us."

"What about the biography?" Kirill asked.

"We have that, too," she replied importantly. "You may make a copy, the paper is in good condition."

The paper was in excellent condition. Vladilen must have bought the most expensive kind in order to perform the solemn act of relating his own life—what a contrast with the yellowed, crumbling, torn, and decayed papers of the family archive.

Kirill was surprised by the handwriting—steady and even, learned at school: the penmanship of the eternal top student. It should be used for writing declarations and award certificates:

not the slightest inaccuracy that would make you confuse letters, no haste, no curlicues in the wrong direction or clumsy connections between letters or even an extra dash; nothing vulnerably individual, human, nothing superfluous. Kirill felt the malevolent meaning of those words.

In fact, there was nothing superfluous in the biography of Vladilen, a man without family or past. Even the grammatical errors were appropriate, even necessary, to stress his healthy peasant or proletarian background, proving that we were dealing with a real, correct Soviet man of that era.

That night Kirill read the manuscript.

Little Mikhail in Tsaritsyn was left in the care of a Kalmyk wet nurse; Colonel Vladilen Ivanov wrote in his autobiography that he was adopted by a commander of the Red forces that defended Tsaritsyn; Naikha must have met someone she could persuade to save the boy's life.

Naikha was killed or died later, Mikhail/Vladilen wrote that he tried to find her in vain. Why didn't she reveal his real name, his parents, where to find them? He wrote that his real parents were "of the working class and died defending Tsaritsyn from the White Guards." Did Naikha come up with that salvation story or did he make it up himself, since he could create any past he wanted?

Great-Grandfather Arseny looked for his son among the nomad Kalmyks, but by that time the officer who had adopted Mikhail was sent to the Higher Military Academy in Moscow. For three years father and son lived in the same city; perhaps military doctor Schwerdt had even met the officer. Then the certified company commander went off to the Central Asian military district, where he died in battle on the border of Tajikistan.

Mikhail, by then Vladilen Ivanov, his adopted name, was officially listed as a son of the regiment and graduated from military school in Tashkent. He related with special pride that the school had a theater club, very much in the spirit of the times, and the students wrote the plays, and he, twice orphaned, performed in a play about the Revolution (which he always capitalized) called *The New Times*; dressed in crimson as Red October, he used his bayonet to chase away the Old Alphabet, portrayed as the silly Church Slavonic letter *yat*, since discarded, the Old Calendar, drawn on a poster, Capitalism in tailcoat and top hat, Religion, a fat-bellied priest with a chamber pot for a censer, and Old Time, dressed in a monarch's mantle.

Arseny's two missing weeks, the cruel war of times and calendars that divided Russia, and now his son, unknowing, chased his father with a bayonet.

Vladilen became a lieutenant, served in Asia, fought in skirmishes with the Basmachi. In 1941 he asked to be sent to the front, but he was kept at the school; that is probably why he survived, by being stuck there during the time of retreats and sieges, the time when armies and fronts perished. It was only when the Germans were approaching Stalingrad that he was transferred to a recently formed unit. The Stavka, the High Command, was moving troops, new tanks, artillery systems, and pack camels to the city on the Volga; in the Far North the Nenets people slaughtered reindeer for meat for the soldiers, in the South the nomads slaughtered sheep for coats and mittens; all this moved along ancient river and caravan paths, much older than Russia, toward Stalingrad.

Vladilen knew Tsaritsyn from childhood and that must have helped him survive the battle; he began as company commander and ended as battalion commander. He crossed the Dnieper and the Oder, he fought in Berlin, he retired as a colonel in 1956. He was the only one to live a life without blots, he didn't lose any family, he married after the war, had two children, became a deputy to the local soviet and then the city soviet and a member of the council of veterans; they almost named a small street after him, but decided on another person; he was given a four-room apartment in the center of town; he did not turn in his party card in 1991 and attended Communist rallies, died in Putin's time, outliving his wife by a year; the children erected a clumsy memorial stone at the cemetery and began fighting over the inheritance, the apartment on Lenin Prospect that now cost many millions.

Kirill read his great-uncle's text and could not understand whom exactly he was hoping to find. The text existed, but not the man: a derivative of time.

Priest, Invalid Soldier, Officer—his strange trio of fellow passengers, two living and one dead—came to mind.

He thought that Mikhail/Vladilen, whose life story was built on fighting Germans, was a man with only one facet; he needed someone else to give his image dimension.

Of the three, Vladilen was clearly the Officer; but just as chessmen on the board need one another, the Officer needed the Priest and the Invalid Soldier; they would frame, illuminate, and set the right point of view on his fate for its providential meaning to be clear.

At first Kirill thought he would find the other two figures there in Volgograd.

He looked for the Priest in Sarepta, in the church of the former German colony that survived in 1942 with the acquiescence of the god of war. But he found only the fraternal grave of Red Army soldiers—during the Battle of Stalingrad the Soviet hospital was located in the colony—three thousand people under a granite obelisk, while around it in a square were the German church, apothecary, warehouse, store, houses, studios, barns "where the flour in the barrel never ran out and the butter pot was never empty": a horrible piece of shared history, a place frozen in the convulsion of an insoluble contradiction, not killed but unable to revive.

He visited Lenin, the concrete idol standing on the spit between the Volga and the Volga-Don Canal, dug by German POWs, the biggest Lenin in the world. Mikhail Schwerdt had been renamed in his honor, perhaps something would be revealed there, on the riverbank, in the shadow of the monument? But it was empty and the day was silent. He traveled to the remote steppe beyond the Volga, where the military prisoner camps had been; there was nothing there but snow-swept emptiness, the kingdom of wind.

Kirill went to where Vladilen had lived. The fourth-floor windows of the now sold apartment opened on the rear courtyard, its walls once brilliant egg yellow in the sunlight. The paint had chipped, the plaster ornaments eaten by water dripping from the leaking drainpipes; the balconies leaned perilously, and the fallen cement revealed their armature skeletons. Maxim had told him that these neighborhoods were built in the first decade after the war, when the city was planned as a temple of Stalin—not the battle—which is why there were no military symbols on the walls: only plentiful wheat sheaves, grape clusters, fruit baskets—images of the postwar heaven for veterans, the embodiment of the dream. Kirill thought these houses were not crumbling in accordance with the laws of decomposition of materiality but with the laws of destruction of dreams, much faster. Vladilen was not here; here were only the many-faced images of the lost generation who had started the war as sergeants and lieutenants and became sacred figures, heroic ancestors whose blood paid for every breath and step of the young.

It was only on his last day that Kirill went to the Mamayev Kurgan, that height overlooking the city, where the statue of a woman wielding a sword, *The Motherland Calls*, towers over the city; he was wary of the place. He took the trolley, underground, which traveled in tunnels like a subway; he made a mistake and got on the trolley that went in the opposite direction, away from the burial mound.

It was a strange trolley line where left and right were reversed; Kirill thought that everything in the city was remagnetized by the immense tension of the battle, the poles switched, the trolley followed the rules of left-side traffic, and Mother Russia with her sword was placed as if she were commanding the Germans to attack.

This was the point where destinies and time were turned 180 degrees, the point where plus and minus, top and bottom, and all meanings were switched.

Kirill went up the long staircase past plaster and concrete soldiers—set into the handmade brick ruins, carrying a wounded comrade, slaying a dragon— through the hall of memory where a white hand, growing out from beneath the ground, held a burning torch, to the chilly area beneath the statue, with its floor, a paved zigzag path of sparkling blue labradorite slabs commemorating the greatest of all heroes, the best of the best, whose lives paved the road to victory. There, in the icy wind smelling of cinders, blowing from the north, where the factories were, where the line of defense once ran, Kirill stopped.

For them to win, someone else had to lose; for Vladilen to become another, someone else had to change; the one who lost and understood what is not known to the winner is necessary; a German priest, a German Invalid Soldier, and Vladilen's alter ego, the Officer who became a military victor because someone else ceased to be victorious.

Kirill understood that the fate of the Priest and the Invalid Solider would come to him later and not here; from this height, where the war was turned around, where one side acquired a future and the other lost it, he could see the ones who did not live to this day. His thoughts moved from the surviving Vladilen Ivanov to all the perished Schwerdts.

***

Kirill was amazed by how few papers remained from the 1920s and early 1930s, when the family had reached the shore of the new era and settled in the new country.

Yes, Sophia's father, a priest, was exiled to the Solovki prison camp, from which he did not return, but no one else was touched; the estate was confiscated, but they were able to keep two rooms in Gustav's former mansion. The children went to school and then—after all, their father was a Red commander—went on to higher education.

You would think there was nothing to hide in that time, no reason to burn papers, but only two or three pages remained, less than from times later and more dangerous.

The estate house had been roomy enough for everyone, family and relatives. But the two small rooms partitioned out of one old room were too crowded for the family. Thus began the diffusion, separation, dispersal; the growing children moved into the corners of friends' apartments or rented rooms. The family quickly fell apart.

Letters were infrequent. Kirill pictured a common subject of silence, the elephant in the room everyone tries to ignore; it was life itself, in which they all found a path and their own measure of loyalty to the Soviet regime; and that most important thing was what no one discussed. Arseny must have been tormented by the fact that he did not get the family out in time and watched helplessly as the children grew away from him. He himself had gone far on the Soviet path, had been an army doctor, but it seemed that he had remained, inside, a hostage of the missing two weeks.

Arseny was arrested in 1937, in October.

Kirill went to the archives, held the investigation file in his hands. He had seen some that contained only six or seven pages—the resolution on opening a case, the transcript of the only interrogation with "confessional statements," and the sentence—but his great-grandfather's file had almost a hundred pages, an incredible amount for the fall of 1937, when people were executed according to quotas. Kirill expected to weep, but he had felt everything in anticipation and his eyes were troublingly dry.

In the 1930s Arseny and Sophia lived in Gustav's old house, which had once been the property of the family. The children were in different cities again; only Karolina remained in Moscow, but she avoided the former residence and did not like visiting.

Arseny had a safe conduct letter from Aristarkh, with the seal of the VCheKa, which said that the Schwerdts "had helped the work of the revolution with all their strength." The letter did not save Andreas, but then it showed its power during the arrests of the 1920s, when formerly bourgeois people were rounded up and charged with participation in invented conspiracies; this was not yet widely proclaimed in the newspapers and only a few trials were announced.

Aristarkh never did take back his real surname and remained Aristarkh Zheleznov (Iron), as Dzhugashvili remained Stalin (Steel) and Rozenfeld was still Kamenev (Stone). In time, before the October Revolution, Aristarkh moved from the Socialist Revolutionaries to the Bolsheviks. During the Civil War, he was not on the frontlines and did not figure in the reports from there. However, through indirect sources Kirill found out that Aristarkh and the other military experts who had switched to the

Reds worked on Soviet intelligence, oriented to the East.

Along with the idea of spreading the revolutionary fire to the West, to Europe, which ended with the Polish expedition of the Red Army in 1920, some Bolsheviks had a semi-mystical dream about the East, an expectation that the new republics of the Land of Soviets would appear there. Apparently, Aristarkh subscribed to that dream; his work in the eastern sector of intelligence, which was not considered the most important, saved him from the first wave of purges.

Aristarkh was arrested in 1937; Kirill found that information in a biographical dictionary. He was accused of collaborating with Japanese intelligence; Germany and Japan were about to sign the Anti-Comintern Pact, and the investigators started searching for German connections, so that they could charge Aristarkh for being a triple agent.

The connection, the only one, was Arseny Schwerdt, army doctor, former tsarist military physician, former nobleman, relative of influential German capitalists involved in the Myasoedov case, a former officer in the Russo-Japanese war, who had been imprisoned by the Japanese and accused by the regiment commander of treason (all the corresponding documents had been thoughtfully saved in the military archives).

For the investigator, this was not mere biographical detail but a gift, thought Kirill. Arseny put too much faith in the power of the safe conduct, like a cleric believes in the power of healing relics.

Aristarkh was interrogated for several months before they started arresting his circle, near and then distant; and then they used a fine-tooth comb in the course of a single night.

That night Karolina was held up at work; the anniversary of the revolution was coming, and she had to write a play for the amateur group. Karolina was known for her ability to write fast, whatever the text, no matter how much her heart and soul resisted; but this time everything went wrong, the typewriter broke, the words wouldn't come, and all she could think of were ribald jokes about the first Soviet leader. She missed the last trolley home; she watched the trolley's rear lights roll into the distance. She went to spend the night with her parents; she had a friend who lived near work, and she usually stayed there on occasions like this, but the friend was having a dalliance, and there was only one room.

The streetlights near the house were meager, one at the start of the lane, the other at the end; you couldn't hear the traffic on the Garden Ring Road. It seemed at that moment, to Karolina, that time was transparent like water and just as malleable, and she could walk into the mansion of her youth to find Iron Gustav's study, and not the housing office, on the second floor of the building.

She went up in the dark to her parents' rooms (it used to be all theirs; now the alien world began outside the bedroom door), and in the dark, as she passed through the new sounds and exhalations of unfamiliar lives, she sensed the old phantom odors that awoke when the new ones fell asleep: the faint scent of the oak parquet, the icy marble steps, whatever remained of the silk drapes, which had been refashioned into underwear by the new residents many years ago.

Her father was out, which was usual, an emergency operation or meeting at the hospital. Her mother offered tea and complained. That something must be wrong with her eyesight, she can't thread a needle. Karolina said she would do it, but couldn't, either her hands were trembling or the thread was jinxed. That incongruity with the needle confused mother and daughter, as if they had done something embarrassing that would have to be reported to Arseny.

He came home around three, driven in the hospital car, for he had declined a personal car and driver. Suddenly Karolina felt such a reluctance to be there, a toxic, corrosive dreariness assailed her at the family home, the sight of her father in a Red Army greatcoat within the rooms where he used to wear different clothes and insignia, that she asked the driver to take her home, she had the galleys of an important book there. It was hasty, awkward, Arseny was always against such services for his family, her mother couldn't understand why she needed to rush off, while she, following a strange impulse to flee, hurried down the stairs. The sweet ghosts of childhood seemed like evil black-mailers, there to remind her that she was as much a centaur as her father; she remembered the balls in this mansion, her little girl's ball gown, her birthday toasts that began, "To the honor-able Karolina Schwerdt."

The car sped off; the driver must have been in a hurry to get home or he wanted to give the chief doctor's daughter an exciting ride. The road ran toward them with the infrequent headlights of oncoming cars that seemed like animals, with yellow and red eyes, radiator grills bared in a snarl. Among the cars was the Black Maria that took her father, whom she never saw again.

She was back in her parents' house the next day; the search was over and her mother called her at work.

For many years now she had visited her parents as a guest—in any case, she didn't look in places that only the family could access: closets and hutches, trunks, suitcases, storerooms, desk drawers, cupboards, kitchen shelves. Only her father's library remained open to her: she read a lot and always borrowed Arseny's books, it was their inexhaustible connection, a secret expression of love.

The library had changed its face; some books, the most valu-able ones, had gone to dealers in the hungry years of the Civil War, and the remaining old books in German—hundreds of them—that had stood in separate cases were now relegated to the back rows, behind books in Russian; Arseny had not only refused to use German at home and at work, but he had also sacrificed some of his favorite things of German manufacture: his cigarette case, his watch. Karolina did not consider that strange, but with the library she felt that there had been a betrayal; she purposely asked for books in German, to force her father to unlock their prison cell at least temporarily and let one or two out into the light.

By cursory observation, it seemed the old things in the house had been left behind in the olden time. Clothing changed, the old furniture vanished, probably given to resale shops, and the everyday trifles like sugar bowl, curling iron, shoe brush, umbrella, rugs, and purses also disappeared one after the other, replaced with new items in the new fashion.

Then the olden time itself ran out: the ancient cuckoo clock broke. Arseny went to a famous clockmaker who had serviced all the Schwerdt timepieces for the last fifty years—Iron Gustav's priceless chronograph, ladies' watches, the grandfather clock with a pendulum in Gustav's study—but he did not find the craftsman nor his shop. Torgsin, the state hard-currency store, had taken over the space. They took him for one of the former aristocrats trying to sell his clock and told him that he should bring only gold, precious stones, or paintings.

This misunderstanding was not as upsetting as the disappearance of the clockmaker, the master of time, as solid as Moscow, for people would wear watches under any regime; some vanished along with the man who had set the family clocks accurately to the second; ever since he was gone, none of the Schwerdt clocks showed the same time.

So Karolina thought that there was almost nothing left of the old things, conquered by the invasion of a horde of trivial monstrosities, pushy and self-demeaning, like beggars.

But after the search turned the house inside out, bringing out all its secrets, she saw that in fact her childhood, which was contained in things, had been preserved. Karolina could not even imagine how so many objects had fit in the closets and storeroom, hidden, tied up, squeezed, compressed, and now the pressure had exploded and thrown everything into disarray, painful as well in the violation of household rules of compatibility, a mocking mixing of everything with everything.

Underwear and letters, shoes, books, coats, dishes, fabrics and threads, documents, writing instruments, photographs, forks and knives, hats—everything lay on the floor, sprinkled with the stale and crumpled down from slashed pillows and duvets, as if a large bird, a fat goose, had been slaughtered and plucked there.

All those things, her father's tsarist army insignia, her mother's old German dream book, the gilded porcelain cupids, the German primer that Karolina studied as a child, the tin candy boxes with German labels filled with miscellaneous trifles; the letters in German, books in German, German engravings, German surgery textbooks—all those things clearly told the investigators who lived here, as if the name Schwerdt were not enough for them to expose, charge, and sentence.

Kirill held his great-grandfather's file; he was not allowed to see the file on Aristarkh Zheleznov, an agent of the security organs, it was still top secret, and neither his connections nor offers of bribes helped.

Under interrogation, Aristarkh admitted that he met with Arseny Schwerdt and received espionage information from him, that both were agents of the Germans even before the revolution and that was why he had given Schwerdt a safe conduct letter from the Cheka.

Kirill opened the pages of the statements. He watched the change in Arseny's signature from date to date—he must have been beaten; six weeks in the interrogation cells and he signed everything.

Kirill knew he would have broken, too, and probably much sooner. He saw the duration of hopeless resistance and the fact that Arseny held out for days and weeks as a heroic deed, and it didn't matter that he gave in at the end. The time until he gave up, measured by the pages of the case file, was a message to Kirill: not to hope, but to endure.

The family was informed that Arseny had been given ten years without the right to correspondence; in fact he was shot in the fall of the same year, and his body burned in the Donskoy crematorium.

The brothers Gleb and Boris, both Red commanders, received urgent telegrams about the arrest of their father on the same day. Gleb was a captain in the artillery, serving near Kiev, while Boris was a major in the tank division, and his unit was near Leningrad.

Gleb was quiet and removed from the family. It seemed that he could never forgive his parents for the three-year separation, the exile in Vladimir with his grandfather the priest: the master of the home, the domestic dogmatist where the children of his daughter who became a Schwerdt were almost like foundlings.

The priest had consented to the marriage figuring that his new wealthy relatives would not leave him and his family to their own devices. Andreas did a lot for them, hired them to work in the factories, helped the young get into universities; but once the war started, the stock of those married to a German went down, the priests were obliged to denounce the demonic attacks of Wilhelm the Antichrist, and the old clergyman launched into the work with zeal, picturing the foreign emperor as Iron Gustav, rich pig and alien believer.

Gleb and Boris looked like each other, but the priest could tell them apart; he claimed Boris for their own and cast Gleb as corrupted. They decided that Boris was Russian and Gleb—German.

And so Boris's life in Vladimir was very different from Gleb's. However, it was not due only to the random assignment of scapegoat or who was older.

Boris had a buoyant and fluid personality, and he knew how to make adults like him, accepting their power and finding a way of getting praise and rewards through obedience, even though he enjoyed the occasional mischief; he was practical and not given to dreaming. Gleb had inherited some traits from Balthasar the apostle, primarily independence and a capacity for solitude.

Character separated the brothers, but without destroying their fraternal feelings. Boris took from his three-year term in Vladimir a liking for his second family and scorn and alienation with regard to his German roots. The grandfather priest did not manage to plant the seed of Orthodoxy in his soul, although Boris gladly attended services; the boy left his Orthodoxy back in Vladimir, like clothing that had done its duty, and subsequently was the first to refuse to pray, take communion, or wear a cross.

Gleb, on the contrary, was drawn to the Orthodox mysteries, and his grandfather took him to church, seeing that as the only hope for saving his lost, poisoned soul. But churches, whether the ancient Cathedral of the Assumption or the small Church of the Purification, somehow did not let him fully in; either he got chickenpox from the communal chalice or he fainted in the stifling heat and candle smoke. Perhaps Gleb had mystical feelings upon entering a church, but his grandfather naturally saw signs indicating the true, sinful nature of the boy.

So Gleb came out of Vladimir with a carefully hidden resentment against his parents and a deep and perhaps not quite healthy desire to attach himself to Russia, to become more Russian than the Russians.

Gleb lived alone, even chastely; he was an eligible bachelor, an artillery captain with family in Moscow, and many women tried to snag him, but their intentions were usually as transparent as a tear, and the wise but unironic Gleb spent a lot of time disentangling himself from their nets.

Boris had recently married the daughter of the head of the tank testing ground, where his unit was trying out the BT-7 with a new turret. Another man might not have given away his daughter to a German, but he was born in the south, living side by side with German colonists in his childhood and youth, and he had no fear of Germans. The officer knew the testing work well, he liked tanks—in the Civil War he fought in trophy Renaults—but he was also no stranger to careerist intentions; on his recommendation, Boris joined the Party, and the father-in-law pictured Boris as a colonel and perhaps maybe even a general; the new bride was already pregnant.

Gleb asked for leave and went to Moscow.

Boris sent an express letter: I do not want to be the son of an enemy of the people, therefore I reject my father and take my wife's surname—Morozov. The voices of his father-in-law and wife could be heard in that letter. His father-in-law was always afraid that he would be accused of sabotage, the engineers or factory directors could blame their mistakes on him; and naturally he passed along his fear to Boris.

Karolina did not forgive her brother; their mother wanted to reply and say, "You'll have to live with God and your conscience," but the daughter did not allow it.

Kirill could not understand the secret of that betrayal. He

understood that there might be no mystery at all, and Boris had acted like hundreds, thousands of others who denied their relatives to save themselves.

But the cold betrayal did not jibe with Boris's hot nature; later, during the war, he fought bravely. Then Kirill figured out that Boris's courage did not come from his ideas of honor and dignity; it was a collective courage triggered by orders from above, in the heated unity of attack against a foreign enemy. When the enemies were his own people and they'd arrested his father, Boris could not find courage, for he did not have any.

Their sister Antonina worked in Leningrad at a secret installation, and she did not write or talk about it. She did not come, but she sent a check for a large amount, she must have hocked the last of her jewelry, diamond earrings left to her by Iron Gustav. Karolina knew that Tonya was with her and her father: the letter ended with "sending you my love," which is how they closed letters in their childhood, when Karolina was with their father at the frontline hospital and Tonya in Petrograd.

Ulyana came, but she was nothing but a burden; Arseny called her a "comma girl" when she was little, and she remained a comma as an adult—someone had to determine the right place for her. Their father had chosen her profession, pharmaceuticals, and she worked in a lab in Saratov for one of Arseny's former students.

But now her father was gone. Ulyana did not seem to understand what had happened; she wanted to go to Lubyanka and ask to be arrested in his place so that he could be released.

The sentence was pronounced: ten years without the right to correspondence. Sophia, stripped of her husband, was convinced that he was innocent. She was certain he'd been arrested for his surname. The letters S-C-H-W-E-R-D-T became an entity in her mind, like the fairy-tale embodiment of Disaster that could hide in a peasant's bag, sneak into the house, attach itself to some-body, and see to his death.

Long ago when she was young, Sophia took sentimental delight in her new, romantic and unfamiliar name; she saw it as a symbol of parting with her former life, her provincial milieu.

Later, during World War I and the Civil War, Sophia felt she was a Schwerdt; the name took on a new significance, and Sophia preserved the family, protected it in the years of calamities.

Arseny, who had chosen her for the talent to survive, the ability to save herself during a shipwreck, could not have imag-ined how hard she would take his decision to send the children to various cities and his inability to gather them together. She did not look older, but inside, old age was prepared to manifest itself mentally and physically at any moment.

The moment had come.

Even before the sentence was passed, Sophia was forced to move out of the rooms in the mansion. Karolina helped her mother pick up the things tossed around during the search, to glue what had been smashed, repair the torn and broken; but the wholeness of mind and body could not be returned. Before, Sophia had secretly believed that Arseny was under God's pro-tection, of which the emerald necklace was the covenant, the necklace made for her, his future bride, in the days when the Russian squadron sank in Tsushima. And now, Sophia, a priest's daughter, could not understand why the covenant had been bro-ken, why Arseny was taken away from her.

The necklace survived the search; they did not find the secret drawer in the old chest. But Sophia did not wish to see it anymore; the emeralds had come to symbolize vain dreams and hopes.

She faded in two weeks, so weak that she was transported to Karolina's room on a stretcher. Her stricken mind, previously so sharp, grew dim and murky; its power was not lost, but she became gloomy and embittered. Sophia began to suspect that Karolina wanted to get rid of her, put her in a home for the aged.

Seeking to understand God's will, Sophia thought back to her maiden days and the precepts her father gave her before the wedding; he told her to remain true to Orthodoxy and be careful, for the Germans had their own fate created by a false God, written by the Pope or Protestant bishops.

She recalled her first trip to the German Cemetery, to visit her husband's ancestors: how chilly and unfamiliar it was amid the stone crosses, weeping marble maidens, how strange to pronounce the German names, and through them feel the dark universe of a foreign language her husband spoke easily and simply.

With growing stubbornness Sophia asserted that the name "Schwerdt" was cursed, and that Arseny was doomed not only for being born a German but also for being a Schwerdt.

The horrible irony was that Sophia was right.

It was the German surname, written in lovely script in the regimental papers and printed in Aristarkh's safe conduct, that was the main evidence against Arseny.

Karolina took care of her mother for over three years and was her final companion and aide.

Kirill knew what happens to time in such situations.

Time is subordinated to illness, reduced to the size of a tablet, a syringe needle, flowing slowly from an IV, flashing as an X-ray, turning into a physician's indecipherable scribble, a waiting line at a famous doctor's office, new streets and houses, where there will be yet another hospital. Illness shows you the city you did not know, demands more trips, anticipation, streets, buses, and streetlights; this city has no theaters, restaurants, bookstores, museums, dance halls, parks, or the apartments of friends—only drugstores, clinics, dispensaries, where every lamppost is covered with posters advertising patient care, where despair whispers about the benefits of badger fat, or an old healer woman, or a holy icon, where the miserable travel the same paths of grief.

Kirill understood now what had happened to the three and a half years missing from his grandmother's life, why they alone of all of her years did not leave any documentary evidence.

Grandmother Karolina had no time to think about what was happening to the country, where she was in danger; even her arrested and vanished father was in a sense sacrificed to her mother's illness.

In the spring of 1941, Karolina's village nanny, her wet nurse, found her. The old woman had come to the city to arrange for a pension and wanted her help, but once she saw the situation, she stayed on and Karolina partitioned off a corner for her in her own room.

The sight and sound of the nanny who had shared her motherhood lulled Sophia; her attacks became less frequent and even the pain seemed to have lessened. Sophia imagined she was at the estate, in Pushcha; Arseny would soon return from Moscow, on a dirigible; in the early 1930s when the dirigible factory manufactured its fledglings and Umberto Nobile was at the height of his fame, Arseny was going to be a physician on one of the expeditions to the northern regions, and now Sophia, mixing up the past with the planned, the near with the far, thought that Arseny always commuted by dirigible.

Flying metaphors peppered her speech, and the nanny, deeply sensitive to such things, said that Sophia was preparing to leave. The nanny insisted that Karolina go away on vacation since the inexorable force with which the daughter wrestled with illness had frightened her weakened mother. Karolina allowed herself to be persuaded and found a temporary job as a counselor in a Pioneer camp.

On the eve of her departure, her mother had her open the secret drawer in the chest and take out the emerald necklace, the last treasure, the source of squabbling among the sisters. Obeying her mother, Karolina put it on; her mother watched as if she were getting ready for her first ball, and then turned away and quietly went to sleep. Karolina thought she could see her mother's dream, eternally present in the treacherous green stones: the restless waves of the Sea of Japan, the *Emerald* tossed onto the rocks, the train traveling through Siberia—the entire chain of memory crystals. She removed the necklace and put it back in the drawer, frightened by her vision, her view into the forbidden.

Sophia died in the first days of the war. The nanny buried her, ordering them to put her maiden name on the gravestone— Uksusnikova—so that the gravediggers did not think they were burying a German woman named Schwerdt.

***

Kirill was brought up in the historical tradition that considered the war the beginning of a new era, "June twenty-second at exactly four o'clock." But Grandmother Karolina left no reminiscences of that day. At first he thought that she was simply shocked by the event. But then he figured that she remembered June 22 perfectly well, but she wanted to forget, because with the first shots at the border she lost all her relatives: she never saw any of them again, and there were no graves.

Captain Gleb Schwerdt would certainly have been recalled from the front like most of the soldiers and officers of German ancestry when Soviet Germans were declared traitors in August 1941, when the Republic of Volga Germans was abolished and all its residents, like Germans from other areas, were deported.

He would have been recalled, but not in time, for the artillery unit in which he served destroyed its weapons as it retreated so they would not fall into enemy hands, and it was re-formed and sent to defend the Kiev fortified district. By late August, the Germans had crossed the Dnieper above and below Kiev, attacking from the rear—an encirclement many did not survive, including Captain Schwerdt.

Major Boris Morozov fought in the Finnish War, since he served in the Leningrad Military Okrug, and he fought successfully, he laid a frozen causeway on the lake ice where tanks were not expected to pass and came out behind the fortified Finnish position that could not be taken head on; he received a decoration and promotion and was sent to train on new KV breakthrough tanks, manufactured at the Kirov Factory in Leningrad.

He was lucky, but the fear associated with that luck was growing. Unconsciously he expected life or God to punish him for denying his father—but nothing happened, as if he were under a spell. He was also tormented by the fact that his brother Gleb had not been thrown out of the army but was never promoted in rank; perhaps he needn't have even denounced his father at all. He talked about this with his sister Antonina; she continued to stay in touch with him secretly because she loved him.

As far as Kirill could judge, Antonina acted first. Intelligent, dynamic, but in a certain sense blind, devoid of instinct about fate, she decided she would not allow the family to be separated again as it had been during the Civil War. The last time, she reasoned, the brothers and sisters were scattered, separated from their parents, and the family suffered through years of wandering; now, having learned their lesson, they had to act differently.

Tonya, using her husband's influence, tried to gather everyone who was not going to go to war. Her sisters Ulyana and Karolina, Boris's wife, Marina, and his two daughters. She managed to do it, in the midst of the chaos and panic of the early months of the war; Karolina was the only one she missed.

At the end of May, Karolina had gone to work at a Pioneer camp near Minsk, and she was evacuated with the camp; the mysteries of administrative planning sent the train carrying the children to Smolensk, then aimed it toward Rostov, and then to Yaroslavl.

No one was prepared to take in an evacuated Pioneer camp, no one could explain why the children were there, yet someone's will pushed the train farther, changing engines and crews, using up coal and water and food. Some of the Pioneers must have been children of commanders and Party bigwigs and now—even at a distance—the powerful parental hand tried to move the train as far as possible from the front.

In the meantime Antonina had gotten everyone together and found them a space to live and a bit of bread. Kirill tried to imagine what resources were needed to do that; he guessed that her husband must have been more than a chemistry professor and had worked on some special state project controlled by the NKVD; what happened later confirmed his hypothesis.

Antonina was certain that they would not give up Leningrad. Her husband, who was better informed than most, explained the same thing to her: defense plants, the naval base, the communications center; it would be hard but better to be together in a big city where there is food and medicine, paychecks, connections, and special rations; the husband could not have been thrilled to have a pack of relatives land on him, but he did not berate Tonya.

Even when the blockade circle closed in early September, Tonya still had hopes of finding Karolina, certain that Russia would break through the circle quickly, and get her to come to Leningrad.

There was talk that people should flee the city, but her husband's institute was working away, handing out special rations, and they stockpiled food for later; however, Boris's wife and Ulyana were mobilized to dig trenches, they came home late at night, numb with exhaustion, and all they got during work was bread and hot water.

Kirill knew that many enterprises were moved before the blockade. He wondered whether the secret institute was not evacuated due to an oversight, or simply because it was not a priority?

Or did it all depend on more than orders from the center but also on the individual directors, which of them had greater power, who got along better with the big bosses, who could put pressure on Moscow; and the window of opportunity was small in terms of time and tonnage for everyone to squeeze in.

Ration cards were introduced. The Badayev Warehouses burned down under German bombs. The daily ration of bread for dependents and children was cut to two hundred grams, but Tonya's husband got food at the special distribution centers and they could continue stockpiling flour for later.

One evening Tonya's husband did not come home from work. She thought he had been arrested. But in the morning she learned at the institute that people came from the NKVD with orders to evacuate several particularly valuable experts; they were convoyed out of the building and taken to the airport and a waiting plane.

Grandmother Karolina met with Tonya's former husband after the war; he found her, traveled from Novosibirsk to see her. He already had a second family, years had passed, but still couldn't look her in the eye and his hands shook.

He told her they were forcibly taken. The guards warned them that an attempt to avoid evacuation would be commensurate to joining the enemy side. The six of them were flown in the bomb bay of an airplane, given boots and padded jackets to keep from freezing, then taken by train, also under guard, all in one compartment, East, beyond the Volga, beyond the Urals, to Central Asia.

The head of the convoy promised that their families would come out on the next flight, and if there were delays, they would receive their husbands' rations. But all six men knew there would be no flight, no food parcels; but they still hoped that wherever they were going, that secret somewhere, they would find the levers to bring out their families, they would find the right people to ask, write a letter to the people's commissar, call the deputy minister…

They did call and write, they tried to get more information, help; in December one of the six men hanged himself; he never even received a form letter telling him his inquiries had been received and his questions would be looked into.

Grandmother did not tell Tonya's ex-husband that the day after he was taken out of Leningrad, Tonya started keeping a diary. It survived: Tonya's friend, the last person to have seen her alive, saved it.

Kirill could not read it. He would open it, scan a few lines, a few paragraphs, and then hastily shut the worn oilcloth cover.

Kirill could listen endlessly to Shostakovich's powerful Seventh Symphony, conducted by Mravinsky. But one look at the handwriting of Tonya—who was suffering from starvation-induced edema—the degenerating letters growing larger, the crooked lines, written almost blind in the dark, drained him.

Tonya was crushed by her husband's disappearance. She had brought them all together under his protection.

Hoping to instill faith in the others, she rushed to find a way to evacuate or to obtain parcels, work, hope. She called, wrote, ran, waited in doorways, tricked her way into meetings, begged, threatened—all for nothing.

Kirill felt that this burst of activity had probably reduced Tonya's already weak prospects for the future. People don't like those who refuse to suffer in silence and who strive for salvation; afterward, in the hungry winter, when life and death depended on a calorie and a gram, Tonya was shortchanged a tiny portion, a crust, a particle of sugar, a dot of fat for she had shown her will to live too soon, had not hidden it.

Of course, the embittered and starving people began recalling that Antonina was a German, that her sister Ulyana was German, and nobody remembered that they were only half-German. The German army surrounded Leningrad, German bombs fell on the city, shells exploded on the streets, and the enemy name Schwerdt could inflame sudden hatred in a queue or the crowd at a bus stop.

Kirill did not know how to weigh all this, if it was provable, but he knew that if Tonya had been Russian, she would have survived, or at least had a better chance; being German was not a final sentence, but it pushed people toward death.

The first to break was Marina. In the summer she had wanted to be in Leningrad, she liked the possibility of remaining there, digging in; now she made it sound as if Tonya had brought her to the city against her will.

There was no communication with Boris. The summer letter with news went to his unit's old address, to a town long held by Germans; the unit itself no longer existed. But Marina was sure that Boris was alive, and she imagined that he was sending letters and money orders to where they lived before; their old place was outside the blockade ring, on Soviet territory. In morbid detail she described the imagined parcels: how much grain there was, what canned goods, how hard was the sugar in the tongs. Tonya did not get into squabbles; she still believed that her husband would find a way to get them, and she was counting on the food she had stored away; she calculated it would last about six months.

Tonya and Marina and the whole family were still living in a Soviet country, in a familiar city, albeit a besieged one. Tonya remembered the revolution in Petrograd, the hunger, the shootouts in the streets, the robberies; now it seemed that the Soviet regime was solidly in place. But there were people in the city who understood that the cold and hunger would attack every house, every source of heat, and the time would come, it was already approaching, when the regime would lose control of the streets.

They came at night, four men in police uniform. Tonya was the only one who was sure they weren't policemen, she didn't want to open the door, she shouted to her neighbors—a military man lived across the hall, he had a gun—but no one interfered.

Someone had told the "policemen" about them. Tonya had not said anything for a long time about storing food, that she had sugar, buckwheat groats, rice, and flour under the bed. But in late summer before the blockade she had generously told friends about her reserves and promised to help if things got bad.

The men said they had orders to search all Germans and confiscate valuables; any resistance meant being shot on the spot. The bandits saw whose food they were taking: two girls and three women. Tonya and Marina begged them to leave a little, some flour, some grain, some salt; the robbers wiped them out, taking everything; you Germans, let your people feed you, they're stationed not far from here.

Kirill supposed that if they had been robbing Russians they might have left a small bit behind for women and children, but Germans were not supposed to get anything.

When she was over the shock, Marina started screaming that it was all their fault, the Germans, damn them; her howling was crass, her accusation vile; but this offensive scandal was better than silence; it was at least a sign of life.

A day after the robbery the rations were cut in half; the bandits must have known it was coming. Antonina went to her acquaintances but came back with very little; an old friend, Olga, daughter of a tsarist fortification officer, gave her some condensed milk, powdered eggs, and a promise of more; she was selling off her family valuables little by little to a receiver. If not for him, she would have been killed, and this way she got a little money. The emerald necklace could have saved the family, but it was in Moscow with Karolina. Tonya had sold her diamond earrings when their father was arrested.

The first to die was Marina's younger daughter. Tonya suspected that Marina intentionally gave bigger portions to the older girl, having decided which one would live and which would die.

They could no longer bury the child; they left the body wrapped in an old sheet closer to the central streets where they were still picking up corpses. Tonya no longer had the strength to go to work to get ration cards.

Ulyana died. They got their water from a burst pipe deep underground; layers of ice formed around the source, and Ulyana slipped, broke her leg, and froze trying to crawl home.

Tonya remained with Marina and her older daughter. Tonya had the first attacks of starvation madness: she thought that Marina was not feeding but fattening up her daughter; they were finding bodies with sliced off flesh on the streets. Tonya used to think of Marina as younger, but realized they were peers; Marina had spent the Civil War not in the city like Antonina, but in the country, where the hunger was more horrible, where they dug up cattle graves, where they baked human flesh; Tonya thought that of the two of them, Marina would survive.

Later, at New Year's, Olga kept her promise. She brought Tonya a hefty chunk of pork fat back: unimaginable, not a delicacy, not food, but life itself—two or three weeks, maybe a month of life. Olga had traded a family icon ornamented with freshwater pearls for the *salo*. The old receiver now paid with the clay-filled bread from rations and drove a hard bargain; he would not have cared about the icon, taken it for a trifle, for a handful of burned sugar mixed with dirt from the Badayev Warehouses, but only Olga knew that the old man was not what he pretended to be. He was an officer who had served with Alexander Kolchak in counterintelligence, he robbed the interrogation victims and grew rich on their valuables. Her father had revealed the secret to her, after he'd recognized the man during the NEP years when he went to him to sell his old medals.

The *salo* vanished. Tonya thought Marina had stolen and hidden it. In the icy house where hard snow fell in the neighboring apartments, because the walls and roof had been destroyed by a nearby bomb, the two women fought on the floor, Marina whispered that she had not taken it, Tonya choked the suspected thief, then Marina gained the upper hand and started choking Tonya. Neither could kill the other, they were too weak.

Hidden in the cellar, far from her mother and aunt, Marina's daughter ate the *salo*. She was dying of a bowel obstruction but kept eating.

Her death took away even the hatred that had connected Antonina with Marina. Sometimes Marina looked at Tonya with a strange wordless affection, as if seeing herself in a mirror and wondering why she looked unfamiliar.

Olga promised to drop in in early February. She was not as emaciated as Tonya, but lived far away, and getting from one end of the city to the other across the Neva was comparable to a North Pole expedition on foot. Tonya started counting the days in her diary until Olga's visit. It was the only thing she wrote.

Marina died on January 24. It seems Tonya no longer had the strength to drag her out of the room.

When Olga came, Tonya was dead. She must have believed that Olga would come on the first day of February, and when the day was over, she died. Olga dragged both bodies downstairs, hoping to return and with someone's help take them to the cemetery. She took the diary, but then was bed-ridden for she had nothing else to offer the buyer, and did not return to Tonya's house until spring.

The bodies were gone. Tonya's apartment had been ransacked and emptied. By the end of the war, the building was gone, declared unsalvageable and demolished. No one knew whether Tonya and the others had been buried in a common grave, thrown into the Neva, sealed in the cellar, or had fallen under a knife or saw, their flesh stolen for the calories.

Kirill could not remember what he had known as a child about the death of his grandmother's sisters. Grandmother Karolina had tiny, stamp-sized photos of Tonya and Ulyana hanging on her wall. Their photo albums had been burned for heat in December in blockaded Leningrad, and Karolina had only these photos of them, which were easily overlooked among the bigger portraits.

Kirill learned that among the dead there are those who get the lion's share of remembrance and those who are remembered only secondarily.

The sisters did not even have a line on the common headstone. Their disappearance without a trace gave Grandmother Karolina the terrible rights of an executor: how they were to be remembered. Had there been a monument, had the letters

SCHWERDT been incised in stone, Karolina Schwerdt would not have been able to turn into Lina Vesnyanskaya.

***

*I*n mid-September, when the command of the Soviet troops near Kiev was falling apart completely, Gleb Schwerdt was captured. His German dossier stated that he had been concussed and caught in the battlefield; the Soviet file stated that he had joined the enemy side voluntarily and taken several soldiers with him. Kirill thought that the German documents were probably more truthful: at that moment, Gleb was more likely to obey fate than consciously switch sides.

In the POW camp he became an interpreter, thanks to his childhood German lessons—both dossiers agreed on this. A low rank, captain, not a member of the Party, half-German, *Volksdeutscher*, his father arrested by the Soviets: the ideal portrait of a collaborator. The Soviet document said that Gleb began reporting on his former comrades, there in the camp; the German document delicately avoided that question, but Kirill guessed that the Soviet dossier was probably right: it would be strange to assume that the interpreter was not required to keep an eye on the other POWs. Of course, no one could say what exactly Gleb told them, whom he saved, whom he turned in, or even whether the camp guards had time for operative work. Kirill thought that Gleb might have worked as an interpreter because there was no one else and life had to be organized, food delivered, the wounded tended to.

As an interpreter, Gleb lived through the winter of 1941–1942 in the camps, when most POWs died of hunger and cold. In the spring of 1942 emissaries started looking in the camps for personnel for the Russian National People's Army (RNNA),

the predecessor of General Andrei Vlasov's Russian Liberation
Army, which collaborated with the German command against
Communist Russia. Gleb was given the rank of corporal and
once again put on the Soviet uniform (captured by the Germans) with new tricolor cockades and shoulder boards.

"I have a burning desire to avenge my father, killed by the
Bolsheviks," he wrote in the German questionnaire.

To avenge Arseny. Kirill realized to his surprise that he himself had no desire for vengeance, as if for him, born much later,
everything that happened to his great-grandfather was like a
natural cataclysm, not subject to the laws of revenge. Gleb's sen-
timent frightened Kirill not so much because he went to work
for the Nazis but by the intention, the confession of readiness to
commit murder.

Gleb's service did not last long. The RNNA fought the partisans, and often the soldiers went off into the woods. One major
operation called for RNNA units to take the commander of the
Soviet paratroopers. But instead, several dozen soldiers joined
the partisans. German counterintelligence suspected Gleb, who
was in charge of a platoon, of treason, that he was a Soviet spy
who took the name of the real Gleb Schwerdt; after being tortured and interrogated, he was shot.

The German dossier noted that Gleb had admitted that he
was not Gleb Schwerdt, that he was an agent left behind when
the Soviets retreated, so that he could penetrate the occupation
administration. The Soviet dossier said that Gleb had compromised the real Soviet agent in the RNNA who was giving the
Germans false clues. Kirill felt that Gleb had been affected by the
reverse stigma: in the 1930s he could have been arrested by the
Russians as a German spy, but he was executed by the Germans
as a Russian spy; the name Schwerdt saved him when he was a
POW and then destroyed him.

At first, Boris had better luck: in June he was in the Urals at a tank factory, in charge of receiving new machines, and avoided the border areas where his unit was demolished. He was not kicked out of the army because he denied his German father at the Party meeting.

But then luck abandoned him. He was a good officer, but the war, which had gone so well for him, was now giving him trouble: his tanks would be bombed as they were being unloaded from a train, or a bridge tested by sappers would break beneath the tanks, or the tanks he obtained would be from a faulty lot, where the recoil would damage the turret, but that would only become evident under enemy fire. He acquired the reputation of an unlucky commander.

The telegram informing him that his wife and children were going to Leningrad was sent to the old address of his unit. When Boris realized that his wife had left home, he telegrammed Antonina, asking if Marina and the girls were with her. But the reply from Leningrad did not reach him; the army was retreating too fast, the weakened units dissipated, changed numbers.

Boris had betrayed his father for the sake of his wife and children, and now they had vanished as abruptly as Arseny. The whole bloody state, to which he had sacrificed his father, was shaken; the fronts collapsed, local draftees were hiding, Soviet officials ran to the east—he must have seen Party and NKVD bosses hastily evacuated, loading official cars with personal property, the people Boris had feared in 1937. He must have had the feeling, Kirill thought, that he had not betrayed his father because the regime was horrifying and the circumstances were cruel, but simply for the sake of it.

Boris must have started a journal around that time, which soldiers and officers were not allowed to do; Kirill saw excerpts from it in the file. There were no military secrets, only doubts that the interrogators characterized as defeatist moods; there was the underlying question of how it was possible for the Germans to be at Moscow's gates. Was it because the Soviet regime, which tortured its people, opened the path for them?

The file also had reports from an informant, one of Boris's subordinates. Reading them, Kirill thought of Lieutenant Kolakovsky and his part in the Myasoedov case: yet again the family crossed paths with this kind of man, a genius of denunciation, an inspired swindler who could create a complex and massive lie using the ideological mindset, and come out looking as though he—the snitch—had exposed a conspiracy responsible for grave damage.

The informant had probably served with Boris back in the 1930s. And therefore he knew what Boris did not advertise: that he was a Schwerdt and not a Morozov.

Boris might have held up his promotion or chewed him out in front of the formation, and the soldier, whose name was hidden under the pseudonym Ermak, compiled a report for the special section of the brigade.

Ermak wrote that in 1937 he had believed like everyone else, like their superiors, that Major Schwerdt had sincerely denounced his father, a traitor of the Homeland, a former German agent; as Comrade Stalin teaches, a son is not responsible for his father. But now, once again under the command of Schwerdt-Morozov, he suspected that the denunciation was false, the trick of a spy so determined in his hatred of the Soviet regime that he was prepared to break family ties, change his name, just to sabotage the land of the Soviets.

At the start of the report, Ermak called him "Schwerdt-Morozov," but on the second page, just "Schwerdt." Even Kirill felt that the two words "Major Schwerdt" created the image of a German agent, an officer of the Abwehr. The name itself implicated Boris, and that was more than enough.

Ermak had no other proof. Except for the fact that Boris went with an orderly to the neutral zone at night and returned toward morning. There was a shot-up German tank there and Boris was studying it to learn its weak points in battle. He went at night because the Germans shot at the tank during the day. But Ermak wrote that Boris had a sort of mailbox in the tank, and once the soldiers saw him come back with papers written in German, a pack of typed pages, and read them in the trench. Boris testified at the investigation that the pack of papers was a technical manual he'd found in the tank, but it was too late.

Ermak also added that he considered the whole Schwerdt family, for Boris had talked about his brothers and sisters, a spy nest, for despite his false denial of his father, Boris continued getting clandestine letters from his sister Antonina, who worked in some secret enterprise in Leningrad and was probably giving him information.

Kirill knew that even if Boris had a high-up patron, no one would dare not act on a denunciation like that. But they didn't arrest him right away, either because they didn't believe Ermak totally, sensing a lie, or because they decided to find all his connections first.

Boris was allowed to fight for another two weeks. He learned that his wife and children were in besieged Leningrad. And his army, the 2nd Shock Army, was headed for Leningrad to break through the blockade!

Boris lost his head and phoned a friend at headquarters to ask about the general plan of the operation, which unit would play what role—hoping to be first to reach the city. The staff officer reported the strange request that violated the chain of command and secrecy; the intelligence people decided that Ermak's report was fully credible and that the German agent Schwerdt was trying to learn highly important military plans.

The final nail in the coffin was a report from the partisans that former Red Army commander Gleb Schwerdt, considered missing in action in September 1941, was discovered in the RNNA as a platoon commander.

So a brother avenged his brother, thought Kirill; for Gleb must have known what would happen to his family if the Soviet authorities learned he was in the RNNA. Did he hope the Germans would win quickly? That his service would remain a secret? Or did he want to sentence his brothers and sisters to death for continuing to live, eat, drink, marry, and have children after their father's arrest?

Boris was arrested and removed to the rear. There was no evidence except his ill-starred name, the stupid inquiry, and his brother's service in the RNNA. There was a chance—one in twenty—the tribunal would have simply demoted him to private instead of sentencing him to death.

But mid-March the Germans counterattacked, and soon the 2nd Shock Army was ensnared. Someone had to answer for the sudden German blow that ruined their attack. Now Major Schwerdt's story was seen in a completely different light; they worked him over so that in two days Boris was ready to confess that he was an Abwehr agent, and his brother Gleb was an Abwehr agent, and his father was also an Abwehr agent. The intelligence people were in a hurry, for they might have been asked how they missed an enemy spy under their noses, and so Boris was shot without delay.

The Myasoedov story came back to the family as a grim ghost, as if back in 1915 the fate of the boy Boris had already been written down to the last letter and had been shown to his parents in the mirror of someone else's drama: look.

Or—the death of a universally calumniated colonel, made the scapegoat for the generals' mistakes, cold-bloodedly sentenced to the noose by a court that knew his innocence amidst the rejoicing in the press and the cries "Hang him!" and then subjected to such defamation after the execution that people were ashamed of the name Myasoedov and hurried to change it. The death of one innocent man became a black funnel that pulled in all of Russia, applauding that death (the way France was almost pulled down to the bottom of shame by the Dreyfus case). Everything that later happened to the country, arrests without trials, mass killings, was just a multifaced reflection of an ancient drama that grew, like a poisoned seed, in the fate of those who applauded and even those who were simply alive then, barely born.

Boris was executed by firing squad in the days when the few remaining tanks of his division were trying to break through the "corridors" to the surrounded Soviet troops, while the German counterattacks from the flanks once again closed those loopholes, narrow strips of swampy land where the soil had already sensed the coming warmth.

Kirill traveled to the place of his execution, a small train station where now peat was extracted. They said that they sometimes found bodies in the peat, the dead of 1942, uncorrupted, sunken in the unfreezing depths.

Everything was low there, the buildings, the platform, the station, so that the old water tower seemed tall, although it would have been lost at a big station. Kirill imagined that they shot people at the water tower: you had to shoot near something, connect death to a target, a sign that meant the end and took some of the responsibility from the guards as if this were the measure allotted the dead man—to live to this point and no further, and the one who pulled the trigger was only following the lines marked by fate.

Kirill looked at the scrubby grass, the dappled tracks of bicycle tires in the dust, and thought how Grandmother Karolina, such a cherished and indispensable force in his life, could easily have been turned into this unsightly dust and brittle earth, in which shards of broken bottles glistened. The secret services could have started an investigation of the other family members, based on Ermak's report. But the remaining Schwerdts had already died in Leningrad, and she, the only survivor, was stuck in evacuation. The case was closed for good, and she lived. If they had found Karolina, there would have been yet another dusty station, a water tower pockmarked by time or bullets and sunbeams on the green bottle glass.

Then Kirill went to the Vitebsk Oblast, to Osintorf, yet more swamps and peat works, where Gleb had been executed. The tidy rotting of swamps, scattered trees, dry switches of reeds drearily rustling in the wind.

In Osintorf, Kirill remembered the German Cemetery and his guess that so many dead were missing from family mausoleums and graves: families destroyed, surviving descendants scattered around the world. The old monument on Balthasar's grave, the limestone altar with the stone book, now seemed like a lighthouse, a sign known to all the dead in his line, in his family. Grandmother Karolina went to the German Cemetery the way people visit places where they saw someone for the last time. She had been spared the blockade, had lived through the war, was called in as a military interpreter, getting her job and measure of food thanks to the dangerous Schwerdt legacy, the German language, and then she waited endlessly at Balthasar's grave for the ones who had been killed by that same legacy.

* * *

*N*ow Kirill returned his thoughts to the German Cemetery: what role it had played in his topography of Moscow, how it had been connected to other places, to the houses of his family.

They walked to the cemetery but rode back, leaving by the other exit, on the trolley. Always, as if it were an immutable law of the universe.

As a child, Kirill had liked the Moscow trolleys. The black stone of the old cobbles showed between the rails, they traveled unknown streets where in the autumn drizzle or winter snows the lights burned sweetly and tearfully in the building windows, teapot-shaped churches flew by, old women shuffled on a store's slippery porch, where a mangy poodle was tied up, called Totoshka or Froufrou, afraid of the local yard dogs and whining at the sharp scent of their urine.

They rode past the pocked snow, icicles on the roof, the signs that read SPORTING GOODS—OCEAN—BARBER—POST OFFICE—VEGETABLES—*GASTRONOM*—APPLI-ANCES—the red *M* at the Metro entrance—GLORY CPSU on a rooftop—MILK—another *GASTRONOM*—MEAT—RUBBER TECHNICAL FACTORY—CINEMA—into the darkness where there was more light in the puddles than in the streetlights, where resin from the discarded holiday trees and dried tangerine peel scented the air.

The trip from the cemetery was special. They didn't go home, but in the other direction, to another Moscow; it seemed so far, not seven stops, but seven meridians, which he liked to count on the old-fashioned globe that showed mountains in relief, oceans with a blue glaze, a caravan of camels strode across the Arabian Desert, reindeer pulled a dogsled in the Siberian tundra, and a sperm whale sent up a spume in the Pacific Ocean; the globe on a bronze turtle pedestal stood in the apartment of Grandmother Karolina and Grandfather Konstantin.

When Kirill was little, he perceived Grandfather Konstantin the way Arseny had seen Balthasar; Kirill thought his grandfather was a mysterious wizard. His apartment was full of marvelous objects like ones Kirill had seen in a museum; no one ever said where they came from, as if they had appeared at the wave of a magic wand.

It was only in ninth grade after a conversation with a friend whose grandfather was a retired general that Kirill understood where Grandfather Konstantin got his mysterious "inheritance."

In his own way, he was a follower of Prince Uryatinsky. The mad grandee imported dwarves, magicians, aphrodisiacs, surveyors, engineers, and agronomists from Europe; Konstantin's colleagues brought back specialists—rocket scientists, designers, chemists, physicists, atomic experts from Germany; Konstantin brought trophy art for Soviet grandees.

Grandfather Konstantin was part of a special army that followed on the heels of the fighting troops; they were armed with sealing wax and seals and shopping lists—the Chief Administration for War Spoils of the Red Army. On battlefields they picked up damaged hardware that could be repaired or melted down; they expropriated reserves of strategic materials, disassembled factories; in the Ore Mountains, special units of the NKVD were in the closed zones around the uranium mines. The ancient castles, libraries, galleries, museums, mansions, and churches were scoured by art historians in civilian clothes, who took away paintings, sculptures, manuscripts, books, altars, and jewels. Grandfather Konstantin was one of them.

Called up from the reserves in the fall of 1941, he served as an interpreter in frontline headquarters, or at least, that was the story he told, and in late 1944, when the Soviet army reached European borders, Grandfather Konstantin got a new assignment. Kirill thought he had initiated the move, had suggested it to someone who had enough military power to make it happen.

Behind the Soviet frontlines in Germany there were hundreds of organizations, thousands of groups with the most varied mandates (Konstantin told him that even the Moscow union yacht club sent people who brought back a trainload of sail boats from the imperial yacht club in Bremerhaven). In that chaos and the general scramble for booty, a determined and qualified man who knew how to recognize a master's brush, the age of the canvas, the value of decorative objects could make a fortune, as long as there were relatively reliable documents, transportation, a dozen loyal soldiers, and the ability to bring the things to the USSR. During the Civil War, the Red commanders had traveled with truckloads of plundered goods, dined on stolen family dishes; the same thing was repeated in Germany.

Naturally, his grandfather did not go into these details; he avoided the question of where he had served and under whose command in the last months of the war.

Kirill understood that at first his grandfather did not have the rank to trophy hunt on his own or to seek out a very high patron. The most he could have had was the unspoken support of a corps or army commander: a pass, five men with machine guns from the commander's personal guard, a truck, and access to the quartermasters.

However, Konstantin's postwar circle of friends, his connections, and his apartment spoke of a different level of marauding. Yet he could not have skipped over the rungs of the Soviet hierarchy.

Kirill solved the puzzle.

There was one man with whom Konstantin was servile and submissive.

As a child Kirill had often visited his grandfather, lived at his house on holidays, and when important guests visited, Konstantin invited him to join the table, carefully building his grandson's future, introducing him into his circle from early on.

But once in a while his grandfather asked him not to come into the living room and go play in another room. He even let him touch the rare toy soldiers, prerevolutionary, made especially for a rich family's son: they were once numerous enough to populate the entire Battle of Borodino. But during the Civil War—as if they had died in the wrong war—the Life Guards Chasseurs, the Pavlov Grenadiers, the Akhtyr Hussars, the French Old Guard, and the artillerymen and their cannons were lost. Some regiments and brigades were lost completely, others had only two or three tin figures left. Konstantin spent decades finding the soldiers with the recognizable maker's stamp and spared no expense. That he would let Kirill play with the Borodino soldiers, a gesture far too extravagant, showed he was afraid of his guest and had lost his usual sense of proportion.

Kirill peeked through the keyhole, for he was worried by this strange guest, who knew how to remain unseen; he always stood so that someone or something blocked Kirill's view of him.

His grandfather had other nondescript visitors: antiques dealers. But the special guest was not one of them: he was a dark shadow hanging over other people. One time Kirill saw his face, which seemed strangely familiar. He recognized the unknown guest—he had always been close, right in the house.

An antique clock under an oval glass dome stood on Konstantin's wide desk. The clock showed a crevasse; silver hunting dogs raced down the bronze slopes after golden, slender-legged deer; none of the dogs could catch a victim. But up on top, on the flat peak, stood a golden hunter in a kaftan and tricorn hat. In his lowered left hand he held a hunting horn and in his raised right hand, a dead silver bird.

Grandfather Konstantin had bought the clock three years after Kirill had experienced the most profound fright of his life, watching the mad Sergeant killing geese. His grandfather showed him the clock proudly; at noon and at midnight the hunt began, the hand with the bird went down and the hunter raised the horn and blew into it.

Kirill froze when he saw it, but his grandfather thought he was amazed by the marvels of the mechanism. He was afraid to approach the clock, he thought the hunter was watching him and knew what had happened at the dacha; when the strange guest showed his face once, Kirill recognized him: it was the face of the triumphant bronze hunter in the clock. He imagined it in every piece of glass in the house: the glass door of the buffet, pitchers, bottles, glasses. Sergeant, Guest, and Hunter were merged into a single figure, and Kirill was astonished that his grandfather did not understand, did not see, whom he had set upon his desk, who kept looking at him with a dead goose in his hand.

Decades later, Kirill recognized his grandfather's visitor a second time, when he found a photo of him in a history of the secret services of the USSR. A major and then lieutenant colonel of state security who had served in counterintelligence in the war, then colonel, major general, who survived all the purges and infighting; he left the system only after Serov, who was head of the KGB, was fired.

That's when Kirill figured out what had happened to Grandfather Konstantin in 1945 and how he had skipped all those rungs on the career ladder. Someone noticed his small group, and military counterintelligence arrested him. When he told them what we has doing, Konstantin was taken away from his previous patron and given more power, more men, and put to work for a new boss.

That's when he met Grandmother Karolina: she was assigned to the unit, interpreter Schwerdt, half-German, daughter of an enemy of the people, sister of a deserter; she owed her life to the security organs and therefore she would keep quiet. She had probably been hired explicitly for such work; otherwise Kirill could not explain how she ended up as a military interpreter with her background, even if she didn't work at the frontlines.

Kirill understood why Karolina had married Konstantin. By the standards of the day, she was an old maid, she had lost her entire family, and now she got a new name and escaped the curse of the Schwerdts. By why did Konstantin marry the daughter of a prisoner and sister of an executed man?

Love? He didn't love her. Sometimes Kirill thought that as an antiquarian, he took her, a formerly upper class woman who was like an object from the past, into his collection of antiques, the most valuable piece in his assemblage; her presence in the house, her role as hostess brought the antiques to life.

Candelabra and silver tray, inkwell and pen, fan and Chinese box, marble paperweight and coffee pot, grandfather clock and painting by a lesser Dutch artist—having been born among them, she connected them all into a microcosm of a home, into a hierarchy of places and functions; she turned a dead collection into an inhabited world. Her manners, speech, and style set the basic tone of the things and did not allow them to degrade or forget their provenance. And Konstantin, who had risen in social strata, a city dweller only in the third generation—his great-grandfather had been a fisherman on Lake Chudskoye who sent his son to Moscow to sell fish—had been taught by an old professor and before the revolution as a gymnasium student had seen literary salons and the mansions where members of high society consorted, their doors closed to him—and he received daily lessons in aristocratic domesticity from his wife.

Kirill thought, but there were so many previously upper class people in the Soviet Union. Konstantin could have even found a baroness, duchess, or princess, who had nothing left but their noble family name. In 1945, Grandfather Konstantin did not yet have a house filled with antiques; he married Karolina—who became from that point Lina Vesnyanskaya—in September, the marriage registered by the military commander of Jena, in Germany.

Konstantin must have sensed something in Karolina. His patrons must have seemed like gods to him, comparable to the cruel gods of Egypt or Mesopotamia, with heads of eagles, jackals, crocodiles, lions, dogs, and cats, guards of the dead and eaters of souls. Grandfather Konstantin selected the correct offerings among the German trophies to earn the infernal favor of the gods; but like medieval miners who took canaries into the shafts, he needed someone who would sense danger sooner than he would. That is why he chose Karolina.

***

*T*he grandparents left Germany in early 1946; the German government was back on its feet and marauders were more likely to be caught. Kirill asked himself, which Germany had they been in? A world of severed ties and displaced persons. Among ruins where "bombs destroyed not just a city but something fundamentally more important, that which kept things and their mission together," as Kirill read in a marvelous novel about postwar Berlin.

That is why Karolina, even if she had wanted to, would not have been able to find the German Schwerdts, who had corresponded with her great-aunts. The country was inhabited by refugees and ghosts of city dwellers, hiding in the ruins.

Grandfather Konstantin told him how one day, when there was still shooting in various parts of Berlin, in the parks and the U-Bahn, they were sent to examine some statues to see if they were worth requisitioning. They left on a foggy, rainy morning. He did not know Berlin or its monuments; the fog hid everything, their experienced driver drove through burned barricades and the gunners armed with submachine guns smoked plundered cigarettes in silence, hungover, and scornful of the civilian officer and his interpreter.

They reached the edge of a park, seared by fire, with nothing left but craters and shattered trees; the sergeant drove on. Suddenly they saw a vague figure; the gunners shot a long round into the fog, out of which came a response, either a shot or a ricochet; the commander ordered them to go around, and now the submachine guns were firing from the side, but the figure, all in sparks, did not fall.

The first ray of sunlight cut through the fog and they saw that they were shooting at a statue, a marble composer with a pile of music in his hands; Haydn was dead—four bullets in his belly, two in the right lung, one in the collarbone, one in the shoulder.

The sun dissolved the curtain of fog, and the Reichstag appeared nearby. It was in the center of Berlin, in the Tiergarten. The sergeant poked his finger in the statue's wounds, nodded at the gunners, good shooting, lads, and looked indifferently at Grandfather Konstantin in expectation of orders.

Thanks to that story, the Tiergarten was a kind of gateway into Kirill's Germany. When he first arrived in Berlin, he didn't know anything except the bullet holes in the marble coat made by the nameless soldier.

He headed straight for the Tiergarten and Haydn; it was late spring, the automatic sprinklers chirped, people sunbathed on lawns, and tourists took photos of themselves with costumed Allied soldiers at the Brandenburg Gate.

He could see the four bullet holes in the belly, two in the right lung, one in the collarbone, one in the shoulder from a distance—exactly as remembered by his grandfather, professionally attentive to detail and photographically recalling scratches and worn spots on antiques. Unwittingly, he repeated the sergeant's gesture, touching the wound in the stone; it was real.

He spent two days in the Tiergarten, wandering among the statues, studying the outline of long-ago battles.

A soldier in the Kaiser's army bidding farewell to his wife—bullets hit her dress and boots and broke off the right hand of the son, watching his father anxiously. An armless Hercules at the Reichstag, the body riddled with bullets. The gods of fertility, goddesses of crafts were to one side; only two or three bullets hit the pedestal, they were untouched. Two decapitated soldiers, a woman without a head and her chest torn open; there was an old man with a banner and next to him an officer in luxurious uniform killed by the sculptor's imagination, falling down—his legs were shot, and a bullet hit his chin, killing the dead man. Goethe in a cape scarred by shards. Cupid with a hole in the hip. A mourning angel with a new marble face to replace the smashed one; a Muse with a pasted-on dead mouth and a marble prosthesis for a shoulder. Beethoven shot in the chest. A wounded bronze Amazon on a wounded horse. A fingerless harpist. Wagner and his executed griffin.

Gods, corpses, maidens, heroes all bearing the mark of death, all dead twice.

The marble wounds, scrapes, cracks, holes, voids, and caverns turned into Braille for Kirill; it was the language of the past here, speaking of the losses, and he studied the language so that he could ask his questions.

Somewhere here in the Tiergarten in 1925 the former Minister of War Sukhomlinov, homeless, froze to death on a bench.

After being fired and arrested following the Myasoedov case, tried by the Provisional Government and amnestied, he moved to Germany.

Bronze stalkers trumpeted, and a dead hare dangled from a hunter's belt; in his raised hand a killed fox bared its teeth, biting its tongue, and the hounds, obeying the call of the trumpet, ran, faster than their breath—just as in Konstantin's clock, measuring the time of the hunt and death.

Kirill entered the spectral gates and came out on the other side, into German history.

***

*I*t turned out that there was a book about Thomas, Balthasar's father. His works and correspondence with his son were in the archives of medical departments. Kirill had not expected to find living German relatives; he thought that he was the only surviving piece of the family history. But the professor who wrote the book gave him his card, and the name on it was so familiar and yet unimaginable in the present time: Schwerdt.

The relatives were suspicious of his telephone call and thought Kirill was an elaborate prankster. But Kirill stubbornly recited names and dates and finally the man asked him to hold on; when he returned some ten minutes later, his voice was friendly, as if he had checked an encyclopedia that confirmed the existence of what Kirill had said.

Subsequently, Kirill saw what the man had used as a reference.

A gigantic sheet of paper, taller than a man, with a genea-logical tree drawn with ant-like scrupulousness: a real oak tree, roots going into the soil and branches penetrating the clouds, hiding a myriad of names and dates in the foliage. This was the

Schwerdt cosmos, a universe of relations, deaths, and births.

Balthasar's line broke off on the tree; there was a note with the number of his children. He took a risk, headed East as an apostle, was lost and forgotten.

The family was not taking revenge, no; there were too many christenings, birthdays, deaths, and marriages, and in the logic of genealogical bookkeeping, the hermit Balthasar was deemed unworthy of the right kind of remembrance, evidence of the practical benefit of family values and the subsequent need to stick together. Pharmacists, burgomasters, lawyers, doctors, officials, priests—they could have remembered Balthasar as a negative example, a lesson for children, but they did not remember him at all, not out of ill will but because the machinery of documentary memory, which seems impartial, also has a built-in mechanism of forgetting, with definite rules.

In Germany, at the request of Thomas's indomitable father, the renegade was forgotten; he became the legendary Grandfather Balthasar, the eccentric who went East a hundred years ago, or maybe two hundred, or maybe never existed at all.

Kirill brought a copy of the tree back to Russia; he had hopes of returning to the house near Munster, where the attic had trunks containing the family archive, similar to what Grandmother Karolina had left him: letters, tickets, newspaper clippings, certificates, including one for racial purity, photographs, postcards, school journals, medical reports—everything they had managed to take with them when they fled to the west from the approaching Soviet troops, to the Allied occupation zone.

Then he got a call asking him to visit a home for the aged in Berlin. The news of his strange and amazing appearance, which was recounted at family meetings, adding spice to evening conversations, repeating all the twists and turns of relationships, all the sluices of love and hate, finally reached the one fate had intended it for.

Now, Kirill could not believe that there was ever a time when he did not know this man. They saw each other briefly, but he, the Priest and Invalid Soldier in one, the alter ego of the Officer, Vladilen Ivanov, fit into Kirill's concept like the clincher in a plot's arc.

His name was Dietrich. He was the great-grandson of the middle brother, Bertold, who had remained in Leipzig when Balthasar and young Andreas went to Russia. Dietrich's grandfather, a physician for delicate female problems, had married well and moved to East Prussia, taking his wife's rich dowry. She was the daughter of a merchant, but their children wanted to become Junkers and tried to be more Prussian than the Prussians; Dietrich's father, Richard, became an army officer and his brother, Maximilian, served in the navy.

The twins were the same age as Arseny Schwerdt, about whom they knew very little, as he did of them, nevertheless their paths crossed, as if by fate.

Young Lieutenant Richard Schwerdt came to Africa, to Namibia, as part of Lieutenant General Lothar von Trotha's expeditionary corps; he fought the Herero and Nama and perhaps in late 1904 in the Angra Pequena harbor saw the battleship *Prince Suvorov* with the admiralty flag, where military doctor Arseny Schwerdt was serving; later the doomed Russian vessels were spotted by Maximilian, who was serving in Tsingtao where the German East Asian cruiser squadron was based.

Their destinies diverged, as if the ships had sideswiped; ten years later the war began and the three Schwerdts were on opposite sides. Arseny survived to die in 1937 as a German spy. Maximilian served on the cruiser *Leipzig*, a small reminder of his recent Prussian origins, and sank with the ship in the Falklands battle, when the German ships were attacked by the British battle cruisers. Richard died in the early days of the war; in Prussia his mounted patrol—officers out for reconnaissance —ran into a Cossack half squadron in the fog of morning.

The widow got a letter from Richard's friend in the same regiment, which described Richard's bravery, how the cavalrymen who accompanied him were killed, and how the Cossacks threw wounded Richard onto the ground and finished him off with spears. The letter was a family relic, a certificate of martyrdom: a semblance of Arseny Schwerdt's Borisoglebsk horror captured on paper.

Kirill was skeptical of the letter. One detail—that the Cossack patrol allegedly on secret reconnaissance in a forested area took along impractical and unnecessary spears that would catch on branches however you carried them—made him think this was a war legend, something like the story of the crucified Canadian soldier that entered the annals of British military propaganda.

Yes, Richard died in a skirmish with Cossacks who outnumbered their small patrol. But the image of riders with terrible spears piercing an unarmed man arose later, when the survivors told their tale, exaggerating the villainy of the foe in order to justify their flight. The officer friend who wrote to the widow—the Germans were retreating, losing battles—gave her this exaggerated, bloody version. He knew that Richard had a son and perhaps he intended this as a patriotic pedagogical lesson; the letter, preserved like a silvery hand of a martyr symbolically depicting the Lord's pointing finger, determined Dietrich's fate.

Richard's Prussian estate went to Poland along with the lands of the "Polish corridor"; mother and son had to stay with relatives, without money or a past. There began the path that first made Dietrich a priest, since his patron was a priest, and later

Dietrich became a field chaplain of the Wehrmacht because, despite the spirit and letter of Christianity, he wanted to avenge his father, killed by the Russians.

Kirill visited the place where the estate had been. It was a grim hilly area, where black peat streams flowed down to the sea, powering water mills, while the wind from the sea powered windmills in the opposite direction. Pagan dolmens that recalled stone knives and blood stood in the deep woods, deer drank at the springs, vultures slept in the trees, and foxes taught their young to catch mice in the yellow fields. Every village had an enormous stone barn; they could hold the entire world and still have room for the harvest. The moss-covered houses bore the year of their construction—1905, 1923, 1934 ... The abandoned old cemeteries at the crossroads of country lanes held the dead from the Franco-Prussian war, and the porcelain plates with photographs and gold Gothic inscriptions looked as if they came from family dinner services. Tall hunting blinds were scattered along the edges of the tilled fields and the oak-lined slopes of ravines to shoot deer in the seeded fields or boars digging for acorns.

On a smooth sunny day that rippled the wheat fields, Kirill felt a strange dark shadow in the air; his imagination connected the hunting towers with barbed wire stretched from pole to pole, creating a concentration camp, the concept of it, just as it had appeared in someone's mind many years ago. He understood the nearness of evil, how it is aroused by a single thought, a leap of the imagination—the important thing was to have the intention already there. This seemed to be a way to show him Dietrich's grim transformation into a new crusader, because Dietrich never spoke of his past.

He had no close relatives. His nieces and second cousins knew that he had been a chaplain, had been part of the expedition to the East, was captured at Stalingrad, and then returned to Germany and served the Church.

Kirill hoped he would get a detailed autobiographical narrative from Dietrich—he had sketched it out for himself: the 1920s, poverty, Catholic school, authoritarian grandfather, desire to avenge his father, the memory of exile from his family home, Horst Wessel, 1933, *Mein Kampf*, Lebensraum, occupation of the Rhine Demilitarized Zone; the scratchy newsreel showed the T-1 tanks, wobbling, almost toy-like machines with bulletproofing and matchstick guns, scurrying larvae of the future Panzertruppen; they would turn into General Guderian's roaring, mobile, biting beetles, which by the end of the war had turned into the T-V and T-VI armored monsters …

Kirill wrote this draft of Dietrich's life from an outline of clichés, commonplace images, presupposing that another's life was like a weathervane blown by the winds of the era; instead, he got a story that was like a thawing block of ice that dissolved into murky water, revealing a new apostle who had headed East.

***

*T*he retirement home was next door to a laundry. Kirill looked through the windows at the washing machines tumbling the gray piles of linens: sheets, pillowcases, blanket covers, towels, and curtains. This concerted movement of dozens of drums made Kirill think not of household maintenance but the desire to whitewash, bleach life, remove its stains, and present it as innocent, white as white could be, remembering nothing.

The nurse met him on the main floor and led him to the room; "Herr Schwerdt, you have a visitor." Kirill stared at the door, a tall white door with a decorative bronze knob; unremarkable to others, it was the door between two worlds for him.

He entered. The room was extremely white—you could go crazy in such whiteness that eliminated shadows, nuances, an emasculated whiteness, a whiteness that meant the death of all other colors.

At the window, with a view of the garden, fir branches touching the glass, an old man lay in a tall bed. Kirill recognized him from the photographs of Great-Grandfather Arseny and of Vladilen-Mikhail, the only one of Arseny's sons to reach old age. A scar crossed the right cheek and his gray hair was thinning.

Another Vladilen was looking at him, as if by God's grace one man was allowed to live two lives: the Nazi priest Dietrich Schwerdt and Communist officer Vladilen Ivanov.

Kirill thought about Stalingrad, where everything was mixed up, where there might be Germans in the cellars and Russians upstairs, or the reverse: a city with walls shot through completely, where enemies could meet—having entered like fleshless beings or spirits, through a ceiling or wall, an apartment where photographs of the owners hang and bomb-damaged dishes are hidden in cabinets—and not shoot, recognizing each other as if in a mirror.

The nurse warned that Herr Schwerdt could not speak for long; his health had deteriorated and he should not be upset. Kirill understood that there were only a few months or weeks left in Dietrich's long life—he had outlived everyone in his generation on both sides—and that he would get only an hour or so of that remaining time; he would not have time to ask questions but only to hear the sudden confession of a dying man who had decided to talk to him, family and stranger at the same time.

Kirill spoke German poorly, even though he understood it well. His inability to ask questions was a kind of filter that let the past flow in only one direction: from Dietrich to him.

The old man nodded, not wasting time on extended

greetings. He spoke calmly, with long pauses, as if enjoying his last conversation, because after that there would be brief chats with doctors, names of ineffective medicines, useless procedures, and then, soon after, words would be said *over* him.

"A soldier told me. An Austrian from the regimental intelligence," Dietrich said, as if continuing a long conversation with himself. "They were sent to that bank of the Volga. There's an island below Stalingrad. They went by boat. Burning spots of oil flowed down the river. Corpses were stuck in the oil, it was thick. They were burning, too. Firebrands. Behind them was a forest where wild apples had ripened. Like paradise. The Austrian said he imagined how many corpses had drowned. The river was full of them to the bottom.

"They were reliable soldiers," he said softly. "Spies. Butchers. No one survived. The last one, the Austrian, I saw in the camp. He had become an informer for the NKVD. That's how he described that island … Truly like paradise. I had stopped believing in paradise."

The nurse peeked into the room, pointed to her watch. Dietrich looked at her and shook his head; she wagged her finger at him and shut the door.

"That Austrian, yes," Dietrich said, seeking the vanishing thread. "He came to me for confession. And then to Lieutenant Kibovsky. No," Dietrich chuckled. "No, of course he went to Lieutenant Kibovsky first and then to me."

Dietrich pulled out his disfigured arm, missing the hand, from under the covers, as if getting an object needed to explain the story; Kirill guessed at the frostbite and the dullness of the instrument—ax, saw, sapper shovel?—that was used hastily.

"Lieutenant Kibovsky was my God," Dietrich said with an ironic smile. "He gave me ham. Slices thinner than cigarette paper. Nothing but the aroma. He could have sent me to clear snow in the city. Even with one hand. People did not come back from that. But he didn't. And I told him all the confessions." Dietrich laughed again, angrily. "And what was not in the confessions. He was tactful, Kibovsky. Put me in the isolation cell and we talked there. They trusted me, believed in me. I didn't have faith, but they had faith in me. Kibovsky understood. In 1943 I was transferred to a different camp, in the Urals. There were confessions there, too." Dietrich paused. "And then a miracle happened. I almost started believing in God again. I was sent home as unfit for labor. In January 1946. The others envied me, said I was lucky."

Dietrich fell silent. Outside on an old fir, a squirrel took apart last year's cone.

"I returned to Leipzig," Dietrich said. "That summer I ran into an old friend. Michael. A minor party functionary. Nazi Party, naturally. He said he'd gotten a job with the Soviet administration in Germany. I wasn't surprised. He wasn't a Nazi. Just a clever crook. He used to have a café near our house in the 1930s. Then he got his military orders ... He said he had reopened the café. For his friends. Illegal. He had coffee and cognac. We went up to the second floor. The first room was like a café of sorts. Even with a coffee machine. Some bottles behind the bar. Two or three tables. Tablecloths. Paper flowers. But Michael led me to the back room. There ... There ..." Dietrich grew agitated, his pale face grew flushed, his Adam's apple stuck out, and Kirill imagined women, an underground bordello, and Dietrich had recognized one of them—a sister, niece, neighbor, his teenage love ...

"And there was Kibovsky," the old man said, lips unmoving, like a ventriloquist. "Lieutenant Colonel Kibovsky. A cup of coffee on the table in front of him.

"Kibovsky worked in Serov's group. They were preparing for the elections on October 20. Kibovsky had my signed receipt for my work." Dietrich laughed out loud, unfettered. "I thought it was back in Stalingrad, with my hand. Rotting in the archives. Paper grew damp very quickly in the camp. We wrote our consent declarations on the back of our staff documents. On the back of our former lives." Dietrich's speech slowed, as if he were going back in time. "I often dreamed that rats were gnawing on my hand. They lay like a woodpile by the hospital—arms, legs …

"And so I began serving God again. Then they passed me over to the Stasi. That was a god no worse than others. Everything was revealed. The Gauck Commission investigating the East German secret police. They have my dossier now. … You think you're hearing my confession," Dietrich concluded harshly. "Let me tell you what I understood. There is no God. But in some room on the second floor, there is always Lieutenant Colonel Kibovsky, reading your personal file. History is Lieutenant Colonel Kibovsky. That is its name. That's what it looks like."

Kirill wanted to laugh, but he suddenly felt the horror of the ex-priest's words, so sure of himself.

The old man flung himself back on the pillows.

Kirill was not allowed to see him the next day; "The patient is feeling worse." Kirill waited another ten days and then left. He couldn't get to the funeral; he returned later, when the autumn flowers had withered on the grave. He drank heavily that night, commemorating Dietrich, whose death outlasted all expectations, left him alone with the necessity of starting the book; he drank, moving from bar to bar because he did not want to return to Moscow, Dietrich's last words echoed in his head; he had no more days left on his visa, he had spent them all on his research in Germany; he drank until the lamps and ceiling spun.

***

*F*og. Fog, as if snow had fallen and left its ghostly light in the air.

Where was he going? He had had too much to drink. Thick red wine. Now it felt as if a warm nauseating ball was rolling around inside him. Where was he going?

Houses. Houses flooded in moonlight. Intervals of dark among the reddish streetlights. A car drove next to him. Two men inside. Looking at him for some reason. His face reflected in the window. He ran his fingers through his hair. His fingertips were cold. He shut his eyes. Darkness. A glowing yellow film and scattered lemon-colored sparks.

A voice. A familiar voice. The warm ball has slipped forward—they had stopped. The doors hissed. Icy cold from the street. Steps. Someone was there.

He opened his eyes.

A dead man. Not yet corrupted. His face was powdered, as if he had been laid out in a coffin.

A dead young woman behind him. Red protruding eyes, dried blood in the corner of her mouth, bite marks on her lips.

A priest on the right. His pale hands held a wooden stake. It smelled of church. Incense. A dead pastor of dead men. They were crowded in the electric twilight of the tram, staring at him with lifeless eyes.

The Priest, he was Dietrich, the old pastor who did not believe in God. Who lost his faith in Stalingrad. But Dietrich was dead. Yes, that was right. Dietrich was dead.

The unholy horde came closer. He recognized the creatures of the abyss; they were a phantasmagorical, demonic reflection of his memory.

Glowing, phosphorescent flasks draped the master of poisons, Balthasar, wizard, murderer; the vicious killer physician in a white coat spattered with blood was Arseny; the thin drowned mermaids with wet wreaths of waterweeds were the Leningrad sisters; the rich fat man in a tuxedo and lemon-yellow face was Gustav; the wounded soldiers leaning on crutches and riddled with bullets were the brothers Gleb and Boris; the sailor with an eye hanging by a thread was Andreas, the Marinated Midshipman; the priest Dietrich was at the head of this gang and next to him stood a broad-shouldered executioner with a poleaxe and a severed head under his arm.

The head opened its eyes, blinked, trying to wake up, find its body.

That's my head, he realized. That's my head.

A cold hand touched his face, scratched it.

He screamed and hurried away, falling from the seat onto his back, pushing with his feet, sliding on his rear along the filthy floor.

There were explosions outside the window, and the colored lights of firecrackers flew up into the sky. The tram slowed down, and the same familiar voice said, "Next stop: S- und U-Bahnhof Alexanderplatz."

A crowd made noise outside; the tram stopped, and the zombie girl held out her hand: get up. The company of costumed dead laughed the way drunken people laugh: hiccupping, oblivious. The executioner lifted up the fake head and showed how the machinery worked: he moved his fingers and the dead eyes blinked again.

It was Halloween.

Slightly more sober, he approached the World Clock.

It was eleven at night in Berlin. Tomorrow was the last day of his visa and he was flying back in the morning.

It was midnight in Moscow.

Kirill imagined the sound of his grandfather's clock striking in the Moscow apartment; he saw the horn in the bronze hunter's left hand going up, and the dead goose in his right going down.

Suddenly, as if the poles had connected, the continents joined up—the hunter in Konstantin's clock reminded Kirill of the nocturnal guest's half-forgotten name, the KGB general who was his grandfather's patron. He should have recalled it sooner, while talking with Dietrich, but he had not because Dietrich's fate existed in his mind only on the German side of world, completely separate, coming into contact only once with the fate of Vladilen-Mikhail; no matter how he had tried to place the Schwerdt history onto a single field, it turned out that the old borders of language and enmity were stronger. But as soon as the name floated up, it appeared as the final, unbelievable completion of the plot, combining the ends and the beginnings like an omen on his road to Moscow.

Kirill breathed out, expelling the syllables as if they were poison: Kibovsky.

In the distance, he saw the blinking red lights of a plane flying out of Tegel Airport.

A new day had begun in Moscow, awaiting Kirill. That day had a face—the face of the bronze hunter. Kirill took out his passport and looked at it with dumb hope, even though he knew: his visa expired today.

*S*ergei Lebedev was born in Moscow in 1981 and worked for seven years on geological expeditions in northern Russia and Central Asia. Lebedev is a novelist, essayist, and journalist. *Oblivion*, his first novel, has been translated into many languages and was named one of the ten best novels of 2016 by *The Wall Street Journal*. Lebedev's second novel, *The Year of the Comet*, has also received considerable acclaim.

*A*ntonina W. Bouis is one of the leading translators of Russian literature working today. She has translated over 80 works from authors such as Evgeny Yevtushenko, Mikhail Bulgakov, Andrei Sakharov, Sergei Dovlatov and Arkady and Boris Strugatsky. Bouis, previously executive director of the Soros Foundation in the former USSR, lives in New York City.

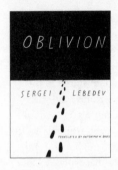

OBLIVION
BY SERGEI LEBEDEV

In one of the first 21st century Russian novels to probe the legacy of the Soviet prison camp system, a young man travels to the vast wastelands of the Far North to uncover the truth about a shadowy neighbor who saved his life, and whom he knows only as Grandfather II. Emerging from today's Russia, where the ills of the past are being forcefully erased from public memory, this masterful novel represents an epic literary attempt to rescue history from the brink of oblivion.

THE YEAR OF THE COMET
BY SERGEI LEBEDEV

A story of a Russian boyhood and coming of age as the Soviet Union is on the brink of collapse. Lebedev depicts a vast empire coming apart at the seams, transforming a very public moment into something tender and personal, and writes with stunning beauty and shattering insight about childhood and the growing consciousness of a boy in the world.

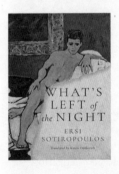

WHAT'S LEFT OF THE NIGHT
BY ERSI SOTIROPOULOS

Constantine Cavafy arrives in Paris in 1897 on a trip that will deeply shape his future and push him toward his poetic inclination. With this lyrical novel, tinged with an hallucinatory eroticism that unfolds over three unforgettable days, celebrated Greek author Ersi Sotiropoulos depicts Cavafy in the midst of a journey of self-discovery across a continent on the brink of massive change. A stunning portrait of a budding author—before he became C.P. Cavafy, one of the 20th century's greatest poets—that illuminates the complex relationship of art, life, and the erotic desires that trigger creativity.

A Very Russian Christmas

This is Russian Christmas celebrated in supreme pleasure and pain by the greatest of writers, from Dostoevsky and Tolstoy to Chekhov and Teffi. The dozen stories in this collection will satisfy every reader, and with their wit, humor, and tenderness, packed full of sentimental songs, footmen, whirling winds, solitary nights, snow drifts, and hopeful children, the collection proves that Nobody Does Christmas Like the Russians.

A Very French Christmas

A continuation of the very popular Very Christmas Series, this collection brings together the best French Christmas stories of all time in an elegant and vibrant collection featuring classics by Guy de Maupassant and Alphonse Daudet, plus stories by the esteemed twentieth century author Irène Némirovsky and contemporary writers Dominique Fabre and Jean-Philippe Blondel. With a holiday spirit conveyed through sparkling Paris streets, opulent feasts, wandering orphans, flickering desire, and more than a little wine, this collection proves that the French have mastered Christmas.

The Eye
by Philippe Costamagna

It's a rare and secret profession, comprising a few dozen people around the world equipped with a mysterious mixture of knowledge and innate sensibility. Summoned to Swiss bank vaults, Fifth Avenue apartments, and Tokyo storerooms, they are entrusted by collectors, dealers, and museums to decide if a coveted picture is real or fake and to determine if it was painted by Leonardo da Vinci or Raphael. *The Eye* lifts the veil on the rarified world of connoisseurs devoted to the authentication and discovery of Old Master artworks.

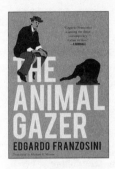

THE ANIMAL GAZER
BY EDGARDO FRANZOSINI

A hypnotic novel inspired by the strange and fascinating life of sculptor Rembrandt Bugatti, brother of the fabled automaker. Bugatti obsessively observes and sculpts the baboons, giraffes, and panthers in European zoos, finding empathy with their plight and identifying with their life in captivity. Rembrandt Bugatti's work, now being rediscovered, is displayed in major art museums around the world and routinely fetches large sums at auction. Edgardo Franzosini recreates the young artist's life with intense lyricism, passion, and sensitivity.

ALLMEN AND THE DRAGONFLIES
BY MARTIN SUTER

Johann Friedrich von Allmen has exhausted his family fortune by living in Old World grandeur despite present-day financial constraints. Forced to downscale, Allmen inhabits the garden house of his former Zurich estate, attended by his Guatemalan butler, Carlos. This is the first of a series of humorous, fast-paced detective novels devoted to a memorable gentleman thief. A thrilling art heist escapade infused with European high culture and luxury that doesn't shy away from the darker side of human nature.

THE MADELEINE PROJECT
BY CLARA BEAUDOUX

A young woman moves into a Paris apartment and discovers a storage room filled with the belongings of the previous owner, a certain Madeleine who died in her late nineties, and whose treasured possessions nobody seems to want. In an audacious act of journalism driven by personal curiosity and humane tenderness, Clara Beaudoux embarks on *The Madeleine Project*, documenting what she finds on Twitter with text and photographs, introducing the world to an unsung 20th century figure.

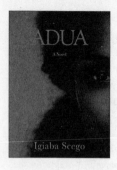

ADUA
BY IGIABA SCEGO

Adua, an immigrant from Somalia to Italy, has lived in Rome for nearly forty years. She came seeking freedom from a strict father and an oppressive regime, but her dreams of film stardom ended in shame. Now that the civil war in Somalia is over, her homeland calls her. She must decide whether to return and reclaim her inheritance, but also how to take charge of her own story and build a future.

IF VENICE DIES
BY SALVATORE SETTIS

Internationally renowned art historian Salvatore Settis ignites a new debate about the Pearl of the Adriatic and cultural patrimony at large. In this fiery blend of history and cultural analysis, Settis argues that "hit-and-run" visitors are turning Venice and other landmark urban settings into shopping malls and theme parks. This is a passionate plea to secure the soul of Venice, written with consummate authority, wide-ranging erudition and élan.

THE MADONNA OF NOTRE DAME
BY ALEXIS RAGOUGNEAU

Fifty thousand people jam into Notre Dame Cathedral to celebrate the Feast of the Assumption. The next morning, a beautiful young woman clothed in white kneels at prayer in a cathedral side chapel. But when someone accidentally bumps against her, her body collapses. She has been murdered. This thrilling novel illuminates shadowy corners of the world's most famous cathedral, shedding light on good and evil with suspense, compassion and wry humor.

THE LAST WEYNFELDT
BY MARTIN SUTER

Adrian Weynfeldt is an art expert in an international auction house, a bachelor in his mid-fifties living in a grand Zurich apartment filled with costly paintings and antiques. Always correct and well-mannered, he's given up on love until one night—entirely out of character for him—Weynfeldt decides to take home a ravishing but unaccountable young woman and gets embroiled in an art forgery scheme that threatens his buttoned up existence. This refined page-turner moves behind elegant bourgeois facades into darker recesses of the heart.

MOVING THE PALACE
BY CHARIF MAJDALANI

A young Lebanese adventurer explores the wilds of Africa, encountering an eccentric English colonel in Sudan and enlisting in his service. In this lush chronicle of far-flung adventure, the military recruit crosses paths with a compatriot who has dismantled a sumptuous palace and is transporting it across the continent on a camel caravan. This is a captivating modern-day Odyssey in the tradition of Bruce Chatwin and Paul Theroux.

THE 6:41 TO PARIS
BY JEAN-PHILIPPE BLONDEL

Cécile, a stylish 47-year-old, has spent the weekend visiting her parents outside Paris. By Monday morning, she's exhausted. These trips back home are stressful and she settles into a train compartment with an empty seat beside her. But it's soon occupied by a man she recognizes as Philippe Leduc, with whom she had a passionate affair that ended in her brutal humiliation 30 years ago. In the fraught hour and a half that ensues, Cécile and Philippe hurtle towards the French capital in a psychological thriller about the pain and promise of past romance.

ON THE RUN WITH MARY
BY JONATHAN BARROW

Shining moments of tender beauty punctuate this story of a youth on the run after escaping from an elite English boarding school. At London's Euston Station, the narrator meets a talking dachshund named Mary and together they're off on escapades through posh Mayfair streets and jaunts in a Rolls-Royce. But the youth soon realizes that the seemingly sweet dog is a handful; an alcoholic, nymphomaniac, drug-addicted mess who can't stay out of pubs or off the dance floor. *On the Run with Mary* mirrors the horrors and the joys of the terrible 20th century.

THE LAST SUPPER
BY KLAUS WIVEL

Alarmed by the oppression of 7.5 million Christians in the Middle East, journalist Klaus Wivel traveled to Iraq, Lebanon, Egypt, and the Palestinian territories to learn about their fate. He found a minority under threat of death and humiliation, desperate in the face of rising Islamic extremism and without hope their situation will improve. An unsettling account of a severely beleaguered religious group living, so it seems, on borrowed time. Wivel asks, Why have we not done more to protect these people?

GUYS LIKE ME
BY DOMINIQUE FABRE

Dominique Fabre, born in Paris and a life-long resident of the city, exposes the shadowy, anonymous lives of many who inhabit the French capital. In this quiet, subdued tale, a middle-aged office worker, divorced and alienated from his only son, meets up with two childhood friends who are similarly adrift. He's looking for a second act to his mournful life, seeking the harbor of love and a true connection with his son. Set in palpably real Paris streets that feel miles away from the City of Light, a stirring novel of regret and absence, yet not without a glimmer of hope.

ANIMAL INTERNET
BY ALEXANDER PSCHERA

Some 50,000 creatures around the globe—including whales, leopards, flamingoes, bats and snails—are being equipped with digital tracking devices. The data gathered and studied by major scientific institutes about their behavior will warn us about tsunamis, earthquakes and volcanic eruptions, but also radically transform our relationship to the natural world. Contrary to pessimistic fears, author Alexander Pschera sees the Internet as creating a historic opportunity for a new dialogue between man and nature.

KILLING AUNTIE
BY ANDRZEJ BURSA

A young university student named Jurek, with no particular ambitions or talents, finds himself with nothing to do. After his doting aunt asks the young man to perform a small chore, he decides to kill her for no good reason other than, perhaps, boredom. This short comedic masterpiece combines elements of Dostoevsky, Sartre, Kafka, and Heller, coming together to produce an unforgettable tale of murder and—just maybe—redemption.

I CALLED HIM NECKTIE
BY MILENA MICHIKO FLAŠAR

Twenty-year-old Taguchi Hiro has spent the last two years of his life living as a hikikomori—a shut-in who never leaves his room and has no human interaction—in his parents' home in Tokyo. As Hiro tentatively decides to reenter the world, he spends his days observing life from a park bench. Gradually he makes friends with Ohara Tetsu, a salaryman who has lost his job. The two discover in their sadness a common bond. This beautiful novel is moving, unforgettable, and full of surprises.

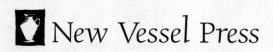

New Vessel Press

To purchase these titles and for more information
please visit newvesselpress.com.